SING FOR LIFE

a novel by

WENDY PERRIAM

For Maurice

Thank you for your wonderful help & support on the way back from Choir – much appreciated.

Francesca / Wendy

ABOUT THE AUTHOR

Wendy Perriam has been writing since the age of 5, completing her first book, *A Pony At Last*, on her 12th birthday (sheer wish-fulfilment, since the only pony in her life was the milkman's ancient nag!) Expelled from boarding school for heresy and told she was in Satan's power – a terrifying verdict for a devout Catholic child whose father had spent 5 years training to be a priest - she escaped to Oxford, where she read History and also trod the boards. There followed a variety of offbeat jobs, ranging from artist's model to carnation-disbudder to carer for the elderly, to researcher on medieval cookery, all of which provided entrées into unknown worlds that find echoes in her work. A former tutor in Creative Writing at Morley College, Lambeth, Wendy now teaches privately.

Her 18 novels have been acclaimed for their psychological insight and their power to disturb, divert and intrigue, while her 8 short-story collections explore themes of loss, rebellion and escape. She also writes poetry, which has been published in various collections and anthologies, has contributed articles and stories to many newspapers and magazines, and was a regular contributor to radio programmes such as *Stop the Week* and *Fourth Column*.

Wendy feels that her many conflicting life experiences – strict convent-school discipline and swinging-sixties wildness, marriage and divorce, infertility and motherhood, 9-to-5 conformity and periodic Bedlam – have helped shape her as a writer. 'Writing allows for shadow-selves. I'm both the staid conformist matron and the slag; the well-organised author toiling at her desk and the madwoman shrieking in a straitjacket.'

By the Same Author

NOVELS

Absinthe for Elevenses
Cuckoo
After Purple
Born of Woman
The Stillness The Dancing
Sin City
Devils, for a Change
Fifty-Minute Hour
Bird Inside
Michael, Michael
Breaking and Entering
Coupling
Second Skin
Lying
Tread Softly
Broken Places
An Enormous Yes
The Tender Murderer

SHORT-STORY COLLECTIONS

Dreams, Demons and Desire
Virgin in the Gym
Laughter Class
Little Marvel
The Queen's Margarine
The Biggest Female in the World
'I'm on the train!'
Bad Mothers, Brilliant Lovers

Sing for life, sing for love,
sing for all the things that you are
dreaming of.
Sing for hope, sing for strength,
sing for ev'rything,
keep singing till the end,
no matter how hard life gets.
Sing for your life.

The anthem of Tenovus Cancer Care "Sing With Us" Choirs

The song, the longed for
song at last.
Can it be
I have emerged, appeared
who lay in the dark so long?

from *Imago,* by Sister Mary Agnes (1928-2014)

For all my inspirational friends in the Tenovus Cancer Care "Sing With Us" choirs (the London and Sutton choirs in particular, but also the melodious Welsh contingent); for our brilliant choir-leader, Vicki Hodges; our fund-raisers *par excellence*, Louise Swindell, Verity Cadwallader and Alexandra Smith; our multi-talented Music Director, Paul Rothwell, and for all those who have helped me on musical and medical matters and on a host of other subjects from skating to stalkers and from hellcats to hot-air-balloons!

Keep singing to the end.

CHAPTER ONE

'I will survive!'

The last phrase of the song was lost in rapturous applause. Veronica gazed out at the audience, the tiered rows of stalls and packed gallery above, both seeming to come alive as they erupted from their former respectful silence into a tide of acclamation. Some people had even risen to their feet and were clapping with their hands above their heads, as if unable to contain their bodily excitement – an infectious excitement now rippling through the whole choir. It seemed completely unbelievable that she could be included in this fanfare: a woman voiceless for over fifty years actually performing in a famous concert-hall! She tuned in to the sound, eager to impress it on her mind: a noise like frenzied hail lashing at a windowpane – not normal cold white hail, but fiery-hot and spangled, deepening as she listened from fuchsia-pink to scarlet.

Katy, their choir-leader, bowed deeply to the audience, then turned around to acknowledge all forty-seven singers, spreading her arms wide, to encompass every one. Before leaving the stage, Veronica took one last, lingering look at her surroundings, drinking in each detail: the elegantly tall windows and elaborate balustrade, the intricately carved organ-screen, and impressive Steinway grand on stage, still amazed to be part of this grandiose occasion, and even more amazed to be applauded. Applause was for celebrities, not for a mere nobody, who had always tried to hide away, lie low. Yet the brilliant June sunshine flooding through the hall and enfolding her in its golden glow seemed a tangible sign that she had indeed escaped her former drab brown chrysalis.

Katy ushered them off-stage and, as they began descending the stairs in twos and threes. Megan took her arm and whispered, 'Bravo, Veronica! That was the best you've ever sung.'

About to demur, Veronica realized with a jolt that it was true. During her first weeks in the choir, shamefully unable to sing a single note in tune, she had simply mouthed the words, or emitted a gruff croak, whereas today she'd actually managed a creditable performance. And, as they all assembled in the foyer, she was aware of a bubbly elation again spreading through the choir, like yeast, as if everybody shared her sense of genuine achievement.

'Who's coming to the pub?' Katy asked, raising her voice above the general hubbub. 'I do want us all to celebrate, because that was the largest audience we've ever had in the history of the choir! And I've booked a private room, so we'll be able to let our hair down.'

A forest of hands shot up, although not Veronica's. She was torn, as usual, between the dutiful voice urging her to go straight back home and her still-tingling-with-excitement body staking its claim to company and conversation.

Megan, however, was already steering her through the door, the pair of them first out into the street.

'Look, I'm not sure if I ought to …'

'No "oughts",' her new friend interrupted. 'I insist on buying you a drink, so daren't you dare sneak off!'

Friendship, Veronica was finding, demanded almost as much practice as singing, both unknown in her life to date. Megan, though, had encouraged her right from the first rehearsal: scribbling pencilled prompts on the song-sheets, providing links to YouTube, where she could hear the songs performed by famous vocalists, and explaining terms like legato and arpeggios. Surely one drink wouldn't hurt?

As they turned the corner to the pub, several people gave them curious glances, dressed as they were in long black skirts - or smart dress-trousers for the men - worn with crisp white shirts and red bow-ties. Katy had insisted on formal dress this evening, instead of their usual 'Larks Ascending' T-shirts, and indeed the attire itself added to the sense of celebration.

Catching a glimpse of herself in the large, gilt-framed pub-mirror, Veronica felt as if she were wearing a disguise; her newly lightened hair and brazen lipstick in such startling contrast to the shabby wreck of six months ago, she barely knew which 'her' was authentic.

Katy led the way to the private room at the back, where they began seating themselves at two large pushed-together tables. Megan had already pulled out two adjoining chairs and now proceeded to introduce Veronica to the tall, slender, red-haired woman sitting on her other side – someone Veronica had noticed at rehearsals, but never actually spoken to in person.

'This is Yvonne - one of our oldest members, oldest in the best sense. She was here when the choir was first founded and, in those days, very small and select.'

Until they permitted duds like me to join, Veronica didn't say, remembering Megan's injunctions not to keep putting herself down.

'Catherine told me,' Yvonne said, once they'd exchanged a few pleasantries, 'that, until you came here, you hadn't sung for fifty years. Is that really true?'

Veronica nodded. 'It was fifty-five years, to be exact. I was told at age four that I was singing out of tune, you see, and must never open my mouth again, because I was obviously tone-deaf.'

'What a dreadful thing to tell a child!' Clive put in from the opposite side of the table. 'Anyway, surely you defied them – sang to please yourself, around the house or in the shower?'

Pleasing herself had been an unknown concept in her childhood, and defiance out of the question. Tonight, however, she was determined to stay firmly in the present. 'When I joined the choir,' she said, deliberately changing the subject, 'I was so appallingly out of practice, I could only manage a sort of growl, which is why Katy put me with the tenors and basses.' She flashed a shy smile at Clive, whose deep baritone usually covered up her lapses. And her friendship with Megan had sprung from the fact they stood side by side at rehearsals, Megan being the only other female singing with the men (not from any musical deficiency but because her recent throat-cancer had left her with a low and husky register).

'Is it also true,' Yvonne persisted, 'that you'd never heard of any of the songs in our repertoire, not even hoary old favourites like *I Will Survive?*'

'But how could you *not?*' Charlotte broke off her own conversation to express her disbelief. 'A world-wide hit like that, which was in the charts for decades? And it was used in various films and whatnot, and there were endless cover-versions.'

Veronica could feel a blush suffusing her cheeks – further proof that she was hopelessly unsophisticated. She should have stopped blushing at sixteen. But how could she admit that never in her life had she followed pop-charts, let alone bought records and CDs, and had no idea what cover-versions *were?*

'I presumed we all grew up with songs like that?' Charlotte

continued. 'I mean, they were always on the radio and ….'

'In fact,' Catherine interrupted, 'I only got through my horrific divorce by playing *I Will Survive* and really latching on to the words.'

That Veronica could understand. When, at last, she had heard the words, very late in life, they had struck her with extraordinary force - their sheer defiance, self-belief – much more so, she suspected, than those whose very familiarity with them had long ago diluted their impact. Even the concept of survival had always been an uncertain one: would she survive her childhood and, later, the early years of her marriage and the all-consuming challenge of Tom?

'And don't forget,' Michael chipped in, with a conspiratorial wink at his partner, Clive, 'it became an important gay anthem.'

Veronica was relieved to see a waiter sauntering over to take their drinks-orders. Until today, she had never said to word to anyone about such trivial matters as her childhood singing-teacher, nor admitted to such shaming general ignorance. The elation of the concert appeared to have shattered her customary reserve and, anyway, she'd been hogging the limelight far too long.

'This is on me,' Megan reminded her, once the waiter was standing beside them, pencil poised, 'so push the boat out and have a glass of bubbly.'

'No, honestly, I'll stick to orange juice.' Impossible to return home even slightly woozy.

'Oh, come on, Veronica, let me twist your arm!'

'OK, a glass of white wine then, but make it a small one, please.'

'And what for you, Barry? I received my yearly bonus last

week, so I'm feeling fairly flush.'

'Thank God for that! I can't afford Sloane-Square prices, not on benefits.'

What Veronica found surprising about the choir was its mix of types and ages, everyone from skint, boyish, Cockney Barry to born-with-a-silver-spoon-in-her-mouth Samantha, who must be pushing eighty.

Once everybody's drinks arrived, Katy called for silence and raised her glass. 'I'm so proud of you all,' she announced. 'You sang really beautifully today, with such conviction and attack.'

Once each person round the tables had clinked glasses with their neighbours, Veronica took a long draught of her wine, as if deliberately defying the stern voice in her head still nagging her to leave. Why *shouldn't* she stay and enjoy this once-in-a-lifetime occasion, instead of making excuses to dash off, as she invariably did at rehearsals? Apart from anything else, it would be a chance to get to know some of those choir-members who were still strangers, more or less, especially the sopranos, who sat some distance away from the tenors and basses. As she glanced around the tables, she was aware of the many friends she'd made already – Megan best of all, of course: the freckled, gawky, plain-spoken fifty-something who'd approached her on day one – but also the tenors Michael, Keith and Theo, as well as several of the altos. All of them had welcomed and accepted her, despite the fact that, as far as singing was concerned, she was still in kindergarten, whereas several in the choir were not far off professional. Yet the reassuring thing about being in a choir was that the stronger voices supported the weaker, so that, notwithstanding her limitations, she was swept into a bigger, brighter sound. And today had been a totally new experience, in which she'd sung with her whole heart and mind and body, as if what Katy called her natural voice had been unlocked, at last.

But it wasn't just the singing. This new community had become almost a new family – her *only* family, in one sense - which was so utterly precious, she damned well would stay longer, break the habit of a lifetime of always putting duty before pleasure; maybe throw caution to the winds and have another drink!

CHAPTER 2

As she strolled back from the tube, she was singing to herself, working her way through the concert repertoire and hardly even caring that passers-by were looking at her oddly. She was 'someone new', as it said in *I Will Survive*, no longer 'a chained-up little person', but a tall, strong, tough survivor.

She stopped a moment to inhale the balmy air, scented with roses and honeysuckle wafting from front gardens in the tree-lined avenue. It was still almost light, only two weeks away from the longest day of the year; her mood so upbeat she actually dared imagine a new life. At her age and in her situation, she'd assumed she had no future and certainly no chance of any new relationship. Yet the songs themselves had worked as some sort of catalyst, especially their emphasis on love: *Can't Help Falling in Love, Make You Feel my Love, Crazy Little Thing Called Love*. How could love be 'little'? Surely it was the biggest, most important thing in the world?

She turned the corner in to her street - a drabber street, with no trees or flowers, although with the same substantial Victorian terraced houses. Theirs was one of the few not divided into flats, and she marvelled, as so often, that she, the daughter of a rootless, impecunious mother, should now own a three-storey house. However, as she fumbled for her door-keys, she was oppressed by a deep sense of guilt at daring even to entertain the prospect of romantic love, which was shamefully disloyal to Colin. She crept in to the hall, relieved at the engulfing silence. Perhaps he'd gone to bed and was already fast asleep. But, as she peered in to the sitting-room to check, the last trace of her ebullient mood collapsed. A wine-bottle had been overturned and a large, still-wet stain crimsoned the carpet; the food she'd left had not been touched, the non-alcoholic drinks not even opened.

Kicking off her shoes and dumping her bag on the sideboard, she tiptoed upstairs to his room, trying not to make a sound, so she could leave him sleeping while she got to grips with the wine-stain before it soaked in permanently.

But he was sitting on the bed stark naked and awake, his huge expanse of belly concealing his genitals, a strong shitty smell dousing any lingering memories of perfumed summer gardens. His underpants, clotted with faeces, had been discarded on the floor.

'How did you get on?' he asked, trying and failing to get up, his slurred, unsteady voice bearing witness to his state.

'Fine,' she said. 'But I need to clean you up, darling.'

She picked up the pants, took them to the bathroom and doused them with a hot blast from the shower, trying not to splash her fancy outfit – hardly appropriate attire for such a task. She then went back for Colin, who lurched his way to the bathroom, clinging to her arm. Little wonder he'd become so heavy when, nowadays, he refused all healthy food in favour of cakes, biscuits, multi-packs of choc-ices, and large bags of jelly babies - all clearly comfort-food. And, yes, he did need comfort in his confused, forgetful state.

'And don't *you* need it just as much?' an inner voice demanded, 'as carer, cleaner, cook?'

Instantly, she silenced the voice. Hadn't she just enjoyed a magical evening, leaving Colin to cope unaided? She tried to make amends by treating him with the utmost gentleness, sponging his stained and stinking body with her best apple-blossom soap, then leading him back to the bedroom and helping him into clean, freshly ironed pyjamas.

Next, she settled him in bed with Peter, the toy dog she'd bought him after the real Peter had died of little more than old age, a month after his seventeenth birthday. It had been sheer serendipity to find a stuffed Dalmatian so closely resembling his namesake – and to find him in a charity shop, languishing in a bin of mostly scruffy animals, some missing tails or ears, the Dalmatian alone fighting-fit and snowy-clean. Colin had loved Peter with a fierceness and devotion he found it impossible to bestow on any human being, so this substitute was another vital comfort.

'Was Peter OK this evening?' she asked, deliberately switching to his favourite subject, in the hope of brightening his mood.

'Hungry,' he mumbled. 'Peter always hungry.'

'Well, why don't we give him some biscuits?' She made a show of ripping open biscuit-packets and piling the contents on the bed. 'You know what he's like! Once his tummy's full, he'll be fine.'

Resettling himself on the pillow, Colin seemed at least reasonably content, so she said goodnight and was about to make for the door, when she heard him murmur, 'Snug down, little Tom.'

Riveted, she stared at him. Tom was no mere toy, but Colin's flesh and blood. And that particular phrase was *hers*, one she had always used when putting Tom to bed, whereas Colin had never, ever uttered those words before, and very rarely put Tom to bed at all. How on earth had he remembered it, when he had forgotten so much else?

'Yes, snug down, little Tom,' she repeated, wondering how much of their past life Colin could recall, and whether he felt any trace of guilt, regret or sadness. Pointless to reflect on such things, since she was unlikely ever to know.

Having finally closed the door, she made instinctively for Tom's old room downstairs – a room she had never changed. Even half his medical equipment was still in situ, and his huge array of prescription-drugs, which she used to pretend were sweeties, and pretend to swallow, too. She lingered in the doorway, glancing at the photos she'd set up for him, to give him a sense of identity, help him recognize his mother and that crowd of strangers for ever coming and going, at least in his early years. In pride of place were the 'Tom' photos, a good three-dozen, arranged on a large bulletin board. He loved looking at himself at various stages of his life, always with the same incongruously cheerful smile.

She turned on her heel and went back upstairs, ruing her folly in allowing such painful memories to intrude on what had been a rare and special evening. Colin she could deal with – he was simply part of her day-to-day existence – but the loss of Tom was still bruisingly raw and recent.

Having checked on Colin - now asleep, but breathing in an uneven, snorty fashion - she went in to her own bedroom to watch one of the videos Megan had flagged up: Gloria Gaynor performing *I Will Survive* at the Mandela birthday concert in 2009. The singer seemed heavier and slower than in earlier performances, yet sang with more emotion than in all her other recordings, as if recalling a whole lifetime of suffering and survival-skills. She herself could identify with that and with the singer's age - just a few months older than she was now – indeed, she found it profoundly moving. And, as the jaunty tune erupted into the room - filtered through headphones on her laptop, so as not to disturb her husband - she began to sing along. Never before had she dared do that, even in the privacy of her bedroom but, gradually, she became still more uninhibited, now jigging and clapping in time with the audience, copying their movements and expressions. And, at the finale, when Gloria kissed her hand to her fans, bowing to acknowledge the exuberant applause, Veronica knew she had no option but to emulate this woman's sheer grit and gutsiness.

Yes, they must both survive.

CHAPTER 3

As Veronica turned into Sebastian's street, her pace slowed with every step. Was she out of her mind to have booked a singing-lesson with a man she had never met and knew almost nothing about? Admittedly, Katy had recommended him, as an up-and-coming baritone who'd already made a name for himself, but that made it all the more inappropriate that he was about to teach an ignoramus.

Having arrived ridiculously early, she had filled the time walking round and round in circles, passing exclusive boutiques and trendy bars and restaurants. Whatever else, he must be wealthy to live in Clerkenwell and, indeed, as she forced herself to approach his house, she saw it was a quite a grandiose one, with two majestic stone lions outside. As she was peering at the snooty beasts, there was a sudden clap of thunder and torrential rain started pelting down, as if some powerful water-feature had been switched on at a theme-park. Wincing against its onslaught, she rang the bell of the smart, olive-painted front door and, hearing footsteps clacking down the hall, tried to change her expression from one of apprehension into the semblance of a smile. But the smile vanished when the door was opened by an imperious-looking woman frowning fiercely at the interruption.

'Yes?' she demanded.

'I've ... er ... come to see Sebastian Lamont.'

'Why the hell can't he *tell* people he lives in the basement?' She gestured tetchily to her right. 'Go down those steps at the side, OK?'

The door slammed on the 'OK', and Veronica was left stranded on the step in the still relentless rain. The basement steps were steep and slippery, but it was a definite relief to see her teacher's name just above the doorbell – certainly a distinctive name, so maybe one he'd adopted in his professional role. There was no answer, however, to her first tentative ring, nor to her second, louder peal. Third time round, she kept her finger on the bell-push. Perhaps the downpour was muffling all other sounds.

As she stood alone and apparently ignored, all her childhood memories of absences and abandonments began lurching in to her mind – those frequent, frightening occasions when no one had been home. 'You're a grown woman,' she rebuked herself, wiping her clammy hands on her skirt, 'not some scaredy kid.' People were often late in London, what with traffic diversions, signal failures, hold-ups of every kind. He'd probably phone her any second to explain the delay and tell her he was now en route.

Unless she had the day wrong - or the time? No, she had double-checked the appointment, confirmed it by email just this morning. She edged closer to his door, which provided a tiny overhang of shelter. Maybe he, too, was sheltering, merely waiting for this torrential rain to abate, so, if she phoned him, at least she'd know what was happening. Yet, barely had she dialled his number, when she cancelled the call, not wanting to sound panicky, or make him think she was hounding him. Best to give him ten more minutes.

After a mere two-and-a-half, the rain stopped as suddenly as it had started, and a fickle sun lit up the puddles in the tiny basement yard. As each remaining minute passed, she began to regret the whole idea of having lessons, although it was Megan who'd encouraged her.

'You're singing so much better anyway, Veronica, but you really need some personal tuition and there simply isn't time for that at rehearsals. So, you owe it to yourself to work on your technique, one to one, with a professional.'

Owing something to herself was not a familiar concept, and it was certainly an indulgence to be forking out forty pounds an hour for what was basically a vanity-project. Megan herself had had lessons, but her case was completely different - more a medical matter, to help retrain her voice, once she was in remission from her throat-cancer.

The ten minutes was long since up, yet still Sebastian hadn't come, so she began to worry that perhaps he'd had an accident. Maybe, at this very moment, he was trapped in the wreckage of a fatal bus-collision, or bleeding to death from a terrorist attack. But just as she was checking her phone for any such atrocity, there was the sound of thudding feet behind her and she swung round to see a striking-looking man descending the steps three at a time, and shaking the rain dramatically from his thatch of bleached-blond hair.

'Desperately sorry Veronica! I'm utterly beside myself to be so fearfully late.'

'Er, that's OK,' she stuttered, taken aback by his inflated words, although glad of their seemingly genuine contrition.

'Our slot overran at the studio, and I just couldn't get away.' Still shaking rain from his leonine head, he went on to explain, 'You see, I'm playing Alberto Roc, one of the big solo roles, in the premiere studio recording of *The Exterminating Angel*.'

The Exterminating Angel meant nothing to her – apart from a vague undertow of doom - but if he was one of the soloists, then he must be even more eminent than she'd thought.

'It's Adès' newest opera, first staged at Salzburg in 2016 and at Covent Garden only a couple of months ago.'

Adès? Who was Adès? She knew as little about opera as she

knew about nuclear physics.

'And what makes it even more of a feather in my cap is that they asked me to take over from Sir Thomas Allen for the recording!'

Another name she didn't know, but she did her best to concentrate, in the hope of eventual elucidation.

'Apparently, Sir Tom had an engagement at *La Scala*, singing Don Alfonso, which had been booked some time ago, before the contract came in for the studio recording. And, just between you and me, Veronica, one of my ambitions is to sing at *La Scala* myself. In fact, I actually feel I'm halfway there already, with all these prestigious contracts and engagements. But, getting back to *The Exterminating Angel*, Adès has written some fiendishly difficult vocal lines, especially the coloratura, which is stratospherically high. But even *my* part is exceptionally challenging.'

Although she nodded in seeming comprehension, she couldn't help but wonder if he intended to stand out here for half her lesson, despite the fact they were both uncomfortably wet?

'I hadn't the faintest notion the studio would need me for so long, but you know what conductors are like – insisting on endless takes, regardless of time-constraints.'

No, she *didn't* know. But she was impressed by the fact that he should be making a recording at all.

'It was quite a triumph for me personally. After the last take of my part, the whole chorus burst into spontaneous applause.'

Whereas *he* was more likely to burst into jeering derision, once he'd heard her raw, uncertain voice.

'Are you familiar with Adès' work?' he asked, still presumably forgetting she had come here for a lesson.

'Er, no.' She didn't even know how to spell the composer's name, which sounded, disconcertingly like 'adders'. Indeed, her musical ignorance did feel like a sort of venom, requiring an instant antidote.

'Well, in that case, you have a treat in store! It's quite wonderfully surreal. And this particular opera is also deliciously decadent and, of course, based on the Buñuel film.'

Although Buñuel meant nothing either, at least Sebastian seemed to be finally aware that she was seriously out of her depth, and, at last, suggested they move inside. Having unlocked the door to the basement, he ushered her in to a cramped and gloomy hall that appeared out of synch with his own tall, stylishness. Over six foot in height, his lean, long-legged figure was emphasised by skin-tight black trousers, worn with a ruffled white shirt, and knee-length calf-leather boots - the latter somewhat inappropriate for this humid mid-June weather, although no one could deny how dashing and distinctive they looked. His slender build made her all the more conscious of her own fleshy plumpness, and his ringing public-school voice seemed to rebuke her quieter, self-effacing tone.

He opened the door to a starkly uncluttered sitting-room, containing nothing but a piano, a small makeshift table and four upright wooden chairs. 'We'll soon dry out in here. Can I get you a tea or coffee?'

Politely she declined – couldn't afford to waste more precious time. Her mind was on Colin, as usual. Should she have left him alone for so long? Had he eaten the food she'd put out?

'Please sit down, Veronica, and, before we start, I'd like you to tell me what you hope to achieve in our lessons, and whether you have any particular problems as a singer.'

'I'm not a singer,' she started to say, before quickly swallowing the words. It was important to be positive and make the most of this session. 'Well, in just over a week's time,' she explained, 'our choir is singing three separate times at Guy's Hospital, for their annual Cancer Survivors' Day. Apparently loads of people turn up and our performances will be videoed and shared on all social media platforms, so I have to admit I'm nervous. We've had audiences before, of course, and, at our last big gig, I did reasonably well – or at least I didn't disgrace myself. But then, just two days' later, at one of our rehearsals, I sang appallingly out of tune, and that really threw me, so I immediately clammed up. And now I feel I'm back to square one – someone who just can't sing.'

'*Everyone* can sing!' he announced, with enviable confidence, standing tall and imposing above her, while she subsided into a chair. 'And "can't" is a word I don't countenance.'

A good thing then, she thought, that he had never met her mother.

'However, as I'm sure you must appreciate, a week is an impossibly short time to try to effect any large or lasting change.'

'Yes, I of course I see that, but I was hoping we might go over just one of the songs we're singing at Guy's – one I'm finding a bit tricky.'

'Well,' he said, frowning, 'I usually start the sessions with standard breathing exercises and some vocalizations to relax and warm up the voice. But, since time is of the essence, I suppose I can make an exception for today. Could you let me have the music, please, of the song you want to work on?'

'I'm afraid I only have the words,' she said, rummaging in her bag. 'You see, quite a few in our choir are unable to read music, so it's deliberately not provided, to prevent people feeling inadequate if others around them can follow the notes, but *they* can't. In fact, there's not even a piano in the hall we rehearse in, so our choir-leader uses a backing-track.'

'Oh, it's *that* sort of choir,' he said, with a shrug.

She bristled at his disparaging tone. 'It's actually a rather special one,' she retorted, albeit softly. 'You see, everyone in Larks Ascending has been affected by cancer in some way. They're either survivors, or carers, or people who've lost loved ones to cancer, so musical ability is considered less important than the benefits of singing – how it boosts one's mood and general health and so on.'

Disconcertingly, he said nothing in reply, so, to fill the edgy silence, she handed over the words of *Can't Help Falling in Love.*

'Oh, you sing *pop*!' he exclaimed, in the same unenthusiastic tone.

She gave a nervous laugh, still confused about the various categories of music. Katy had called the song a 'classic' – a word she'd assumed applied to Beethoven or Mozart, although in truth she was just as ignorant about such 'classical' composers as she was about the lighter stuff. 'Again, it's democratic,' she tried to explain. 'Choosing familiar songs that everybody knows' (except me, she didn't add), 'rather than more rarefied pieces.'

'Well, I must admit, I don't know that song myself. But no problem - I can Google it.' He strode over to the table, opened his laptop and, in seconds, the tune was echoing through the small, stuffy room. 'I see it's an Elvis Presley number,' he remarked, giving the name a note of undisguised distaste. It took him almost no time, however, to seat himself at the piano and play the tune with a passion and intensity she couldn't help but admire.

'Right,' he said, gesturing her over, let's get down to work. Do you sing alto or soprano?'

'I actually sing with the tenors and basses,' she mumbled, awkwardly.

'Surely that's not wise? It could damage your pharynx and strain your vocal chords, and it won't open up your higher register, either.'

'I don't have much higher register – that's the problem.'

'I'm not surprised. You're not giving yourself a chance. But, since we're pressed for time, you'd better sing your normal part for now and I'll pick it out as best I can. Start with the first two lines, OK?'

Despite it being the bass part, the first line was challengingly high, and, nervous as she was from this whole unpromising start, she managed only a strangled screech, instantly stopping short. 'I'm sorry,' she said, mortified. 'I'm afraid I'm a total dunce.'

'Veronica, before we go any further, you need to change your whole approach to singing. If you keep putting yourself down, your subconscious will pick up that negative message and we won't get anywhere. Instead, I want you to cultivate an attitude of defiance.'

That word again – and still not one in her vocabulary. Could one learn defiance in the last quarter of one's life, when one was far more used to submission?

'I want you to simply tell yourself that you can and will sing well, and cultivate an upbeat, can-do spirit. But first it's essential we work on your posture. Look at you, Veronica! Your shoulders are hunched, you're stooping badly, and you're looking down at the floor, and all that contortion makes your breathing very shallow, which sends you a completely contrary message – one of doubt and apprehension.'

She willed herself to vanish in a puff of smoke. It was no longer just her voice - now her stance, her body, her breathing, were all equally at fault.

'I want you to move from introversion to extroversion,' he continued, getting up from the piano and coming to stand beside her. 'And that means thrusting your chest forward, holding your head up higher and looking straight ahead.'

As one hand straightened her shoulders and the other tipped back her head, literally moulding her into shape, she felt a frisson of excitement ripple through her body. It was so long since she'd been touched. Indeed, never in her entire life had she been touched by any young, attractive man.

'Posture is all-important for singers,' he reiterated, watching eagle-eyed, in case she let her new position slip. 'And the key element of posture is alignment. You need to align your feet to your knees, your knees to your hips, your hips to your shoulders, and your shoulders to your ears.'

She was already confused, yet the barrage of instructions continued. At every rehearsal, Katy gave them a few basic tips about standing tall and keeping their stomach muscles loose, but never such an elaborate drill.

'Rotate your pelvis slightly, to unlock your knees.'

Even that was a puzzle. How were her knees and pelvis

connected?

'Now, place your feet shoulder-width apart and lean forward just a little, so that most of your weight is on the balls of your feet.' His frown deepened as he examined her stance. 'Your chin should be roughly parallel to the floor and your hands relaxed and held loosely at your sides.'

Relaxed? Was he joking? She felt like a contortionist, trying to hold her body in a totally unnatural pose. And she was all too aware of the clock on the mantelpiece, reminding her that she ought to rush back for Colin and dreading what might have happened in her absence. On the other hand, because of their late start, she'd had nowhere near her full hour's lesson and hadn't yet sung a single note.

'It's vital, Veronica, that you rid your body of all tension. Otherwise, it can spread to your tongue and jaw and throat and so fatally affect your voice.'

Yes, fatally was the word. She already felt like a broken reed. 'The problem is, Sebastian, I *do* feel a bit het up, what with this being my first lesson and the pressure of having to sing well at the Guy's gig, in little more than a week.'

'OK, we'll have to cut some corners right now, but I don't intend to make a habit of it. Next week, we'll start with the basics, but, just for today, we'd better use the remaining time to have another try at the song. Just the first two lines again, OK?'

She strained every muscle to think confidence, defiance, extroversion, relaxation, however unfamiliar the concepts, since she knew full well that if she trekked all the way back to Clapham without having done any singing, she was bound to feel deeply dejected. And, by some miracle – or fluke – she managed to make some rough approximation to the tune.

'That's better. Now continue, please. The next two lines - *For I Can't Help Falling in Love With You* - are the crux of the whole song and repeated four separate times, moving step by step. So, I want you to enunciate all those vowels and consonants as clearly as you can, roll them around your mouth and really try to *enjoy* them!'

It was less enjoyment than embarrassment she felt singing such lines to a man she'd only just met and young enough to be her son. And, because falling in love was, for her, another whole area of ignorance, she felt doubly out of her depth. Her mother's frequent abortive attempts at 'love' had left them both deeply distrustful of the sentiment, the string of hapless lovers now seeming little more than a crude but desperate search for security. Nonetheless, the memory was so upsetting, her voice faltered on the very word 'love'.

'Would it help if I sang with you?' Sebastian offered, with noticeable impatience, breaking off his accompaniment as she broke off the song.

'Yes, *please*!' She was bound to feel far less exposed if she was no longer singing solo.

'Right, we'll take it from the top again, OK?'

His richly expressive baritone was so resonant, so powerful, she tried to hook her own wavering voice to his, as if connecting with some energy-source. And the technique seemed to work, since she heard herself singing with less hesitancy and doubt, as she allowed his sonorous voice to carry hers along.

'That's a definite improvement,' he said, his face at last expressing a modicum of approval. 'So, let's try it once more, but this time we'll take it right through to the end.'

Again, she tried to imbue herself with confidence and, yes, defiance, remembering to breath correctly and hold her head up higher before they launched, once more, into the opening lines. And, despite her awkwardness and apprehension, she had to admit there was a certain excitement in singing a duet with such a handsome and distinguished man. Indeed, as they reached the final verse, she allowed herself a moment's ludicrous fantasy: she was his age now and he was singing to her, personally and specifically, with all the passion and devotion she had only ever known from romantic books and movies.

CHAPTER 4

'So, let me end where I began and welcome you all again – patients, staff, families, friends, carers and supporters – to our Cancer Survivors' Day.'

Veronica applauded enthusiastically as the Chairman of Guy's Hospital stepped down from the stage. He'd explained at the start of his talk that the day was a Celebration of Hope and hope did, indeed, seem tangible, symbolized by the multi-coloured bunting and balloons, the swarms of excited children sporting face-paint and fancy dress, and the rollicking tune just struck up by the band.

As the audience began dispersing, Charlotte rallied their small Larks Ascending group. 'We still have an hour in hand before our first performance, so where shall we start? Do you fancy a bite to eat, or a tour of all the stalls, or how about attending one of the talks?'

'The one about lymphedema is a definite must for me.' Michael gestured to his bandaged leg.

'I'd prefer a pony-ride,' Yvonne joked. 'They have some Shetland ponies here, so someone told me earlier.'

'For the under-tens, I imagine, though,' Charlotte put in, tartly, 'not the over-eighties.'

'Well, whatever else we do,' Dorothy insisted, 'I can't miss the Fashion Show. I promised Samantha I'd support her and I have to say it must take guts to strut your stuff as a model at the age of seventy-nine and after a double mastectomy.'

'That's not on till four, though.' Clive was flipping through his programme. 'And the lymphedema talk is later still, so how about some food first? Has anyone had lunch?'

Almost no one, it appeared. Getting here by early afternoon had meant a rush for most, especially those with long journeys and/or families.

'Let's eat outside?' Catherine suggested. 'It's such a gorgeous day. I noticed a food-stall, when I first arrived, selling sandwiches and cakes and a few decent-looking hot dishes.'

'But can we sit down out there?' asked Michael, noticeably hobbling as they all made their way towards the exit.

'Yes, there's plenty of tables and chairs, even a couple of beach-umbrellas, if anyone wants shade.'

As they ambled in twos and threes towards the food-stall, Charlotte linked her arm through Veronica's, much to the latter's surprise. The woman was often acerbic, not given to displays of affection, although, in today's celebratory atmosphere, she appeared to have thawed and mellowed. And, once they were all seated round the table, eating, drinking, chatting, the sense of camaraderie was as warm and substantial as the creamy, chunky fish chowder Veronica had ordered. She couldn't help reflecting on the huge distance she had come since joining the choir six months ago: a non-singer, then, an outsider, indeed, an abnormal person who never shared meals or activities with anyone. Now, though, she was accepted as one of the crowd, and, even Megan's absence – away with her pregnant niece on a spa-weekend in Newbury – couldn't spoil this gratifying feeling of belonging and togetherness.

'Veronica's an unusual name,' Michael remarked, leaning across to pour her a glass of wine.

'It still seems a bit strange to me, to tell the truth. I was always called Ron as a child, you see, and right on through my adult life, and only switched to full, formal Veronica when I joined the choir. And, since my maiden name was Simon, and my mother, Denise, was known as Den, there was nothing very girly about us. So, it's quite a treat to have a feminine name!'

Everybody laughed, although she herself had to make an effort to suppress the painful truth that her single-parent mother had most vehemently not wanted a child, let alone a girl-child, and had made no secret of the fact. Had the 'Ron' been an attempt to make the highly inconvenient baby daughter a fraction less unacceptable?

'I was called Lottie as a child,' Charlotte observed, 'a shortening I abhorred. But the more I made my aversion clear, the more my three brothers used it, simply to annoy me.'

'It's not as bad as Dotty,' Dorothy countered. 'That's a real handicap!'

'Well, at least my name can't be shortened' - Barry paused to take a massive bite from his cheese-and-ham baguette - 'although I'm not mad-keen on it. I was called after my Dad, see, and he was a right chancer!'

Veronica was invariably fascinated by these glimpses of people's families. As a child, forced to fit in with her mother's nomadic life, she'd had little idea how other people lived and whether some of them might be equally cut off. Anyone with siblings, though, must surely feel less isolated, so she had dreamed up a couple of comfort-sisters (one older, one younger, both loving and affectionate), not only to fill the gap, but to prevent her mother's unpredictable mood-changes being directed at her alone.

When the conversation turned to Barry's father – a hard drinker and a gambler –Glenys, sitting on her other side, took the chance to lower her voice in a private exchange, 'May I ask you a favour, Veronica?'

''Course! Go ahead.'

'I wondered if you'd mind helping me choose some sort of headgear.' She gave a nervous laugh. 'You see just last week, a child in the street stared at my bald head in horror and asked its Mum, "Is that a man or a woman?", so I feel it's high time I made myself more presentable! And today's the perfect chance, because there's a specialist shop right here in the cancer centre, just a hop and a skip away. I've already had a quick recce, but there were so many styles, I couldn't make up my mind. You always look so elegant, so it would be great to have your advice.'

A good thing, Veronica thought, that Glenys hadn't seen her during all the years she'd been looking after Tom. 'Elegant' was hardly the word for the baggy tracksuits, stain-proof fabrics and sturdy lace-up shoes the role of carer had necessitated. Yet, weirdly, that messy, shabby self still seemed the real one, while her new 'choir self' remained something of an imposter.

'Yes, I'd love to help,' she said, glad to have this chance to get to know Glenys better, since, despite several confidential exchanges, they hadn't yet cemented any real or lasting friendship. 'In fact, let's go right away, to give you time to try on various things. We've both finished eating, so ….'

'But don't you want a coffee?'

'We can have that later on. We're here all day, remember, and Katy's scheduled lots of breaks in our programme.'

While the others returned to the stall for dessert, she and Glenys slipped away, re-entered the main building, and squeezed through the crowds clustering round a range of stalls selling everything from hospital T-shirts to hand-made jewellery. It was much quieter in the shop, where the array of wigs prompted Veronica to count her blessings in having hair at all -doggedly thick hair, indeed - rather than facing the dilemma of whether to display an undisguised bald head, or don a hot, heavy wig in today's temperature of thirty degrees. Glenys had told her in private that her hair had fallen out in great, distressing clumps and that she'd also lost her eyebrows and lashes. 'There are no eyebrow-wigs,' she'd joked, the jest disguising the courage it must take to come to terms with such losses. And that same courage was in evidence from other choir-members who had suffered still more seriously, losing breasts, wombs, large sections of skin, even limbs and organs. And, although mercifully 'intact' herself, Veronica felt a bond with them, since her long years of looking after Tom had demanded similar bravery and strength.

Glenys clearly disliked the idea of a wig and, after some discussion, the two of them decided that a turban was the best option. 'What we need to establish first,' Veronica said, sorting through the rail, 'is whether you want to make a statement or merge into the crowd.'

'Oh, make a statement any day!' Glenys replied, more assertively than usual.

'Well, in that case, how about these animal-print ones – the zebra or the leopard? Or, look - this one's rather special, with those ruffles round the bottom and that rather fetching scarf-thing down the back.'

'Oh, yes. I love the colours. I shan't merge into any crowds in that brilliant gold and scarlet!'

'Try it on then.' Tactfully, she looked away, as Glenys removed her tatty bandeau, which failed to cover a few sad clumps of greyish stubble. Once the turban was in place, the saleswoman came gliding over to purr her compliments, which seemed a shade fulsome when all three women knew perfectly well that *hair* would look infinitely better than any mere cover-up. Her well-intentioned disingenuousness reminded Veronica of certain cancer websites that depicted ever-smiling women so ravishingly gorgeous they made one almost *want* to go bald, with no terror in their eyes of the dread disease reoccurring, or fear of long-term complications; just airbrushed rose-pink prettiness all round. Yet the reality was rather different. Having seen a photo of Glenys before her illness, the contrast with her present self was cruel - not just lack of hair, but the loss of her attractive curves and former healthy glow. She was now achingly thin and as greyish-pale as the dregs of milk in a cereal-bowl.

As Glenys continued checking her reflection in the mirror, Veronica couldn't help but wonder how much her changed appearance upset her. Did mirrors become the enemy for cancer-patients – a constant reminder of a self destroyed? 'Try a few more,' she urged, desperately wanting her to find the perfect headgear. 'There's plenty of time before the fashion show and you need to be sure there's nothing you prefer. How about this, for instance?' She was doing her best to pick out styles suited to Glenys's colouring, whilst providing a touch of panache

Eventually, however, Glenys returned to her first choice. 'The more I try on, the more I tend to dither, so, let me go and pay the bill, then we can have that coffee you missed. And coffee's on me, by the way.'

'Forgive me asking, Veronica,' Glenys said, as they sat with cappuccinos and cream-filled cakes in the ground-floor coffee-shop, 'but I wondered if *you've* had cancer.'

'No, I'm blessed in that respect. It was my stepson who had it, sadly.' She deliberately didn't mention the fact that Tom's cancer had come as an unexpected blow on top of his lifelong disability, the latter diagnosed when he was barely one-year old. The memories were too painful to revisit, so she explained instead how she had come to join the choir. 'There was a notice up at the hospital where he was having his cancer treatment. I have to say I ignored it at first, because I've never been able to sing and was fearfully busy anyway. But, when Tom died, my whole existence sort of ground to a halt – you know, without him to look after, and with no outside job or anything. So, one of the oncology nurses suggested I go along to the choir, just for a trial session, for support and companionship more than the actual singing.'

Paralysed by grief, it had taken her more than eighteen months to act on that advice, but no point boring Glenys with more details of her personal life, so she concluded, briefly, instead, 'And now I try my best never to miss a Thursday.'

'But you *did* miss last week. What happened?'

'Oh, just a last-minute hitch.' How would Glenys understand Colin's sudden frightening tantrum as she was on the point of leaving, when she herself could barely fathom what had upset him so profoundly?

'I'm sorry, Veronica, I intended to get in touch to check you were OK, but things have been mega-hectic, with my brother and all his family staying. Still, the only thing you missed, besides the singing, was Katy's announcement that we're setting up an official fund-raising group. She gave this little spiel after the rehearsal about the choir's finances being rather rocky and how she wants us to pitch in ourselves with lots of money-making ideas. She told me later, in private – and do keep this confidential – there's a danger of the choir actually having to close.'

'Oh, *no*!' The 'no' came out like a wail – and with reason, for God's sake. Without the weekly rehearsals, Veronica would lose the only place she felt normal and where she could interact with other people, converse, confide, even *laugh*. Just entering the hall seemed to transform her into a different person, whereas returning home to Colin, a mere couple of hours later, she became a Cinderella whose ball-gown had changed back to rags, and whose melodious name, Veronica, had contracted back to discordant Ron. Indeed, without the choir, this second self she'd created, so vastly more appealing than her unvarnished original self, would lose its whole context and setting, and would simply, ignominiously, collapse.

'Don't worry. We intend to fight that prospect tooth and nail! I say "we" because she's asked me to be the chairperson, in light of the fact I've already had experience of raising cash for charities. And she herself is working on it flat out, despite all her other commitments. She's just negotiated a special rate to hire a room adjoining the hall that should suit us very well, since it's small and cosy and much less institutional. And, of course, people are far more likely to join the group if the meetings are held in the same place as our rehearsals, either just before choir, or straight after. We decided *before* would be better - except for the first meeting, which has to be an evening, because I've invited a professional fund-raiser who won't be free till then. He's quite a charismatic type, so I hope he'll start us off with a bang! Anyway, put the date in your diary, because I'd love you to come, Veronica – it's Thursday 13 July.'

She didn't answer for a moment, aware it would mean leaving Colin alone for an additional hour or two. He was so obstinate, he refused to allow a carer to set foot in the house and had driven away the entire social-work team, despite their offers of help and support, which for her would have been a godsend. Today, she'd been forced to resort to subterfuge and beg her next-door neighbour, Beryl, to pop in several times, on some fabricated pretext, to ensure that Colin was upright, coping and continent. 'Can I let you know that same week?' she asked. Evenings were especially difficult, because Colin started drinking as early as four or five - his way of blanking out the reality of his physical and mental state, which only made both worse, of course.

'Absolutely. On the day, if you want. But, look, here I am, rabbiting on, when it's just ten minutes till the Fashion Show! We ought to make a move right now, if we want to get decent seats.'

In fact, the others had forestalled them and were sitting in the very front row, two spare seats in the centre piled with bags and cardigans.

'Quick, sit down!' Michael urged. 'We've had quite a problem keeping these two free.'

Once they'd settled themselves, Catherine admired the new turban. 'And, would you believe, it exactly matches these chairs!'

The chairs in question – gold with scarlet seats – helped give the sense of a proper Parisienne fashion show, especially once the band struck up and the models started sauntering in, striking dramatic poses to display their finery. Men were in a definite minority: four male models as against some fifteen females, the latter displaying a variety of outfits, from a hobble-skirted cocktail-dress to a beaded turquoise sari, and even a Scottish kilt in a vibrant black-and-yellow tartan. Every model was smiling and the smiles were so infectious, Veronica found herself smiling, too, as she joined in the rhythmic clapping initiated by the audience in time to the catchy music – a veritable cannonade of applause.

Samantha, however, proved the star of the show in a full-length evening-dress spangled blue and silver, with an exotic feathered headdress in the same vivacious blue. The minute she appeared, the applause grew still more exuberant, accompanied by spontaneous cheers – cheers that changed to laughter when Geoffrey strutted in and broke into a song-and-dance routine, sporting nothing but a black top-hat and ultra-brief Lycra shorts. Despite his skimpy attire, he was sweating profusely – one of the side-effects of the hormones he took for prostate-cancer. He joked openly at rehearsals about his hot flushes and night-sweats and how, any day now, he'd be forced to buy a bra for the breastlets he was sprouting.

Courageous again, Veronica thought, to laugh away such threats to his masculinity. But courage was an integral part of this day, and, after the finale – with all nineteen models assembled on-stage, twirling paper windmills in time to the fervent applause - it was very much in evidence once more, when three cancer-survivors recounted their personal stories.

The final speaker, Isobel, made the greatest impact, on account of her youth and her long and gruelling saga, involving multiple surgeries, repeated cycles of chemo-and radiotherapy, and even a bone-marrow transplant.

'But I'm still here,' she concluded, on a note of jaunty triumph. 'In fact, I'm very much alive - not just surviving, but positively thriving!'

Veronica couldn't help but feel a certain scepticism. Was this woman's stance another type of airbrushing, emphasizing the happy outcome, whilst concealing a host of daunting after-effects? Yet the phrase itself, 'positively thriving', had hit her with a jolt, since it went against the grain of her entire life-experience. No one she knew had 'positively thrived', least of all her mother, who'd simply muddled through in face of often self-created difficulties. Yet why follow Den's example of inbuilt pessimism? It had done damage enough in her childhood, but she was grown-up now, almost *old*, for pity's sake. And, in all that time, she had escaped the blight of cancer, side-effects and all, and was still alive and healthy and, today, surrounded by new friends. In fact, couldn't she agree that she was, indeed, positively thriving – if only here, now, for this one, short, special day?

And, a little later on, *she* would be performing and – thanks to Sebastian's tuition - able to sing at least one of the choir's extensive repertoire of songs loud and clear and, yes, very nearly confidently.

CHAPTER 5

Veronica broke into an uninhibited dance, trying to copy the wildly sensual gyrations she was watching on her laptop, the video so blatantly raunchy, her chaste, pink-pastel bedroom seemed to blush a deep, incriminating crimson. Never before had she seen such a sexy mover, the camera now lingering on his buttocks, as they swivelled from side to side, the sheer suggestiveness of the motion emphasized by skin-tight red-leather trousers. He was naked to the waist, the rippling flesh of his torso gleaming in the stage-lights, his wide-lipped, sensuous mouth pumping out each word of the lyrics with total conviction and commitment. As the song reached its climax, she increased the tempo of her own manic dance, then collapsed on to the bed, amazed at her reaction to a singer she'd never even heard of when they'd first rehearsed the song two weeks ago - a new one in their repertoire.

Fortunately, she'd learned to conceal her ignorance, since Freddie Mercury, apparently, was one of the greatest singers of all time, and only seriously peculiar people would not have known his name. However, this last fortnight, to make up for her cluelessness, she'd been watching all his videos online, especially the different recordings of *Don't Stop Me Now*. Its sheer, exhilarating hedonism was the complete antithesis of her upbringing, when 'stop' had been a constant injunction: 'Stop talking.' 'Stop slouching.' 'Stop messing up your room.' 'Stop scuffing your shoes on the pavement.' She'd wondered sometimes if her mother meant 'Stop *living*.'

The others in the choir scarcely seemed to register the full force of the words, their responses probably dulled, as so often, by their very familiarity with both the singer and the song. To her, in contrast, each and every line had the impact of a breaking wave, flinging up great spumes of spray, upending every maxim she'd been taught: not discipline and self-control, but rebellion, pleasure, self-indulgence. But, while Freddie insisted he was having far too good a time to stop, her mother denounced him with equal conviction: 'And that's the very reason you *should* stop, you degenerate!'. Den's wrathful bellow, however, didn't quite obliterate a peevish cry from downstairs.

'Ron! Ron! Where *are* you?'

Guiltily, she sprang up from the bed, turned off her laptop and dashed down to the sitting-room, where she had left Colin watching the cricket. Her husband's shambling, pregnant-bellied figure was in such contrast to Freddie's lithe, leaping, lunging body, she felt anger with them both: the former for his lumpen torpor, the latter for stirring feelings in her that were bewildering at her age, if not downright dangerous.

'What's wrong?' she asked her husband.

'There's someone at the door.' His voice was rising querulously. 'They've been ringing loudly for several minutes. Why didn't you come down?'

Because she had failed to hear the doorbell, having deliberately turned the sound up high, to drown out her mother's nagging with the exuberant force of Freddie's counter-messages. 'Don't worry – I'll get it now.' She sprinted along the hall and opened the front door, dismayed to see her next-door-neighbour, Beryl, who, for some inexplicable reason had turned up two hours early.

'I know you said five, Ron, but now we're into this new regime, I thought we'd need some extra time, so you can show me the ropes and explain things.'

'Er, it's *not* a new regime ….' Beryl was still standing on the doorstep and, for the sake of common courtesy, should be invited in.

Veronica struggled between politeness and annoyance. She'd already told Beryl – indeed, only yesterday - that she'd be doing exactly what she'd done before, namely, keeping a surreptitious watch on Colin, the only difference being that it would now be a paid job, with a proper hourly rate. It seemed exploitative not to reimburse her neighbour for what would be several hours 'on duty' this evening. She was lucky to *have* the money – something she never took for granted, even after forty years with Colin.

'But what about your husband's supper?' Beryl was asking now.

'I'll do that before I go.'

'Or getting him to bed?'

'Time enough for that when I return.'

'To be honest, Ron, what I still don't get is why I have to sit in a different room. I mean, how can I keep a proper eye on him if we're separated by a wall?'

Impossible for Beryl to understand Colin's idiosyncrasies, especially his dislike of being in the same room as anybody else, including his own wife, or sharing meals with anyone. She couldn't blame it on his dementia; all their married life, he had felt a certain unease about any sort of intimacy, and that, coupled with a deep desire to escape his disabled child, had often driven him from the house. Although he'd never articulated his feelings, she knew he regarded Tom's pitiful condition as reflecting on him personally in a highly adverse manner, since no normal, macho man would have produced a 'spastic' son.

'Look, you'd better come in,' she said, feigning a smile for Beryl, while her mind continued to dwell on the past and on Colin's repeated efforts to put a distance – geographical and emotional –

between himself and Tom. For many years, work had proved a very handy excuse – no one could argue with meetings, deadlines, business crises – while his membership of a small, local Business Association provided ample reason for his frequent evening absences. And, even now that he was confined at home, with no Tom to avoid, he absented himself in a different way, sitting alone with the television and shutting her out with cricket, football, golf. All the years she'd known him, he had never cultivated friends, and even acquaintances were kept strictly at arm's length, since they, like wives, might wish to get too close.

'Don't worry, Beryl,' she said, ushering her neighbour into the dining-room, 'Although you may not be able to see him, you'll hear him easily. He's right next door in the sitting-room and, before I go, I'll make sure both doors are open. And, anyway, you can pop in every now and then, just to check on him, like you did two Sundays ago.'

'But won't he think it's odd I'm here at all?'

'He won't ask. If it does cross his mind, he'll just assume you've come to help me with some computer problem or ....'

'But surely he'll know you're out?'

'Maybe, maybe not. He forgets a lot of stuff and, with any luck, he'll fall asleep while he's watching the box. But, I'm sorry, Beryl, I really must get changed now, so if you like to make yourself comfortable in here, I'll get you a tea or coffee.' Far better for her neighbour to pop back home and show up again at five, as asked. But, gritting her teeth, she went to fetch her a drink and a snack and a pile of magazines, before returning upstairs.

She was keen to spend some time on her appearance, not only for the usual choir-rehearsal, but because it was the first meeting of the fund-raising group. Since joining the choir, she'd been experimenting with new clothes and different hair-colours, and now sat down at her dressing-table mirror to reappraise the Clairol Vivacious Red. Although she'd chosen it for its name, it was in fact a pleasingly subtle auburn and a definite advance on the rather brassy brown she'd tried originally when still a hair-colour virgin. Colin wouldn't have noticed if she'd worn a sky-blue-pink wig, or put a live chicken on her head, but her Thursday friends were more observant and decidedly more complimentary. Catherine had even told she had a good figure and great dress-sense - impossible to believe, having been criticized throughout her childhood as an ugly, clumsy carthorse. Whatever Catherine might say, the carthorse stubbornly stayed around, refusing to give place to a gazelle.

Yet, the minute she turned on the video again, its wanton words and intoxicating rhythms caught her in their spell once more, and, in time to the music, she kicked off her shoes, pulled the brown-patterned top over her head, and dragged down her gravy-coloured skirt – both chosen on account of Colin, because any staining didn't show too much. This evening, however, she was dressing not as a carer but in honour of Freddie Mercury and had bought herself a vivid scarlet top to match his skin-tight trousers, as if his own flamboyant flair had leeched out from the video to transform her usual low-key clothes. Red was a new colour for her, signalling desire, passion, anger, revolution – all exciting, although highly dangerous forces.

Only when she returned downstairs, did her usual worries return. Could she rely on Beryl to stick to rules she must find odd in the extreme, and also to contact her immediately in the event of an emergency? Would Colin resent the woman's presence if she happened to barge into the sitting-room, rather than peek in unobtrusively? How much booze might he knock back during the long spell she'd be gone?

Before she left, she poured him the new, non-alcoholic drinks she'd selected on account of their kick - a so-called 'Fiery' ginger beer, a Norfolk Punch, fierce with spice and ginger, and a sparkling pear-juice fizzing with semi-convincing bubbles. Yet, even as she set down the glasses, she knew her wish to wean him off the hard stuff was totally and utterly futile, however zingy these alternatives. With a sigh, she returned to the kitchen to fetch his supper, first checking with Beryl if she too would like a meal.

'No, I'm more than happy with this cake, dear.'

'OK, I'd better be off, then. I've pinned up my number on the board in the hall, so you can't fail to see it.'

'But I know your number, Ron. There's no need for all this fuss. I'm not a cretin.'

She winced at the word. In the early days, before things improved, cretin was one of the words used for people like Tom. Cretin, spastic, retard - all infuriatingly unfair for an innocent baby injured during his protracted, hazardous birth.

Still torn between anxiety and a strong desire to escape, she popped in to Colin one last time. 'I'll be a bit later than usual, darling, but not to worry, Peter will look after you.' She had already settled the dog beside him, as a reassuring influence. 'And I know,' she added, placing Peter's nose just over the edge of the plate, to remind Colin food was there to be eaten, 'he'll love this nice cheese flan.' She had long since stopped cooking messy foods like stew or curry or pasta, which he would only spill on himself, his clothes and the carpet, and now tried to steer a course between convenience and reasonably good nutrition.

Only when she was out of the door and halfway down the street, did she realize she herself hadn't eaten a thing since breakfast.

Who cared? Food and drink hardly mattered when she was about to be sustained and nourished by company and conversation.

'Silence, please!' Katy called, waiting till the chatter had died down and she'd secured everyone's attention, 'Now, as most of you know, we're holding the first meeting of our fund-raising group this evening, straight after our rehearsal, and in the smaller room right next to this hall. Some of you have already signed up for it online, but if anyone else would like to come along today, you'll be extremely welcome. And, if anyone has questions, please do ask them now.'

There were only a couple, after which Katy asked all who were well enough to get up to their feet. 'Right, let's get started and kick off with a few relaxation exercises. I'd like you all to imagine you're highly-strung Persian cats, clinging to the curtains with tense, hysterical claws, your eyes and faces screwed up really tight.'

Veronica's nails were digging into her palms with the sheer effort of making herself the tensest cat imaginable, and muffled giggles were escaping from the others as they, too, followed suit.

'Fantastic! Now I want you to change into nice, calm, soppy Labrador pups – eyes wide open, tongues hanging loose, paws stretched out in front of you in a relaxed and open stance.'

'Fabulous! Now change from cats to dogs six times in a row, and very fast.'

Veronica relished the sense of *playing*. In her childhood, playing had been discouraged as unsafe, unnecessary. However, the new choir-member, Christopher, standing right beside her, was certainly entering into the spirit of the thing, his cat-dog switch so rapid it resembled a speeded-up movie. Indeed, his young, attractive presence was a fillip in itself, making her feel a full-blooded female, rather than nursemaid to a dilapidated octogenarian husband. Although guilty at such disloyalty to Colin, she couldn't seem to help the fact that, in the last two weeks, the combination of Freddie Mercury and a few fanciable tenors like Christopher and Keith were reigniting a sensuality she'd assumed had vanished for ever.

'Next, we're going to work the jaw and mouth muscles. So, pretend I've made you a nice, big, squidgy chocolate cake, and stuff a huge great slice of it, whole, into your mouths and chew really hard and vigorously.'

Veronica chewed until her mouth ached. Whatever the scientific reasons for these exercises, for her they were important games that changed her from the anxious carer she had to be at home into a carefree kid at playschool – a kid constantly praised and encouraged for doing almost nothing.

'Brilliant, all of you! Really, really good! And let's follow that with a few vocalizations, OK? I want you to start with "ssss-ssss' and hiss like angry snakes, up and down the scale.'

Veronica turned herself from playschool kid into dangerous python, hissing with all the venom she could muster. Not to be outdone, Christopher's hiss was so comically exaggerated, it made them both shake with laughter.

'Wonderful! You're all in really great form tonight. Now change to 'ma-ma-ma' and repeat it over and over, starting higher each time.'

As the ma-ma-mas rose and fell around her, Veronica wondered, as so often, why her mother had never let her call her Mama, Mum, or Mummy, but always and only Den – the only answer, presumably, being that then her mum could pose as young, available and unhampered by a child.

'Perfect! And now we've done the warm-up, we need to work on our new song, which I know some of you are finding a bit difficult. But, for goodness' sake, don't let that inhibit you. You know what I always say: "Wrong but strong is miles better than right but mute." I've noticed a few of you just mouthing the words with no sound coming out, which is the very last thing I want.'

'Strong but wrong', Veronica reflected, was the polar opposite of all her mother's dictums. According to Den, women could *never* be strong – mainly on account of men's overbearing deficiencies – and, as for being wrong, that was highly reprehensible. So, it was thrilling to have permission to make a hash of something, yet not be punished for it or put down. Indeed, Katy's usual response to any choir-member's mistake was a happy, kindly laugh, not a tirade of abuse.

Indeed, their choir-leader was laughing now, even doing a little dance on the spot, as if to encourage them all to let go. 'Even if you're not sure how it goes, just sing out loud and proud, then, if anything's not quite right, we can work on it together.'

'Loud and proud' was equally liberating, Veronica thought with pleasure, after a lifetime of being ssshhed: 'Pipe down, Ron. Shut up! No one has the slightest interest in hearing what you have to say.'

'But, what I suggest is we slow things down a bit and take the song line by line, OK, starting with the tenors and basses.'

Ejecting her mother from the hall, Veronica tried to make her mouth as mobile and wanton as Freddie's, as she joined in with the men, her voice blending seamlessly with the great fanfare of sound. And, there and then, she made a fervent vow that no one and nothing would stop her being a hedonistic, self-indulgent Freddie Mercury tonight, rather than a self-denying Ron.

'We're extremely lucky,' Katy said, smiling at the short, silver-haired man standing on her left, 'to have Alex Sutherland here with us tonight. Alex is the CEO of one of Europe's leading PR, Marketing and Communications firms, where he heads up a large, specialized team. He's more used to raising funds for major corporations, so the fact that he's helping us in our much more modest efforts is a tribute to ….'

Veronica could barely concentrate, transfixed as she was by Alex himself – the spit-image of Leonard, the only one of her mother's lovers she had ever liked, indeed, admired, and whom she had kept alive in her mind and heart since the age of twelve-and-a-half, when Den had first brought him home. She stared at Alex in fascinated disbelief: the same thick silver hair, the same unusually dark-blue eyes, not far off navy in shade, the same smart suit, the same upright, almost military bearing. Hair, clothes and posture had all endowed him with gravitas, made him seem reassuringly old and safe. Although too young then to tell grown-ups' ages, it was obvious he was old enough to be her father and, having never had a dad, she'd been searching for a substitute since very early childhood. However, her mother's string of highly unsuitable men had caused her to lose hope, until the evening Leonard appeared. He wasn't tall or even good-looking; his appeal lay in the fact that he didn't see her as an irritating impediment to his making out with Den, but took the trouble to talk to her, even asked her opinion on things, which no one had ever done. And he made wonderfully silly jokes and bought her loads of presents – always the right gifts, as if he knew her tastes instinctively.

After only a month of his visits, she had begged her mother to marry him, daring to hope they might become, at last, a proper family – father, mother, daughter – and live in Leonard's clean and tidy house. Up till then, they seemed to have been forever moving from one scruffy flat to another, or even from one country to another, if Den's current lover happened to live abroad. And, of course, those constant moves from 'home' to 'home' involved frequent changes of school, and she'd be struggling to learn new teachers' names, or even learn a new language, only to be yanked away again and transplanted somewhere else.

'Alex has set us a target,' Katy continued, gesturing to the whiteboard on which were written various figures, 'of twenty-thousand pounds. That's peanuts compared to the substantial sums he's used to raising in his day-job, but it will still take a lot of work and application for our choir to find that sum. And that's where you all come in.'

Veronica tried to concentrate, but it was *Leonard's* voice she was hearing, *Leonard's* face she was seeing - weirdly similar to Alex's, but with a gentler and less arrogant expression. She could even smell the Lifebuoy soap he used, feel the rough graze of his duffle-coat, which he used to leave on the peg in the hall, when upstairs with her mother. She would lay her cheek against it, do her best to blank out what was going on between the pair of them in bed, pretend it was *her* he'd come to see, dressed in her best frilly frock, not disgustingly naked Den.

'Alex has been kind enough to put together a video presentation, with some really helpful clips of all the different ways his clients have raised money, be that holding a grand ball or a barbecue, or taking part in a sponsored run or cycle-ride, or commandeering your local pub for a quiz-night or a karaoke session.'

Veronica did her best to keep her mind on karaoke and cycle-rides, yet could barely understand what was happening to her internally. Extraordinary as it sounded, she was re-experiencing the anguish she had felt at Leonard's disappearance, all those years ago. He had lasted a mere two months, discarded by her mother as too old, too staid, too stuffy – a ridiculously wrong decision, since the whole point of fathers was they *must* be old and staid.

Only the sound of wine being poured jolted her back to the present. Clive and Michael had begun passing glasses around, presumably on Katy's instructions, although, if there'd been an announcement, it had completely passed her by, entangled as she had been in the past, recalling her desperate hope that Leonard might return, or her mother change her mind. In little more than a week, however, Den had shacked up with a different man - decades younger, but a noisy, bad-tempered brute who shouted and slammed doors and patently disliked any child who might keep him from Den's bed. Fortunately, he, too, had been discarded almost as soon as he'd arrived.

Despite the subsequent succession of men forever in pursuit of her mother's brassiere-popping breasts, it was Leonard she herself had retained somewhere deep in the recesses of her mind. Every night, in her fantasies, he would tuck her in, read her a bedtime story (although she was far too old for them), and, every weekend, they would set off for the sweetshop together and he'd give her half-a-crown to splurge on sherbet lemons. Half a crown was a fortune and, even after the change to decimal currency, Leonard's pockets continued clinking with half-crowns and threepenny-pieces – at least in her imagination. The halfpenny had a ship on, the threepenny-bit a bird, and the shilling featured a happy-looking lion standing on a crown - all infinitely more magical than the new coins.

'Alex has brought us all a Fund-Raiding Pack that features many of these ideas. So, Glenys, if you could pass them round ...'

Veronica took her pack, its glossy professionalism rebuking her distracted mind, although, when Michael offered her a glass of wine, she accepted with alacrity. She had eaten nothing since breakfast and it was unwise to drink on an empty stomach, yet she needed some resource to help her come to terms with this extraordinary coincidence of Leonard 'reappearing'.

Once everyone was settled with their drinks, Alex wiped the whiteboard clean and used it as a screen to project his laptop images, full-size. She forced her attention back to him, determined to scrape him free of Leonard and take some interest in this presentation, behave like a cooperative and rational grown-up, rather than a lovesick adolescent.

'Thank you, Alex,' Katy said, with a genuinely appreciative smile, 'for that fantastic presentation and also for your patience in answering all our questions. I'm sure we all have a much better idea of what we need to do to save our choir. And I must impress on everyone here that there is a serious danger of Larks Ascending having to close if we don't reach our target figure. So, I want you all to go away inspired to do your bit for this really vital cause. I promise not to delay you much longer, but our Chairperson, Glenys, wants to say a few words.'

Glenys, new turban in place, went to stand in front of the assembled group. 'Well, as Katy said, we all need to choose our individual way of raising money and to encourage our friends and families to join us in our efforts. But all I want to do, before we disperse, is appoint the other officers needed for the group – Vice-Chair, Treasurer and Secretary. The Vice-Chair must be ready to take over the meetings, if for any reason I'm not here, the Treasurer must clearly have financial nous and knowhow, while much of the work of the Secretary can be done at home by anyone with good computer skills.'

Before Glenys had finished speaking, Veronica's hand shot up. 'Could *I* be Secretary?' she asked, astonished at putting herself forward in so brazen a fashion, before anyone else had had a chance to volunteer. Had the wine gone straight to her head? Or was she still stuck at age twelve, trying to impress Leonard, as she had indeed done back then: learning new words from the dictionary, or pretending to enjoy boring books like *Ivanhoe* and *Silas Marner*?

'Yes, perfect, Veronica – thank you. As I said, most of the work can be done from home, but you will, of course, need to take the minutes at each meeting.'

Instantly, she was tempted to withdraw. How could she get to all the meetings if Colin's condition deteriorated, or Beryl decided she no longer wished to help out? Yet Leonard was looking in her direction, nodding in approval.

'Good for you, Veronica! It's always encouraging to have an immediate response. Do you mind me asking, have you had any previous fund-raising experience?'

'Yes, quite a bit,' she said, again aghast at herself for admitting things she had told no one in the choir as yet. 'My stepson had cerebral palsy, so I was very much involved in trying to raise money for what in those days was The Spastics Society and later became Scope. Again, I did much of it from home, but I've certainly had plenty of practice in setting up donor databases and doing all the admin and suchlike.'

'Excellent!' Alex was all but purring his approval. 'That's

exactly the sort of thing we need.'

While Glenys pressed for volunteers for the other two posts, Veronica sat torn between her wifely duty and a deep desire to branch out in a new direction. All the years she'd been looking after Tom, any sort of outside job had been obviously impossible and, in the two years since his death, she had assumed it was too late for anyone to employ her - and she could offer little anyway as an unskilled woman only eight months short of sixty. But here was the perfect compromise: meaningful work involving other people, yet much of which could be done at home, to fill the lonely hours when Colin was in another room and they'd barely exchanged a single word all day. No way would she ignore his needs – that would be cruel and remiss - but it was hardly an easy task spending so much time caring for a man who frequently forgot her very existence.

Besides, she would never forgive herself if Larks Ascending was forced to close and she had played no part at all in trying to save it. Admittedly, that was a selfish impulse, since the choir was her vital lifeline, her way of keeping sane between one Thursday and the next. Indeed, just the thought of having a new role was rejuvenating and cheering in itself, so, selfish or not, she refused to withdraw her offer. She had been accepted by all present as the new official Secretary and, although her mother's beyond-the-grave putdown was already resounding in her head – 'You'll be rubbish at it, Ron' – for once she intended to ignore Den.

It was Leonard who had prompted her to volunteer in the first place – Leonard, the only person who had ever praised her as a child - so, however irrational and ridiculous that prompt might seem to others, she vowed solemnly to stick to her decision.

CHAPTER 6

Veronica gave the glasses one last (unnecessary) polish, desperate to stay as long as possible. She had volunteered to clear up, purely for that reason, and was now spinning out the chore. All the others had left, except for Glenys, who was having a final word with Alex at the other end of the room from the open-plan kitchen. She kept glancing across, as if hungry to get her fill of him and, all at once, he looked up and met her eye. Gratified by the approving glance he threw her, she hoped he was reflecting that, if she lavished such devotion on a mere domestic chore, he could count on her to bring the same commitment to her secretarial role. Yet she was also painfully conscious that this was their first and last encounter – a one-off, granted as favour to the choir, before Glenys took over as official fund-raiser.

As she swabbed the surfaces – third time - she tried frantically to come up with some scenario whereby she could meet this man again, however unlikely or impossible that seemed. Finally, however, she had no choice but to leave, not only to get back for Beryl, whom she feared would be getting restive at this lengthy caring stint, but because Glenys might appreciate a brief spell with Alex on her own, without the noise of clinking glasses or running water.

'Well, I'll be off,' she said, her casually cheerful tone concealing the anguish she felt at the thought of 'Leonard' disappearing for ever, a second time.

Glenys gave her a farewell hug, Alex a formal handshake. As her hot hand encountered the cool grip of his fingers, she imagined him hugging *her*: the sheeny texture of his wool-and-mohair suit pressing against her breasts, his hands clasped tightly round her back, as she inhaled his musky aftershave, so different from her husband's smell of poo and pee and gravy.

Was she out of her mind? She had definitely drunk too much – only a couple of glasses, admittedly, but they had bypassed her stomach and gone straight to her ditzy head, making her behave like a lovesick teenager.

As she stepped out in to the street, the sight and sound of a fierce and sudden downpour brought her swiftly down to earth. With neither raincoat or umbrella, she gave silent thanks that she lived a mere three streets away and should be home in a matter of minutes. Head down against the deluge, she battled her way along the puddled street, starting in surprise as a taxi swooped to a halt beside her.

'Hop in,' Alex shouted, winding down the window, 'and I'll give you a lift. Only ducks should be out in this weather!'

Gratefully, she clambered in and was about to reassure him that her home was so close by, she would barely take him out of his way. Yet, for some unfathomable reason, the words failed to take shape in her mouth and, when he asked directly where she lived, it was as if a puppet had commandeered her voice and she heard herself saying, 'I'm actually staying with a friend in Kentish Town tonight,'

She had no friend in Kentish Town, simply knew it was a good long drive from Clapham and that she must resort to any means to extend her time with Alex.

'Perfect! *I* live in Camden, so if the cabbie drops me off first, it's only a short drive for him to take you on to your friend's. In fact, you've saved me the price of a stamp! You see, just before I left, I was showing Glenys some detailed information on networking and the use of social media and setting up a blog and all that sort of stuff, and she thought it might be useful in your role as secretary. So I can hand it over in person now, rather than put it in the post.'

As he reached for his briefcase, the taxi gave a sudden lurch, throwing their bodies together, the momentary contact sending shockwaves through her system. And the steamed-up windows had created a sort of fug within the cab, their own private, intimate space as they sped through rain and darkness. As always, she was fighting two contradictory voices in her head: one strongly disapproving, telling her it was ludicrous, for the sake of a pointless lie, to have to catch the tube from Kentish Town and trek all the way back to Clapham in the still relentless rain, and that she was behaving irresponsibly, in leaving Beryl to cope with Colin far longer than was necessary. Yet, as another lurch sent his knee pressing into hers, a different, more persuasive voice was murmuring, 'You're *alone*. With *Leonard*. Anything could happen!'

CHAPTER 7

'Welcome!' Megan exclaimed, ushering her in to an arty-looking hall, its vibrant deep-purple walls, hung with a series of modernist prints. 'I can't believe it's taken all this time to actually persuade you to come round for supper! Which is all the more ridiculous considering what near-neighbours we are.'

Near in one sense, Veronica thought, but distant in another. Megan might live less than a mile away, but this particular part of Clapham was far more gentrified and trendy than her own shabbier, 'left-behind' area. 'Well, I shouldn't be here even now,' she said, her mind tracking back to Colin, as usual.

'But isn't Beryl holding the fort?'

Veronica nodded. 'Yes, but that doesn't stop me worrying. Still, the good thing is she seems only too happy to earn another whack as Colin-sitter. I just thank my lucky stars that nothing went wrong last Thursday, so she now imagines she's the perfect, natural-born carer.'

'Well, maybe she is. Her great advantage is that she's not related to Colin and that always lessens the tension. When my mother went doolally, I was the absolute worst person to look after her but, if I left her with a friend or neighbour, she was all sweetness and light, not the cantankerous old cow she always was with me! I was luckier than you, though, in that she never actually lived with me and I'd see her only at weekends or pop in for an hour or so mid-week. And, anyway, she died surprisingly peacefully before her Alzheimer's made her totally deranged. But let's not waste our time on her or Colin. I'm dying to know what happened with Alex, so come in and have a drink and spill the beans!'

Veronica immediately regretted having confided in her friend – an impulse phone-call she had tried, in fact, to terminate even while she was speaking. But Megan had refused to ring off before making her promise to come over as soon as possible, for the express purpose of recounting the whole saga – a prospect that now rendered her increasingly uncomfortable.

'Oh, I love your place!' she enthused, deliberately playing for time. Megan had opened the door to a large, light-filled room, with a spotless parquet floor and more abstract paintings making vivid splashes of colour on all four walls. 'And what a beautiful table!'

The table, constructed of highly polished, blue-grey steel, was laid with elegant white china, crimson paper-serviettes and an austere centrepiece of bare twigs and pinecones. Impossible, she thought, ever to invite Megan back to her own shabby, cluttered house, with its stained carpets and ingrained, unpleasant odours. Here, the only smell was the heady scent of roses from the vase of scarlet floribunda on the sideboard.

'This room feels so serene. I'd no idea you were such a homemaker.'

'Oh, it's easy when you live on your tod – no one else to inflict their rotten taste on you or mess the whole place up! My ex was hopelessly untidy, so, once I was rid of him, not to mention his equally messy predecessor, I deliberately moved to a modern new-build flat and started afresh, as it were.'

Ridding herself of two husbands made them sound like vermin, Veronica reflected, a temporary infestation you could remove with traps and poison. She found Megan's toughness enviable, in one sense, yet also disconcerting. How could any woman be so brazenly self-sufficient – something she herself had never been and probably never would? But to have a friend so different from her was part of the attraction – indeed, to have a friend at all, when, for most of her life, friendship had been difficult, whether due to Den's constant house-moves, or Tom's all-consuming neediness, or her present reluctance to let anyone see Colin in his lamentably vacant state. As a child, she had envied bananas in bunches, or peas in pods. How wonderful to be securely joined to others, or have a row of identical siblings nestled reassuringly close.

'Do sit down, love, there's some prosecco chilling in the fridge. Or would you prefer a fruit-juice?'

'Prosecco sounds perfect.'

As Megan went out to the kitchen, Veronica settled herself on the ice-white sofa, ruefully reflecting that her own current furnishings had to be strictly Colin-proof, which meant mainly multi-patterned or mud-coloured.

Megan returned with two frosted glasses and a tray of nibbles: tiny cubes of cheese and ham, a blue ceramic bowlful of black olives, a tub of humus and some fingers of warm naan bread.

'Oh, Megan, you shouldn't have gone to all this trouble.'

'Hardly trouble. Just a few snacky things from Waitrose, and even the supper itself owes more to Waitrose than to me!'

'But those glasses look really special. How on earth did you do them?'

'It's dead simple, to be honest. I was given the tip by a barman, donkeys' years ago, although I rarely bother these days. But,' she added, with a self-deprecating shrug, 'I wanted to make things nice for you.'

Veronica felt genuinely touched. It was rare in the extreme for someone to make her a meal at all and, as for sitting down to eat with a friend at a beautifully laid table, that was a treat of the first order.

'OK, so what's all this about Alex?' Megan asked, having passed her a glass and put the tray within her reach.

Hold on, not so fast! Veronica wanted to shout, having not yet sorted out all the confusion in her mind, or whether she should be telling Megan at all. 'Wait a sec. First, I want to hear about your day in Margate.'

'Oh, that went surprisingly well. The town's changed a lot since I knew it as a child, mainly because of Turner Contemporary.'

'The new Tate Gallery on the seafront,' she explained, seeing Veronica's puzzled expression. 'Well, not so new now. It opened about six years ago and transformed a place that was, frankly, a bit of a dump, full of sad old pensioners.'

'We'll be sad old pensioners ourselves, given a few more years,' Veronica observed, reaching for an olive.

'Speak for yourself! I've no intention of being either old or sad, at any age.'

Fortunately, she then veered off at a tangent, describing some exhibition at the Gallery, which she'd caught on its last day, and which included some unusual sculptures, made of wire, wax and string.

Veronica did her best to concentrate whilst simultaneously reshaping her account of what she could and would tell Megan about Alex. All he'd confided about his painful divorce and two rebellious teenage sons must definitely be censored, since she had no right to divulge such details of his private life.

Only once they had sat down to eat, did Megan start probing

again, leaving Veronica little option but to expound at least some of the saga, starting at the point when Alex got out at Camden. 'So, then he paid the driver to take me on to Kentish Town and ….'

'Why Kentish Town, for heaven's sake?'

Veronica's blush felt as fiery as the Waitrose Chicken Madras they were eating. 'Oh, because ….' She left the sentence hanging, quickly ploughing on before Megan could interrupt again. 'Anyway, once I'd waved him goodbye, I suddenly realized to my horror that he'd left his briefcase in the cab and guessed he'd be frantic at losing it. I had no way of returning it, because I didn't know his address, you see, and, although I searched all through it, to try to find a business-card or some such, there was nothing personal at all, except his phone and that was locked. Besides, I was already terribly late and feared Beryl might have given up on me and simply left Colin on his own. So, I took the briefcase home and, once I'd mollified Beryl and then got Colin into bed – both of which took some doing - I had another thorough search, but still nothing to identify him. So, next I Googled his Company and managed to find his office number, but of course at that hour there was only an answer-machine.'

Anyone normal and responsible would have left a message: *Please tell Mr Sutherland I have his briefcase safe and sound, and it can be collected from* …... Then, his PA could have dealt with the matter as soon as she picked up the message, sent a cab for it, perhaps, or instructed some colleague to fetch it. Veronica, however, hadn't been feeling either normal or responsible; indeed, she'd had the sense, however fanciful it sounded, that, for once, benevolent Fate was playing into her hands. Alex had left her with part of himself, a vital, indispensable part he would desperately want returned, so why involve some snooty PA, when she could return it herself, in person, and thus ensure another encounter with him?

'So, you left a message?' Megan prompted.

'Well, no, actually I didn't. I was worried it might get lost or fail to be passed on - you know what those machines are like. So, I reckoned it would be safer to take the case to his office first thing in the morning, and go by cab, to save leaving Colin too long.'

The next morning, however, Fate turned from benign to punitive, in that Colin suffered a violent attack of vomiting. Whether Beryl had given him some totally unsuitable foods was something she would never know and preferred not to explore.

'Unfortunately, Colin wasn't well,' she explained, 'and that delayed me hugely. And I still felt anxious about leaving him at all, so I had to call on Beryl again and she took her time coming over, so it was almost noon before I called a cab to the City and ....'

'But why on earth didn't you ask the cab-driver to deliver the wretched thing, instead of flogging all that way yourself?

'It seemed, er – you know, risky. He might take my money but dump the case.'

'Come off it, Veronica! He could lose his licence doing a thing like that. Anyway, what's wrong with you today, not trusting either answer-machines or cab-drivers?' Megan's smile didn't quite disguise the sting in the remark.

'I suppose I was tired,' Veronica countered, lamely, 'not thinking straight.'

In fact, she had felt anything but tired as the cab approached the imposing-looking office building in Bishopsgate. A tingling excitement seemed to be turning her blood to quicksilver, her legs to an Olympic athlete's, as she ran full-pelt up the flight of marble steps.

'Could you please tell Mr Alex Sutherland that I'm here to return his briefcase,' she said, having given her name, but omitted the 'Mrs'.

'I'm sorry,' replied the willow-thin receptionist, once she had tried his phone. 'He doesn't appear to be answering, but no problem, I can get the case sent up to him.'

No! she all but shouted, horrified to think that all her attempts to look glamorous, not to mention her uncharacteristic extravagance in taking a cab such a distance, were so much wasted time and money. 'I, er, actually wanted a word with him in person. But don't worry, I'm happy to wait.'

'Well, do sit down, in that case.' The receptionist gestured to a clutch of squishy black leather chairs positioned opposite the lifts. 'Claire, his PA, normally answers his phone, but as soon as she's back at her desk and picking up, I'll tell her you're here.'

Was she on a hiding to nothing. Veronica wondered, miserably, as she subsided into the black, clammy embrace of a chair? The PA was bound to say that Mr Sutherland was extremely busy, or had meetings back-to-back, or some such, and, if Veronica had a message for him, she, Claire, would pass it on.

'Well, what next?' Megan pressed, with a touch of impatience. 'Did you get there OK and hand it over?'

Veronica had to clamp her lips together, to abort the stupidly triumphant smile that rose spontaneously every time she thought back to the next fortuitous twist of fate. Just as she was sitting in reception, fidgeting with nerves and worrying over Colin, she suddenly spotted

Alex emerging from one of the lifts. The sight was a blue touch-paper setting off a rocket, as she leapt to her feet with his briefcase.

'Oh, thank God!' he exclaimed, his expression changing to one of profound relief. 'My secretary's been ringing around like a lunatic, to try to track this down – or you!'

Her words were the rocket's flaming tail, streaking and scorching in fevered, impetuous bursts, as she did her best to apologize, explain. 'I'm terribly sorry .... I should have returned it hours ago .... Or at least rung to say it was safe. But I didn't have your number ... And then I was seriously delayed this morning and ....' At least the latter statement was true, although she invariably felt guilty about any lie. Yet wasn't it something of an irony that she'd been brought up to be scrupulously honest, whilst Den herself resorted to wholesale deception?

'Don't worry, I'm just so glad to have it back. I've had a frantically busy morning, with barely a minute spare to give any thought to the problem. In fact, I was just going out for an early lunch, to try to clear my head and decide what else to do to track it down. But' – he broke off with a shrug - 'since you've relieved me of that chore, why not join me for a bite to eat?'

She needed no persuasion, whatever her worry over Colin. And, once Alex had left the briefcase in reception, with a joke about not risking it again, he steered her through the grand entrance, down the steps and along the street.

'Do you like Italian food?' he asked, stopping outside an elegant-looking restaurant, with a dove-coloured canopy and a row of well-manicured bay-trees standing to attention in gleaming mahogany planters. 'Fernando's is our local, so to speak, and I can guarantee the food's top-notch.'

His phrase, 'a bite to eat', had suggested a quick snack at Starbuck's, not this exclusive establishment. But, before she could say a word, he had swept her inside, where he was greeted effusively by the Maître D, whose sleek black suit matched his sleek black haircut.

'Ah, Mr Sutherland, how lovely to see you! And your usual table happens to be free, so you're in luck.'

As was *she*. They'd be wining and dining at leisure here, rather than grabbing a sandwich at one of the chains, with little time to relish it. She vowed to leave all guilty thoughts of Colin outside in the gutter, as the Maître D showed them to their table, pulled out their chairs and presented Alex with the wine-list. She had never seen such exorbitantly priced wines, yet Alex ordered a fifty-pound Shiraz as casually as if it had been a bottle of Coke.

'Veronica!' Megan complained, banging down her fork to attract her friend's attention. 'You keep breaking off with a beatific smile on your face, yet you've hardly told me a thing so far. You said on the phone you wanted to ask my advice, but what the hell *about*, for heaven's sake?'

Veronica wiped her mouth, almost surprised to see a red paper-serviette, rather than Fernando's crisp white linen napkin. And the fervid Chicken Madras was in total contrast to the delicate fillet of sea-bream she had eaten at that enchanted lunch. Indeed, Megan's lively spices were inflaming her already sizzling mood, as she thought back to the amazing fact that all her normal shyness and uncertainty seemed to have been swept away by the sheer buzz of sitting next to Alex, his knee tantalizing inches from her thigh. And, as droves of waiters competed to indulge her every whim, she, too, became someone of importance, as if she were picking up his gold-leaf-lustre by a process of osmosis.

'OK,' she said, determined to focus her attention on Megan, if only out of common courtesy. 'Well, I managed to hand over the case, at last, and then we, er, stopped for a spot of lunch.' 'A spot of lunch' hardly did justice to the food: a starter of steamed courgette-blossom filled with lobster mousseline, followed by the bream and, to finish, Crostata di Ricotta e Cioccolato, an exquisitely creamy, chocolatey dessert. 'And then, over coffee, he said, just sort of casually, that he happened to have two tickets to Convent Garden and would I like to go with him to see something called *La Bohème*?'

'Ye gods!' said Megan, with a grin. 'Now we're getting somewhere! It's one of the best-known operas in the repertoire, and tickets to Convent Garden can cost an arm and a leg, I hope you know. So, I take it you said yes.'

'Well, that's where I need your advice, Megan. I didn't know what to say. I mean, he doesn't even know I'm married.'

'What the hell's that that got to do with it? He's invited you to the opera, not for a dirty weekend!'

'Yes, but he doesn't have the faintest idea how hard it is for me to get away.'

'That's equally irrelevant. And, anyway, you have Beryl now. And, if she isn't available, I'll gladly come over myself and keep an eye on Colin, if it means you're free to go.'

'But I'll be terribly late back, Megan. You see, he wants to take me to dinner afterwards with a couple of VIPs. I'm not sure who they are, except that they're connected with the opera production in some way, which means they'll be frighteningly musical. I'm scared I'll be struck dumb and not have a clue what to say.'

'Knowing most artistes, they'll be only too glad to hog the limelight. They're usually so narcissistic, all they want to do is talk about themselves. And, since you're a wonderful listener, both parties should be happy.'

'But I've never moved in such circles before.'

'All the more reason to start!'

Veronica scooped up a forkful of rice, only to let it fall back on to her plate. 'Actually, I thought I'd say no to the dinner, because it means I won't be back till the early hours and I can't expect Beryl to hang about that long. As far as I can gather, she's normally in bed by nine!'

'I've told you, *I'll* hold the fort. In fact, I can easily stay the night, if it'll put your mind at rest. You don't want to be a Cinderella, counting down every minute to midnight!'

'Meg, you're a saint! But what do I tell Colin – I mean, as to why you're there and I'm not?'

'I doubt he'll make much sense of it, whatever you say. But, if you insist on an excuse, tell him my computer's crashed and I've come round to use yours.'

Veronica abandoned her attempt to finish up her rice, head too full of worries and misgivings. 'Yes, but I still feel awkward about Alex spending all that money on me – not just another lavish meal, but the tickets. He told me they were the best seats in the house.'

'OK, so the cost will be astronomical, but he's most unlikely to have shelled out for them himself, so don't worry your head about it. People who work in PR get offered loads of freebies – centre-court seats at Wimbledon, entry to the Royal Enclosure at Ascot – you name it. Most of his clients will want to twist his arm, you see, or get into his good books.'

'But he'll probably be shocked to the core to discover I've never been to an opera in my life. It's the first night of a new production, he said, and started going on about the conductor and the director, as if he knew them personally, whereas it was all double Dutch to me.'

Megan shrugged. 'He sounds a right show-off to me! And, anyway, just because he hobnobs with the in-crowd doesn't mean he's any great shakes when it comes to being musical himself. I know for a fact that some of these wealthy folk who are given free tickets to Glyndebourne are bored to tears within minutes. I even heard of one who nodded off during the overture of *Figaro* and began to snore so loudly, he had to be removed!'

At least Veronica knew what Glyndebourne was, although only because her singing-teacher had a friend who was performing there this summer. 'OK,' she said, changing tack, 'I'm not likely to snore, admittedly, but I've nothing remotely suitable to wear.'

'Honestly, Veronica, you're being utterly pathetic! Can't you just enjoy this treat without coming up with all these footling objections? I'd willingly lend you a frock myself, if we weren't such different shapes. But, don't worry, I intend to march you to the shops and insist you buy something in keeping with this grand occasion. And don't start saying you can't leave Colin. I'll hire a wheelchair, if necessary, and trundle him round Harrods' Dress Department!'

Veronica had to smile, just imagining the scene: Megan blithely ignoring Colin's incoherent protestations as she whizzed him past rails of evening-gowns or feather-boa wraps.

'Just give me the date, and I'll pencil in a shopping trip in my diary.'

'Well, actually, it's not till September 11.'

'Veronica, for pity's sake! That's a whole two months away. I assumed it was next week, the way you've been going on.'

'It seems worryingly close to me – I mean, a mere two months to mug up on the opera and try to be worthy of those *artistes*, as you call them.'

Megan all but exploded in irritation. 'You don't *have* to be worthy of two jumped-up little strangers. You're enough in yourself, don't you see? Just enjoy the occasion, can't you, rather than treat it like an exam you have to prepare for. Anyway, it's good we have loads of time, because there are quite a few places I think we should try for your outfit – not Harrods, in fact, but Selfridges, and Zara, and possibly John Lewis.'

'But, Megan,' she said, shaping the remaining rice into a large, wonky M on her plate, 'why on earth should you do all this for me?'

'Because we're friends, you chump! And also because I'm determined that you allow yourself to be indulged, for once, without feeling you don't deserve it, or coming up with a thousand reasons why you have to refuse. But, don't worry, I intend to demand my pound of flesh in return! I expect you to invite me round to supper at your place, the same week as the opera, so you can give me a blow-by-blow account. And don't think you can fob me off with a phone-call, or wait till we I see you at choir. I'll expect chapter and verse while the whole thing's still fresh in your mind.'

And, with that, Megan cleared away the dirty plates, then returned from the kitchen carrying a seriously-dark chocolate mousse, decorated with contrasting white-chocolate curls and little pouffes of whipped cream. Hell, Veronica thought, I'm now presented with a double challenge: first, to be a suitably glamourous, musically knowledgeable companion to Alex, and, second, to lay on a meal that matched her friend's demanding culinary standards.

Both equally impossible.

CHAPTER 8

As Veronica stepped in to the Champagne Bar, its spectacular proportions raised her spirits as high as the soaring roof itself, and its glitter of glass and steel seemed to express her own tingly surge of excitement - an excitement tempered with an undertow of apprehension? Did she really belong in this place of privileged opulence?

Stealing a glance at her reflection, she knew Colin would fail to recognize his usual stained and shabby carer, now transformed to striking elegance in a red-and-gold two-piece, her hair glossed to a chestnut sheen, her legs looking longer and slimmer in high heels.

'Get out!' she hissed at Colin, having promised Megan not to let her mind keep drifting back home to Clapham, not to phone or fret or agitate. 'He's my responsibility this evening – all night, if you want, love - and all you have to do is enjoy Alex and Puccini,'

But would she even find her escort amidst the crush of well-heeled people, who all seemed effortlessly superior in their appearance, accents and general demeanour? She was adrift in this whole new world of affluent entitlement, amidst those who thought it their natural birth-right to imbibe wealth and culture along with their mother's milk.

Just as she was feeling increasingly awkward, she suddenly spotted Alex, sitting right near the entrance and clearly keeping an eye out for her, as if aware she might feel daunted.

'Veronica!' he exclaimed, springing to his feet, 'it's so long since we last met, I'd forgotten how stunning you look!'

His genuinely admiring glance made her almost believe the compliment - and certainly justified the huge amount she'd spent, egged on by Megan's own extravagance. Besides, she now looked a worthy companion to him, clad as he was in a slim-cut, tailored dinner-jacket and a velvet bow-tie in a subtle shade of aubergine.

'I intended taking you out well before this,' he continued, having ensconced her at his table, where a bottle of champagne was already chilling in an ice-bucket. 'But life got in the way. First, I was travelling all over the place on business, then I went down with that dreaded summer flu that seems to be doing the rounds.'

About to say that Colin had caught it, too, she rapidly changed tack, trying to blank out all the worry about her husband's abnormally high fever and her ensuing panic as to whether he would recover by this evening.

'July was fairly reasonable, thank God, as far as my work was concerned, but August was a write-off, to be honest.' He paused to fill their glasses, before adding with a mock-grimace, 'It's a bit of a dreary month altogether, don't you think, with everyone away and pretty rubbish weather, like as not.'

Why were they talking about the weather, when her instincts - and the champagne - made her want to throw herself into his arms and dispense with all conversation?

'Anyway, at least we're both here and in one piece!' he said, passing her a platter of smoked salmon, decorated with nasturtium flowers, radish roses and long, tapering strips of cucumber-peel.

The whole thing looked far too artistic to eat, but, as she hesitated, he leaned towards her, all at once, and placed his hand on hers, the touch of his fingers seeming to echo the fizzing, foaming bubbles in her glass.

'How have you been?' he asked, his unusually dark blue eyes

meeting hers with such intensity she was forced to look away.

'Oh, fine,' she stammered, determined to forget the perils and alarms of the last fraught weeks, and all its tedious busyness: sponging Colin's sweaty body, trying to tempt his failing appetite with smoothies and milk-jellies, all of which he pushed peevishly away.

Fortunately, Alex sat back in his chair again and sampled the champagne. Whatever her crazy instincts, this was only their third meeting, so safer not to go too fast. And, in an attempt to stick to the truth, rather than conceal her musical ignorance (only to be rumbled later), she plucked up the courage to do what Megan had advised and come clean about the fact that this was her first experience of opera.

'Well, in that case, I'm sorry it should be *La Bohème*. It's not the most challenging of works - a bit of a tear-jerker, to be frank.'

She was immediately confused, having heard from Megan and several other choir-members that it was one of the opera greats.

'But,' he continued, with a shrug, 'at least it's very approachable and this new production should undoubtedly be interesting. I met the conductor at a party last week & he struck me as incredibly energetic and committed.'

Veronica didn't trust herself to reply. Not only was she unsure whether she was about to experience a masterpiece or a sentimental piece of kitsch, but the only conductors she had even met were old-style bus-conductors. Mercifully, Alex was in full flow, sparing her any risk of making some *faux pas*.

'Tony's an interesting fellow altogether. Apparently, he grew up on a council-estate and is just as interested in football and pop music as he is in the highbrow stuff.'

She began to warm to this 'Tony': full name Antonio Pappano, the Royal Opera House's Music Director, as she'd learned from a little judicious reading, in her attempt to prepare for this evening. 'Little' was the operative word, not only on account of Colin, but because, before he was laid low, her main intellectual efforts had been focused on the challenges of fund-raising, which seemed to require equal application. So far, she'd attended three meetings in her role as Secretary, spurred on by pretending that Alex himself was due to preside at all three, and thus it was imperative to impress her with her expertise.

Hastily, she returned her attention to the potted history he was now recounting, from when Pappano's parents arrived in England with nothing but a fiver and one suitcase, to the family's eventual move to the States, when Tony was just thirteen, and finally outlining the young prodigy's meteoric rise as he embarked on a multi-faceted career.

'His life has changed out of all recognition from that early hand-to-mouth stuff. Now, he can earn close on a hundred grand in just one night!'

'You're joking!'

'Not at all. He's one of the highest paid conductors in the world. And some of these maestros feel entitled to more than mere cash. Claudio Abbado wanted ninety-thousand trees to be planted in his home-city of Milan, in return for just two performances.'

Alex continued to regale her with the eye-watering sums paid to the musical equivalent of Rooney and Renaldo, only breaking off to refill her glass. Surely he didn't intend them to finish the whole bottle before the opera had even begun? Disgracing herself musically was one thing; keeling over in a drunken stupor would be infinitely humiliating. Nor could she forget the cost. Some of these champagnes were £350 a bottle, which might be nothing to millionaire conductors, but, after the deeply engrained restrictions of Den's lifelong economy drive, seemed very nearly obscene. Yet, to be drinking such liquid gold at all was so exhilarating, she could almost feel herself expanding to fit the majestic scale of the bar, as if Alex's very presence lent her magnitude and distinction.

'But that's enough about Tony,' he said, taking an appreciative sip of the bubbly. 'Since this is your first opera, I need to fill you in a bit. But just one word of warning – I strongly advise you not to read the English surtitles.'

Seeing her puzzled expression, he added, 'They're projected on screens around the auditorium, so that people can follow the words as they're sung. But doing that can distract you from the subtleties of the music and, anyway, some of the banter in the opening scenes may strike you as banal. The four rumbustious artist-friends are joking about how cold and hungry they are, so the words are hardly momentous, but the music itself is surprisingly dense in its themes and textures. And there's a constant shifting and diversity as each new character appears, so, I suggest you focus on the complex orchestration. And I ought to point out the very obvious influence of Verdi's *La Traviata* on the score.'

Veronica said nothing. Complexities of orchestration were totally beyond her and, as for Verdi's *La Traviata*, she had never heard of it. But, rather than deplore her ignorance, she tried to recall Megan's counsel: if Alex had invited her in preference to some musical genius, then he must appreciate her company, rather than her ability to tell an oboe from a *cor anglais* or recognise a key-change. 'Just admit you're an opera virgin, love, and if he wants to feel smugly superior, why deny him the pleasure?'

Alex *wasn't* smug in any way, but then Megan had never met

him and thus failed to understand that he was simply doing his best to enlighten her.

'And the same goes for those VIPs at the dinner afterwards. If it turns them on to patronize you, that only proves how shallow they are.'

Dreading the very thought of being patronized, Veronica had vowed to keep mum at the dinner and let the cognoscenti enjoy the limelight.

'I have to say I'm a bit snooty about Puccini,' Alex admitted, taking a piece of smoked salmon. 'And he is definitely a manipulative composer, working shamelessly on our emotions, yet there's no denying there are some truly ravishing melodies in *Bohème* and many magnificent musical moments in the score. When Mimi first enters, for instance, there's a rather delicious shiver in the strings.'

Delicious shivers she well understood. Since her first glimpse of Alex, two whole months ago, delicious shivers had been stealing over her at the most inappropriate of times: when wiping Colin's bottom, or helping him cough up greenish phlegm.

'But I think we should take our seats soon' - Alex gave a quick glance at his watch - 'We're right at the front of the Grand Tier, and bang in the middle, so, once we're settled, no one will need to push past. But, first, are you sure I can't offer you a refill?'

She shook her head emphatically, already feeling light-headed. In her life to date, champagne had been like opera: an exotic, unknown pleasure. Fortunately, he didn't press the issue but, instead, took her arm to steer her down to the auditorium, she warming to the notion of being thought a couple by the throng of fashionable people they were passing. It was achingly long since she and Colin had gone out together and, even in the early days, almost any prospect of socializing had been put paid to by Tom's condition. Besides, Colin had always been more a man's man, preferring to mix with his business associates and, later, becoming virtually a recluse. Alex, in contrast, seemed to relish her company, admiring her outfit once more and thanking her for 'giving up' her evening. How could 'giving up' her frequently stomach-turning Colin-chores be considered any sacrifice, when the alternative was this glittery occasion?

As they entered the auditorium, she paused a moment just to drink in the atmosphere: tier after tier of gold-and-crimson glory, soaring up to a magnificent domed ceiling. The sound of the orchestra tuning up mingled with the hum of conversation, to create a buzz of anticipation. And, when they reached their seats, she could see for herself they were undoubtedly the best in the house, with a full-on view of both the stage and the orchestra. Yet, knowing they had cost a cool five-hundred pounds (even if Alex himself hadn't had to pay), she couldn't help reflecting on Den again, aware that, in her childhood, the pair of them could have lived on that sum, food and rent included, for a good three months or more.

Once settled with a programme, she was glad that last night's final stint of 'homework' had familiarized her already with the synopsis and the cast, so no need to study it now. Instead, she could sit and listen to Alex talk about the various quirks of the soloists, as if he knew them all personally – as indeed he might. Far from being a show-off, as Megan had unkindly suggested, she was beginning to see he was simply steeped in musical culture, like a priceless brandy matured in oak to vintage golden perfection. And, as she watched the house gradually filling up, each cluster of new arrivals increased her sense of being present at a momentous occasion.

Soon, almost every seat was taken and the air of expectation deepened as the house-lights began to dim. She could barely contain her excitement, when, under cover of the encroaching darkness, Alex insinuated his hand caressingly into hers, the touch of his skin seeming to intensify in the fevered hush.

And then a second thrill as the conductor entered - Tony in the flesh – and all the members of the orchestra rose from their seats in a gesture of respect. He took his bows from the orchestra-pit, reaching his hands out to the audience to acknowledge their rapturous applause, she herself clapping with palm-aching enthusiasm. As he raised his baton, there was a moment's pregnant silence, which suddenly gave way to a surge of full-throated sound. None of her paltry homework had prepared her for the sheer impact of the orchestra, the sense of being immersed and engulfed in the great resonant fanfare now rising on all sides, so arrestingly close and immediate. Impossible to distinguish all the different instruments, or concentrate on anything in depth; there were just too many other elements competing for her attention: the bleakly realistic set (a bare and draughty attic), the relentlessly falling snow outside its window, the surtitles flashing up on screen - impossible to ignore, whatever Alex said. Just half-an-hour ago, she had alighted at Covent Garden tube, in mild September weather and with still-light autumn skies, now she was plunged into the black night and bitter cold of Christmas Eve in Paris's Latin Quarter.

Two student-friends were already on stage, their shabby costumes in tune with their poverty-stricken surroundings. Indeed, the total lack of amenities reminded her of some of the cheerless lodgings she and Den had inhabited. Their standard of living, back then, had depended totally on the vagaries of her mother's affairs; one month living in style with the latest lover, the next forced to rent a bug-infested bedsit, after some shrieking, terrifying scene had put paid to the romance. She couldn't help regretting that she'd been unable to leave home until her marriage, and had never personally experienced any carefree student days - a lack made all the more apparent by the four exuberant students now larking about on stage. But why hark back to her unhappy past when she was enjoying this glorious present, with Alex's hand, still linked to hers, seeming to scorch a hole in her exultant palm?

Only when a timid knock on the attic door heralded Mimi's arrival - the other students having gone out on the town, leaving Rodolfo alone - did Alex loosen his grip on her hand, as if to mark this all-important moment. And, indeed, the whole atmosphere on stage had changed: no longer student japes and complaints, but the first stirrings of romance, as Rodolfo chanced to encounter Mimi's frozen hand and sought to warm it in his own. The former short exchanges gave way to a passionate outpouring, and the sheer intensity of Rodolfo's voice seemed to dissolve Veronica's boundaries, so that now she *was* Mimi, responding, with identical passion, to the ardour of a poet. It no longer mattered whether she was musical or not, or if she could understand each word, it was the *feelings* she recognized, as if she had known them at some instinctive level from way back in her past, but buried and denied them until this very moment. The longing and emotion in the music needed no translation, the orchestra itself echoing and amplifying the voices. And, as Mimi responded, her pure, sensuous soprano seeming to rise to the very skies, it was she, Veronica, pouring out her long-concealed frustration and desire.

Her own acute reaction was peculiar, unsettling, and entirely unexpected. It was as if she had left the normal world behind and was inhabiting a sphere of raw, undiluted passion, where all her usual uncertainties simply flowed away in this insistent tide of melody. And, when Mimi, too, began to sing with the same forcefulness and conviction, the two intertwined and soaring voices seemed to symbolize the sexual act itself – sex as she had never known it, yet imagined in some region of her mind. Only now did she realize, through Mimi and Rodolfo, how she, too, might be capable of such heightened sensuality – even this late in her life, should the opportunity somehow come her way in some as yet undreamed-of future. And she also realized, with a sunburst of surprise, that such love - although closed to her for decades - had been there all along, throbbing through poetry, music, songs, as a great universal force she was only just beginning to taste, and which lay far beyond the monotonous commonplace that had constituted her life to date.

When the three student-friends reappeared, trying to lure Rodolfo out to join them, her instant reaction was to cry, "No! Don't go! Stay with Mimi, with Veronica." And, as if conscious of her plea, Rodolfo begged his friends for a few more minutes' grace, then, alone with Mimi again, broke into a declaration of love, a love admittedly irrational in its speed and its intensity - how could they possibly know each other after so brief an encounter? - yet the music itself seemed to be insisting that love, of its very nature, *was* irrational - an overwhelming, animal force. Mimi knew that in her very core, as she sang fervently, ecstatically, '*Tu sol commandi amore*!', but even she, Veronica – run-of-the-mill singer and inexperienced when it came to brute desire - repeated the phrase with equal ardour and conviction:

'Ah, love, you rule alone.'

CHAPTER 9

As she strolled from the tube to Sebastian's flat, Veronica was singing – or *trying* to sing - one of Mimi's arias, having bought the libretto and memorized the Italian words. She ought to be exhausted, having spent most of yesterday spring-cleaning the whole house, ready for Megan's visit this evening. And, because she'd been on a permanent high since Monday's opera and dinner, she had spent the last two nights less in sleep than in churning excitement.

As she rang the bell to the basement, she was relieved to hear footsteps echoing down the hall. Sebastian's unpunctuality had become an increasing source of annoyance, so maybe her sharpish words last week had finally hit home. However, the door was opened by a young girl in an ultra-short skirt, with bare, grubby feet and a mane of uncombed hair, who casually announced, 'Seb's just texted to say he's been a bit delayed and would I let you in.'

Veronica's frown of displeasure went unnoticed, as the girl introduced herself as Tilly, apologized for being frightfully busy, then dashed back into one of the rooms leading off the hall.

Veronica fumed in silence. Sebastian's cavalier attitude seemed all the more remiss compared with Alex's reliability and old-world courtesy. Refusing to stand in the draughty hall, while Sebastian took his time sorting out some last-minute hold-up or crisis, she marched into his room and tried to use the time profitably by running over the new song they'd been learning at last week's choir-rehearsal. Yet her irritation made it difficult to concentrate and her mind kept straying back to Colin, as usual, although in fact, he was used to being on his own while she was at her lessons. Mornings were easier anyway, in that he rarely drank before noon and was usually reasonably content watching daytime soaps. And, in any case, he had seemed noticeably less intractable since his bout of flu, as if it had disabled the childishly perverse streak that made him deliberately flout her. Nonetheless, with Megan there, she'd be unable to keep her usually strict eye on him and, although she'd considered calling in Beryl again, there was a limit to what she could keep shelling out on Colin-sitting, so she'd resorted to his favourite DVDs - Kenny Everett and Bergerac – praying they'd keep him glued to the box.

She checked her watch – again – riled by Sebastian's continuing absence. Hearing footsteps outside, she dared to hope he might have turned up, but it was only Tilly re-emerging.

'Sorry, but Seb's just rung again to say there's been another delay. But the good news is he should only be fifteen minutes' longer.'

The 'only' was a downright cheek, in that fifteen minutes was another quarter of her lesson lost. 'Couldn't he ring me directly?' she asked the girl, snappishly.

'He said he tried but couldn't get through.'

That she didn't believe, since she'd had her phone switched on since early morning. More likely he feared another dressing-down from her – and rightly so.

'I'll make you a cup of tea, OK?'

Before she could refuse, Tilly instantly pranced off again, as if powered by rocket-fuel, returning with a chipped china mug over-full of what looked like greyish dishwater. Certainly, no self-respecting tea could have had time to properly brew in the few seconds she'd been gone. This time, the girl perched on the edge of a chair and launched into a rambling monologue on Brexit. Perhaps Sebastian had instructed her to engage in distraction-tactics, although how he imagined she'd be mollified by Tilly's half-baked views on the Single Market was beyond her comprehension.

Taking a sip of tea – tasteless and unsugared – she made an effort to calm herself by tuning out of Brexit and into *La Bohème*. She was still amazed by all the different skills and occupations required to stage an opera: not just orchestra and singers, but set-builders, stage-managers, movement-directors, sound- and lighting- technicians, acting-coaches - and dozens more. They'd all come together as a flawless whole on Monday, as the opera moved beyond the garret of Act One to a street-scene of stylish shopping-arcades, and then to a highly realistic restaurant, complete with waiters, white-clothed tables and wealthy diners in top hats. But, for the final act, it was back to the garret – and, when Mimi assured Rodolfo she would be with him for ever, whilst actually breathing her final failing words, she had wept unashamedly, despite fearing Alex would be embarrassed by her tears.

However, he had told her later, much to her surprise, 'I envy the way you reacted so spontaneously and genuinely. I feel such a blasé old cynic in comparison.'

The 'blasé old cynic' had seemed enchanted by her enthusiasm in general, when she went on to praise every scene and moment of the opera, and, once Alex had informed her that Puccini himself had wept when writing the death-scene, she no longer even worried about sounding naïve. What she hadn't divulged – and would never tell a soul – was that she, too, would gladly pay with her life, if that was the price demanded for an awesome, overpowering love.

'Well, we'll definitely go again,' Alex had promised. 'Or how about a ballet next time? One of the dancers in the new production of *Sylvia* happens to be a good mate of mine, so I can easily get tickets. It's not exactly highbrow entertainment, but there is some brilliant dancing and really clever choreography.'

'Veronica!'

Sebastian's voice cut through her happy reverie` of a second glitzy evening, as, all at once, he bounded into the room, shedding coat, scarf and his usual maddeningly inflated apologies.

'I'm absolutely devastated to keep you waiting again.'

'Well, if you're so devastated,' she dared to say, amazed at her own courage in standing up to him for once, 'couldn't you ensure that you're not always rushing from one engagement to the next - as you were last week and the week before - with never enough time to fit everything in?'

Clearly taken aback by her uncharacteristically acerbic tone, he began detailing all the pressures he was under: his new, prestigious teaching post, apparently unheard of for someone of his age, the commission for what he claimed was the best Youth Symphony Orchestra in the whole of the UK, the incredibly high standards demanded by some international singing competition he'd entered (and been tipped to win) - etcetera, etcetera. Most of his explanations, she noted, were more boasting than apology.

'And on top of everything else, I've just been awarded the principal role in a ground-breaking new opera, which is a real feather in my cap, but of course increases my load enormously. You probably don't realize, Veronica, but singing a role like that is a major athletic challenge, as well as a vocal one.'

'Obviously,' she said, 'I rank low in your priorities compared with all that high-powered stuff; nonetheless, I still expect you to turn up on time.' Never before had she spoken to anyone in such uncompromising terms, so Alex's view of her as someone worthy of attention and respect must have changed her usual submissive attitude. And, of course, Megan had played her part in the process, constantly urging her to stop accepting slights and put-downs, and speak up for herself and her 'rights'.

'I've said I'm sorry, haven't I?' It was now Sebastian's turn to sound peeved, but perhaps aware, for once, he was in the wrong, he added in a more conciliatory tone, 'How was *Bohème*, by the way?'

'Wonderful!'

'That's good to hear,' he said, with the semblance of a smile, only to add, 'Personally speaking, I've very little patience for any opera after Monteverdi or before Berg. All that nineteenth-century Romantic mush leaves me completely cold.'

Determined not to get side-tracked or to allow Monday's peak-experience to be diluted and disparaged by his snooty attitude, she stood her ground and suggested they immediately get down to work for what was left of the lesson. 'This is our new song,' she said, handing over the words of *Put a Little Love in Your Heart*, 'and I'd like to have at least a basic grasp of it by our next choir-rehearsal tomorrow.'

He nodded, giving the song a cursory glance. 'I have to admit, though, I find it deeply depressing that your choir doesn't stretch you more. To be perfectly frank, this is second-rate stuff, with no real musical challenge and no poetry in the words.'

'Maybe,' she said, tersely, 'but our choir doesn't exist to be "stretched", as you call it. The whole point of it is for people to enjoy their singing and hopefully forget their troubles, at least briefly. Some of our members are terminally ill, as I've told you several times, and others are struggling with the side-effects of chemo or loads of other ghastly drugs, so Katy deliberately chooses easy, upbeat songs.'

Although he merely shook his head in reply, she must have shamed him into action, since he powered up his laptop to Google the track, then sat at the piano and picked out the tune with an ease and rapidity she couldn't help but admire – only to break off after a couple of minutes.

'Veronica, I'm not at all happy about you singing without any warm-up, or even any basic breathing-exercises.'

'Well, in that case, you need to allow time for the warm-up, which we certainly don't have now. There are exactly nineteen minutes left of my sixty-minute lesson.'

At least he had the grace to apologize again and even to sound genuinely contrite. 'In normal circumstances, I'd gladly stay longer and make up your lost time, but I'm afraid I'm due at my first opera rehearsal, so I just have to get off really sharp today.'

'OK,' she said, testily, annoyed by the fact he was still trying to fit in far too much and thus invariably cutting things fine.

'Anyway, let's get back to work,' he said, launching into the tune once more and asking her to sing the first three lines.

Despite, or perhaps because of her annoyance, she sang with new attack, but far from praising her new assurance, he again criticized the song.

'Whoever wrote this drivel clearly couldn't manage even the simplest of rhymes, and, as for the sentiments, they're pure Pollyanna, crossed with Patience Strong. What pains me about your choir, Veronica, is the way they ignore nine whole centuries of outstanding choral tradition, and instead feed you a junk-diet of mainly pop and rock.'

She forbore from saying that if *he* put a little love in *his* heart, he might be less disparaging of both the song and of their choir. Instead, she muttered, tersely, 'Could we please continue?'

Once they were halfway through the song, he stopped again, this time to advise her. 'There's an important key-change here, where you hold the long B natural, go up a semitone to Middle C. then you're in the key of F, a fourth above - the C being the dominant of F.'

She immediately felt thrown. During their rehearsals they were never given such instructions, since many of the choir - herself included, of course - were unfamiliar with many of the musical terms Sebastian banded about so freely: rubato, syncopation, grace-notes, sostenuto. And, although she knew what a key-change was, she couldn't actually recognise one without it being pointed out. As for specific notes like F or Middle C, they still meant very little to her. Nor did thirds, fourths and suchlike, which she'd now learned were called 'intervals', but knew nothing much beyond that. The jaunty, 'go for it' confidence Katy aimed to instil in them all, regardless of their musical expertise, Sebastian saw as misplaced ignorance. However, aware of time-pressures, she did her best to comply with what he had asked and, somehow, they reached the end of the song and, with it, the end of the lesson.

'I'm desperately sorry, but I just have to dash off now. If I'm late for the first rehearsal, it'll make a really bad impression.'

'As you've already made on me,' she muttered, sotto voce, reluctantly preceding him into the hall. It had barely been worth her while trekking all the way to Clerkenwell for this severely truncated lesson.

Indeed, once she'd wished him a curt goodbye and told him she'd settle up later (refusing to pay a full hour's price for less than twenty minutes), she grabbed her phone as she marched towards the tube. 'Megan, would you believe, Sebastian kept me waiting even longer than usual and then had the cheek to leave five minutes before my hour was up.'

'I certainly would believe. You must sack the prat, Veronica, refuse to return for more lessons. They're just a source of extra stress – as if you didn't have enough already! I'll never forget that time he cancelled when you'd already left for Clerkenwell. Does he think he's some great god, or something, to mess you about like that?'

Veronica tried to keep listening, as she squeezed her way along the crowded pavement, dodging other people similarly glued to their phones, and despite the noise of workmen digging up the road.

'You don't even *need* more lessons,' Megan was insisting now. 'You're singing so much better and, anyway, I reckon Katy gives us enough help each week to see you through our repertoire, without Sebastian attempting to train you for *La Scala*!'

Veronica couldn't help but smile, although the sound was distorting as she reached the tube and began descending underground, so she suggested they discuss the issue this evening.

'Yeah, 'course. And, talking of this evening, please don't go to any trouble. As I've told you ad infinitum, I'm coming not for the food – bread and cheese will do me fine – but to hear about *Bohème* and Alex, and more about your life in general.

Bread and cheese indeed! She had planned a decent three-course meal and already done the shopping for it, even made the starter and the pudding, both now chilling in the fridge. Nonetheless, she still felt highly apprehensive about her non-existent cooking-skills. Her mother had never cooked a proper meal in her life, the pair of them existing on pizzas or pot-noodles, or, when money was especially short, making do with packets of crisps or bowls of Instant Whip. And, even after her marriage, she soon discovered Colin had no wish to join her and Tom for meals, claiming evening after evening to have been 'kept late at the office', despite the fact he had always been his own boss. Admittedly, Tom was a messy eater, his many medical problems making chewing and swallowing difficult, but whereas she accepted his drooling, Colin found it too disgusting to endure. And, since all Tom's food had to be mashed or puréed, her culinary expertise had never stretched much beyond the electric blender or a simple fork and sieve. However, she could hardly serve Megan a plate of soggy mush, so she'd invested in a copy of *Cooking For Dummies*, choosing three of the simplest courses and refusing to resort to shop-bought food, even if Megan herself had done.

She was actually looking forward to playing hostess, and had even laid the table in advance, so she'd be free to cook the main course as soon as she got home. First, though, she would indulge her husband with all his favourite dishes – a form of shameless bribery, to keep him quiet, since most of those favourites were highly unhealthy puddings and ice-creams. Whether he'd be able to eat them was another matter entirely, as he'd woken with a bad stomach-ache and, on her suggestion, gone back to bed to rest. Frankly – and unkindly – she was hoping he'd continue to feel a bit below par, since then he'd be less likely to drink too much once Megan had arrived.

As she waited on the platform, her mind was still preoccupied: should she continue with her singing-lessons, would Megan find the house a shambles, despite this morning's major clean-up, could she trust Colin to behave himself, without her checking on him every second minute? Yet when the train arrived, she stepped into the cheery sound of a three-piece brass-band playing in the carriage. Such performers seemed increasingly common and, of late, she'd seen a juggler, a skiffle-group playing Irish jigs, and a lone guitarist with less talent than exuberance. But, as far as she could judge, this trio sounded surprisingly professional and their happy, buoyant music set her foot tapping to the rhythm and was mercifully effective in submerging her anxieties. Indeed, when the train stopped at the next station and one of the players went round with a collection-box, she not only poured in all her loose change, she tossed a fiver on top, simply to thank them for changing her mood.

CHAPTER 10

'Colin!' she called, as she opened the front door, hoping there'd be no response. If he shouted a reply, it meant he wasn't resting, as she'd urged, but maybe prowling around, in danger of a fall.

No answer. Her sigh of relief, however, was cut short as she proceeded into the hall, all but gagging on the reek of diarrhoea. And, to her horror, she saw she'd actually trodden into a squelch of the brown stinking stuff, which was pooling into the carpet she'd shampooed only yesterday, so lovingly and thoroughly, ready for Megan's visit. Indeed, after her marathon efforts, the whole house had smelled clean and fresh (with a little help from a jasmine room-spray), yet now it was like stepping into a sewer.

Picking her way between the fetid brown deposits, she went straight to seek out Colin, passing the open dining-room-door on the way. Glancing in a moment, she stood transfixed in shock. The new white lace tablecloth, bought in Megan's honour, was now awash in a lake of red wine, the best wine-glasses and side-plates she'd arranged so tastefully had been smashed into cruel-edged shards. Worse, the luxurious flower-arrangement – orchids, roses, Madonna lilies – sent by Alex yesterday – was lying toppled on its side and dripping yellowish water on the floor. Several flower-stems had snapped off, blooms decapitated, loose petals strewn everywhere.

She surveyed the wreckage, torn between rage and disbelief. Surely Colin had neither the strength nor the motivation to wreak such havoc. She had left him in bed, wearing his usual thick pad and incontinence-pants, and promising to stay put till she returned. So how come the diarrhoea in the hall? How come the assault on her elegantly laid table, and on the bouquet in particular?

She gripped the door-frame, a hundred questions churning in her mind: had he grown suspicious at some level, become increasingly uneasy when first Beryl and then Megan turned up to look after him? Had he somehow intuited that she'd been out with another man?

No, that was plain ridiculous. He would simply assume she'd bought the flowers herself – if he gave the matter any thought at all. The card that came with them, thrillingly inscribed, 'Thank you, lovely Veronica, for your enchanting company', was now well-concealed beneath a pile of sheets in the linen-chest – although in fact she intended keeping it for ever. In any case, there was nothing really wrong about accompanying Alex to the opera – well, apart from that one passionate kiss. But to imagine her husband knew about the kiss and was now hell-bent on revenge was totally improbable.

She continued on upstairs to his bedroom, found him still in bed - naked, poo-stained, yet fast asleep. Peter was curled in the crook of his arm and the very sight of their intimacy ratcheted up her anger yet another notch. Her husband had started sleeping in another room, as early as the second year of their marriage, choosing Peter – the *real* Peter, still very much alive then – as his nightly companion, in preference to her. By then, she'd come to understand his psychology - dumb animals were less threatening, in that they wouldn't make emotional demands on him, as a wife was bound to do – nonetheless, it had hurt her deeply to be left to sleep alone when still a newish bride.

She shifted her gaze from Peter to the sheer mess and chaos of the room: all the more infuriating after the effort she'd expended on yesterday's spring-clean, when she had hoovered up myriads of tiny black flakes from the soles of his ancient slippers, which had been coming loose and flaking off for weeks. She had then chucked the offending slippers in the bin and replaced them with the new pair she'd bought him ages ago, but which he stubbornly refused to wear. So, it was obvious he'd retrieved them, against her strict instructions, undone all her efforts to make the house welcoming and shipshape for the first friend she'd invited in literally years.

As she listened to his smugly calm and regular breathing, she, in contrast, seemed to split apart with stress, and, all at once, she darted back to the dining-room and let out a shriek of unadulterated fury, in face of the senseless destruction. She ought to be sorry for Colin – afflicted with diarrhoea, losing his mind and his memory, maybe wrestling with suspicions he could neither identify nor articulate – but, far from feeling pity, she was choking with a frenzied rage, as if a dam had burst and the forty years of resentful acrimony that constituted her marriage had come pouring out in a black, stinking torrent.

'Fuck you, Colin! 'she yelled, blindly grabbing at pieces of smashed china, limp and fading flower-corpses, wine-soaked linen napkins, all littered on the floor. 'I wish I'd never met you,' she shrieked, hurling back the detritus she'd collected, in a red-mist paroxysm of wrath. 'I gave up my life for you and Tom,' she hissed, speaking to the walls, the floor, as it they could bear witness to a truth she didn't know she knew, and astonished at the words issuing from her mouth – words never consciously formulated, that seemed to be erupting from some dark, long-denied region of her mind. 'Tom I don't regret,' she shouted. 'He's dead now and I miss him. It's you who made my life so bloody difficult.' Her heart was beating so furiously it felt as if it were breaking into bits, like the smashed crockery, the dismembered flowers. Her throat hurt from shouting, her guts were churning in queasy spasms, her head pounding with such pain and rage she felt in danger of a stroke. 'You never lifted a finger for Tom,' she accused the toppled vase, as if holding it responsible. 'Yet he was *your* bloody son, not mine.'

No, this *couldn't* be her. She never swore, never used four-letter words, had never before complained in all those forty years, let alone lost control. Nonetheless, it *was* her – a new, terrifying, rebellious her, continuing to shout poison-darts of invective, the words catching in her throat and seeming almost to draw blood.

'Fine for you!' she stormed at the tense, tight-lipped Colin staring from their wedding-photo, pewter-framed on the mantelpiece. 'You could escape whenever you chose, swan around with your business-friends, but *I* was tied to your son, your house, the regime you imposed.' In the photo, she looked so touchingly young and hopeful, as if daring to believe that things could and would work out, yet how wrong she'd been back then, not realizing she was trapped and had been since her wedding-day. And, as she paced round and round the dining-room, she did indeed feel like a caged beast, with no chance of breaking free, or breathing the wilder, purer air of the jungle or the rain-forest.

'Shut up!' she snapped at her mobile, its sudden intrusive shrill enraging her still more. Why bother to answer the sodding thing, when it was probably the geriatric clinic with details of Colin's brain-scan, or Social Services offering him yet another assessment? But, once the date came round, he'd refuse to have the scan, as he had refused the previous ones, and, as for the Social Services, he invariably dismissed them as 'do-gooders' and 'busybodies'. Just the thought of his pig-headed rejection of all services or investigations that might actually ease his situation – not to mention hers – made her start sobbing in despair, as it dawned on her that, if Colin lingered on, the present wretched impasse might continue for another decade. The prospect was all the more intolerable now she'd been given a glimpse, through Alex, of a different sort of life, one with affection and romance, togetherness, companionship, one that made the sheer waste and deprivation of her actual life hit home with desperate force.

Collapsing onto a chair, she remained leaning over the table, as if its mutilated state symbolized her own existence, and only the scratchy hoarseness of her throat sent her blundering out to the kitchen to fetch a glass of water. New outrage met her eyes there: both fridge and freezer had been left open and water was trickling on to the vinyl floor-tiles she'd polished to a shine only hours ago. And the starter and the pudding she'd made for Megan first thing this morning, and left pristine in the fridge, had both been raided and despoiled. The avocado mousse was all but finished up, the lemon posset streaked with green, where Colin had used the same spoon as for the starter. It was totally inexplicable, in that he never normally helped himself from the fridge but always left *her* to bring his food, and, in any case, he detested avocado. Besides, he had told her when he woke that he wasn't the slightest bit hungry on account of his tummy-ache, although only now did she realize that he must have been going down with the gastroenteritis bug that had caused his violent diarrhoea. Why and when his appetite had mysteriously returned, or why he'd eaten *Megan's* food, instead of the snacks she'd left beside his bed, she was never likely to know, since she and Colin could never communicate or engage in rational dialogue.

All the frustration of living with someone with memory-loss seemed to come to a seething boil in her head, as she recalled the frequent occasions when he clean forgot what had happened only hours or minutes earlier. In fact, it struck her, all at once, that her recent outburst – so precipitate, so vehement, so totally unprecedented – had been simply wasted breath. Colin, peacefully slumbering upstairs, had failed to hear a single word. And, even if he had heard, he would never admit he'd been at fault, but deny all accusations, since whatever he had done this morning would have long since been consigned to oblivion.

She was determined to go and wake him, though, however fruitless any attempt to tell him how upset she was, or how unlikely any coherent conversation. But, as she began striding towards the staircase, the sudden peal of the doorbell stopped her in her tracks. If it was the postman, he could go to hell; if Beryl, the woman could go straight back home and stay there. She wrenched open the front door, tears streaming down her face, her hair dishevelled, the smart clothes she'd put on for Sebastian now plashed with red wine and dirty flower-water, yet not caring who might see her.

'Veronica,' Megan exclaimed. 'What on earth's the matter? I heard you shouting from halfway down the street!'

Veronica froze in shock. Why in God's name had her friend arrived at lunchtime, rather than for supper? How much had she heard from 'halfway down the street': the 'fuckings', the abuse, the intemperate accusations?

'What's *happened*?' Megan asked again, stepping into the hall and off-loading into Veronica's arms the bunch of flowers she'd been clutching to her chest. 'The only reason I'm here at this hour is that I picked these from the garden and thought I'd drop them in early, to save you the hassle of having to find a vase and arrange them at the last minute. I've been trying to phone you, to say I was passing your house anyway, so would it be OK if I popped in for a second, but you didn't pick up.'

Veronica was too ashamed to speak. Instead of the gracious welcome she'd planned, Megan had been confronted with a screaming harridan, utterly at odds with the serene, upbeat persona Veronica tried to present at choir. She could hardly bear the humiliation of knowing Megan had seen her in such an uncontrollable state, had heard the dark and terrible things she had never voiced to anyone. Would their friendship even survive?

'You're *shaking*, love. You'd better come and sit down.'

She let Megan take her arm and lead her into the sitting-room. Only then did she notice that the new throw she'd bought to cover the shabby sofa was now stained with wine and diarrhoea and had been tossed on to the floor. Just the sight of it was enough to add a racking misery to her existing mortification, and she sank down on to the now uncamouflaged sofa, again weeping bitterly.

Megan sat beside her, rock-solid and supportive, one arm around her shoulders, the other hand held tight and comfortingly in hers, until haltingly and gradually the sobs subsided into uneven breathless gasps.

'I'm so *sorry*, Megan,' she stammered, once able to speak, and so desperate to explain now, the words emerged in a garbled rush. 'I wanted everything to be nice for you, but now it's all wrecked and the whole place smells like a shithouse. And I can't bear to think you heard me screaming like that and saying God knows what. And, as for our supper, that's all ruined too. Colin's already eaten the first course and the pudding, and if I don't get down to the cooking soon, there won't even be a main course.'

'Hush, love. The food doesn't matter, as I've told you umpteen times. If this is Colin's doing, then we need to get the place to rights. But I insist you sit and rest, and let *me* take over, OK? Just show me where you keep your cleaning stuff, and I'll have everything spick and span in a jiffy. It'll do me good to work off some of the flab!'

Megan ignored her protests, ordered her back to the sofa, brought her a cup of strong, sweet tea, then got to work on the hall with the shampooer and the disinfectant and an impressive show of energy.

For a shaming minute, Veronica merely sat and watched, barely able to believe that, far from losing Megan's friendship, here was someone so genuinely supportive she didn't balk at clearing up diarrhoea, and could negate her own afternoon plans, to come to the immediate rescue. Yet, mixed with her gratitude were a thousand accusing guilts: guilt towards Megan, of course, and towards Colin for wishing him dead, even guilt on Tom's behalf, for allowing herself to resent his pitiful condition, if only for a moment. And also guilt for sitting useless now, while Megan slaved cheerfully away. Making a supreme effort, she rose, still trembling, to her feet, only to be rebuked by Megan, who insisted she stay put. And she was, indeed, so exhausted by her outburst, she appeared to have lost her usual willpower and resolve, and simply allowed her friend to overrule her, gratefully aware that she had managed to find everything without even needing to ask: cups and saucers, teabags, sugar, brooms and floor-cloths, carpet-shampoo, pine disinfectant, a sturdy green-glass vase.

Finally, Megan popped in one last time, with a second cup of tea and a tasteful arrangement of her garden-flowers. 'Where shall I put these?' she asked, inhaling the scent of the floppy-headed rambler-roses.

Suddenly realizing how precious that scent was – more so even than the smell of Alex's long-stemmed hothouse roses -Veronica knew she must get a grip on herself and salvage what was left of the day. Megan had seen her at her unutterable worst, so she had to make amends and afford her friend at least some dregs of basic hospitality. 'Let's take them into the dining-room,' she said, forcing herself to sound more engaged and upbeat, 'and I'll give you lunch instead of supper – if you're sure you have time to stay, that is?'

'All the time in the world. I'd planned nothing for this afternoon except catching up on emails, which I'm only too happy to postpone!'

'The only problem is there *isn't* any lunch! The main course I'd planned will take ages to cook, so I'll have to cobble together some sort of stopgap meal instead.'

'Look, I came to see you, as I've told you all along, not to award your kitchen its fourth Michelin star!'

'OK. Let me just check on Colin. I'm amazed he hasn't woken up with all the noise.' As she made her way up to his bedroom, she wondered for a second if he was dead. Surely otherwise, he'd have come barging down to see what was going on, peevishly vociferous at being so rudely disturbed.

Yet, to her astonishment, he was still deeply asleep and still breathing calmly like a placid child. Could this be the self-same man as had caused all the wanton destruction? Perhaps she'd overreacted, blamed him for things beyond his control, forgotten to make her usual allowances for the difficulties he couldn't help.

She returned to Megan, trying to put her confusion into words. 'I just can't understand what was going through his mind to make him behave like that. It's as if he somehow knows about Alex and decided to pay me out.'

'How could he possibly know, Veronica? I'm the only person you told about it, and the evening I was with him, we barely exchanged a word. I kept checking on him, of course, but, every time I went in, he was completely engrossed in the telly and, even when I got him into bed, he made no fuss at all and didn't even ask what I was doing there. In fact, he seemed a total, docile, little pussy-cat!'

Veronica gave a sudden hooting laugh. The notion of Colin as a pussy-cat strained credulity too far.

'That's better, love! The way you looked earlier on, I thought you'd never smile in your life again! Now what I suggest is that we get some bread and cheese, or something really simple, and sit and eat it in style in the dining-room, and you can tell me what on earth's been going on – not just with Colin but with Alex.'

They finally settled for beans on toast, with some of Colin's ice-cream for pudding – hardly the elaborate fare she'd planned, but, as Megan said, who cared? And at least they had flowers on the table, and Megan had found some paper serviettes: unseasonable Christmassy ones, adorned with jolly Santa Clauses, but they somehow added to the sheer relief Veronica felt at patching up her shattered plans and being safely with her friend, notwithstanding all the screaming horror of the last two hours. The circumstances might have altered, the meal might be a scratch one, but this amazing woman was so genuine, so caring, it seemed to more than compensate for everything.

CHAPTER 11

'Forgive me being blunt, love, but why did you ever marry Colin in the first place?'

Thrown by the question, Veronica paused to sip her wine. There'd been so many different, complicated factors, including a shaming lack of self-knowledge at the time, a desperate desire to matter to someone, and an overwhelming urge to separate herself from Den. 'I know it sounds pathetic,' she said, at last, 'but I wanted to be needed, above all else, and here was a man who'd just lost his wife in a car-crash and been left to care for his severely disabled son. Tom was only three at the time and totally distraught without his mother.' She didn't explain that the so-called car-crash had been widely seen as suicide on Daisy's part, because, as Tom grew out of the baby stage and became increasingly handicapped, Colin's first wife had apparently found it harder and harder to cope. 'You see, Daisy was only twenty when she died,' was all she said to Megan, 'so the whole situation was terribly harrowing.'

'But you can't have been much more than that yourself when you took Tom on. I mean, if Colin's twenty-four years older …'

She nodded. 'Yes, I married at nineteen and my husband-to-be seemed so wise and mature and dependable in comparison.'

'Maybe so, but why make such a sacrifice, when you could have married a much younger guy, with no dependents and not trailing all that tragedy in his wake?'

Veronica gave an embarrassed laugh. 'I actually felt grateful that anyone wanted to marry me at all! My mother never thought I'd amount to much, and I'd grown up feeling a burden to her and …'

‘From what you told me earlier, she sounds completely toxic.’ Megan banged down her glass, as if to express her disapproval.

‘No, that’s unfair – honestly. You don’t understand how difficult things were for her. You see, I was … illegitimate.’ She all but choked on the word – one she never used, since, from earliest childhood, Den had given her strict instructions to tell anyone who asked that her legal, loving father had died of a heart attack a few weeks after her birth. In point of fact, the mystery-man had scarpered the minute he heard that Den was pregnant, and the inconvenient daughter had never once laid eyes on him or seen so much as a photograph. ‘Having a child out of wedlock was a terrible disgrace back then, and Den’s own parents disowned her, so she had no support and was desperately short of cash. So it was only natural she’d resent me.’

‘I’m sorry, but I disagree. It’s not natural to resent your own child, illegitimate or not.’

Veronica was feeling increasingly uncomfortable, having already said far more than she’d intended. In any case, it was unlikely Megan could understand, coming as she did from a stable, loving family, with two hands-on parents and an affectionate younger brother. She deliberately hadn’t mentioned Den’s string of ever-changing lovers, knowing such behaviour would be widely condemned as promiscuous, whereas she had finally come to understand it as a desperate bid on her mother’s part for security and love.

She passed Megan the bowl of fruit salad, which she’d made a mere five minutes ago, having discovered a few tired fruits in the salad-drawer of the fridge. They had long ago finished the beans on toast and a whole carton of Raspberry Ripple, but, since the meal still seemed so inadequate, she had added this little extra.

Megan helped herself, whilst continuing the conversation. 'From what you've said, Veronica, it strikes me that you've been trying to make amends for most of your adult life – to be "needed", as you put it, and prove you *weren't* a disappointment and hadn't disgraced your mother.'

Veronica wished they'd never started on this subject – one she barely understood herself. 'But what you're ignoring, Megan, is that I gained a lot from the marriage. I mean, just to have a settled, permanent home, for the very first time in my life, seemed little short of miraculous. I was so used to living in a succession of rented bedsits and sharing a bedroom with Den – sometimes even sharing her bed – that to have this Clapham house made me feel really rooted and secure. In those days, Colin was doing well in business, and he'd even paid off the mortgage, would you believe? In fact, you *could* see me as a gold-digger, rather than a Mother Teresa!'

'For heaven's sake, Veronica, anyone less like a gold-digger I can't imagine. Having agreed to devote your life to someone else's disabled child, the least you could expect was a roof over your head!'

'Well, I certainly got that, but what I didn't expect – and which was much more precious actually - was Tom's complete, unconditional love. Obviously, it took him a while to get used to me and recover from his mother's death but, once he began to trust me, we forged an incredibly close bond.' Again, she felt uneasy, aware how much she was concealing: the sheer strain and challenge and day-to-day exhaustion of caring for a child who couldn't walk or speak or do the slightest thing for himself. Nor would she admit that part of her bond with Tom lay in the fact that she, too, had been unwanted and resented, made to feel a burden just by being born.

She went to fetch her favourite photo of him and placed it on the table, next to Megan's plate. 'See the way he's smiling – that utterly radiant smile? Well, that was reserved for me and me alone. Every time he saw me, his face lit up like a flash-bulb, so I'd feel I was Father Christmas, come with a sack of toys, or his Fairy Godmother, about to wave her magic wand. OK, he needed me, and I did my best to meet his needs, but I needed him every bit as much, to make me feel useful and important and all the things I'd never felt before.'

As Megan studied the photo, Veronica feared her friend was seeing only his handicaps: his slumped posture in the wheelchair, the skeletally thin arms and twisted hands, the drooling mouth that never quite closed over his uneven teeth. Quickly, she returned the photo to the mantelpiece, not wanting him to be criticised or pitied.

'Yes, but don't you see,' Megan persisted, 'that got you into the habit of thinking you *had* to be useful - a giver and a carer, rather than simply enjoying life. I mean, look at you now, waiting on Colin hand, foot and finger, when, as far as I can gather, he never did a thing for you or Tom.'

Veronica flushed. 'It was extremely hard for him to come to terms with having a handicapped son. He was very much macho-man, so he saw it as a source of shame and stigma that reflected really badly on him. His parents used to refer to Tom as a "cripple" and their aversion made things even worse. So, it wasn't surprising that he failed to develop any sort of rapport with Tom, whereas *I* soon came to see him as my own child. And, when he died, I was completely knocked sideways. I'd not only lost my son but my whole role and purpose in life, and all the things that filled my day – not just the routine care, but the hospital appointments and endless sessions with physios and speech-therapists and the army of other specialists who tried to stop him slipping into greater helplessness. It may sound dreary, Megan, but that type of life can be fulfilling and worthwhile.'

'Maybe.' Megan sounded far from convinced. 'And, of course I understand what a shock his death must have been. But surely it occurred to you, at some point, that now you were actually free? You could have put Colin into a care-home and started living your own life.'

'Oh, Megan, that would be cruel – to send him packing now he has dementia.'

'It could be seen as *kind.* I mean, lots of geriatric homes lay on dementia programmes and reminiscence-sessions, and all that sort of stuff can be really valuable for people with Alzheimer's.'

'He actually has vascular dementia, although, in some respects, it's not that different from Alzheimer's. But, because it came on fairly slowly, I didn't grasp what was happening for a while. First, he just seemed forgetful. He'd lose track of where the cups and plates were kept, or he'd muddle up people's names, or continually lose things, then blame me for hiding them and snap at me non-stop, or go into these awful silent furies. I understood his anger - he couldn't bear being so incapable when he'd once been Mr Control-Freak – so it was almost a relief when, gradually, he began talking less and less. At least I was no longer in the firing-line! But it was also horribly isolating. He's forgotten so many words and concepts, we're barely able to communicate at all these days. And because he's lost all memory of the things we used to do and people we used to know, it's as if the entire past history of our marriage has been wiped out, like someone wiping a blackboard clean. Mind you, even in the early days, when he was completely compos mentis, he was never a great talker and never mad-keen on company. In fact, his favourite bird is the albatross, on the grounds that it stays away from home for months at a time, while it crosses the ocean on the wing. That would suit him perfectly!'

Megan gave a disbelieving snort. 'He's hardly on the wing, love, just stuck here day in, day out, driving you insane.'

'Well, I must admit I find it daunting, and I'm also constantly worried about the dangers – you know, if he leaves fires on, or the oven, or wanders outside with no coat and not the faintest notion where he's going. But the worst thing is knowing I'm his one and only carer, yet with no idea of what the future holds or how much worse he'll become.'

'All the more reason for you to get out while you can. You could start all over again, Veronica, if you'd only put your own needs first, for a change.'

'But that's exactly what I am doing!' Veronica deliberately adopted a more cheerful tone, aware Megan must be sick and tired of her tedious domestic problems. 'I mean, just agreeing to go out with Alex was a real step forward for me.'

'Ah, Alex!' Megan gave a long, suggestive sigh, 'We haven't even mentioned him yet, although I've been dying to ask you how you two got on.'

Veronica tried to suppress her now spontaneous Alex-smile, more than happy to discuss him, rather than her husband. 'Oh, Megan, it was out of this world! He's so bright and successful and on the ball and seems a different generation from poor old doddery Colin, but also – which I *didn't* expect – he was amazingly attentive. He made me feel I was the only woman in the universe!'

'That's brilliant! As far as I can see, you've never had a soul who really paid you attention before – well, Tom, maybe, but certainly not Colin or any other adult. And attention seems to me a basic human need, to stop us feeling lonely.' Yes, Veronica thought, she had undoubtedly felt lonely throughout her forty-year marriage, despite Tom's physical presence. He might be with her most of the day, but, of course, the poor lad had no insight into her situation, or, indeed, his own. It was Megan herself, in point of fact, who - better late than never - gave her that all-important attention, as she'd been doing today non-stop, reversing a lifetime's experience of receiving little in the way of solicitude or affirmation.

'So, did you arrange to meet again?'

Veronica hesitated. 'Er, yes. He's invited me to the ballet. We haven't fixed the date yet and he didn't give me many details, but it appears to be another plush affair, with another glitzy dinner afterwards. Oh, and talking of dinners, the one on Monday was really something, Megan! The restaurant had these huge gilt-framed mirrors on almost every wall, and so many chandeliers, the whole place glowed and sparkled – just as *I* was doing inside! He's obviously a regular there, because the staff were all over us, the minute we walked in, and they treated me like a celebrity just because I was with him. I'd planned to keep quiet and sort of fade into the background, so I wouldn't let him down in front of his sophisticated friends, but I was so elated by the whole occasion, the words just seemed to flow, and, believe it or not, they found what I said of interest, even funny.'

'Why the hell shouldn't they? You always put yourself down and ignore the fact you're attractive and intelligent and extremely sensitive and caring. I reckon all that time looking after Tom gave you loads of patience and compassion, and people tune in to that instinctively.'

Veronica tried to wave away the compliments, while she wrestled with a dilemma: should she admit to Megan that Alex had suggested she come to his flat long before the ballet – as early as next week, in fact – for what he called an 'intimate little supper'. The very thought both terrified and thrilled her. Indeed, the way he'd kissed her just before they'd parted, was proof enough that he wanted to take the relationship to a completely different level from that of mere casual acquaintance. It was so long since she'd been kissed that when he pressed his entire body against hers and used his tongue to explore the deepest recesses of her mouth, it was as if she'd been electrified, every cell and limb and organ responding to his touch. And, since Monday night, she couldn't stop herself reliving that extraordinary sensation of rampaging excitement, as her whole soul and self and essence seemed to open to him, merge with him, and she had to stop herself from shouting, 'More! Don't stop! Yes, *more*!'

There *hadn't* been more. She was a married woman, yoked to Colin, who was awaiting her return any minute, as, on that magical evening, Megan herself had been. So, if she had succumbed to some wild, spontaneous fling in Alex's flat, or allowed him to lure her to a Convent Garden hotel, she would have aroused the strongest suspicions when she eventually returned, flushed, exultant, and exuding guilt from every pore.

'Hey, what's that noise?' Megan held up her finger for silence.

Oh my God, Veronica thought! The moans of passion and wild, orgasmic cries echoing through the ceiling from Colin's bedroom could mean only one thing: her husband had succumbed to his intermittent porn habit and was playing *Lesbian Lovelies* or *Busty Blonde Babes* on his computer. Crimson with embarrassment and hastily excusing herself, she rushed upstairs to turn off the video, found him furtively masturbating, while a bevy of big-breasted beauties caressed and pleasured each other on-screen, to a panting, thrusting soundtrack. She struggled between fury and a guilty awareness that she'd neglected Colin today, deliberately leaving him in the bedroom, so he'd be well removed from Megan, and checking on him only twice during lunch –

both cursory checks, in her haste to return downstairs.

Sternly, she re-zipped his trousers and replaced the Lesbian Lovelies with an old video of Morecambe and Wise. However, his expression of mingled shame, resentment and disappointment only increased her own guilt and, in a bid to make amends, she went down again to fetch the box of Magnums from the freezer and brought him up two Double Caramels. No way could she subject her friend to a second instalment of breathless gasps and whoops, so distraction-techniques were justified today.

'Why are you so busy, Ron?' he asked, querulously. 'I've barely seen you since breakfast. I don't like your friend. I don't want her here.'

'Well, you'll jolly well have to lump it,' she muttered sotto voce, realising with a jolt that Megan's forthright views threatened to undermine her own former submissive attitude. Indeed, she refused to stay with him now, whatever his wishes and complaints, and, as soon as he'd unwrapped one of the Magnums and begun laughing at Eric and Ernie, she returned to the dining-room.

'I didn't know Colin was into porn,' Megan remarked. 'I'm far from being a prude, as you well know, but I have to say I detest the whole porn industry. It's so fake and meretricious and makes us women feel frigid if we can't come six times in succession, or cope with twelve-inch cocks rammed down our throats. And we're forced to shave off our pubic hair, because, compared with the Brazilian-waxed brigade, it now seems unsightly and disgusting.'

Veronica's discomfiture was growing. She had never discussed such things before, let alone in such frank terms. Besides, she found herself conflicted, as so often. In theory, she supported the anti-porn stance, but if Colin sometimes craved comfort in his pitifully truncated life, wasn't it better to turn a blind eye to it, since he'd only overrule her anyway? She just wished he'd waited till Megan had left, rather than making an already difficult lunch still more awkward. What riled her most, however, was that her husband should sit slavering over such no-holds-barred excesses, when he personally had always been a half-hearted, tepid lover. Indeed, the reason why Alex's kiss had made such a deep impression on her was that, having never known real passion in her marriage, she had exploded like a touch-paper to his deliciously dangerous advance.

Suddenly, and probably unwisely, she found herself blurting out the whole saga to Megan, no longer able to bear the stress of being torn both ways. 'So you see,' she concluded, 'I just don't know what to do. If I agree to supper at Alex's place, I'm pretty sure there'll be more to it than food, and never once have I cheated on Colin, not in all these years. On the other hand, he and I haven't actually… done it for decades. He may watch porn, but, to be perfectly honest, he was never that mad-keen when it came to our own sex-life.'

Megan gave an unexpected laugh. 'That's typical of men, don't you think? They spurn the real thing in favour of exaggerated fantasy, where all the females have 44-D breasts and never have periods or headaches or off-days!'

Veronica laughed too, although Megan's frankness still had the power to shock her. 'I'm in this churn of indecision, changing my mind every second minute, first deciding I will go to Alex's, then thinking of all the reasons why it would be madness on my part.'

'Why madness?'

'I keep telling you I'm married. And I've always taken marriage very seriously, right from the word go. You see, I wanted all the things my mother never had: one man in my life who'd stick around, for better, for worse, and a happy settled home.'

'It was hardly very happy, judging by what you've said.'

'Yes, but it was secure, and not just in terms of bricks and mortar. Colin was so relieved that his son was now thriving – as far as any child with cerebral palsy can thrive – no way would he have rocked the boat by having affairs.'

'I should jolly well hope not! I mean, he must have realized that, as Tom's full-time carer, you've been tamped down and circumscribed for decades, with no scope to be your own person.'

Veronica doubted if he *had* realized. He probably simply saw it as his right to accept her help and support, leaving him free to develop his various business ventures, or pursue his various hobbies.

'And you're still tied down, more's the pity. Remember that gig we did at the Marsden and the rest of us all trooped off for a coffee afterwards? Well, you missed all the fun and gossip, because you had to rush back for Colin. He's too selfish and stubborn to let you employ a proper carer, so you're stuck with that role. I'm sorry, love, but I feel you need an escape-route, otherwise nothing will ever change. So, for goodness sake, take advantage of this opportunity and at least give Alex a chance?'

'Oh, I couldn't possibly escape, Megan, or not for any longer than a few strictly rationed hours. Colin would be completely thrown trying to manage on his own.'

'Well, just escape for those few hours, then, and simply be open to what happens. There's no need to see it as a great life-and-death issue, just go for the sheer hell of it. If you've never had an affair in all that time, then I reckon it's high time to start!'

Last night's vivid dream seemed to have been saying the same thing. For hour after brazen hour, a rugged but faceless man had made violent, vehement love to her, the two of them totally, voraciously insatiable. It was as if all her natural sex-drive, bottled up since adolescence (when Den forbade all boyfriends save her own), and even stoppered throughout her marriage, had exploded in a storm of passion that went beyond all boundaries. She had woken in a sweat, astounded at herself. Never before had she experienced such heights and depths of desire, or even known they were possible, save through clues and hints in some of their choir songs and the all-consuming passion in *Bohème*.

Trying to suppress the dream, she reiterated the fact that two-timing Colin would seem fundamentally wrong. 'Besides, I'm completely out of practice when it comes to - you know …. And far too old, in any case.' As far as she could gather, many women of her age were only too happy to be 'left in peace', and even Megan had admitted today that, since she'd ditched her last live-in lover, she hadn't once missed all the heaving and thrusting, or the damp patches on the sheets!

'Alex is older, though, and not exactly an Adonis. I doubt he's likely to attract whole hordes of gorgeous young babes when he's short and plain and beginning to thicken round the waist!'

Appalled to hear Alex described in such unflattering terms, she was about to object, when Megan put in breezily, 'Anyway, don't they say sex is like riding a bicycle, something you never forget?'

'It may sound pathetic, but I've never actually ridden one. Den's lifestyle wasn't conducive to bikes – nowhere to store them, for one thing, and she'd never have let me go gallivanting off on my own.'

'That was donkeys' years ago, though, and now you are

branching out on your own. Take the choir, for instance. When you first joined, you were so shy and tongue-tied, you barely said a word, but of late you've really blossomed. Everybody warms to you and quite a few of the younger ones turn to you for help and advice. And, since you took on the job of Secretary, you've developed a whole raft of different skills and been a huge help to Glenys.' Megan paused to eat her last two peach-slices, before continuing. 'Well, all I'm suggesting is that you do the same in your private life and let Alex give you some of the things you've lacked. You don't have to stop looking after Colin, or do anything drastic like breaking up the marriage, just live a little and see how things work out.'

'But he's talking about next week, Megan, and how can I possibly be ready in time?'

'What do you mean, "ready"?'

'Well, physically ready – primped and primed and so on – and emotionally ready, in the sense that I won't feel such extremes of guilt, the whole thing will be counterproductive. Besides, I can hardly ask Beryl to Colin-sit if I intend to cheat on him while she's there? How could I look her in the eye when I got back?'

'Don't worry - you won't have to. *I* intend to hold the fort and, before you start objecting, it's absolutely no trouble. I'm as free as a bird, with no ties, not even a cat, and anyway I quite enjoy being in your house.'

'I can't think why, when yours is so much less shabby and cluttered.'

'There you go, putting yourself down again! Anyway, it's settled, so no more argument. Just give me the day next week and I'll be there.'

About to express her thanks, a sudden wail from Colin, now on his way downstairs, jerked Veronica to her feet. 'Oh, Lord! What's up with him, for heaven's sake? Look, would it be a cheek, Megan, if I left you to make some coffee, while I go and check?'

'Actually, I need to push off home now, if that's OK? I've been here hours, although the time went by in a flash. I'll see you at choir tomorrow, anyway, and we can chat more then. But one last thing before I go – I want your solemn promise that you'll sack that nerd of a singing-teacher.'

'Oh, Megan I can't! He's so tremendously talented, I doubt if anyone has ever given him the push.'

'High time they did, then! Don't you see, Veronica, it's all part of the same thing? You've just got to stop putting up with shoddy treatment, whether from Sebastian or Colin or –'

Colin's crescendoing wail cut through Megan's voice. Veronica could see him halfway down the staircase, proceeding at his usual slow, unsteady pace. Torn between concern about him and her duty as a hostess, she hurried down the hall to wave a hasty goodbye to Megan, before she went to his aid. But, as she closed the front door, her friend had the parting shot.

'Don't be at hubby's beck and call, love. If he has to wait two minutes for his next nappy-change, or ice-lolly, or mug of Ovaltine, it'll teach him patience, do him the world of good!'

CHAPTER 12

'Mm, these are really more-ish!' Kevin spoke through a mouthful of chocolate muffin. 'Can I be a pig and have another?'

'Go ahead.' Veronica passed him the Tupperware carton. 'I made them specially for choir.' This, her first-ever baking session, inspired by post-Alex elation, had proved a surprising success, the recipe from *Cooking for Dummies* extremely lavish with both butter and chocolate. She had got up early this morning, not only to make them, but to ensure she spent a good chunk of time with Colin before leaving him (with his own muffin-supply) while she attended this Thursday rehearsal.

'And one for me, ta.' Barry reached across to help himself.

As more people clustered around her, Veronica savoured what had now become her favourite part of choir: this pre-singing socializing in the crowded church-hall kitchen, when members caught up with each other's news, made themselves hot drinks, and enjoyed a laugh and a joke. When growing up, a kitchen had been a rare luxury, since she and Den usually made do with a gas-ring or a Baby Belling, stuck in the corner of some bedsit. And there had certainly never been congenial people around. It was either just the isolated two of them, living cheek by jowl, or – worse – one of Den's lovers staying over, which meant cowering somewhere out of sight and covering her ears so as not to hear the weird, disturbing sex-sounds.

'I like the pink, Veronica,' Marianne observed, 'especially teamed with that orangey scarf. I always admire the way you co-ordinate your colours.'

Veronica smiled her thanks, having learned, at long last, not to demur at every compliment. Indeed, she was coming to believe that perhaps she did have a natural sense of style.

'I would never wear such vivid colours, not at *my* age,' Charlotte put in – an obvious put-down, since she was much the same age as Veronica. But, as Megan had pointed out, Charlotte had a sharp tongue and seemed almost to take pleasure in other people's discomfiture. 'She's jealous of you, that's all, now you're doing so well as Secretary. But then in a choir as big as ours, there are bound to be a few awkward cusses.'

And also a few windbags, Veronica didn't say, as the garrulous Theo made a beeline for her and continued last week's saga about his enrolment in a trial of a new anti-cancer drug. Trapped by his monologue, she exchanged a complicit smile with Megan, who had just arrived with some plums from her garden to share. As Theo veered off on a tangent about a new source of Swiss funding for the drug, Veronica continued valiantly nodding, having long ago accepted that, if the choir was her new family, then there would be good and bad among them, a few shy or downright unsociable ones, a few chronic complainers, and one or two New-Agers like Frances, who believed in crystals and Flower Essences and insisted 'all would be well', even in the face of terminal illness. What mattered overall was the sense of community, of joint purpose and shared bonds, and nothing could ever destroy that.

'What's happened to Katy?' Charlotte asked. 'She's usually here on the dot of five-thirty. If she fails to turn up, *you'll* have to step in, Veronica, and take over the conducting.'

Veronica winced at this dig at her inexperience, relieved when Anna wove her way towards them, mercifully interrupting Theo by brandishing her phone in front of their noses. 'I promised to show you my new grandchild. Well, here she is, with my daughter, just hours after the birth.'

Real family, Veronica thought, peering at the photo on the screen. The tiny, podgy infant reactivated her long-suppressed desire to have given birth to her own child. Instead, she'd simply fallen in with Colin's view that, since all her time and energy would be required for Tom, it would be unwise for them even to try for a baby. Yet, had she married someone different, she might be a great-grandmother by now, sharing her own family photos and relishing the comfort of being part of a large, supportive tribe.

Her long talk with Megan yesterday had left her feeling generally confused, 'needs' and 'rights' being daunting, unfamiliar concepts. Indeed, in one way, submission was easier – no need for hard decisions then, or to put her head above the parapet and have to face possible dissension. And, in any case, she had always been ambivalent about biological motherhood, for fear she might have inherited Den's genes and condemn her child to a lifetime of bad mothering.

'Terribly sorry to be so late!' Katy swept into the kitchen, wearing a Hippyish patchwork coat and shedding a long, woolly scarf too hot for this mild September. 'I feel really bad about keeping you all waiting, but there was a signal-failure on the tube. Still, let's get cracking right away, so finish up your drinks, please, and join me in the hall.'

She began chivvying them out of the kitchen and, once everyone was settled, asked those well enough to run through the usual stretching, bending and general limbering-up exercises.

'And, now, to warm up our voices, we're going to learn a limerick and sing it in four parts. First, we'll just get to know the words, so repeat after me, please:

There was an old lady from Ryde
Who ate too many apples and died.
The apples fermented inside the lamented
And made cider inside her inside.

The words provoked much hilarity, Trevor's honking laugh prompting yet more giggles. The general atmosphere was exceptionally light-hearted this evening, Katy leaping about exuberantly as she taught them the simple tune. Veronica couldn't help reflecting that Sebastian would be appalled by such levity and, still more so, by them singing a limerick, rather than some gem from the classical repertoire. But the last thing she wanted was to dwell on Sebastian, since, lacking, as she did, Megan's gift for plain speaking, the prospect of giving him the sack was daunting in the extreme.

Once they'd sung the limerick straight through, and then in parts, Katy began conducting them faster and faster and faster, until they all collapsed in hysterics, unable even to form the words at such a crazy speed.

'And now for something more serious,' Katy announced. 'We're going to learn *A Nightingale Sang in Berkeley Square* – which I'm sure you all know pretty well already.'

Amidst the general chorus of assent, with some people even breaking into the tune, only Veronica shook her head, to Megan's obvious bemusement. 'You *must* know it, love. It's an absolute classic. And, in all these years, you can't fail to have heard it on the radio. It was certainly one of my mother's favourites. She had several different recordings of it and often sang along to the tune!'

She hadn't yet admitted that she and Den hadn't owned a radio, let alone a gramophone, knowing how peculiar that would sound to normal people. And her severely disruptive schooling had made any chance of learning an instrument, or even any repertoire of songs, more or less impossible. And, even after marriage, her demanding daily round with Tom made it most unlikely that they'd be sitting listening to music. But things had vastly improved now, in that she was learning a new song every month at choir and – an unexpected advantage - the words had a far greater impact on her than on those who knew them off by heart and so no longer really registered their meaning.

And these particular words spoke to her with exceptional force: the sense of magic in the air since Alex's phone-call this morning, confirming tomorrow week as the day of their 'intimate supper' - indeed, more than magic, a sense of seismic upheaval, as she struggled between excitement and sheer terror. And, although guilt and indecision were all fatally churned up with elation and arousal, no way would she change her mind now– she just knew she must be there.

She let her voice ring out loud and clear, despite not knowing the song, since Megan had impressed on her that, having never been 'heard' in her childhood or in her married life, she needed to be more forceful and vociferous. Mercifully, Katy was making it easy, not only because she'd begun by coaching the basses, but because she was running through just two lines at a time.

And these two lines were easy to sing with rapturous conviction, since they focused on love and she *was* in love – already - however crazy that might sound, in that she still barely knew Alex in any sort of depth. But hadn't it happened in *Bohème*: two near-strangers experiencing an instant rapport, the first tiny seeds of passion burgeoning like Jack's Beanstalk?

'Well done, basses! That was excellent. You're singing with real musicality today.'

Veronica lapped up the praises like a once-starving cat gorging on clotted cream, even accepting Katy's congratulations on their 'truly stupendous sound'. That was rank hyperbole – and Sebastian would be suitably appalled - but since the 'stupendous' and the 'excellent' matched her inordinately upbeat mood, she simply revelled in the adjectives, rather than working out whether or not she deserved them.

'Romantic', they sang, the word a slab of sweetest butterscotch melting in her mouth, because *Alex* had proved himself so gloriously romantic, from the moment he'd swept her into Fernando's on only the second day of their acquaintance. One ingredient of his magic was that he was still overlaid with her beloved childhood sweetheart, Leonard - so much so it was impossible to disentangle the two. Indeed, the extraordinary phenomenon of 'Leonard' having resurrected in her adult life seemed so fortuitous that, when it came to believing nightingales might sing in urban Berkeley Square, it caused her no problem whatever. In fact, after Friday night, she was pretty certain that every London square would be full of melodious nightingales singing their blissful little hearts out.

'Veronica, before you push off, could you spare me a minute?'

'Yes, 'course,' she told Glenys, buttoning her jacket. The two had not yet spoken during this rehearsal, since Glenys had turned up uncharacteristically late, then taken her seat with the sopranos at the other end of the hall. 'Is it about the new fund-raiser?'

'Sort of.' Glenys lowered her voice. 'But I can't really discuss it here. Have you time for a quick coffee?'

Veronica nodded, although disappointed not to have her usual 'escort' – Christopher on one side, Keith on the other, the three of them laughing, joking, chatting, until she turned off into her street, while they and most of the others made their way to the tube. Instead, she said her goodbyes to everyone, before she and Glenys peeled off to the small coffee-shop opposite the hall.

'I'll get these,' she said, going up to the counter. 'What do you fancy?'

'Just tea, please, strong and sweet.'

Once settled with their drinks, Veronica noticed how tired and strained Glenys appeared, sitting in oppressive silence, rather than embarking on any discussion. 'Have you had more bad news about the choir finances?' she prompted, aware Glenys might feel awkward about revealing some new shortfall in their coffers.

'No,' Glenys suddenly blurted out. 'I've had bad news about my cancer. It's spread to my bones. I only found out yesterday, after a bone-scan and an MRI.'

Veronica stared in horror, too shocked to know what to say. She reached for Glenys's hand across the table, trying to compensate for her clichéd words through the warmth and concern and pressure of her grip.

'It means another op, unfortunately, followed by more chemo, but don't worry, I'm determined to survive! The problem is I shan't be able to function as Chairperson for at least the next few weeks, so what I want to ask is could you possibly take over and run the meetings for me, while I'm having treatment?'

'Yes, of course,' Veronica reassured her, despite a spate of doubts and worries. Was she even qualified to be Chairperson and, anyway, how could she fit in more engagements with Colin likely to cause more mayhem if she left him on his own too long? And, to her eternal shame, she was also thinking, selfishly, that such bad news had come at the worst time for her, when she longed to sustain her upbeat mood and devote her energies to furthering her bond with Alex. Guiltily aware that such concerns were mere flimflam compared with the horror of secondary cancer, she tried to concentrate instead on what it meant for Glenys in terms of suffering, side-effects, uncertainty, disruption and deep-rooted fear of the future. And, to make things worse, Glenys was on her own, widowed long ago and childless not by choice, but because after years of trying to conceive, it turned out that her husband was firing blanks - or so she'd confided recently.

'I'll help in any way I can, Glenys. I mean, apart from taking over as temporary Chairperson, perhaps I could come with you for your chemotherapy sessions and take you home afterwards.' It would mean leaving Colin even longer, especially as Glenys lived far out in Wembley Park.

'Oh, that would be great, Veronica - at least for just the first one.'

'I'll try to be there for them all - if I possibly can,' she added, as more worries about Colin surged into her mind.' If necessary, she would have to remove Alex from the equation by postponing Friday week and desperately hoping he wouldn't assume she'd changed her mind about the whole relationship. Appalling as that prospect was, she couldn't leave Glenys to face this crisis alone.

Glenys took a sip of her now cold and scummy tea. 'You know, I was thinking on my way to choir about our two most reviled C-words and, in my opinion, cancer's the worse!'

Veronica gave a rueful smile. In her present situation, even the other C-word had been causing her no little concern since Alex first suggested supper at his flat. Not that she ever used that word, let alone Den's still more vulgar alternative of 'cock-sock', but had always thought of hers, vaguely, as 'down there'. But, whatever the semantics, 'down there' had been so long out of operation, she feared it would prove wanting if called on to perform, or even cause her discomfort, rather than any vestige of pleasure, whereas her whole mind and heart and body longed for the passionate consummation of *Bohème*.

CHAPTER 13

'Stupid how het up I feel.' Glenys made a conscious effort to relax back in her blue padded leatherette chair.

Veronica noticed, though, how one fist was tightly clenched and the fingers of the other hand fidgeting and fretting on her lap.

'I mean, you'd think with all the chemo I've had, I'd simply romp through it by now!'

'"Romp's" hardly the word,' Veronica said, with a smile, determined not to admit that she, too, felt nervous, surrounded as she was by some twenty other patients, all hooked up to drips, like Glenys, and trailing wires from their arms.

'I can't thank you enough for coming. Having you here is a wonderful distraction - stops me focusing on all the things that might go wrong. I'll never forget, during my very first chemo session, my immune system suddenly crashed and I was rushed into Intensive Care.'

Veronica gave silent thanks that, far from any such crisis, everything appeared to be proceeding smoothly. Yet it was hard to relax in this atmosphere, with shrill, insistent beeps going off, staff scurrying around, checking drugs and drips, and the patient in the adjoining chair visibly distressed, tears running down her parchment-pale face. The poor woman was also completely shiny-bald, in contrast to the patient opposite, who was wearing a cold-cap to prevent further extensive hair-loss – too late for Glenys, alas. 'Oh, I brought you this,' she said, reaching for her bag and passing across a small, soft, tissue-swathed package. 'I thought you deserved a new one!'

Glenys exclaimed in pleasure as she unwrapped the gold-and-turquoise turban, with its frivolous gold fringe. 'But, the greatest gift is your presence, as I said, so you really shouldn't have bought me anything.'

'Oh, they're only tiny things.' She rummaged in her bag for two more packages, wrapped in the same pink tissue. 'I know bed-socks seem a bit granny-ish, but these are cashmere, so they'll be nice and warm for when the weather turns colder. And this is a CD of soothing nature sounds, which you might like to play this evening, once I've taken you home.'

'You're spoiling me rotten, Veronica, but honestly there's no need to take me home. I can easily get a taxi right here outside the hospital.'

'No, I want to be sure you're OK. And, if you feel up to eating by then, I can make you a spot of supper and maybe see you into bed before I push off.'

'But what about Colin?'

'He's fine' Hastily, Veronica blanked out the fuss he'd made on hearing Beryl would be there again today – *and* tomorrow, when Glenys would need another visit, to ensure she'd had no bad reaction to this new combination of drugs. By then, it would be a mere three days to her supper with Alex – and again some blanking out was necessary, to censor the tantalizing images already throbbing in her mind. It seemed truly reprehensible to let her own selfish lusts and longings take precedence over Glenys' needs, so she had already decided to cancel the supper, if necessary. And she must certainly give the Thursday rehearsal a miss, since she couldn't possibly leave Colin four days running. 'Glenys, if you prefer to close your eyes and just be quiet, please do say so, won't you. The last thing I want is to tire you.'

'No, it's great to chat. It keeps my mind off all the nasty "what-ifs". But, actually, what I'd love is for you to read me a few snippets from the paper. My concentration's shot to pieces, so if I try to read it for myself, I find I'm thinking about the future – or what future I have left - rather than the News.'

Veronica unfolded the *Metro* she had picked up on the tube and started leafing through it, carefully avoiding any mention of terrorist attacks or downbeat reports about climate-change or the dire state of the economy. 'Ah, this is interesting! Apparently, one in eight eighteen-to-twenty-four-year-olds have spent so little time in the countryside they've never seen a real cow in their lives.'

'That seems a hell of a lot, but then I grew up in a remote part of Shropshire with almost more cows than people! Glenys had the bed-socks on her lap and was stroking them like a fluffy cat.

'And a fifth of that age-group,' Veronica continued, 'have never left their home city.'

'Well, I suppose at least that gives them roots.'

Veronica nodded, aware she herself lacked any concept of home, in the sense of a place of security and permanence. She had done her best, however, to provide such a concept for Tom – although thoughts of her stepson were undoubtedly unwise here, since they sparked memories of his own terror-stricken reaction to chemotherapy. His fear was hardly surprising when the poor lad had no way of understanding what was happening to him, or of articulating his feelings. Dragging her mind from Tom, she turned a page of the paper, wishing there were fewer bad-news stories. 'I don't know whether you're into mermaids,' she said, 'but one of the short-listed contestants for this summer's Miss Mermaid UK, was later disqualified because she lacked professional diving qualifications.'

'Oh, I assumed it was just a beauty pageant – you know, the girl with the longest hair and the perkiest tits.'

'Far from it, according to this. Each contestant has to train as a free diver, as well as taking singing lessons. We'd be fine in that respect, at least!'

Another unwelcome subject, Veronica thought, in that it reminded her of Sebastian's cold fury when she'd informed him yesterday that she wouldn't be returning for further tuition.

'Well done you!' Megan had said, approvingly. 'If he wants to sulk, that's his affair. What matters is you've made it clear you won't be messed about. People can see you're a pushover – that's the trouble - so they take advantage and treat you badly.'

Megan's bluntness was hurtful at times. Being a 'pushover' – vile phrase - had often been the only possible option when faced with intractable circumstances or highly critical people. She resumed her reading, swapping the *Metro* for *House and Garden*, one of several glossies she'd bought for Glenys this morning. 'Hey, how do you fancy a nine-hundred-grand, Georgian manor house?' she asked, turning this time to the property pages, 'complete with a swimming pool, a vineyard, a fully stocked wine-cellar and fishing rights on the adjoining River Otter?'

'Fine, so long as it has staff quarters, with all the staff in situ, ready to do my every bidding!'

Their light-hearted chat was skirting all the unspoken questions, lying between them like unexploded bombs. How long did Glenys have? How aggressive was this new cancer? How frightened was she beneath the veneer of bravado? Veronica had seen already, with other choir-members, how implacably the dread disease could encroach on lives, claiming more and more of a person's time and energy, as they trekked to all their various appointments, battled with side-effects, waited for what could seem an age to see the oncologist or get results, or were just too dog-tired to engage with once-routine activities. And this very room, she guessed, must be awash with pain and loss: patients who'd lost their confidence and femininity, along with their breasts, and could no longer bear to look in a mirror, those who'd lost their fertility, forced to face a childless future, those who'd lost a husband who maybe couldn't cope with what he saw as a mutilated wife, those who'd lost jobs, mobility, sense of purpose and basic trust in life. For all she knew, Glenys might prefer her to confront such issues head-on, rather than indulge in the trivial distractions of the property pages. Yet, she took the coward's way out and returned to the safer subject of bricks and mortar, resuming her cheery tone.

'Ah, this sounds just the job! A farmhouse here in Somerset, with five-hundred acres each of pasture and woodland, extensive outbuildings, and -'

She was interrupted by one of the nurses, a Hispanic lady with comfortable curves and hair a vehement shade of auburn, who had glided over, to check on Glenys's drip. While the two were conversing, Veronica found herself wondering whether future generations would look back on current cancer treatments as disfiguringly barbaric, if more merciful procedures happened to be developed. And she couldn't seem to stop harking back to questions more related to her own life, such as how would she cope as Chairperson, given her lack of experience, and what if Glenys didn't return as Chair, so the role became hers long-term? But, annoyed by such petty worries, she deliberately allowed herself a mini-break with Alex – or rather with Rodolfo. She now knew his words from the first act of *Bohème* almost off by heart, and here, in this most unlikely of settings, secretly thrilled to them again.

Already I taste in spirit
the heights of tenderness!
Love trembles in our kiss!

Surely there'd be another kiss – a whole evening of kisses, maybe - perhaps even a declaration of love. As she closed her eyes for a moment, the chemotherapy suite gave place to Rodolfo's draughty attic-room, the glaring hospital lights now replaced by shimmering moonlight; the nurse's murmur overlaid by her lover's voice, passionately repeating over and over: '*Nel bacio freme amor.*'

CHAPTER 14

Veronica sorted through the two packed rails of lingerie, torn between her natural preference for plain white no-nonsense underwear – the sort of unobtrusive style she'd worn throughout her life - and Megan's prompting to choose something sexy and provocative. In her life to date, there'd been no reason to indulge in pants so skimpy they wouldn't have covered a bee's bum, or in bras that were mere nipple-shields. Indeed, she hadn't even known the existence of this shop, despite it being a mere half-mile away.

She picked out a few pairs of pants, only to bung them straight back on the rail. One was composed of nothing more than criss-crossed silken ribbons, one bore the words *I adore big bongs*, written right across the crotch, and the third had no back at all. She feared such things might repel Alex rather than attract him, although, with her limited knowledge of men, she had no real way of telling. Colin was the only male she'd ever known in any depth, and *his* attitude to sex – when it came to real women rather than porn-stars – was one of inhibition, even prudishness, coupled with an obvious fear of getting too close to anyone, in any sense.

'May I help you, madam?'

The salesgirl's mouth was a scarlet slash across a tropically-tanned complexion, and her stiff, spiky, iron-railing lashes meant she could barely blink her eyes.

'Er, I'm looking for something a little more low-key than these.'

'No problem, madam. What colour did you have in mind?'

Megan had suggested black or red, but her own instincts again urged caution. 'Well, I'd prefer a fairly subtle shade, if possible.'

'And d'you want a set of matching bra and pants?'

Veronica nodded, whilst keeping a wary eye on the time. She'd been gone only a scant twenty minutes, whereas normally on a Thursday she spent a good two hours at choir, so Colin should be OK on his own, at least for a short while longer.

'How about these?' The salesgirl had ushered her over to a (presumably) less blatant rail and was pointing to a duo in the palest maroon silk, the pants cut not too brazenly low, the bra giving some support, and not a bow, rosette, or slogan in sight.

'Yes, they look fine.'

'Would you like to try them on, madam?'

If she was quick about it, she should have time. This was her sole errand, after all, and, once back home, she could then stay with Colin for the rest of the day and all evening.

The fitting-room, with its pink-and-black frilled curtains and photos of pouting sex-kittens on the walls, induced a monumental surge of guilt. The very fact of being here proved she was actually *preparing* for seduction – which, in plain unvarnished terms, meant preparing for adultery. Megan had been telling her all week to take the whole thing less seriously and simply enjoy tomorrow without so much shame and self-blame, and even with far less expectation. What happened happened, be it disastrous, bathetic or ecstatic. Easy for Megan, who'd had a whole succession of affairs, to adopt so sanguine an attitude, but for *her* tomorrow was a one-off – a flagrant betrayal, in one sense, but a turning-point and milestone in another.

She gazed at herself in the mirror, unable to prevent the tiniest smile of satisfaction at seeing her transformation from plain, white, no-

nonsense Ron to glamour-puss Veronica. And both bra and pants fitted remarkably well, which spared her the need to waste precious time trying on a whole raft of other styles and sizes.

She hadn't reckoned with the bill, however. A stupefying £275 for two flimsy bits of silk seemed not far off an outrage, when single mothers like Den still struggled in this day and age to bring up kids on much less than that a week. She was about to tell the salesgirl that she was sorry but she'd changed her mind, when Megan's voice intruded. 'For God's sake Veronica, spoil yourself for once. You deserve a bit of indulgence after a lifetime of slaving your guts out for Tom and Colin. And, even this last week, you've been rushing back and forth like a steam-train on Glenys's behalf.'

'It's the least I can do, when she's so ill.'

Megan knew as well as she did that secondary cancer was, basically, incurable and, although some lucky patients survived for years, no one could ever count on it.

'OK, and I admire that. But you spent all yesterday in her flat, cleaning and cooking and getting in masses of shopping - and, knowing you, probably washing the curtains and shampooing the carpets, just for good measure - so now you're owed some "me-time." And, anyway, it sounds as if she can cope perfectly well on her own now.'

Certainly, Glenys had recovered surprisingly quickly from the chemo and even her initial nausea was now being well-controlled by drugs. All that had proved a relief, as had running into one of the neighbours, a small, sparrow-like woman who lived in the flat opposite and had promised to pop in tomorrow, giving Veronica the certainty of knowing someone was on hand in case of an emergency. She was also mightily relieved for her own sake, in that she appeared to have been given the green light for tomorrow's date with Alex.

And, as she walked out with her purchases into the genial September sunshine, she felt a tiny ripple of triumph darting down her body - even clad as she was in her functional white cotton underthings and still struggling with fears and misgivings. Tomorrow, she dared to hope, her pale-maroon-silk finery would banish all the angst and leave only the brazen glamour-puss.

As she crossed the road from the shop, she broke into the first lines of *Nightingale*, despite the fact those were the sopranos' lines and, stuck as she was in the bass section, she had never sung so high before. Nonetheless, her voice rang out loud and true, and, as she sang the first poetic words, she could almost see the Angels dining at the Ritz. Throughout her life, she'd been starved of poetry and beauty, yet now she could enjoy them in many of the choir-songs, and was on such a high at present, her very surroundings seemed transformed, lavish beauty flaunting all around her in the trees' autumnal colours and in the blaze of crimson berries and gold chrysanthemums in the front-gardens she was passing. And, even in her own treeless street, the mother-of-pearl shimmer on the ever-shifting clouds reflected her own inner radiance.

'I'm back!' she called to Colin, as she unlocked the front door and strode into the hall, stopping in horror to see him spread-eagled on the floor at the foot of the stairs, clearly unable to get up and moaning in pain.

'Wh … what happened?' she stammered, quickly darting over and kneeling beside him. He was always super-careful on the stairs since the time he'd tripped, three months ago, when he'd first become unsteady on his feet. She had tried to insist at that juncture that he moved his bedroom to a safe ground-floor level, but he'd opposed the idea so fiercely, she'd eventually given in and settled for his solemn promise to go up and down as infrequently as possible, always at a snail's pace and always clinging firmly to the banisters. He'd complied, so far, much to her surprise, so she was all the more shocked by this fall. 'Why were you going upstairs at all?' she asked, suddenly noticing his ankle, which was visibly swollen and hot to the touch.

He let out a cry of pain as her fingers explored the swelling, then added with a groan, 'I wanted to see Tom.'

'*Tom,*' she echoed, bewildered? The boy had slept upstairs only for his first couple of years, when his mother was still alive. Once diagnosed with a permanent handicap, his bed had been moved downstairs and his new room fitted with all the equipment he'd need: hoist, wheelchair, activity-chair, gait-trainer – sad, clumsy objects, they had always seemed to her, however vital they might be.

'No, don't get up, for heaven's sake!' she warned, seeing Colin struggle to change position. 'We need to see what damage you've done before you put any weight on that ankle. Promise to keep still, darling, and I'll try to make you more comfortable before I phone the paramedics.'

His only answer was a gasp of pain, so she darted into his bedroom to fetch a couple of pillows and a blanket, along with Peter, whom she hoped would provide some comfort. Then, having arranged his head on one pillow and positioned his foot on the second, she covered him with the blanket, and then phoned 999.

'Emergency. Which service do you want?'

'Ambulance.' The very word seeded new fears. Suppose he never walked again? She'd heard stories about people his age breaking a bone and eventually landing up immobile. Indeed, she felt a surge of pity at seeing him already so reduced, floundering like a beached fish on the shore and emitting pathetic wails of pain.

A woman had come on the line and was asking a series of questions. 'So how did your husband fall? And how long ago? Did he lose consciousness at any point? Has he vomited?'

Since she'd been absent when he fell, her answers could only be approximate – a factor that increased her guilt at seeming to the outside world a faithless, feckless wife.

'And, apart from the swollen ankle, does he appear to have any other injuries?'

How remiss of her that she hadn't even checked. Quickly, she drew back the blanket, unbuttoned his shirt and unbuckled his belt, looking for wounds and grazes. And, yes, the large purplish bruise on his arm was clearly a carpet-burn, presumably resulting from his attempts to get up from the floor. Had he been lying here the entire time she'd been out? And why had he taken his shoes off, when tackling the stairs in his socks would only increase his risk of a fall?

Her own unanswered questions jangled in her mind, as the call-handler continued to quiz her. As usual, though, she would never know the answers. Even long before the onset of dementia, Colin had been a closed book, never permitting her to open his cover and peer into the secret pages of his mind.

At last, the woman promised an ambulance would be dispatched, although warning it could take half an hour, depending on the paramedics' schedule.

No thirty minutes had ever passed more slowly. Her uncomfortable position didn't help, squatting next to Colin on the scratchy hall carpet, and trying to stop him moving. While she waited, she placed Peter gently on his chest, glad to see him reach out for the dog and start stroking his droopy ears.

'Peter's in the wars,' she said, keeping her voice deliberately low and gentle, to establish an atmosphere of calm.

'Yes, Peter's in the wars,' he agreed.

The dementia booklets all advised supplying frequent memory-prompts, to try to take the patient back in time – apparently an effective distraction-technique. 'Do you remember when Peter gobbled down that whole fancy cake I'd ordered for Tom's eighth birthday?'

Colin looked confused, so she added a few details. 'It was a chocolate cake, wasn't it, with chocolate-fudge icing? Tom loved chocolate, and so did Peter!'

'Yes, Tom loved chocolate,' he echoed, and she wondered for the millionth time, what his true feelings were for his disappointment of a son. Since the boy's death, had Colin experienced any guilt, remorse, regret, or were those *her* type of emotions, mostly alien to him? How sad it seemed that two people in a marriage, meant to be one flesh, barely knew each other, either physically or emotionally. And, all at once, her sense of isolation ratcheted up to panicky proportions. Without a child or a single living relative, she alone was responsible for Colin, however dire his future might be, in terms of total immobility, full-scale dementia or an increasingly worrying drink problem. Of course, Megan's help was fantastic – a precious, unexpected bonus - but Megan wasn't 'family', in the sense of blood-ties and a tribe of 'loved ones', to use the phrase so frequently bandied about. Indeed, she found herself wondering, at this desolate moment, whether she had actually had any loved ones since Tom's death.

Appalled by such self-pitying thoughts, she reached for Colin's hand. *He* was the casualty, not her. 'Are you hungry, darling?' she asked, aware it was getting on for lunchtime. She'd planned this morning to make him a cheese-and-strawberry-jam omelette – the only sort he'd eat these days, with his increasingly sweet tooth. Every savoury food had to be disguised beneath a coating of honey, syrup, jam or even condensed milk, and she found herself sometimes absent-mindedly eating the same weird savoury-sweet combinations.

He didn't answer, just tried to change position on the floor, which resulted in a shriek of pain.

'Try to keep still,' she urged, knowing that, even if he were hungry, it would be unwise to give him anything to eat until he'd been examined by the experts.

'Are we waiting for Tom?' he asked, fretfully.

'No, we're waiting for someone to come and see what you've done to yourself.'

A sip of water wouldn't do him any harm, but she decided not to risk fetching it, since he was continually fidgeting and shifting and, if she disappeared even for a moment, might attempt to get back on his feet and only aggravate his injury.

The eventual ring on the doorbell was so welcome, she sprang up from the floor and rushed to let in the paramedics: a broad-shouldered, solid-looking guy, and a girl with a long blonde pigtail that bounced and jiggled on her back with her every movement.

'I'm Greg and this is Linda. Where's the patient?'

'Right here,' she said ushering them in to the hall, and introducing herself and Colin.

'Hello, Colin,' Greg said, kneeling beside him on the floor. 'I need to examine you. Is that OK?'

'And perhaps you and I could sit down,' Linda suggested, 'while I ask you a few questions.'

Having taken her into the sitting-room, Veronica answered most of the questions with a 'no'. Did he have a carer? Was he registered disabled or diabetic? Had he ever broken a bone before? Was he taking statins, or blood-thinners?

When she returned with Linda to the hall, the two paramedics proceeded to lever him up from the floor, and, with an impressive combination of gentleness and strength, manoeuvred him onto a trolley-bed they'd brought with them from the ambulance.

'I've checked his vital signs,' Greg told her, 'and there seems no cause for alarm, but he's obviously injured his ankle. It could be just a strain, or maybe a fracture, so we'll need to take him to A & E and let them have a look at it.'

She glimpsed several neighbours – although thankfully not Beryl - watching from their front rooms, one trying unsuccessfully to conceal herself behind the curtains.

Linda climbed into the driving-seat, while Greg clamped the trolley-bed securely in place, secured Colin with a strap, then took a seat beside him and motioned Veronica to the spare seat. It wasn't until they'd pulled away – lights flashing, sirens wailing – that the full impact of what had happened hit her with sudden jolting force. She'd been operating on auto-pilot, reacting to the crisis rather than dwelling on its implications, and only now did she see that this incident had administered the death-blow to tomorrow's date with Alex. It was maybe even a punishment, a warning from Fate that, if she put her adolescent lusts before her loyalty to her husband, she couldn't expect to escape with impunity.

She reached for her mobile to ring Megan, relieved to get the answerphone. Obviously, Megan must be informed as soon as possible that she would no longer be needed to 'Colin-sit' tomorrow, yet, knowing her friend would try to change her mind, she was glad to be spared a whole argy-bargy of discussion and debate.

There was no argument. She must return to grim reality and consign Alex to the realm of fantasy, of dream.

CHAPTER 15

'Veronica, how lovely! Do come in.'

The minute she stepped into his flat, Alex drew her urgently towards him. And, despite the wild emotions and churning indecision of the last fraught twenty-four hours, the sheer risk and thrill of being here – indeed, being so physically close to him - suddenly hit her with full force. And, as she inhaled his spicy aftershave – a heady blend of sandalwood and musk – she pressed right against his body, as if to feel his very bones.

At length, he let her go, but still held her with his gaze. 'Every time I see you I'm struck by how stunning you look.'

A good thing he hadn't seen her at the hospital this morning, with her hair unwashed and clad in her workaday clothes. But, somehow, she had managed to effect a major transformation since leaving Colin in the orthopaedic ward, awaiting surgery and mercifully sedated.

'I love your flat,' she said, glancing around at the oyster-coloured walls and pale-oak parquet floor, in a deliberate attempt to distract herself from hospitals and husbands.

'I'm afraid it's all a bit stark, as yet.'

'That's the very thing I like – how clear and clean and uncluttered it is. I live with just too much *stuff*, and, although I keep vowing to chuck it out, it seems to sit there breeding more!'

'Well, I've only just moved in, so I haven't had much time to accumulate possessions.'

Presumably, since his divorce, he'd been ejected from the

family home. From the little he'd told her, the rift had been bitter and acrimonious, and his sons were still suffering from the fallout. But that subject had no place here, any more than did her own grim saga with Colin.

He took her coat, allowing his hand to linger on her waist. 'I really chose the place for the view, though. Come and have a look.'

He ushered her over to the huge floor-to-ceiling window, where, spread below, was a kaleidoscope of rooftops, church-spires, London squares and a cluster of smaller buildings clinging like children round their skyscraper-mothers' glass-and-steel-clothed skirts. Dusk was falling and the lights all coming on, a blaze of illumination, reflected and refracted in the dazzling shimmer of the Thames. 'Wow, that really is a view to die for!'

'I find it helps to put things in proportion. If I've had a frazzled day at work, I just come back here and gaze out for a while, and it always seems to calm me down.'

Exactly what *she* needed after her own mega-frazzled day. So, she did her best to take in long, healing draughts of the view, as if it had been prescribed by her GP as a tranquilising medicine.

'Champagne?' he offered, leading her to the sofa, where a bottle of Moet was chilling on the glass-topped coffee-table. Champagne seemed as normal for him as common-and-garden tap-water was for her – not that she had the slightest objection!

'The only furniture I have so far,' he explained with an endearing smile, 'is this sofa and table, and the larger table over there.'

It was all brand-new, she noticed: the sofa upholstered in sleek black leather, the dining-table strikingly modernist in its clean lines and polished-steel pedestal. Had he chosen it himself, or simply dispatched his PA to arrange the purchases? And had it been sad for him to lose all his possessions and have to adjust to bachelor living without the comfort of a family? She knew so little about him, as yet, including what he might expect of her this evening. If his wife had been skilled in erotic techniques, or had experienced the tumultuous, high-decibel orgasms that Colin's porn-stars achieved with enviable frequency, then he was in for a disappointment. Being a musical ignoramus was one thing, but proving a crashing disappointment in the bedroom would be truly mortifying.

She took two hasty swigs of the Moet, using it as another type of tranquilizer and, indeed, the bubbles seemed to have instantly entered her bloodstream and were popping and fizzing in a manner both welcome and disconcerting.

'Cheers!' he said, touching his glass to hers. 'I'm delighted that you're here.'

And I'm delighted to be here, should be her natural response, but it was impossible to pronounce such words while there was so much jittery to-ing and fro-ing in her mind, so she simply sat clutching her glass.

'Oh, by the way,' he said, as if to fill the awkward silence, 'remember I mentioned us going to the ballet? Well, I've made a few enquires and I can easily get tickets for *Sylvia*, if that appeals.'

Although she'd just about heard of *Swan Lake, Sylvia* was an unknown quantity, but she decided to come clean and admit her ignorance.

'It's rather a spun-sugar, whipped-cream confection'- he gave a deprecating shrug - 'very far from cutting-edge. And there's a lot of bogus orientalism.'

She had noticed already how, in intellectual circles, it seemed compulsory to run things down, rather than react, as she did, with naïve, untutored approval.

'But the two principal dancers are said to be outstanding, so it might be worth going just to see them. The role was originally created for Fonteyn and remains extremely challenging for any ballerina.'

'I'd love to go,' she said, refusing to tone down her natural enthusiasm - part of her new bid to try to be her true self, rather than continually adjust to other people's views and expectations. Besides, any ballet would be a first for her and she was keen to amass more 'firsts'.

'It runs from late November to mid-December, so, when you next have access to your diary, let's discuss dates, OK?'

Late November was a good two months away. How could he be sure he would still want to see her by then? If things went wrong this evening, they might never meet again.

'Then I can have another word with my contacts at Convent Garden. Which reminds me,' he said, getting up from the sofa. 'I have a little something for you. Won't be a sec.'

Just that brief moment while he nipped to the other room was enough to drag her thoughts back to Colin. Suppose he'd reacted badly to the anaesthetic? Would he be confused, or even angry, to find Megan sitting by his bed when he returned from theatre, instead of her, his loyal wife? And how the hell would he feel if he ever got to know that, at this very moment, the 'loyal wife' was quaffing champagne with another man?

She struggled to dismiss such fears as Alex came back in, seating himself beside her again and putting a small package into her hands. 'I thought you might enjoy this. It's not the performance we saw together – I'm afraid that's not available – so I chose another recording of Bohème, but one with Tony conducting. And I asked him to sign the CD-cover for you.'

She sat staring in excited surprise at the flourish of a signature - Antonio Pappano – scrawled beneath a personal message to her, Veronica. 'Oh, Alex, it's incredible!' she said, aware of the trouble he must have taken to obtain both record and signature, and in so short a time. It's the best present I've ever had!'

'Well, it's hardly the Kohinoor diamond! I just hoped you'd find it interesting to compare this version with the Convent Garden production. The soloists are very different in voice-quality, and Tony takes it at a slightly slower tempo.'

Such subtleties would be lost on her, but the gift itself was priceless – all the more so because Pappano's signature had been written right across a picture of Mimi and Rodolfo united in a passionate embrace, as if to stress the parallels that arose often in her mind between her and Alex and the two operatic lovers. 'I simply don't know how to thank you.'

'No need. I'm just glad you're pleased.'

She placed a warning hand on top of her glass, as he leaned over to refill it. There hadn't been a moment all day to grab so much as a chocolate-bar and she feared too much bubbly on an empty stomach might make her throw caution to the winds. Of course, one part of her longed to do just that, but vivid images of Colin's supine body, perhaps still on the operating-table, after some unexpected complication, and of her own body remaining stubbornly frigid in face of Alex's advances, continued to act as a restraint.

'Shall we have a spot of supper first?' he suggested, as if aware of her natural caution. 'I had to skip lunch today and, to be honest, I'm ravenous.'

'Me too,' she admitted.

'I'm just sorry it's not a more ambitious meal. I was so pressed for time, I had to settle for a few bits and pieces from our local delicatessen. But at least we can eat in style and christen my new dining-table!'

The food was already laid out on the modish mirror-glass-topped table. 'A few bits and pieces' in Colin-lingo would mean a couple of Mr Kipling cakes, an ice-lolly or three, and a packet of cheese and onion crisps. Rather different was this array of matching smoked-glass dishes, filled with exotic-looking antipasto and salads – everything from caviar and prosciutto, to a whole Camembert and a selection of speciality breads.

Having passed her an elegant oval plate, he began helping her to each dish in turn, first checking her tastes and preferences. Did she like game pie? Would she fancy a few artichoke hearts, or some of the stuffed aubergine? Colin was totally unaware of her preferences, or even needs, and had always left her to buy and dispense the food, so this was true indulgence.

'I feel bad about you going to all this trouble, on top of a long, hard Friday.'

'No trouble at all. The deli's on my way home. But you must come for a proper meal next time. I can actually cook, unlikely as that might sound!'

Not unlikely in the slightest - Alex had every talent in the book. And she certainly relished the prospect of a 'next time', while simultaneously wanting to slow things down, spin out the supper, and postpone the 'intimate' aspect as long as she could – perhaps even to another evening. She decided to ask his advice about standing in as Chair of the Fund-Raising group - a safe, acceptable subject that would provide a welcome breathing-space. 'I have to admit I'm nervous about the prospect, when I've had so little experience.'

'I presume you've watched Glenys in the role?'

'Oh, yes, but she can do it standing on her head! She used to fund-raise for a major charity, you see, whereas my own efforts were much more amateurish, and ages ago, in any case.'

'Well, if you give me some idea of which particular aspects you'd like me to advise on, I'll be only too happy to help. Obviously, every fund-raising group works differently, depending on its aims and ambitions and how much cash they have. But the one thing I would suggest is to draw up a timetable for the whole of next year. Then everyone in the team knows what's planned for 2018, starting with January and right on through to December. And that helps you see exactly what's needed for each event, be it printing tickets for a black-tie affair, or enrolling helpers to set up tables for a wine-and-cheese evening, or obtaining permission to sing in a public place, if your choir plans on doing gigs.'

'Actually, Glenys is already working on a timetable. And we have quite a few ideas pencilled in for next year.'

'Great! That sounds as if she's well-organized. And, of course the two of you can keep in touch, even if she's having treatment or whatever. And one big advantage is that your particular charity should be extremely popular, unlike those for mental health or asylum-seekers, which tend to turn off much of the public. Most cancer charities encourage people to open their wallets, and choirs are all the rage at present, so it's a winning combination.'

He started running through various money-spinning ideas, until, fearing he must be tired of talking shop, she switched subjects back to *Sylvia.*

'It's actually a story of gods, nymphs and Love conquering all,' he observed, with a wry smile, as if to remind her they were here for love, rather than for business talk. And, to emphasize the point, he leaned towards her and ran an exploratory finger along the outline of her lips, then slipped the finger teasingly right inside her mouth. The contact of his soft finger-pad lingering against her teeth was arousing in the extreme, but at that very moment, her thoughts leapfrogged back to Colin, as Megan's voice resounded through her head.

'It's dead simple, love. All you have to do is say you've gone down with a sudden cold, so you can't possibly visit Colin this evening, or you'll spread your germs to him and half the hospital.'

'But that's a lie,' she had objected on the phone, having rung her friend this lunchtime from Emergency, following Colin's diagnosis of a bimalleolar fracture of the tibia and fibula.

'For heaven's sake, Veronica, if you cancel now, all you're doing is continuing the same old habit of putting other people first. From what you've told me, your mother did the exact opposite – imposed *her* needs, *her* lovers, *her* erratic lifestyle on you, the innocent child. And Colin repeated the pattern. He got what he wanted in the shape of someone to run the house and be full-time carer to Tom, leaving you to fit in with his wishes, regardless of what *you* might want.'

Megan's constant blithe assumption that she was dutiful and virtuous made her increasingly uncomfortable. What Megan failed to realize was that her apparent unselfishness had always been prompted not by virtue but by fear. If she wasn't needed, indeed, indispensable, she might be abandoned and betrayed – a far more chilling prospect than continuing her role as care-giver. In point of fact, that role had always paid off, by increasing her sense of security and rootedness, and warding off serious criticism. As long as she was looking after some sick or vulnerable person, she was far less likely to elicit disapproval – the sort of disapproval she had come to expect automatically, after experiencing it non-stop from Den. Therefore, far from being a selfless martyr, she was merely trying to make her adult life less onerous than her childhood.

'What's wrong?' Alex asked, clearly puzzled by her silence and her palpable change of mood.

'Nothing,' she lied, swallowing several olives in succession, if only to bar him access to her mouth.

She could tell he was piqued, as he slumped back against the sofa. And she was equally annoyed with herself by harking back to Colin, Tom and Den, when she'd promised Megan to leave behind all anxiety and guilt.

They continued the meal in a manner somewhat constrained, she desperately seeking subjects that might engage him, whilst preventing any further advances on his part. When had he first met Pappano? Did he prefer opera to ballet? How had he got into Fund-Raising? Yet, even as she babbled on, she cursed her own indecisive temperament. Having ached to be here this evening, now she actually was here, all she seemed able to do was plague herself with second thoughts. Even a second glass of bubbly failed to rouse so much as a tingle, as if her punitive persona had taken charge and was barring any chance of pleasure or excitement. And, soon, the conversation itself appeared to be petering out – and little wonder. He hadn't invited her here to discuss his friendship with 'Tony', or detail the various stages of his career. All she could hear now was the impatient sawing of the bread-knife, as he cut a slice of ciabatta, and the sudden mournful hoot of a passing riverboat.

They both glanced in its direction, then, all at once, he sprang to his feet with a delighted exclamation. 'Oh, look!', he cried, pointing to the window, where a huge, multi-coloured hot-air-balloon had drifted into view, soaring high above the river, like a visitor from a celestial world.

'It's incredibly rare to see them here,' he enthused. 'There are loads of restrictions on where and when they can fly, plus all the palaver of them needing the right wind-speed and a favourable wind-direction. So, you normally need to be quite a distance out of Central London, to catch so much as a glimpse of one.'

'There's something written on it,' she said, peering up to try to make it out.

'Probably just an advertising slogan - Martini or Virgin Media or some such. Let's take a closer look.'

They both moved towards the window, and she spelled out the words 'RED-LETTER DAY', written in emphatic scarlet against the citrus, aqua and emerald swell of the balloon. The message hit her with a jolt, in that it seemed to be intended for her personally, making the point that this could be a red-letter day, if only she changed her outlook, as Megan had been urging for so long. After all, if it was apparently so rare to see a hot-air-balloon in the City, wasn't it peculiar that one should appear at this very moment, as if dispatched by Fate to remind her that it symbolized all the things she denied herself yet craved: adventure, leisure, enjoyment, flying high? So, couldn't *she* soar with it to new unfathomable heights, even tug free of her strings, for once, and be answerable to no one?

The thought was so liberating, she was aware of her body physically relaxing, as she and Alex stood side by side at the window. And he immediately picked up on it, slipping his arm around her waist and swivelling her towards him. And, once they were face to face, it seemed perfectly natural that his lips should seek out hers in a passionate kiss. And, suddenly, it was the night of *Bohème* again, his tongue exploring the astounded secret recesses of her mouth, her whole body responding voraciously, as he half-steered, half-carried her towards the door and on into his bedroom. And, without knowing how it happened, they were lying entwined on his bed and he was unbuttoning her blouse, his clever, seeking fingers warm against her naked flesh, as she exulted in the knowledge that this could be – *would* be – truly a red-letter-night.

CHAPTER 16

'Veronica, I'm so *sorry*!'

'What for?' she asked, confused. If anyone should apologize, it was her.

'For coming so quickly,' he said, with an embarrassed laugh. 'That was your fault, though,' he added, reaching out to trace the curve of her breast. 'You turned me on so wildly, I felt like a young lad, unable to hold back!'

She stored the words in the pantry of her mind, as future sustenance, as she lay relishing the unprecedented sensation of feeling, sensual, attractive, deeply desired. The very fact he was content to lie here beside her, stroking her hair, caressing the line of her thigh, was alluringly different from Colin's habit of getting up the minute he had climaxed and returning to his own bed. 'Coming and going' she had called it in her mind, and it had set the pattern for all their sexual encounters – a hurtful refusal to linger with her afterwards, caressing her, maybe, or just contentedly talking. Whereas Alex seemed eager to prolong their time together, apparently still hungry for her as he lay cupping her breasts and gently squeezing them together.

And, she, in turn, couldn't stop gazing at his body, still awed by the fact that this was the first man, apart from Colin, she had ever seen naked – and a man infinitely younger and fitter than Colin. No way should she be comparing the two, yet an image of her husband's chest somehow slipped into her mind: fleshy instead of firm, with fatty little breastlets above a paunchy stomach, whereas Alex's torso had muscles, definition, and looked unambiguously male. He had also felt different inside her – so excitingly different, in fact, that, within minutes, she had lost Ron, lost Veronica, and become only and totally Mimi: young, ardent, free of all ties, free to respond to her Rodolfo with no guilt, regret or fear. And, as she heard herself crying out - and no longer even caring about the noise she must be making - she realized that her sexual self, so long gagged and bound, had found its voice at last, and that she had been finally awakened from passivity, stagnation.

Alex was now flicking his tongue against her nipples – a provocation so exquisite she couldn't bear it ever to stop. But he pulled away a moment to ask is she was thirsty. 'There's some elderflower cordial chilling in the fridge – unless you'd prefer more champagne.'

'No, elderflower sounds perfect.' And again, so different from their drinks at home. When not quaffing the hard stuff, Colin liked obstreperous Dr Pepper and bellicose Red Bull.

The few minutes Alex was gone, she lay with her hands across her naked breasts, her whole body still pulsing and throbbing, as if with an electric current. Yes, he had come too quickly – with more of the urgent impetus of a rocket-launch than the slow ascent of a hot-air-balloon. Nonetheless, it had still been a total joy-ride - adventurous, audacious, pioneering.

Alex returned with two tall glasses and stood by the bed, gazing down at her. 'You look incredibly sexy like that, stroking your breasts.'

I'd rather *you* stroked them, she longed to say, but that would be audacity too far. Instead, she sat up and sipped the sweet, fruity cordial, which rippled through her body like the aftertaste of those earlier, more headstrong pleasures, bringing with it the never-before sensation of things being *right* with her, and with the world.

Once he'd drained his own glass, he lay back again, beside her, and did exactly what she had wanted: ran a slow and lingering hand across her breasts, the skilful fingertip startling her nipples. This completely new experience of lying beside a man who had time and inclination to focus on her body made her feel someone of consequence, worthy of attention, of devotion, even.

'I was actually quite nervous last night,' he said, with an awkward laugh, 'lying here, thinking about this evening – the whole young lad thing again, I guess: would I come up to scratch?'

She could hardly believe that successful, confident Alex could ever be nervous, yet his honesty was both surprising and endearing. And she warmed to the fact that he, too, had worried, which, in itself, seemed to bond them closer.

'Do you like that?' he asked, breaking off a moment from tracing the coil of her ear with his tongue-tip, a tongue-tip every bit as artful as the fingertip.

As with the food, it was a new, gratifying experience to have someone ask what she liked. In fact, there were many things she liked about this man: the animal heat of his body, the smooth feel of his cheek against her skin, compared with Colin's can't-be-bothered stubble, the contrast between his pale, velvet-smooth chest (recently waxed, she would guess) and the jolting darkness and coarseness of his pubic hair. Suddenly, and brazenly, she allowed her fingers to feather through that hair, moved them even lower, aware of him stiffening in response.

He closed his eyes, as if to focus on the sensation to the exclusion of all else. 'What are you *doing* to me, woman?'

Yes, he had made her 'woman' – elemental, voluptuous, uninhibited – and, as he thrust into her again, all the fire and fervour and sheer sensual solemnity of Puccini music seemed to be resounding through the bedroom, resounding through her body, enlivening its every cell, nerve, sinew, limb and muscle.

CHAPTER 17

'Your coffee, madam.'

As the young Italian waiter put down her cappuccino, Veronica smiled to see a perfect, cream-coloured heart created on the surface of its chocolate-sprinkled foam - wonderfully appropriate, now that her mind refused to shift from Alex. She could even smell the subtle tang of his aftershave, as if she'd been determined to retain at least some trace of him before they'd kissed goodnight in the early hours this morning. Not that she needed much reminding of the time they'd spent together in bed, the way he'd lobbed a stick of dynamite into her sluggish, unawakened self, kindling secret parts of her body she'd barely known she possessed. And, even today, after waking luxuriously late, all her senses were still on full alert, so that she was aware not just of the aftershave, but of every smell around her: the eye-watering kick of frying onions seeping from the café kitchen, the acrid whiff of unripe conkers prised prematurely from their spiky green shells, the aroma of freshly brewed coffee, rising from her cup. Her taste-buds, too, were sharper: coffee, chocolate and cinnamon all tingling on her tongue as she spooned up the foamy outline of the heart.

She tipped back her head to enjoy the warmth of the sun on her face, marvelling that even the weather reflected her upbeat mood: a serene, late-September morning, with trees and grass and café tables sparkling in a self-important sun. How life-denying it seemed that, in all the years she'd lived here, she had barely visited the Common till today, despite it being so close, hadn't even known the existence of this friendly Italian café, with its out-of-doors overspill and its happy clientele of dog-owners, joggers, and parents of young children. Carefree kids were sprawling on the grass, or clambering over the bandstand, or shuffling through the fallen leaves, and, despite those drifts of brittle brown, most of the trees were still in lush green leaf. Indeed, the sky was such a braggart blue, it seemed that summer was reluctant ever to give way to autumn, ever to fade or shrivel.

'And your toasted sandwich, madam.' The waiter had returned, setting down her plate with a flourish, his smile revealing a flash of gold tooth.

Another first - to be having breakfast out and breakfasting so late, when normally she'd be stuck with Colin, working through the chores, or trying to persuade him to eat a healthy egg rather than gorge on sugar-laden Frosties. Today, though, was a gift from Megan, a whole day to do exactly as she pleased.

'Veronica ...' Her friend's tone had been formidably strict – 'I'm sorry, but you can't come near the hospital this weekend. I told all the nurses on Colin's ward that you'd gone down with a filthy cold, so they simply won't believe that you're suddenly as right as rain a mere twenty-four hours' later. No arguments - it's all in hand. *I'll* visit on both Saturday and Sunday, and only phone you if any problems arise. By the way, I've bought him a couple of colouring-books for adults, because that nice cuddly nurse, Miranda, happened to remark that they're soothing for patients and becoming quite a craze in general.'

Although hard to imagine Colin finding solace in a colouring-book, rather than in half a pint of whisky, Veronica had accepted Megan's gift with guilty gratitude, knowing she would be busy enough tomorrow, preparing for Colin's homecoming. He'd be on crutches, with severely reduced mobility, so she would need to move his bedroom downstairs to Tom's old room. She'd already booked a couple of odd-job men to come first thing Monday morning, to shift the actual furniture, but *her* job was to clear out both the rooms in advance. In fact, this was her one rare chance to chuck out the loads of clutter her husband had accumulated, which normally he forbade her to touch. For now, though, she was determined to keep her promise to Megan and do her best to relax.

'No point having a day off if all you do is fret about Colin. Just kick him out of your mind, love, and indulge yourself for once.'

And part of that indulgence was to sate herself on replays of her bewitching time with Alex: the indescribable sensations of his lips on her 'down there'; the way he'd grazed his teeth across her nipples with slow, tantalizing languor; licked up and down each finger and the space between each finger, startling her with the gentle acrobatics of his tongue. As she bit into her sandwich, she imagined that ingenious tongue swirling up the drool of melted cheese dribbling down her chin, then slipping between her lips to electrify her mouth. In point of fact, he was spending the weekend with his sons, which endeared him to her even more, as a responsible, hands-on father.

Just at that moment, a small, obstreperous boy stampeded up to her table to retrieve his ball, which had rolled beneath her feet. He was followed by both parents and two older sisters on scooters and, as she handed him the ball and exchanged greetings with the mini-tribe, she felt her usual pang at never having had her own child. She was cut off from this throng of blessedly complacent parents not only in that respect, but in the fact of her stepson's disability. Most parents took their normal, healthy kids for granted, along with their normal family life, in which mothers, fathers, children all ate together and went out together, in one companionable unit. She, in contrast, could barely remember a single occasion when she and Colin and Tom had enjoyed a trip or outing *en famille*, or had even sat down as a threesome to a meal at home.

Annoyed with herself for revisiting that unhappy past, she shifted her attention to the spurt of conflicting flavours unleashed from the first bite of her sandwich - bland cheese, fierce mustard, darkly bitter rye-bread - and then to the taste of Alex's mouth and the way he'd rendered the very concept of a kiss so wondrously different from Colin's brief, superficial pecks. It seemed little short of miraculous that he appeared more than keen to continue the relationship. Their next date was already in the diary and due in less than a week: a Private View at some trendy West End gallery, followed by a second 'intimate supper' at his flat. She'd had no idea what a Private View even was, until she Googled it, but she realized now that, besides discovering new regions of her body, he was also opening up for her a whole wealth of artistic delights.

Having drained the last of her cappuccino, she paid the bill and set off across the Common, deliberately slowing her pace to a stroll, to break her normal habit of dashing everywhere. Without Colin to rush back for, she felt extraordinarily liberated, a newly hatched lady of leisure with all the time in the world to stop and admire some particularly handsome tree, or the first splash of autumn colour on a russet-tinted bush, or to watch a skitter of ducks on the gloopy green surface of the pond. More smells here, in the stagnant reek of the pondweed and the dank odour of waterlogged leaves, competing with a sweeter note from the honeyed blossoms of one lone flowering bush.

She had no intention of returning home until dusk, having planned the whole day in line with Megan's injunction to devote it to enjoyment: lunch out in one of the High-Street cafes, followed by a movie – a romantic movie, of course, in which *she* would play the role of the glamorous, young female lead, whilst Alex starred as the love-interest. His bed had been crowded enough last night, with *three* men in attendance on her – Alex, Rodolfo and Leonard – and now she was adding a clutch of male film stars, as her mind raced ahead to their next encounter. It was downright reprehensible, if not patently ridiculous, for a post-menopausal almost-sexagenarian to be indulging in such adolescent fantasies, but she was coming to accept that she was clearly a late developer, tasting many new pleasures when already well over the hill, and no longer even caring if she made herself a laughing-stock in the process.

Suddenly, she broke into song: *Put a Little Love in Your Heart* – although the title was a misnomer. There was already so much love in her heart – Alex-coloured love, pulsating with passion, brimful of enchantment – that if she crammed in even a little more, her heart would break with bliss. Still singing uninhibitedly, she branched off along a narrow path that led between a cluster of slender, silver-dappled birch trees, aware, with satisfaction, that she was perfectly in tune. Megan was right: she didn't need a singing-teacher and, now that she'd recovered from her first guilty disquiet at ending her lessons with Sebastian, felt only relief to be rid of him, and pride at having taken a tough line. He had rubbished this particular song, but she could relate perfectly to that sense of the world being a transformed and better place because someone special loved her - someone who'd renew that blazing love on the night of the Private View.

'Colin, you *bugger*!'

In her mind, fury fought with a certain grudging admiration for his cunning, as she retrieved half-a-dozen beer-glasses from the bottom of his wardrobe, all stuffed with the remains of several barely-eaten meals. The food was now mouldy and stinking, an open invitation to mice or even cockroaches - partly *her* fault, though, for not having checked all his cupboards before this. In the major clear-up she'd done prior to Megan's visit, she had made a start on this room, but limited her efforts to hoovering and tidying. Now, however, with his imminent discharge from hospital, in a weakened, vulnerable state, she had no choice but to remove all the health-hazards and chuck out most of the clutter, since Tom's bedroom was much smaller than his, with fewer drawers and cupboards. She remained kneeling in front of the wardrobe, removing the jumbled pile of clothes and shoes he had heaped on top of the beer-glasses, in a sly effort to conceal them.

She dumped most of the stuff into a large black dustbin-bag, including clothes so ancient they dated back twenty years and would no longer fit his paunchy figure, and smart slim-line shoes he would never dream of wearing now, rather than the Velcro-fastening boats he found infinitely more comfortable. She should have cleared all this out an age ago, but if ever she suggested that he no longer needed a certain shirt or tie, he would react like an aggressive bird sitting on its nest, determined to guard its brood against the slightest threat of attack and shouting peevishly, 'Let me be! Leave things alone!' But, in his absence she could complete the task slowly and methodically, without him raising hell as she consigned to the bin a load of poo-stained pants, ragged tops, gym-gear he would never need again, and a good two-dozen elegant silk ties he used to wear for business meetings – all now superfluous.

A stack of unread magazine had been wedged between the wardrobe and the door. Although he no longer had the concentration for reading, he nonetheless refused to cancel his subscriptions to journals he would barely understand these days, so she filled another bag with ancient copies of *The Economist, Business Weekly, Accountancy Age.* One part of her wanted to chuck him out, along with all the detritus, yet the thought induced a sudden surge of panic. Could she actually manage on her own, and without the role of carer? Den had told her so often that she was damaged goods, fit for nothing, so how could she believe in her own competence and coping-skills?

Although, with Megan's help, with Alex's, could it be a different story?

Heartened by the thought, she went downstairs to make herself a coffee, took it into the sitting-room, as a brief respite from the shambles elsewhere. However hard it might be to preserve this room and the dining-room from Colin's depredations, she was determined to try her best, so she could entertain her friends more often – not just Megan, but Glenys and maybe the two gays, Clive and Michael. Her goal was to become a normal, sociable woman, no longer living as a recluse with one probably autistic man, but laying on cosy little suppers for her favourite members of the choir, lingering over coffee with them, chatting, laughing, exchanging confidences. In fact, her goals extended further, in that she longed to transform the whole place from top to bottom, re-carpet and re-paint, maybe buy some attractive house-plants or even modernist ornaments. But what invariably stopped her was the near-certainty that her shambling, incontinent husband would knock over the plants and spill wine or leak stinky faeces on any new carpet she bought.

He would also stand in her way if she ever contemplated moving somewhere completely new, starting again, without all the mess and damage, and minus the unhappy memories that stained the place as much as did the material stains. Wherever she moved, she would still have Colin in tow, so how the hell could she create the sort of stylish, pristine surroundings that both Megan and Alex enjoyed, with clean lines, clear spaces and a sense of basic order? Yet to live apart from Colin was equally impossible. Having never lived alone in her whole life, she feared she might collapse without him as a 'prop', despite the fact that she was the one doing all the propping up. Besides, to wish him eternally absent seemed the height of betrayal, and she began reproaching herself for such ill will until, all at once, Megan's last words on the phone to her re-echoed in her mind: ‘For pity’s sake, Veronica, he’s bloody lucky that you haven’t actually murdered him as yet. And I doubt if any court of law would even find you guilty if you had simply bumped him off.’

The remark had horrified her, yet now it made her laugh - laugh out loud, in fact, surprising herself with the unaccustomed sound. Laughter had rarely featured in her life. Den had never laughed, Colin only rarely and, despite Tom’s radiant smile, there hadn’t been much to laugh about as he and she struggled together to negotiate the intractable challenge of his condition. Post-Alex, however, laughter seemed easy, if not natural, and she let out a delighted whoop as she realized that Megan had come up with the perfect solution. If she bumped off her husband, she’d be free to move in with Alex and enjoy not only his perfect, pristine flat, but revel in erotic thrills morning, noon and all beguiling night.

CHAPTER 18

'Oh, hi, I'm Colin Matthews' wife, Veronica, and I'm here to take him home.'

'Hold on a minute, please.' The nurse at the desk, clearly harassed, snatched up her long-unanswered phone and, having concluded a brief, staccato conversation, turned her attention back to Veronica. 'First, I'll need to speak to the nurse in charge, OK?'

She disappeared a moment, returning with another nurse, whom she introduced as Charlene, an older, solid-looking woman with close-cropped, iron-grey hair.

'Ah, Mrs Matthews, could you take a seat for a moment.' She gestured to a clutch of chairs just inside the entrance to the ward. 'The surgeon wants to have a word with you before we discharge your husband. He's doing a ward-round right now, so he shouldn't be too long.'

As Veronica perched on the edge of the seat, she feared some new complication. Could Colin have contracted an infection, or – worse – had his surgery been unsuccessful? No, Megan would have informed her and, anyway, whatever might have happened, she had no intention of ringing her friend for at least a week or more, since she'd left last night for Godalming, to help her niece, Lavinia, through the last, difficult stage of her pregnancy. Although typical of Megan's kindness to go from one mission of mercy to another, the last thing she needed at present was any more of Colin's problems.

As the minutes ticked by, Veronica's mind kept leaping from peevish, incapacitated Colin to agile, thrusting Alex, the latter prompting a fantasy about this coming Friday night. Indeed, she was soon so involved in the details, she was surprised to look up and see an irritable-looking fellow, in an ill-fitting, crumpled suit, standing over her, instead of gloriously naked Alex.

'Mrs Matthews?' His voice was gruff, impatient.

She nodded, aware that she was blushing as she rose to greet him, as if he had seen into her mind.

'I'm Mr Thompson, your husband's orthopaedic surgeon. I'm afraid the wound's still oozing a bit, so he's not really fit to be discharged, but he's been so appallingly non-compliant, there's no point keeping him in any longer. He's disobeyed every single instruction he's been given. He even started to weight-bear the very day of the surgery, despite all my strict warnings to keep off that leg altogether. The actual operation went well, I'm glad to report, but, notwithstanding everything I said, he tried to walk on the injured ankle almost straight away. That caused some of the screws to come out, which in turn caused an issue with wound-healing. The nurses did their best to persuade him to co-operate, but this is an extremely busy ward, so they simply haven't time to argue with bolshie patients who seem hell-bent on making things worse for themselves as well as us.'

Embarrassed by these revelations, Veronica let forth a flurry of apologies, along with excuses for her own absence and an explanation of Megan's role in the saga.

'Yes, your friend was a tower of strength, but even she couldn't make your husband see sense.'

Megan must have deliberately spared her all this information, so that she could enjoy her time with Alex without additional worry, a fact that increased both her indebtedness to Megan and her irritation with Colin. Weren't 'bolshie' and 'non-compliant' the perfect words to describe him, whether with regard to his diet, his drinking, his obstinate refusal to wear an incontinence-pad, or even to keep the place reasonably tidy?

'He'll be coming home in a below-the-knee cast, which I want him to wear for a total of six weeks. After that, we may put him into a walking-boot and, of course, we'll follow him up regularly and I'll be seeing him again in clinic in a fortnight. Meanwhile. I've prescribed painkillers, antibiotics and some medication to prevent a blood-clot, and we've put in place a care-package, so he'll have help with washing, dressing, shaving and suchlike.'

Except he'll refuse point-blank to let a carer near him, Veronica refrained from saying, aware that any surgeon was bound to be pressed for time.

'Nurse Charlene will take you to the ward,' he said with a brief, dismissive nod, before hurrying off down the corridor.

She followed the nurse into the ward, walking past two rows of beds with patients in various stages of disability, legs in plaster or hoisted up in traction, arms in slings or rigid casts. Conflicting smells wafted past her nostrils: urine, Bovril, disinfectant, and, continuing to the far end of the ward, she caught snatches of conversation, barked instructions from a nurse, incessantly ringing phones, and a sudden warning beep-beep-beep from one of the machines. It struck her suddenly that all these suffering people had been lying here immobile, whilst she and Alex were disporting in the bedroom – a thought that prompted guilt, shame and triumph in equal parts.

On finally reaching Colin's bed, at the far end of the ward, she was shocked by the change in him: how much older and more haggard he looked, his skin ashen-pale, his body smaller and frailer, as if the operation had shrunk him in size. He was sitting on the bedside chair, his leg immobilised in an already grubby plaster-cast that stretched from knee to toes, his crutches beside him, along with three empty wine-bottles.

'We've no idea how he got hold of the wine,' Charlene said disapprovingly, seeing her glance down at them. 'It's extremely unwise of him to drink while he's on those particular drugs. I did explain that several times, and we confiscated the first bottle, but somehow, he managed to lay his hands on more. I'm sorry to say he's been very non-compliant in general.'

That word again, bringing with it another wave of anger and dejection. Could he have actually bribed a fellow patient's relative to bring in the wine for him, or greased the palm of a cleaner, porter or volunteer? And how the hell was she expected to keep him strictly teetotal throughout the course of his medication, when there'd rarely been a day in his entire adult life when he hadn't had a drink or three?

'Hello, darling.' She tried to sound normal and cheerful, as she leaned over his chair and planted a kiss on his cheek.

'Where've you *been*?' he asked querulously, without returning her greeting. 'I haven't seen you for weeks.'

Two-and-a-half days, she corrected silently, before repeating Megan's story of having gone down with a bad cold. She detested lying, although he seemed not even to have heard and was pulling tetchily at her coat, whilst begging her to take him home.

'Yes, we're going right now. But we need to wait for the ambulance.'

'That's all been sorted out,' Charlene interjected. 'It's actually a mini-bus, which takes quite a few patients at once, then drops them off in stages to their various different homes, so I'm afraid the journey may take some while. But let's go down to the Transport Lounge and see when they intend to set off, OK?'

Having transferred Colin into a wheelchair, Charlene laid his crutches across his lap, gave Veronica the suitcase, then followed closely as the porter trundled him towards the lift. As they descended, the nurse made bright, inconsequential remarks. Wasn't the weather glorious? Had she seen the new Emma Stone movie? Was she watching the cricket? Despite answering politely, Veronica's attention was mainly focused on the problem of Colin's disability. Up till now, he'd been able to reach their local shop, with the aid of his walking-stick - and abetted by a fierce determination to lay in stocks of alcohol without her rationing his supplies. Now, however, he'd be completely housebound, and maybe unable to go beyond his one small bedroom. She had seriously deluded herself spinning dreams of a new life with Alex, when, in point of fact, she could no longer leave her husband even for a scant half-hour, without the risk of him falling, trying to get to the shop, or putting weight on the injured leg again. And she could hardly entrust him to Beryl in his present incapacitated state – or indeed to anyone. In her lovelorn mooning over Alex and their rapturous transports in bed, she had blanked out the grim reality of what she would actually be doing: shaving Colin's stubbly whiskers, washing his dirty bum, trying to deal with his fury and frustration at being forbidden even a thimbleful of booze. And, as for looking to carers for some respite, Colin would send them all packing the minute he laid eyes on them, as he had invariably done before.

As the porter manoeuvred him out of the lift and wheeled him along the corridor, Veronica rebuked herself for sheer callous selfishness. Her husband was in pain, immobile, weakened, and all she could think about was her own petty inconveniences and an interruption to a love-life forbidden by its very nature, which she should never have embarked on in the first place.

'I'll leave you here, then,' Charlene said, cheerily, as the porter parked Colin by a seat. With a muttered instruction to him not to move a muscle, Veronica went up to the desk, where a woman checked the paperwork before directing her back to sit beside her husband, joining the cluster of elderly patients, in various stages of decrepitude, awaiting transport home.

Well, she thought, with a grim smile of resignation, at least I'm well prepared for dealing with disability, after my years of practice with Tom.

'But *why* do I have to sleep here?' Colin's wail of protest rose higher and shriller.

'I've told you, darling, because you can't manage the stairs on crutches.'

'But this is Tom's room.'

'Well, it *was*, some time ago, but I've made it *your* room now. See, I've put your best pyjamas out and your nice, cosy dressing-gown, and Peter's there already, waiting to welcome you home.'

Uncharacteristically, he ignored the dog completely, repeating petulantly, 'This is Tom's room. I want to sleep in *my* room.'

'Well, maybe at a later stage, but just at present you simply can't get up there. Now, how about some lunch? I've made you your favourite shepherd's pie, with the cheese and tomatoes on top.'

'I'm not hungry.'

'Yes, but Peter is. We can't let Peter starve.'

Again, he refused to take the bait and, although she managed to keep her voice calm, she was weeping inside as she gazed at the Zimmer-frame, which the driver had brought in from the mini-bus. As for the wheelchair, the fellow had taken it back with him to the hospital, once he'd deposited Colin in the house. She knew her husband would resist all attempts to learn to use the Zimmer or, indeed, his crutches, so both he and she would be grounded, stranded, cut off from the outside world. And, here in Tom's old room, she was also mourning her stepson again, having dismantled this former shrine to him, removed his photo-gallery and all his once-cherished possessions. Such acts seemed disrespectful to his memory, as did Colin purloining his old room, when he had sought constantly to avoid his son throughout the latter's life. Indeed, it had been part of her unspoken role, back then, to try to keep the two of them apart, to avoid unease for either. Nonetheless, she had retained a few of Tom's things for herself: his favourite Mr Froggie puppet, the empty pill-bottle he used to store red Smarties, the photo of his mother, Daisy, in tribute to her short, sad life. Yet the very pathos of the objects only reawakened her regret about his restricted life and her intense grief at his death.

'Shall we watch a bit of *Fawlty Towers*?' she suggested, turning on the television, which she had transferred to this room, so that he could see it from both the bed and the chair, without having to get up.

'I want to watch it in my room.'

'This is your room now, darling. And Peter likes it in here, don't you, Peter?'

Again, he ignored both her and the dog, slumping back in his chair, in a posture of disconsolate defeat. It was not quite one o'clock yet and the day stretched endlessly ahead. Colin might not be hungry, but *she* was, frankly, ravenous, and in dire need of a cup of tea. Yet she dared not leave him, even for ten minutes, in his present agitated state, since there was no knowing what he might do - perhaps even try to tackle the stairs in an attempt to reach his old room. She tried talking to him about upbeat, anodyne subjects, in an attempt to lift his mood, but his expression failed to change from one of abject gloom.

'Be quiet, Ron!' he snapped, suddenly. 'You're making my headache worse.'

'How long have you had a headache, she asked, concerned, but his answer was lost in a loud ring at the front door. Beryl, maybe? The postman? Or some pesky official come to quiz her about the proposed changes to their refuse-collection schedule? She decided to ignore it, but the noise continued pealing on and on, as if the caller had their finger on the bell-push.

'Colin, promise you won't move, OK? I'll only be two ticks and you must stay absolutely still until I'm back.'

At least, in this downstairs room, she was only seconds from the front door, which she opened in hasty annoyance. Standing on the step was a large, curvaceous black woman, with a prodigiously big bosom straining against the buttons of her silky, leopard-printed blouse.

'Hello, sweetheart,' the woman said, her radiant smile displaying teeth of such unlikely whiteness they could surely only be false, 'I'm Pearl.'

'Pearl?' she repeated, wondering who in heaven's name this sexy female could be. had she been dispatched as a singing telegram and was about to break into a rendition of `happy birthday` or `get well soon`?

'Didn't they tell you I was coming?' Without waiting to be invited, Pearl had stepped into the hall, and now placed a reassuring hand on Veronica's arm. 'No need to look so worried, sweetheart. I'm an official carer, here to help your husband.' She fumbled for her pendant name-badge, which had become trapped within the deep fold of her breasts, and flashed it in front of Veronica.

'Oh, I see. Please do come in,' Veronica said, superfluously, since Pearl was already halfway down the hall.

'And where is your lovely Colin?' she asked, again disconcerting Veronica with the steep valley of her cleavage and the dazzle of her smile.

'Er, just in here.' Veronica ushered Pearl into his bedroom. Fortunately, Colin hadn't moved and was still sunk dejected in his chair. 'Say hello, darling,' she prompted. 'This is Pearl, who's come to help us.'

Instead of the tirade she'd expected, Colin said nothing at all, failing even to look up or spare the woman the briefest glance.

'Now what I suggest, my angel' – the woman's hand was on her arm again, hot, damp and sweaty, although patently affectionate – 'is that you leave me on my own with your hubby, so we can get to know each other.'

'Can I make you a cup of tea first?' Veronica enquired, uneasy at Pearl's suggestion. Surely she and any carer should establish some measure of formality and maybe start with a private chat, to explain Colin's medical problems and his likely hostility to what he would see as 'interference'.

'Don't you worry about me, sweetheart. I'm here to give you a break, so the last thing I want is you waiting on me!' She gave a throaty chuckle, before wiping a film of sweat from her face. 'Why not make that cuppa for yourself, my love, and take the chance to put your feet up?'

Reluctant to leave Colin with a virtual stranger who had no idea of his attitude, she slunk into the kitchen and stood by the open door, ready to dash back at the first sound of any protest from her husband.

None came.

Heartened, she filled the kettle, grabbed a couple of biscuits from the tin and ate them standing up, while she waited for the water to boil. By the time she'd finished her tea, there was still no sound from Colin, only Pearl's cheery babble, punctuated by an occasional booming laugh. Well, at least he hadn't attacked her as yet, as he'd once tried to do with a draconian Polish carer, who had lasted all of ten minutes.

No way could she relax, though, whilst straining her ears continually to catch Colin's wails of protest. Instead, she took the chance to wash up all the cooking utensils she had used for the shepherd's pie. Once she'd done the shopping and cooking this morning, there hadn't been time to clear up the kitchen, so she began tackling that chore right away.

Despite listening acutely, she couldn't hear Colin's voice at all. Perhaps this woman was a con, come to drug him and rob him – the sort of scam one read about in the tabloids. Indeed, rather than fearing Colin might attack her, it might even be the other way round. She should have checked Pearl's name-badge more thoroughly, phoned the council for confirmation, or at least quizzed her in person before leaving her with Colin. To calm herself, she scoured the frying-pan, put the rest of the stuff in the dishwasher and swabbed down all the surfaces, trying to use housework as a tranquillizer. The oven-clock said one-thirty, and still not a murmur from Colin. He never failed to raise his voice when necessary – or often when *unnecessary* – and the kitchen door was wide open, so any sound would carry. She'd better go and check on him, if only to reassure herself that he wasn't lying bludgeoned on the floor, while Peal ransacked the place for valuables.

Notwithstanding her lurid imaginings, she knocked politely on Tom's bedroom door.

'Come in!' Pearl called, and Veronica entered apprehensively, blinking in disbelief at the sight that met her eyes. Colin was still in his chair, but now leaning over Pearl, who had pulled the second chair right up close beside him, her plump arm cradling his shoulder. His face was pressed against her majestic bosom, his eyes closed in an expression of near-ecstasy, while Pearl crooned softly to him.

'There, my little love. You go to sleep now, Colin darlin'. Everything's going to be all-righty-right.'

Veronica couldn't drag her eyes from the image of her husband's cheek smooched against Pearl's cleavage. Surely such intimacy was wrong – abusive, even - yet there was no denying that all Colin's former agitation and irritability had vanished at a stroke, and his whole mien and posture now spoke of calm contentment. She gazed at the pair, uncertain whether to intervene and rebuke this so-called carer, or simply give thanks that the woman had managed, by however unconventional a method, to bond with a highly intractable patient. While she stood debating, Pearl interrupted her soothing lullaby of endearments to ask if there was anything she needed.

'Er, no,' Veronica murmured. 'It seems you have everything – um, in hand.'

CHAPTER 19

'Welcome everyone!' At least, Veronica thought, with relief, she'd completed two words without visibly shaking or stuttering to a halt, although she remained distinctly anxious about taking centre-stage. 'As most of you know, our usual Chairperson, Glenys, is not too well at present, so I'm deputizing for her in her absence.'

'Well done you, Veronica!'

Recognizing Megan's voice, she gave silent thanks for her friend and for all the other choir-members who'd stayed behind after today's rehearsal, to support her in this daunting new role. Whatever happened she mustn't let them down, least of all Katy, who was sitting right bang in the front. Having their choir-leader present only increased her fear that her voice would betray her nerves.

'Those of you who were here last time will remember Glenys wanted us to draw up a programme of fund-raising events for the whole of next year, so I've printed these calendars for us to work on together. Our aim will be to fill every month with some event or other, whether a big, black-tie affair or a low-key bake-sale. We also need to map out some additional events, covering Christmas and New Year. Some of you have generously volunteered already. Dave, you've persuaded your local estate agent to fund a winter ball early in December, so if any of you can sell tickets for that, or buy a few for yourself, that will help swell our coffers. And you, Christopher, are taking part in the London-to-Paris cycle ride, and I'm sure most of us here will happily sponsor you. And another person who deserves our full support is Ann-Marie, who's bravely offered to do a sponsored head-shave.'

All eyes turned to Ann-Marie's cascade of naturally chestnut hair, most of them aware what a sacrifice she was making, because, although not all patients lost their hair in the course of chemotherapy, few could boast such a thick, luxurious crop.

'But please don't worry if you can manage only something small-scale, like hosting a coffee-morning or selling raffle-tickets. *All* your efforts are welcome.'

Megan caught her eye and gave her a nod of encouragement and Veronica realized with surprise and pleasure that, whatever her inner turmoil, she was actually sounding confident and professional. Indeed, she could barely believe the huge strides she'd made in just the last few weeks – since meeting Alex, in fact.

'One of the great strengths of Larks Ascending,' she went on, 'is that we're not just any old choir. We're bonded not only by singing but by our shared experience of cancer. And another special feature of this choir is that it's open to everyone. We deliberately don't hold auditions or expect members to read music, because it's not a question of us shining as individual divas, but of the choir binding us together and supporting those who are ill. It also helps boost confidence for anyone like me who implicitly believed I simply couldn't sing and that was the end of the matter. OK, I admit I'm still more of a discordant crow than a melodious lark, but, even so, I can personally assure you that if a musical dunce like me is welcome here then there's hope for everyone, including the tone-deaf!'

Her words prompted a burst of laughter and, aware of the friendly, accepting atmosphere, she continued with greater assurance, following the agenda she'd drawn up with Alex's help.

'Fund-raisers need passion,' he'd told her, adding with a seductive smile, 'which I know from personal experience you're hardly short of, my darling.'

That 'my darling' had been thrilling, as had his actual remark. She was so accustomed to the stale, almost meaningless 'darlings' of her marriage, Alex's use of the word endowed it with new magic and allure.

'And I also know how passionate you are about the choir,' Alex had gone on to say and that's a real plus-point when it comes to raising funds. People are far more likely to donate to a cause when they realize how much good it's doing and how deeply its members care. And all that stuff you've told me about Larks Ascending being almost a substitute family and how therapeutic singing can be in itself, will go down well with potential donors - that I know for sure.'

She had deliberately told him some of the accounts, confided by choir-members, of how they'd discovered new sets of loving, understanding 'parents', by being members of the group, or had acquired extra 'children' with whom they'd established an instant bond. And that many described the rehearsal-hour as a blessed period of forgetfulness, when stress and illness and loneliness all tended to fall away. And since that was profoundly different from the big, impersonal projects he presumably must work on, she hoped it might secure his continuing support.

She'd also come to realize, through Megan's encouragement, that she already possessed certain qualities essential for her role - punctuality, efficiency, organizational skills – and that she must block out her mother's disapproving voice echoing from beyond the grave. 'Who are you to hog the limelight, Ron, when you're bound to make a mess of it? Step down now, for pity's sake, before you make a total fool of yourself.'

Giving Den a fierce kick on the shins, she began distributing the calendars: full-colour, glossy and professional-looking. She had also printed posters, brochures and banners for use at all the various events. Her online courses at the Virtual College, in Design and Digital Business Skills, had definitely paid off and, indeed, it seemed astonishing that, at this late stage of her life, when she had given up all hope of self-development – and, even more so, of love, admiration and a sexual relationship - all those things appeared to have fallen into her lap. Although she attributed them entirely to Alex, Megan kept insisting that she should take the credit and not continually look to a man for self-worth and affirmation.

'I'd like you all to keep October 30 free,' she announced, in a more assertive (Megan-prompted) tone. 'It's the day before Halloween, and I've arranged for us to sing, between six and seven in the evening, outside South Kensington tube. It's usually pretty busy then, with people trekking back from work or going out on the town, so it should attract quite a lot of interest. I needed permission from the Council, but that wasn't difficult.' Thanks to Alex, she didn't add, knowing that, without his help, it would have been a stretch for her to get to grips with all the rules and regulations that governed the granting of licences and permissions required to stage various events. Simple busking was generally no problem, but when it came to rattling collection-tins, one had to get clearance from the Metropolitan Police, which involved masses of red tape. 'I'll email you all with details of the repertoire and dress-code and –'

'We could all dress up as witches or ghosts or pumpkins,' Theo interrupted, 'to capitalize on the Halloween theme and put people in a more festive mood.'

'No,' Charlotte objected, 'if we do that, there's a danger we'll be seen as just a bunch of trick-or-treaters. If we want to be taken seriously, shouldn't we wear our formal Larks Ascending gear, like we do for important gigs, then people can tell we're a well-turned out, professional choir that's really worth supporting?'

'It's great that we're exchanging ideas,' Veronica said, approvingly, 'and, of course, we've already planned to cash in on all the big national fund-raisers, like this month being Breast Cancer Awareness Month. So, don't forget our after-choir Pink Party in just a fortnight's time. Katy's already reminded us to bring pink-themed food and drink, but remember the dress-code is also pink, and that includes all you gents. In fact, we expect you to outdo the ladies in just how much pink you can pile on: pink shirts, pink ties, pink trainers, pink hair, pink face-paint!'

'Yes, I'm wearing my puce-pink thong right this minute,' Barry put in, with his trademark vulgar laugh.

Once the titters had died down, Veronica suggested that, since they hadn't stopped for a coffee-break straight after the rehearsal, they should have a brief one now and combine it with a brainstorm. 'So, over coffee, I'd like you all to come up with ideas – however weird and whacky – for raising money between now and this time next year.'

As people moved towards the kitchen, Veronica used the chance to make a quick phone-call to Pearl, reassured by the woman's relaxed, easy-going voice.

'No need to worry, sweetheart. Your hubby's just fine with me. I'm giving him his supper right this instant.'

Which meant she'd be literally spoon-feeding him, having established the ritual from their very first meal together, Pearl adding a sing-song recital of 'One for Colin, one for Pearl, one for Peter, one for Ron', as if he'd returned to babyhood and needed encouragement to get each spoonful down. It had worked wonders in persuading her normally fussy husband to eat eagerly and fast - although a return to babyhood was hardly the right description for something so weirdly sexualized. During each meal, Colin would lay his head or cheek on Pearl's magnificent bosom, clearly glad to have his hands free, so he could explore the enthralling valley of her cleavage, while she spooned in curried goat or seasoned callaloo. It seemed almost unimaginable that her conventionally English husband, who refused to eat the tiniest morsel of moussaka or chilli con carne (both dismissed as 'foreign muck'), was now wolfing down large platefuls of exotic dishes from Pearl's native Jamaica. Colin, however, was so enamoured of this new porn-star-in-the-flesh, he'd have probably gobbled down sheep-shit, so long as Pearl was the one spooning it in. Their bond was undoubtedly eccentric, probably wrong, yet wonderfully enabling for her personally, in that she could pursue her own life without being tied full-time to home and husband. Pearl, for her part, had needed little persuasion to quit her job with the Council and come to work for her at home at a much increased hourly rate.

At first, she had jibbed at spending so much money on herself, in what was, at base, a bid to shirk her wifely duties, but Megan had pointed out that, since Pearl was freeing her to take over as Chair and thus help to save the choir, that role involved a host of other people and so couldn't be classed as selfish.

'Yes, but my private dates with Alex are nothing to do with the choir and Pearl is covering those as well.'

'And earning a damn good wage in the process, which she need to feed and clothe her kids. How many did you say she had?'

'Five. All girls.'

‘Lord! Rather her than me.’

‘Well, she’s certainly the ultimate earth-mother and Colin responds to that amazingly well. To be honest, I feel a bit guilty that’s she’s so much better with him than I am.’

‘You’re lacking in the boobs department, that’s all. You told me once Colin’s always been a tits’-man, so I guess you need to be a cup-size triple-D before he’ll become all sweet and obliging!’

Aware her mind was wandering, she was propelled back to the present by Pearl’s voice booming down the phone. ‘There’s nothing whatever to fret about,’ the woman reassured her. ‘So, you just enjoy your evening, pet, and I’ll see you later, OK?’

Veronica quickly concluded the call, anxious not just to return to her agenda, but also to get off the phone, in case Alex was trying to get through. He’d been hoping to come in person this evening and might just make it in time, depending on his other engagements. She still found it hard to believe that a man of his eminence should want her in his life at all. When she’d first met Colin, he, too, had seemed a mover and shaker, but disillusion soon set in, as all the businesses he established proved short-lived, often shaky and liable to fail. Alex, in contrast, headed one of the leading Communications firms in Europe, and had a string of professional qualifications on top of a Cambridge degree, whereas Colin’s education, which he liked to portray as substantial, had been, in truth, more a matter of sandwich-courses, evening-classes and home-study, plus a short spell at an undistinguished polytechnic.

But who was she to criticize when she herself was more or less uneducated, apart from what she’d managed to glean from an ever-changing succession of new schools? Which made it all the more extraordinary that a man of Alex’s calibre appeared to enjoy her company. The thought was so consoling, it gave her the boost she needed to kick off the discussion, once everyone had reassembled in the hall. 'I want you all to chip in with your suggestions, but I'll go first,' she said, following Alex's advice of always offering a lead. 'Three ideas, just off the top of my head, are a Great Gatsby Night, a Hymns-and-Pimms Sunday and a Murder Mystery Weekend. And I also want to propose that, if our South-Ken gig goes well, we extend it to other tubes and mainline stations, and to public places, such as the V & A or the British Library.'

'Or how about the South Bank,' Yvonne suggested. 'That already has a strong tradition of happenings and performances?'

'Yes, excellent idea. London bursts at the seams during the tourist season, and I reckon many of those tourists would really enjoy seeing a free choir perform and would probably give very generously. I've ordered some more collection-tins, although actually we're not allowed to rattle them too aggressively or shove them under people's noses! The public don't like being pressurised, so better for us to grab the crowd's attention by handing out leaflets or even doing a little impromptu dance in time to our songs, for those of you with the energy!'

She was amazed by all she'd learned already: how to persuade local businesses to support their choir, financially and personally, the protocol for approaching supermarkets, to obtain free food for events, or be allowed to hold collections on their premises, the importance of drawing up an agenda for each meeting, and the tact required to cut short longwinded monologues on the part of those choir-members who loved to ramble on. She was certainly much busier these days, trying to fit in her daily singing-practice, on top of a taxing home-study course – not to mention the time and vigour demanded by a passionate affair.

As if on cue, her phone vibrated with a text from Alex - *On my way. With you in ten minutes* – the text setting off its own vibration, a ripple of excitement deep within her body. No one must ever guess, though, that she and this VIP were actually having an affair. The very thought brought its usual backwash of disbelief, elation, guilt and shameful lust. In their hours together after the Private View, he had discovered parts of her body she simply hadn't realized could be so stirringly responsive: the coil of her ears, the backs of her knees, her insoles, eyelids, navel. And, under the skilled touch of his mouth and fingers, she had responded so wildly, she could hardly credit that she, the once-naïve, unawakened, long-married almost-virgin could be making such a brazen din.

As other people contributed their ideas, she welcomed the buzz of discussion in the hall, if only because it returned her to the business in hand. Indeed, she let it flow unchecked for a while, before calling for silence, so she could announce the imminent arrival of their distinguished visitor.

'Those of you who were here for our first meeting will remember Alex Sutherland, who was kind enough to share his long experience of fund-raising. Well, he's going to be with us again, in just a matter of minutes, and he has some exciting news to impart. But I'll leave him to speak for himself.'

Her timing was perfect, because, just at that moment, Alex swept into the hall, looking effortlessly stylish in a camel-coloured cashmere coat and a jauntily checked scarf. Once she'd introduced him, she seated herself beside him, doing her best to make her expression one of safe neutrality, despite the frisson that refused to stop fluttering through her limbs.

'One of the advantages of my job,' he began, in his confident, well-modulated voice, 'is that I get to know a large number of wealthy, influential people. Some of those owe me favours and what better way for them to repay such favours than to make a contribution to your choir. And one of those people – a very long-standing friend, in fact - tragically lost his daughter to cancer when she was only thirty-nine, so he was particularly keen to help. He happens to head a small, family-owned car-dealership, and he's offered to donate us a brand-new Mercedes Cabriolet, as a Larks Ascending raffle-prize.'

Gasps from the audience were followed by a spontaneous burst of applause.

'Lordy, Lordy!' Samantha cried, 'that's a change from the usual bottles of plonk and boxes of Boots' toiletries.'

'And I'm determined to win it,' Keith laughed. 'I've always fancied myself at the wheel of a Merc!'

'My friend has also volunteered,' Alex added, 'to take the car to various big shopping-centres and suchlike, to publicize the raffle and your choir. So while we're showing it off, maybe you could lay on a bit of a concert, give out leaflets and sell raffle-tickets to every man, woman and child you can possibly persuade to part with a quid or three. It's imperative we sell a lot, to reap all we can from this one-off opportunity of such an extravagant prize. So I want every one of you to take several books of tickets and do your utmost to flog them - either pester your friends and family, or approach your local shops and ask if you can sell them there.'

'The only raffle-prize I've ever won,' Theo put in, with a groan, 'was a game of Chinese Chequers, and even that had half its pieces missing. So, if I know I'm in with a chance of winning a Merc, I'll buy literally dozens of tickets. It would do wonders for my image compared with riding a third-hand bike!'

'And my second piece of good news,' Alex continued, once he'd shushed those in the choir still exclaiming and emoting over his first announcement, 'is I've managed to arrange a substantial donation from a major Life Insurance firm, whom I'm happy to say have pledged us ten-thousand pounds a year for a period of two years.'

'You mean twenty-thousand in total?' Samantha asked, astounded.

'That's correct,' Alex confirmed. 'And the only thing they've asked for in return is that your choir wear T-shirts printed with their logo and sing at certain public events they organize. They've even offered to obtain your Public Liability Insurance and your licences to use specific music.'

'So, you seem to be saying,' Theo said, in a tone of outright jubilation, mingled with a note of incredulity, 'that we've already met our target, all in one fell swoop.'

Alex nodded. 'Absolutely.'

'But it does tend to put our piddling little cake-sales in the shade,' Patsy remarked, with a certain wry dismay – understandable in that she herself was a prodigious baker who had already raised a considerable sum from her state-of-the-art cupcakes.

'Don't worry, Patsy,' Barry chortled. 'You can sit back on your arse now and leave it all to Standard Life, or whoever, to bring in the bucks.'

'Certainly not,' Alex reproved, with mock-severity. 'In no way does a big donation negate all your individual fund-raising projects. Those are precious in themselves, not only to raise more money, but to give the choir publicity, which will attract new members and secure its future. And, don't forget, we need to factor in the cost of keeping the choir going, each and every year, which includes the hire of the hall, the choir-leader's fee, the printing costs for the song-sheets, brochures, marketing materials and suchlike, the various licence fees, the expense of the PA system, and even things like the teas and coffees.'

'And not forgetting the biscuits!' Theo added, stuffing two chocolate-digestives into his mouth.

'Even so,' Charlotte remarked, 'what you've done, Mr Sutherland, is little short of miraculous.'

'Absolutely,' Veronica said, although secretly she was applying the word less to the stupendous donations than to the truly miraculous happenings between Alex's sheets. Indeed, the memory was so bewitching, she had to force from her face the incriminatingly blissful Cheshire-cat smile.

CHAPTER 20

'Barry, you look amazing!'

Veronica marvelled at how many different shades of pink this one short, skinny fellow had managed to meld together in his outfit: baggy pink harem-trousers, Hawaiian shirt with blowsy pale-pink roses splashed across a deeper puce ground, two-tone pink trainers, worn over strawberry-coloured socks, and a pink fright-wig, with matching false beard and moustache. Of course, Barry was a natural extrovert, but even the more bashful men were sporting at least a pink tie, sometimes teamed with a pink shirt and, in one case, hipster trousers the exact shade of bubble-gum. And the ladies had gone all out with a vibrant variety of pink tops, skirts, jeans, scarves, turbans, nail-varnishes and lipsticks.

She herself had invested in a silk-and-linen-blend dress, in the palest petal-pink, bought really for her ballet-date with Alex, now only five weeks away – a more upmarket creation than anything she had ever bought before, but justified, she felt, in that Alex had arranged a pre-performance dinner with a famous ballerina and her composer-husband, equally renowned. She was gradually picking up tips from the high-powered people he knew on how to choose her clothes – ones that broadcast a message of understated privilege, rather than bargain-basement or charity shop.

More and more people were flocking into the hall, placing their contributions of food and drink on the pink-clothed trestle-table set up at the back of the room. She was struck by the fact that, just as each individual, bringing his or her small share, resulted in a veritable feast, so each individual singer in the choir contributed to a full-throated wave of sound. This sense of community was something she still never took for granted, since it had been so rare in her previous life, whether in terms of a settled local neighbourhood, a long-term school, or even a group of like-minded people. Indeed, to acquire this large extended family at the age of fifty-nine had been totally unexpected, especially the bonus of a loving, supportive sister in the shape of Megan. Not that she'd seen much of her since the birth of Flora Megan, Lavinia's lusty nine-pounder, named in her great-aunt's honour and still barely a fortnight old. Having never had her own kids, Megan was taking a fierce maternal interest in the new arrival and, at this very moment, was showing off her baby-photos to a small cluster of choir-members.

Veronica had seen them already and, secretly, had felt no wild attraction to the bald and podgy infant, who resembled a miniature boxer rather than a flower-like little girl. So, she turned her attention instead to the pink-themed assortment of dishes on the table: shrimps, prawns, smoked salmon, tamorosalata, and enough sweet things to rot everybody's teeth: boxes of pink marshmallows and Turkish Delight, cartons of pink popcorn, pink trifles and pink jellies, and an impressive show from the contingent of home-bakers in the choir, who had brought pink cupcakes, pink meringues, pink macaroons, and several different variations on large pink-iced cakes, most of which outshone the one she'd made specially and exclusively for Glenys. Since her friend was at present in hospital, recovering from her operation, she planned to leave the party early and visit her this evening, to take her a selection of the festive food and give her an account of the proceedings.

She set down Glenys's cake - iced with the message, *We miss you, Glenys. Come back soon!* - amidst the array of other plates. Now that the more serious part of the evening was over – the rehearsal and actual singing – people began pouring drinks, all pink, of course: pink champagne, rosé wine, pink lemonade, pink smoothies. Katy had even signified the change of mood by donning a festive hat decorated with a garland of pink flowers. And everybody present seemed to be consciously relaxing as they blew up more pink balloons, to add to the string already looped around the hall, laid out pink serviettes, printed with flamingos, along with matching paper-plates and cups, or placed posies of pink flowers in the few small spaces left on the table.

Just at that moment, Catherine burst in, having missed the whole rehearsal, but sporting a tropical tan and a fondant-pink straw sunhat.

'Better late than never, folks! My plane touched down only an hour or so ago, but I had no intention of missing this knees-up.'

Veronica was impressed by her resilience, not just in discounting jet-lag, but in having gone away at all, when her cancer was not yet in remission.

'So how was your holiday?' people started asking.

'Idyllic.' Needing no further encouragement, Catherine began displaying a succession of photos on her phone, all too perfect to be real: silver sand, turquoise ocean, cloudless azure sky. 'This was the view from our hotel window and it truly *was* like that, as if filched directly from a hyped-up holiday brochure! Oh, and Veronica,' she added, 'I bought you a souvenir. Sorry you're the only one to get a present, but I thought you deserved it as our new Fund-Raising Chair. Careful now. It's heavy!'

As Veronica unwrapped the layers of tissue paper, Catherine explained the gift as a Barbadian speciality, known as a monkey-jar and made of the local red clay. 'They're designed to keep water cool and probably totally superfluous in our world of fridges and freezers, but I thought it was slightly more original than a T-shirt or a keyring!'

'I love it!' Veronica said, running her hand across the reddish-brown, spherical surface, and touched by the fact that Catherine had thought of her at all. Her own sense of Alex-induced benevolence made her want everyone else to be similarly content, and she longed to magic away all the cancers, problems, difficulties faced not just be Catherine but by many others in this room and waft them into her personal cloud of rose-pink euphoria.

Well, at least the setting was perfect, with food and wine in profusion, party-games and singsongs promised, and that uplifting, heartening sense of friendship almost tangible in the air she breathed.

As Veronica was about to leave, Katy picked up her guitar and started strumming the accompaniment to *For She's a Jolly Good Fellow*. Everyone joined in the song, Veronica assuming that the tribute was to Glenys in her absence, until, at the end, people began calling out, 'Bravo, bravo, Veronica!'

Blushing at so unexpected a send-off, she stood at the door to the hall, carrying not just the weighty jar, but also Glenys's cake and the huge bouquet the choir had clubbed together to buy for their absent Chairperson, and the embossed get-well card all of them had signed. And, although hampered by this baggage on the tube-journey, nothing could dilute her elation until she actually reached the hospital, where she made a conscious effort to descend from the heights of Cloud Nine. Glenys would be sore, weak, and highly anxious about the future, and *Get well soon* was, in her case, less an expectation than a cruelly unlikely hope.

A nurse ushered her in to the ward, where she found Glenys wired up to a drip and looking worse than she'd feared, her face drained of all colour save for a fierce red rash on her neck and forehead. Her mood, however, seemed surprisingly upbeat – more so when she saw the cake and flowers.

'I'll ask the nurse for a vase,' Veronica said, 'and maybe someone in the kitchen could cut the cake into manageable pieces. But, first how *are* you, Glenys?'

'A bit sore,' Glenys said, wincing as she moved, in demonstration of her words, 'But still very much alive, so I've nothing to complain about! And, in fact, I have some good news.'

'About your prognosis?' Veronica asked, wondering, with mixed feelings, if and when Glenys would be back as acting Chair. Although she was enjoying her new role, it was nonetheless intimidating and, anyway, she could only continue in it so long as Pearl was free to Colin-sit. The woman showed no sign of quitting, but of course anything might happen to disrupt the arrangement, given she had five still youngish children.

'No, that's still distinctly iffy. This is something else entirely. But, before I get on to that, tell me how the party went.'

Veronica gave her a brief resumé, then the conversation turned – again - to the two big donations Alex had secured, Glenys expressing her delight once more.

They were interrupted by a nurse, come to take Glenys's blood pressure. The curvaceous black woman reminded her of Pearl – again - and Veronica gave silent thanks that at least her trusty carer was holding the fort this evening and, indeed, making this visit possible at all. When she'd rung her, en route to the hospital, to check on Colin, she had received the usual reassurances, seasoned with endearments, and Pearl had concluded by saying that she'd just introduced Colin to a Jamaican beverage called Tamarind Fizz.

'Your husband loves it, sweetheart – in fact, he seems to believe it's our native champagne, although I assure you, pet, it doesn't contain a drop of the hard stuff.'

If Pearl could solve his drinking problem, Veronica thought – admittedly with a large dose of disbelief - she'd gladly harvest every tamarind tree in the world and award Pearl a laurel-and-tamarind crown.

'So, what's your good news?' she prompted, once the nurse had filled in Glenys's chart and left the two of them alone again.

'His name is Robert,' Glenys said, with a smile. 'And I met him at my second session in the chemo-suite. He happened to be sitting in the chair right next to mine and, after a while, we struck up a conversation and it turned out we had masses in common. We're both exactly the same age, to start with, both grew up in the wilds - me in Shropshire, he in Northumberland - both went to Bristol University, both worked for the Civil Service, and were both widowed quite a while ago. And another coincidence is that he even has breast cancer, same as me, although it's extremely rare in men. Well, once the chemo was over, we went for a coffee together and stayed talking for literally hours. And the amazing thing was I didn't have any of my usual post-chemo symptoms like nausea, or exhaustion, because Robert took me out of myself and made me laugh. You should hear his views on what he calls "Smile To Survive" – you know, how us cancer patients are more or less duty-bound to be everlastingly positive and put on a brave face, and how everything is presented in terms of "winning our battle". He even quoted some hilarious sayings he'd found online about how cancer can be the best thing in our lives by teaching us the value of each remaining day, and how it's a precious gift that can lead us to the Divine – whatever the Divine is! To be perfectly honest, Veronica, I've often felt impatient myself with all that relentless cheeriness, but I could never find the courage to say so, for fear of seeming a killjoy. But Robert has no such qualms and he made me literally cry with laughter when he started on about the cutesy pink teddy-bears promoted on the breast-cancer websites – Hope Bear and Love You Forever Bear and Wish-Upon-a-Star Bear, and all the other pink merchandise, most of which is utterly naff, not to mention infantile.'

Veronica was feeling a trifle awkward, having just left a party where some of those very bears had featured in the celebration, one teddy wearing a turban very similar to Glenys's, as if to conceal its chemo-induced baldness. And there had been goodie-bags of, yes, naff pink trinkets: angel-pins, candle-holders, fridge-magnets, fake rhinestone bracelets. She was also surprised to see this other side of Glenys, who had always struck her as conformist, not a rebel. Yet she knew from her own experience how a new man in your life could change you profoundly, overturn your views and values, make you almost a different person. 'So, it seems as if you're quite smitten with this guy.'

'Oh, Veronica, I know it sounds utterly ridiculous, but I think I fell in love with him over that very first coffee.'

'Not ridiculous at all,' Veronica countered, longing to confide to Glenys her own equally precipitate passion for Alex. She was beginning to see that the concept of Great Love – sudden, overwhelming and, yes, probably irrational – was the one vital thing that made daily life worthwhile and meaningful. Her past existence had been, of its very nature, lamentably mundane, the endless routine chores involved in caring for Tom - mopping up his drool or changing his incontinence-pads – and, later, caring for Colin, which, drool apart, wasn't hugely different. Love's siren-call, however, was showing her a rather different reality - one that had been present all along, in art, literature and music, like a seam of gold in a coalmine - but which she had completely failed to recognize, because she'd been given no access to the requisite mining-tools.

Glenys lay back against the pillows, running an absent-minded hand through her non-existent hair. 'So, you don't think I'm making a fool of myself?'

'Absolutely not. You and Robert both have more than enough to contend with, so if you can make things better for each other, then go for it – no question.'

'Well, it does help enormously that we're both in the same boat. I mean, if I'm not up to talking or I've entirely lost my appetite, I don't need to explain. And because we both have secondary cancer, he never says things like "I know you'll be fine" or suggest useless remedies like shark-oil or elixir of mistletoe! And we plan to go to each other's upcoming appointments with the oncologist or whoever. But it's not *all* cancer, by any means. In fact, we've just decided on a plan where we'll take it in turn to suggest an outing – on our good days, of course, when we're physically able. We've already drawn up a list of ideas: a day-trip to Windsor, a cruise down the Thames to Greenwich, even a weekend in Harrogate, where Robert's sister lives. And having things like that to look forward to makes a world of difference.'

Veronica nodded, thinking of her own weekend away with Alex – the weekend of the ballet, in fact, when they planned to drive straight from the Royal Opera House to a boutique-hotel in Sussex, owned by one of his clients and said to be the most luxurious new hotel in Europe.

'Nurse! Nurse!'

The shrill call from the patient in the adjoining bed silenced them a moment, and Veronica was inexorably drawn back from her sensuous Sussex imaginings to the reality of pain and distress, all around her in this ward. One of the staff came running and, from a sense of tact and respect, she and Glenys didn't resume their conversation until the disturbance was over and the woman made more comfortable. Even after that, though, the constant beeping of pumps and monitors was a sobering reminder that the people here were, for the most part, seriously ill. Nevertheless, Glenys seemed keen to continue her account and, having leaned in closer, whispered, in a distinctly awkward tone, 'You'll probably be shocked to hear this, but Robert and I have already been to bed together.'

She was, in truth, less shocked by the news than by this new, confessional Glenys, although she suspected that was Robert's doing too, just as her own affair with Alex had prompted her to confide in Megan. Going to bed with anyone new was such an overwhelming experience, one longed to share and discuss it.

'I was terribly on edge beforehand about how crap my body looks, with the mastectomy scars and everything, but Robert was amazing. And, of course, he has his own scars and his own libido problems, but he simply joked about them and we ended up giggling like a couple of teenagers, which actually bonded us more than any amount of high-octane sex. Obviously, we had to be careful to avoid any painful or uncomfortable positions, but he turned even that into fun, by suggesting we write our own Breast Cancer Sex Manual. And he started inventing these crazy chapter-headings and giving me demonstrations, right there and then! Yet, despite all the larking around, I did experience some genuine sexual ….'

Glenys broke off suddenly, visibly embarrassed by her own uncharacteristic candour. 'I'm sorry, Veronica. You don't want to hear all this. My only excuse is that it was all just so unexpected and …. well, near-miraculous at my age, I feel I want to tell at least one other person.'

'You don't need an excuse. I understand completely.' Indeed, it was all Veronica could do not to blurt out her own exploits with Alex - as supremely special to her as the bond with Robert clearly was to Glenys.

'And it was so healing afterwards just to lie together and be able to fall sleep. When I'm on my own, I often lie awake for hours, thinking up dread scenarios, or hating the fact I can't make any solid plans for the future. But Robert's so accepting and laid-back, just being with him helps me to relax'

'Oh, Glenys I'm just so glad for you.'

'Promise not to breathe a word, though, will you, not to anyone? I feel a bit of a prat, to be honest. I mean, mooning over a man at my age, or even having sex at all when in the eyes of the world I'm totally undesirable.'

'But if Robert desires you, that's all that matters, surely?'

'Yes,' said Glenys, simply but contentedly.

A good point to leave, Veronica decided. The last thing she wanted was to tire Glenys out and, anyway, however willing Pearl might be to stay on all hours with Colin, she mustn't take advantage of this true-to-her-name treasure. 'Look, I'd better be going, if that's OK with you?'

'Yes, of course. I'm just so grateful to you for coming all this way and for all the time it must have taken to ice that magnificent cake. In fact, before you push off, we'd better do it justice and have a large, fat slice each! Be an angel, would you, and see if any of the nurses have had a chance to cut it yet?'

Veronica got up to investigate and, although the cake was still as she'd left it, a younger nurse-assistant found her a knife and two plates, and Veronica did the cutting herself, giving Glenys the piece with her name on. Having carried it back to Glenys's bed, she poured them each a tumblerful of fizzy pink lemonade, purloined from the party.

'I want to propose a toast,' she said, passing Glenys her glass. 'To you and Robert, long life and true love!'

And, as she walked back along the ward, she added under her breath, 'And to me and Alex, eternal, boundless, immeasurable, infinite love!'

CHAPTER 21

'Right,' said Katy, calling the choir to attention, having finally lined them up in position, after some preliminary regrouping, outside South Kensington tube, 'we're starting in five minutes, so on your marks, please, folks! Clive and Charlotte, you're in charge of these two collection-tins, and will you also try to hand out brochures to any spectators we manage to attract, so they know they're supporting a good cause. But, first, I'd like you all to take a few deep breaths, relax your bodies and pay attention to your posture.'

Veronica made a conscious effort to release all physical tension, although it was hard to relax as the seconds ticked on and the sense of anticipation mounted. Dusk was falling, lights coming on in the buildings, and a steady stream of commuters heading for the tube –their potential audience, with any luck. Christopher and Frances had brought along their guitars and now began playing the accompaniment to *I Will Survive*, the first song in the evening's repertoire. And the sound in general was guaranteed to be strong, since Katy had borrowed a socket from the adjoining flower-stall, to power her portable amplifier, ensuring that their voices would resonate at full volume above the backing-track.

Quickly, Veronica ran over the words in her head, pleased and surprised to acknowledge that she was surviving better than she had ever dared to hope. And, as Katy lifted her baton and she and the other basses belted out the first line, she could truthfully acknowledge that the fear that had ruled her life to date had all but dissipated, just as the song affirmed. In fact, it reminded her of this morning's heavy rain-showers, which had given way to a crisp and cloudless evening, and which she couldn't help regarding not as a mere quirk of the weather but due totally to Alex, however irrational that might be.

The bright, upbeat sound was already having its effect – busy, irritable people, who normally fought and jostled to get into the tube, heads down, eyes blind, ears heedless, were now slowing down and relaxing, as they paused to listen to this unexpected diversion. Some were taking photos on their phones, and a couple of women joined in with the song, their voices thankfully strong and tuneful. Then, a young Asian man began jigging about to the music, looking wonderfully incongruous in his formal pinstriped suit.

The finale was marked by a storm of applause and a satisfying rattle from the collection-tins. She looked up to see the pinstriped fellow donating a twenty-pound-note, and the two women showering in pocketfuls of coins, all presumably grateful to be entertained for free before embarking on what could be tedious journeys.

As Katy rallied them for the second number, *Can't Help Falling in Love*, Veronica reflected that, more than four months later, she could still recall everything Sebastian had taught her on that song. Yet, she didn't miss her teacher in the slightest - no longer even needed him, having finally accepted that singing was a natural gift and one she no more lacked than the ability to breathe.

As they reprised the refrain, she was aware that this, and every number in their repertoire, had personal relevance to Alex. No, she couldn't help falling in love with him, and, yes, nightingales *were* now regularly singing in every London Square, and yes, again, his love *was* lifting her higher and higher and higher.

More and more people began gathering around, attracted not just by the singing, but by the choir's formal dress of black and scarlet, set off this evening by the single red rose each of them was wearing, the flowers donated by a wealthy florist-friend of Samantha's. Larks Ascending was creating its own little happening, recorded for posterity on countless camera-phones, and the sound-effect of laughter added when an over-excited Labrador bounded up to investigate the proceedings and began barking its own bass-baritone descant.

As applause broke out again, Veronica tried to preserve for ever the rare and heady pleasure of being approved of and acclaimed. There was something truly liberating in letting her voice ring out loud and proud, to use one of Katy's favourite phrases, as if she'd been granted permission to do all the things forbidden as a child: to dress up, show off, cut a dash, strut her stuff. Indeed, it was if she were inhabiting the persona of the pinstriped extrovert, who began exuberantly leaping around again, once the choir had embarked on *Don't Stop Me Now*, rivalling even Freddie Mercury in his sheer uninhibited élan. Katy's own enthusiasm was also wildly infectious, as she used her hands, body and facial expressions to communicate what she wanted from her choir.

The evening did indeed feel magical – the cool breeze on her face, the dramatic night-sky, with its three-quarters-full moon seeming to grow brighter along with her own elation, and the empowering sense of unity, as every voice contributed to the overall tide of sound. She was aware of the comforting pressure of Megan's arm gently nudging her on one side and, on the other, Keith's strong, resonant voice lifting and fortifying her less accomplished effort.

Once they'd completed this third number, Katy took the chance to introduce the choir to those still clustered around, explain its mission and plead for financial support, Clive and Charlotte backing her up by raising their collection-tins right above their heads – a better ruse, they'd decided, than shaking them too vigorously, which might alienate the crowd.

During the lull in the singing, Veronica glanced up at the moon again, impatiently conscious that it would be full on 4 November – her next 'intimate' evening with Alex, now less than a week away. In her mind, she saw the two of them standing at his huge picture-window, watching the moonlight carve a golden fretwork across the sombre urban landscape, and feeling the sensuous glide of his hand stroking slowly down her throat and down further to ….

Could she really wait five days? Would it be totally out of the question to phone him once this gig was over and suggest she popped round there and then? Considering they were lovers, wouldn't something so daringly spontaneous be forgivable? The word 'lovers' seemed so cathartic, so emancipated, she still found it hard to associate it with the staidly faithful wife who, in forty years, would no more have dreamed of straying than of riding bareback on a buffalo across the African savannah. But her new, Alex-induced incarnation had very different horizons, which did, indeed, stretch far beyond mere terrestrial savannahs and right up to the moon. And Pearl, of course, permitted such expansion, as if she had provided a personal moon-craft to whiz her employer anywhere she chose and release her from the need to constantly check the time or worry over Colin's welfare. In fact, the woman had actually asked if she could work additional hours this evening, since she needed to earn more money to buy new shoes for daughter number five, whose oversized feet apparently refused to fit into her elder sisters' cast-offs. Veronica's natural instinct was simply to pay for the shoes as a gift, with no request for extra hours in return, but Pearl's strong work-ethic meant she'd probably jib at the offer, so why not stay out later and please herself as well as Pearl?

With her mind still on Alex, she found it hard to concentrate on the last part of the recital, as if he were a wanton wasp which had flown right into her head and was buzzing about with such restless vehemence she could think of nothing but his deliciously penetrating sting. And only when they took their final bow, was she returned to the proceedings by the sheer excitement of that bow, fervent applause rising all around them, mingled with rousing cheers. The financial response was equally extravagant, judging by the jingle of coins showering into the collection-tins and the flurry of ten-and even twenty-pound notes being flashed liberally around.

Once the crowd had finally dispersed and Katy had stowed away her gear and congratulated them all, before saying her farewells and setting off for home, several choir-members suggested going for a coffee in the *Prêt à Manger* opposite the tube. Although tempted to join them, Veronica was diverted by the lively threshing of the wasp, goading and inflaming her, spurring her not to *Prêt,* but to the thrill of Alex's bed. So, having made some vague excuse about having to go home to Colin, she headed down to the tube - not to Clapham, but to Monument, ringing Alex once she was on the platform.

The impersonal tone of his answerphone was like a slap in the face, and left her uncertain as to where he might be – in his car, perhaps, or out at some event, or had his phone simply lost battery-power? Still dithering, she sat down on a bench, debating whether to go straight back to Colin or take the chance of finding Alex at home. He had mentioned no engagements this evening and might, at this very moment, be on his way back from the office, either driving or on the tube. And, even if he weren't, wasn't it worth risking one short, possibly wasted journey even for the slightest hope of seeing him? At least it would please Pearl if she delayed her return to Clapham, and it needn't even be a wasted journey if she used the time to make notes on the gig and try to ascertain if anything needed changing or adjusting before she arranged any similar events.

However, once on the train, she found she could think of nothing but that incorrigible wasp, whose sting was so provokingly addictive she felt she would die of deprivation if she didn't find him at home. And, indeed, when she rang his doorbell she feared she might have started already peeling off her clothes in the short time it took him to open the front door.

In fact, he *didn't* open it, although she could hear voices and footsteps echoing from inside. If he had company, it was her obvious duty simply to turn tail and disappear, since unexpected callers could be highly inconvenient. Instead, her finger reached up to the bell-push once more, against all her natural instincts of caution and good manners. Why was she acting in this precipitate manner, taking the risk of offending him, when she might well regret such folly?

She was about to dash off, chastened by her own indiscretion, when the door was flung open by a tall, willowy woman clad only in a skimpy dressing-gown. The two females stared at each other, Veronica sickeningly aware that this 'rival' was a good twenty years younger than she was and disquietingly attractive. She also realized that her own attire was unusual, to say the least: a long, black formal skirt, worn with a frilly white shirt, a scarlet bow-tie and two matching red roses clipped rakishly in her hair.

'Er, I'm sorry to disturb you,' she said, finding her voice at last, although a mere rag and shred of a voice by now, 'but I wondered if Alex was in.'

'No', the woman said, curtly, with no further explanation.

So why the voices and footsteps? Could he have lent his flat to family or friends? Was she harbouring entirely misplaced suspicions and this woman was a mere innocuous relative? Yet there was something about the dressing-gown that continued to torment her: its brief length and flimsiness displaying the body underneath – a naked body, judging by the bare legs. Why was this intruder here and what the hell was going on?

'I can give him a message if you want,' the woman said, grudgingly.' But please be quick about it – I'm in a tearing rush.'

'Don't worry,' Veronica said, snubbed by the woman's impatience and turning away with what she hoped was a casual shrug. 'It really doesn't matter,'

But, as she stumbled back the way she'd come, she knew it mattered horribly and hugely - more than anything had ever mattered before.

CHAPTER 22

'So, is Colin all right?' she asked, anxiously, having found Pearl sitting on her own, watching a weepie on TV.

'Absolutely fine, pet. He's been as good as gold all evening. But then he always is.'

With *you*, maybe, Veronica thought, suppressing a twinge of bitterness.

'But, come eight o'clock, the little lamb said he wanted to go to bed. That's very early, I know, but I prefer to let him do things *his* way. You see, in my job, sweetheart, I always try to see the person underneath the patient and respect what he or she wants. You wouldn't believe some of the care-homes I've worked in, over the years, where the staff lay down the law and impose strict rules on the residents, without giving them any choice in how they live their lives.'

Veronica said nothing, aware she was sadly lacking when it came to respecting Colin's wishes. But it was markedly easier, she guessed, caring for a comparative stranger than caring for a spouse. Besides, when Pearl was looking after him, Colin always pressed for an early night, knowing his voluptuous carer would tuck him into bed, sing him Jamaican lullabies and smother him with kisses - and, if he asked nicely, would cheerfully repeat the whole process all over again.

'Well, I'd better be on my way,' the woman said, heaving herself up from the sofa, her silky skirt straining over impressively Rubenesque thighs.

Veronica handed over a wad of notes from her purse. 'The extra's for Kerissa's new shoes.'

'No, my love, I couldn't possibly ....'

'No arguments!' Veronica wondered what she'd done to deserve so superlative a carer – not just genuinely kind but without an avaricious bone in her body.

However, once she'd seen her off, her mind shifted back to Alex, and any relief or gratitude she felt to Pearl was immediately replaced with doubts and racking jealousy. There was surely something suspicious about a half-dressed woman being in his flat, yet what the hell could she do about it, without sounding either possessive or persecutory? Even if she rang him, the woman herself might answer, which would only cement her fear that this mysterious stranger was entrenched in both his flat and in his life. Or was she jumping to unwarranted conclusions, and there was a perfectly reasonable explanation for her presence? Perhaps one of his sons was staying for a sleepover, together with a friend from school, and the 'interloper' was simply the friend's mother. Or maybe the daughter of one of Alex's longstanding friends had begged him for a London bolthole for the night. Or was the woman just ...?

Unable to stop such fruitless speculation, she poured herself a small glass of sherry, as a much-needed tranquilizer but, rather than sitting down to drink it, began prowling around the house, glass in hand, unable to settle or relax, but wishing fervently she had gone to *Prêt* with the choir, instead of making that impulsive dash to Alex's. She and her fellow-singers could have spent a happy hour or two laughing and talking together, discussing the gig, even exchanging ideas for the next one.

'*Stop* this!' she said, out loud. Regrets were pointless and she was deadbeat anyway, after all the stupid agonizing, so wouldn't it be more sensible to go to bed and try to forget the whole incident, rather than continue to fret all night?

First, she went to check on Colin, found him peacefully sleeping, with Peter in his arms and a look of bliss on his face, as he re-lived, perhaps, Pearl's kisses and caresses. In her husband's presence, she was more aware of *Alex's* kisses and caresses, and the guilt they invariably brought. Whatever Megan might say, in the eyes of the world she was a culpably faithless wife. Yet that glorious adultery continued to enthral her, its expansive, rumbustious repertoire in such delirious contrast to Colin's inept fumbles and his insistence on tensely silent sex.

'Goodnight,' she murmured to the comatose form in the bed, envying his ability to sleep. Whatever the problems – indeed, tragedies - of his early life, he had never been prey to insomnia, as she had.

And, in fact, once she'd gone upstairs and undressed and prepared for bed, she feared sleep would prove elusive, if not, impossible, and she lay rigid and on edge, recalling all the other times she'd been unable to sink into blithe oblivion. The problem had its roots in childhood, when she'd shared a bed with Den, who bitterly complained that her daughter's restlessness kept her awake with its constant tossing, turning and fidgeting. Ironically, she had tried so hard not to make the slightest disturbance, in the end, she'd kept *herself* awake. And, even after her marriage, the sleeplessness had continued, although for totally different reasons. She found she actually missed her mother, having never before been parted from her in all her nineteen years, and feeling ridiculously uprooted and insecure – even missing the nagging, which had become to seem essential. It had also felt peculiar to share a bed with a man, his boozy breath exhaling in her face, his rank male smells too close, his scratchy stubble unkind against her cheek. And she'd felt perpetually threatened when the small, guileless thing between his legs grew, all at once, inflamed and obstreperous, swelling to double its size. And not just threatened, but worried about Tom, whom she feared might overhear them and react with terror to something apparently violent he couldn't understand. Little wonder she had eventually welcomed Colin's suggestion that they sleep in separate rooms.

Yet now she longed to share a room with *Alex* – as she'd be doing during their Sussex weekend. Surely that was still in the diary? How could the fleeting appearance of another woman cancel a solid hotel-booking?

The very thought was so distressing, she got up again to fetch her phone, deciding to ring Megan, if only to air the problem and see if her friend considered she was simply overreacting and there was nothing substantial to worry about. To her annoyance, she got the answerphone and, knowing Megan rarely went to bed early, wasted more time wondering where she might be and how many times it was worth trying her number again.

Indecisive, she read her texts instead: one from Keith offering to host a combined barbecue and fireworks display for Guy Fawkes, to raise money for the choir; one from Catherine, saying they'd missed her at *Prêt* and hoped she'd found all well at home, and a third from Clive, reporting the good news that they'd raised close on £300 from just this evening's gig. Any elation she might have felt, however, was instantly doused by her mind's maddening inability to stop circling round the mystery of Alex's 'other woman'.

She remained slumped on the sitting-room sofa, glancing at the photos on the mantelpiece: her wedding photo, one of Den, in a provocatively tight pink boob-tube, and her favourite shot of Tom, his plucky, ineradicable smile making her smile back automatically, despite her desolation. Her father's photo was notable by its absence. She had never even known his name, let alone what he looked like. He was just a gap, an emptiness, someone who categorically hadn't wanted a baby, blamed Den for falling pregnant, who in turn blamed her, the child, for the loss of any prospect of a settled. happy relationship. Den's disillusion with him had extended to all her subsequent lovers and she'd eventually concluded that men in general were impermanent and unreliable, at best a disappointment, at worse a disaster. Only Leonard had seemed to break the mould – hence her fervent hope in childhood that *he* would be the one who proved her mother wrong, transformed her from bitter single parent to happily married wife, providing sanctuary in the process for both her daughter and herself. And Leonard was back in her life now, not just his physical lookalike, but a man with the same outstanding qualities, a man worthy of love and respect.

But, she agonized, dragging herself wearily upstairs again, despite the prospect of a sleepless night, *was* he back in her life, or would she simply have to accept, as she had with the original Leonard, that he'd been nothing but a passing hope, a transitory dream?

CHAPTER 23

'Oh my God! Oh, Alex! That's *wonderful* – amazing! Go on. Go on. More, more, more, more, more, more! Don't stop, I beg you. Don't stop!'

She shut her eyes to focus fully on the twin sensations of his penis pulsing deep inside her and his tantalizing finger touching her in the exact same place, as he threshed beneath her on the bed. As the finger probed still deeper, she let out an ecstatic cry, screwing up her face, her eyes, unable quite to bear the sheer paroxysms of pleasure roller-coastering through her body. And Alex, too, seemed more urgent than ever before, as he hurtled towards his climax, the pair of them wild beasts, unruly and ferocious. His hands were gripping her so tightly, she relished the fact they might leave deep, red marks, imprinted on her body – proof that he was hers again and all spectres of other women had slunk away, abashed.

Tightening her muscles to prevent him slipping out, she arched her back so that her breasts were thrust towards him, an open invitation for him to take them into his mouth, first one and then the other. While his teeth and tongue explored the right breast, the left seemed to pant and pester for its turn, and she felt still so aroused, so galvanized, she wanted to stay here in his bed for ever, never put back her restricting clothes, or return to the restrained and decorous self she was forced to be in public.

'You're *crying*,' he said, reaching forward to brush away her tears. 'Whatever's wrong, my darling?'

'Nothing,' she said, the word contradicting her still streaming eyes. How could she explain that these were tears of exhaustion, after five days of uncertainty and anguish, or make him understand her desperate relief that all her fears about a rival had been banished at a stroke?

Reluctantly, she rolled off his body, but remained lying close, glorying in his animal heat, his sweat-sleeked skin and the wild pumping of his heart. 'But I'm sorry for you,' she whispered. 'It must be quite appalling to have a stalker.'

'Well, yes, it was a strain, I must admit. But all that happened ages ago, which is why I'm all the more astonished hat Fiona should have showed up again – *and* in my new flat. How the hell she let herself in I'll never know. But, don't worry, I intend to notify the police first thing tomorrow morning, to make sure they chase her up, so it can never happen again.'

'But that's all more nuisance for you – I mean, involving the police and having to make a statement and …'

'Can't be helped,' he shrugged. 'And, unfortunately, there's always a risk in my job that some female I work with will try to attach herself too closely. I guess it's a power-thing –if they can wangle their way into the boss's affections, they assume a whole host of perks and privileges will follow!'

His laugh was unconvincing, an obvious attempt, she guessed, to play down the stress of such situations, in order to be his usual sanguine self. Although touched by his desire to spare her some long account of his ordeal, she could well imagine how upsetting it must be to have some hated woman actually intrude into his private space, disrupt his home-life and his peace of mind, with no idea what outrage she might be planning next. 'So, did Fiona work with you once, then?' she asked.

'Yes,' he said, tersely. 'And, to be brutally honest, she was trouble from the start. But let's not talk about it.'

In fact, she herself longed to know more than the brief outline he'd provided when she'd first raised the subject earlier this evening. Had the two been lovers? What was the woman's background? Had their relationship been amicable before the stalking began? But, seeing what distress the matter caused him, she deliberately desisted. It was enough that Fiona was over, an unpleasant relic from his past, and about to be officially barred from ever bothering him again.

'I'd much rather lie here quietly and just admire your body.' He ran a caressing hand along her flank. 'Look! Your nipples are still erect, like they're sitting up and begging for more. And, talking of "more", I've never known you so noisy before. Thank goodness this flat has very effective soundproofing!'

She flushed, still unable to believe that this noisy, greedy female could truly be her. It was as if Alex had roused from hibernation the sleeping giant that had lain dormant in her body since her teens - a giant now demanding every sensuous experience it had denied itself for decades. 'Well, you only have yourself to blame' - she gave a shame-faced laugh - 'for turning me on so wildly! When I first met you, I was innocence itself, but now I find myself, even in formal situations, thinking the most unseemly thoughts about your penis.'

'I like the way you use its proper name and not all those abominations like prick and cock and dick and – horrors - ding-a-ling. I read somewhere there are some hundred-and-seventy-four different words for the male organ!'

She herself knew only three or four of them and had actually never glimpsed a penis until her wedding-night. Her mother, of course, must have seen dozens, in her time, but when she had a lover with her, the bedroom door was kept always firmly locked and she, the unwelcome child, turfed out, to sleep on the sofa or curled up in a chair. Thus, male anatomy had remained a mysterious subject, strictly off-limits, until Colin appeared on the scene.

'I discovered recently that the word penis comes from the Latin for tail, and I have to say that threw me a bit – feeling I'm an animal!'

'A very fine one, though!' She dared to fondle the 'tail', gratified when it stirred and swelled beneath her touch. It astonished her that, at his age, he could recover so quickly, when even young men, according to Megan, had no such staying-power.

'Let's have a drink first,' he suggested, 'something cool and refreshing. There's some sparkling elderflower wine chilling in the fridge, or just common-and-garden fruit juice, if you prefer.'

'No, the elderflower sounds perfect.' Anything that fizzed and sparkled would match her present mood.

And, when he returned with two frosted glasses and led her towards the window to look out at the full moon, she gloried in the fact that she, once bashful, stay-at-home Ron, had transmuted into passionate Veronica, now standing naked with a lover, feeling as potent and effervescent as the elderflower itself, and ready for whatever erotic refinements he initiated next.

The night sky looked so dramatic, it seemed to have been laid on as a backdrop specifically for this evening, a swirling ferment of black and silver, as the great golden orb of the moon continually fought for predominance with the dark clouds threatening to engulf it. And the river beneath it repeated the same colour-scheme, inky depths of water rippling and shimmering in a swathe of dazzling light. Suddenly, a single rocket shot in to the sky, reminding her it was Guy Fawkes Day tomorrow, when a long stretch of the Thames would be ablaze with fireworks. The rocket zoomed still higher, as if trying to reach the moon itself, before expiring in the latter's superior brilliance. As she watched, all the songs she now knew about the moon seemed to re-echo in her head: *Blue Moon, Moon River, Walking on The Moon, Dancing in The Moonlight, Fly Me to The Moon* – all redolent with love and longing.

And, with Alex beside her, their bare bodies dappled with moonlight, she needed no rocket to transport her to the moon. She was already there, dancing up and down its craters, leaping from moon-rock to moon-rock, soaring so exuberantly high and shining with such radiance, the moon slunk away in envy and conceded her pride of place.

CHAPTER 24

'Veronica, you mustn't keep bringing me things! Just your coming all this way is present enough in itself.'

'It's nothing.' Veronica unloaded the contents of the bag on to Glenys's kitchen table. 'All I've brought is some stuff for our lunch, a few flowers from the garden and a box of chocs, which won't do your health any good!'

'Never mind my health! You know what a glutton I am for any sort of chocolate. But sit down and I'll make you a coffee.'

'No, I'll make it. You're the invalid. And how are things, by the way?'

'So-so. I'll know more on Monday, when I see the oncologist, but let's not talk about all that dreary stuff. And I certainly don't want you waiting on me. So why don't I make the tea and you arrange your lovely flowers? I can't believe you still have roses in your garden on December the first!'

'Well, only these mingy few.' Mingy or not, the vibrant crimson of the blooms seemed an expression of her own elation that, for the first time in years, she was actually in tune with the coming Christmas season. Normally, she viewed it as the most depressing time of the year – a season of hype and hysteria, rather than of celebration – and the sense of being totally out of kilter with the general festive mood. But, in less than a week, she would be driving to Sussex with Alex, to spend four whole days with him – the longest by far they had ever been together. *That* would be her Christmas, she'd decided, and she would salve her conscience by devoting herself to Colin during Christmas proper, when Pearl would be on leave, having arranged to take some time off with her family. Those four days in the hotel were all the more precious in being the first holiday she'd had since her honeymoon forty years ago – a honeymoon that had lasted all of forty-eight hours, due to their pressing need to return home to Tom.

Aware her mind was wandering, she forced her concentration back to Glenys, who was asking about Colin. 'Oh, he's doing pretty well now. I have to say I was worried for a while, because every time I took him back to the hospital for a change of plaster-cast, or a walking-boot, or whatever, the doctor seemed concerned about how slowly the fracture was healing. But, since then, he's made reasonable progress and he can weight-bear now and he's even agreed at last to have some physio.' Thanks to Pearl, she didn't add. The woman had worked her usual wonders in making Colin less obstinately opposed to any intervention the medical team might propose. Without such an exemplary carer, her own life would be infinitely more frustrating, so never a day went by without her blessing the woman's arrival. Indeed, she, as well as Colin, was beginning to see her as a mother-figure – the loving, caring, upbeat Mum she had always secretly craved.

'That must be a relief,' Glenys said, setting down a polka-dotted china teapot and matching cups and saucers. 'I remember you saying it was quite a nasty fracture, so let's hope he's on the mend now. And how's the fund-raising going?' she asked, having poured the tea.

'Well, I think I already told you I've joined the Institute of Fundraising.' Veronica began arranging the roses in a cut-glass vase too pretentious for the faded, fragile flowers. 'And that's given me loads of ideas. And I've also signed up for a one-day course they run, which covers the basic principles and the various legal requirements for attracting donors and supporters, and also the whole ethical side.' The last thing she wanted was for Glenys to feel pushed out, or, worse, expected to deteriorate and thus be incapable of resuming her role, so she added quickly, 'You see, I feel I need to catch up, so I can do a reasonable job until you're back as Chair. I mean, you know all this stuff backwards, whereas I'm still very much a novice.'

'No way! In fact, when Catherine came to see me last week, she enthused about what a grand job you're doing at all the fund-raising meetings. Which I have to say was a huge weight off my mind.'

'Yes, but there's still a lot I don't know, especially this whole business of GDPR.'

'Well, it doesn't come into force until next May, so no need to worry at this point.'

'But it's so horribly complicated, I'll need all that time to get my head around it. And when I read about the enormous fines they intend to levy for any breach, I break out in a cold sweat!'

'Oh, Veronica,' Glenys reassured her. 'You're far too conscientious ever to commit a breach.'

'I ought to be more clued up, though – not just about all the data issues but about fund-raising in general. In fact, I had this mad idea just the other day that maybe I'd apply to do the Institute's Diploma.'

'Why d'you call it "mad"?'

'Well, just suggesting such a thing seems ludicrously ambitious for someone like me who's not even done any O-Levels. I mean, it's loads more work than just the one-day course, and it also costs a fair whack. On the other hand, if I could only get a proper qualification, I know it'd boost my confidence. But please be honest, Glenys – d'you think I'm overreaching myself?'

'Not at all. I admire your dedication. And it could lead to a whole new career.'

That, in truth, was her secret hope and dream: to reverse the past, move from the E-stream of her childhood by gaining some sort of academic credibility, even build a new life and future, independent of Colin. Indeed, when the idea had first occurred to her, she'd felt the same exhilaration as Alex himself induced in her – and the two were linked, of course, since he backed her decision one-hundred-percent and was even investigating possible grants and bursaries to cover her Diploma fees.

'It probably sounds pathetic,' she continued, keen to discuss the issue with Glenys and so gain another perspective, 'to a thorough-going professional like you, but even the most routine things like being given a formal syllabus and a reading-list, and expected to sit exams, gives me a sense of real excitement. I suppose because, in my teens and twenties, all that sort of stuff seemed only for *other*, clever people, and not for the likes of me.'

'That's not pathetic, Veronica – it's jolly enterprising. Still, you're right in that it *is* a major challenge and will involve a heck of a lot of study, which I guess could prove a problem with Colin the way he is. But, whatever you decide, you need to ensure that life's not all work and no play – and start *now,* I mean, before you take on the commitment of a demanding course. I hope you're managing to fit in some R and R?'

'Oh, yes. In fact, I'm going to the ballet on Thursday. It means missing choir, which I hate to do, but someone's offered me tickets for that particular evening.' She longed to confide in Glenys, change that anonymous 'someone' into Alex, and share all the bewitching details of the affair. But it would be extremely irresponsible to risk the slightest taint of gossip compromising his professional position.

'Frankly, I've never been a great ballet fan,' Glenys admitted, passing Veronica a plate of chocolate biscuits, 'but that's probably my loss.'

'Well, I've never even *seen* a ballet – except this one, *Sylvia*, which I've already watched online.' It had been part of her preparation for the evening, so she could familiarize herself with the story, and be able to make at least a few pertinent comments. 'The actual dancing was incredible – these fantastic leaps in the air and really fast pirouetting, and so much energy on the part of the principals, I just wished I could bottle it and use it like a tonic!'

What had struck her most about *Sylvia* was not just the dynamic dancing, but the ballet's emphasis on love, and, having watched Eros, the god of love, fire one of his potent arrows into the heroine, imbuing her with helpless love for Aminta, she had prayed to him that evening, enlisting his help in binding Alex to her with equal force - although she could hardly admit that to anyone without seeming as mad as two March hares and a hatter. She was learning fast, however, that tempestuously good sex was the strongest glue holding any couple together, and, indeed, the ballet's series of wedding-dances had even made her start imagining her own and Alex's nuptials in the not too distant future. But she simply mustn't dwell on Alex any longer, or she might be tempted to disclose too much, or just let something slip by lowering her guard.

'Actually, Sylvia herself reminded me of Megan – both such feisty females, and a match for anyone!'

'You're close to Megan, aren't you?'

Veronica nodded, deeply appreciative of the friendship. 'Yes, it happened almost by chance, because of sitting next to each other at rehearsals. But I've come to see she also provides all the things I lack myself – confidence, conviction, optimism, self-sufficiency.'

'You're too hard on yourself, Veronica. *We* all see you as confident and optimistic.'

How extraordinary, she thought, aware of the still yawning mismatch between her own self-deprecation and others' apparent approval. And, indeed, when Glenys had asserted last week that she, Veronica, had an almost perfect figure, she'd felt a total imposter, knowing Glenys had never seen the podgy, overweight child, rebuked by Den as 'a great galumphing elephant'. Admittedly, she had shed two stone just before her marriage, but the elephant refused to budge, remaining part of her self-image even now. 'But that's quite enough about me. I want to hear about Robert. The last thing you told me was that you'd been to Kew Gardens and had a steamy kiss in the Palm House!'

'Yes, it was so hot and humid in there, it seemed to turn him on, despite all those drugs that dampen his libido. Maybe they should include that in our general cancer-care package – regular visits to Kew!'

Veronica laughed, her mind shifting from tropical palm trees, as she suddenly noticed Glenys's smeary, crumb-littered kitchen surfaces, which had escaped her attention previously. Before she left, she must find time for a bit of housework, as she now endeavoured to do on all her visits, knowing how hard it was for those undergoing cancer treatment to keep abreast of the chores. Glenys still lived in the small, compact maisonette she had purchased with her second husband, over a decade ago, but, compact or not, it was still a lot to keep in good order.

'If you've finished your tea,' Glenys suggested, 'let's move to the other room. It's more comfortable in there and, anyway, I have some rather exciting news.'

'About Robert, you mean?'

'Yes, but it's so over-the-top, I hardly dare explain.'

'Oh, come on, Glenys. You can't spike my curiosity like that, only to clam up!'

'Promise you won't laugh?'

'Promise.'

Glenys laughed herself, an awkward, embarrassed laugh. 'We…. We're getting married.'

For a second, Veronica was too choked to speak, overcome by the news – news worthy of *Bohème* in its defiance of illness and death, and its insistence on love as the vital ingredient in life, taking precedence, by its very force, over prudence and common-sense. 'Oh, Glenys, that's fantastic!' she said, finally recovering her voice.

'I know it must seem ridiculously fast-track, when we've only known each other ten weeks. But having a terminal illness does tend to concentrate the mind! I mean, anything could happen to either of us, at any time, so we decided to tie the knot while we're still compos mentis and fit enough to say "I will".'

'It's a wonderful idea – absolutely inspired.'

'Not everyone's as charitable as you. Some will see it as stupidly impetuous, or even as tempting fate. So, we don't intend to broadcast it and we're planning a very simple wedding, with no one there but our two witnesses. Which is where you come in, Veronica. We wondered if you'd agree to be one of the witnesses, along with my brother Skip?'

'Oh, Glenys, I'd adore it!' she said, feeling touched, excited, honoured, all at once.

'We've decided on Chelsea Registry Office. It's an attractive building and nice and central, and has a truly lovely female registrar. We had to give quite a bit of notice to both our local registrars, and provide a load of documents, but Robert's sorted all that out, and we've fixed a provisional date for December the fifteenth. I just hope that's not too close to Christmas for you? If so, we still have time to change it.'

'No, the fifteenth sounds perfect.' Pearl wouldn't be starting her Christmas leave until the following week, so she could rely on her to stay with Colin all day, if necessary. Presumably, there'll be some sort of jamboree after the ceremony and, if nothing had actually been planned, she herself would lay it on as her wedding-gift to Glenys and Robert.

'And it's a Friday, so you won't need to miss choir.'

'Glenys, for heaven's sake, I'd miss every choir between now and then just for the joy of being part of the occasion.'

'Oh, Veronica, I do love you.'

Again, Veronica was lost for words. Countless times in the past, she'd heard female friends say 'Love you!' to each other – such a brief, casual phrase and one she'd assumed would never be addressed to *her*. Yet, these days, love seemed in plentiful supply – Alex's love, and Pearl's, Megan's deep affection and now Glenys's, as well. In some deeply gratifying way, she had forged a lasting bond with each and all of them, and every such bond endowed her life with more meaning and more joy – a word she'd never imagined using with reference to herself.

'But please *don't* miss choir, I beg you. They need you, Veronica. And, if you do decide to do the Diploma, you'll soon be more knowledgeable than me and Alex put together.'

‘That I don’t believe! But, hold on a sec – we simply must toast your engagement. I actually brought some sparkling elderflower wine for our lunch, without realizing we’d have anything as momentous as this to celebrate.’

Having fetched the wine from the fridge, she brought it into the sitting-room, along with two tall-stemmed wine-glasses. ‘Elderflower’s a new discovery – a sort of fruity champagne.’ *Alex’s* discovery she thought, suddenly zooming back to his elderflower-scented kiss, and the way his each and every kiss ignited some deep region of her being, as if transmuting the blood in her veins to the sparkliest, most potent champagne. ‘To Glenys and Robert,’ she said, clinking her glass to Glenys’s. ‘Wishing you the greatest possible happiness together.

‘And to Alex and me,’ she mouthed, adding another impassioned prayer to Eros: to pierce her lover’s heart with one of his supercharged arrows, ensuring his love for her could never fade or falter.

CHAPTER 25

'Blast! There's someone at the door. Promise not to move, Colin, while I go and see who it is.'

It wouldn't be the postman on a Sunday - perhaps someone collecting for charity, or asking her to sign a petition. She scooted along the hall, her expression changing from debonair to horrified, as she saw, standing on the doorstep, the most unwelcome visitor she could possibly imagine – a woman she recognized but looking rather different than at their previous encounter – now the epitome of glamour, in a Russian-style fur coat and six-inch heels. Fiona! The *stalker* – come to harry *her*, instead of poor, defenceless Alex.

'You won't know me,' the woman said, in a well-modulated but distinctly frosty tone.

'Well, actually I do,' Veronica countered, her fury rising on Alex's account. 'You used to work with someone I know, and, from what I gather, harassed him unmercifully.'

'I presume we're talking about Alex Sutherland?' Fiona gave an ill-disguised sneer.

Veronica nodded, too aghast to speak. How dare this brazen female turn up unannounced on a Sunday lunchtime?

'Let's get a few things straight, OK? I've never worked with Alex and frankly never would. I'm his wife, in point of fact – Louise Sutherland.'

Never, ever, had he mentioned a Louise. And, as for this upstart claiming to be his wife, that was downright provocation. 'He's divorced,' she retorted. 'I know that for a fact.'

'Facts for Alex are extremely malleable.' The woman gave a mocking laugh. 'I'm surprised you actually believed it, to be honest. It's just the line he takes when he fancies some new bird and is trying to get his leg over - although I have to say the little sluts are usually years younger than you, so I presume he's getting desperate.'

About to make an outraged protest, Veronica suddenly glimpsed Beryl watching from next door, only half-concealed behind the front-room curtains. Even if she couldn't hear, her neighbour might well pick up the gist of any acrimonious contention, and would have no compunction in broadcasting some garbled version of it to half the street. 'Look, I think you'd better leave,' she told the woman, through gritted teeth.

'Absolutely not! It took me long enough to track you down, for God's sake, and now I'm here, I intend to tell you a few home truths. I'm well aware you're having an affair with my husband, so don't even try to deny it, OK? But it's got to end this instant, do you understand? It's not *him* I'm concerned about. He's a serial womanizer and increasing age seems to have only made him worse, so now he can't resist anything in skirts. No - my concern is for my kids. They're only eight and ten and the last thing they need is any more disruption in their lives. It was bad enough with his last little piece on the side, & I simply won't put up with any more.'

Veronica could hardly make sense of this angry torrent of words. Alex always referred to his sons as teenagers - the elder due to leave school in the summer, the younger already embarked on his A-levels – not vulnerable little boys of eight and ten. But how could she trust this snake-in-the-grass, who might be lying through her teeth, out to do still more damage than she had already wreaked on Alex?

'Ron, Ron! Where *are* you?' Colin's petulant voice echoed down the hall. Without his beloved Pearl, who often took weekends off, he was invariably out of sorts, and all the more incensed right now because his lunch had been delayed.

'Look, you'd better come in,' she said, resentfully, trapped between her husband's recalcitrance and Beryl's still unabashed and persistently gleeful spying.

As the intruder stepped into the house, she all but collided with Colin, who was dragging himself along the hall, still unsteady on his two latest hospital-issue walking-sticks, and shrank in visible distaste from his shambling gait and baggy, food-stained clothes. Only then was Veronica aware of her own shabby tracksuit and messy hair – a total contrast to her uninvited visitor's soignée elegance. 'This is my husband, Colin,' she said, deeply embarrassed by the encounter, but trying to observe the proprieties, however appalling the situation.

'Oh, so *you're* married, too – which I didn't know. Not that it would give my husband the slightest pause for thought. If he fancies a piece of skirt, a minor matter like marriage-vows isn't likely to stop him using his wiles, not to mention his endless supply of freebies, to wheedle her into bed.'

'I'm hungry, Ron,' Colin wailed, still weaving about on his sticks. 'You said you were getting my dinner.'

'I'm afraid you'll have to wait. This lady's come to see me about a very urgent matter, so we need to be on our own for a while.'

'Who *is* she?' Colin peeved, recoiling from the visitor with as much obvious displeasure as she had displayed to him. 'I don't *want* her here.'

Any more than *I* do, Veronica thought, with increasing

desperation, equally pressured by the two of them. Did she attend to her husband, at the risk of goading this belligerent female into still more furious outbursts? 'Fiona, could you please wait a moment, while I ….'

'My name's Louise,' the woman cut in, 'so at least do me the courtesy of using it.'

'OK, Louise.' Veronica spoke the name grudgingly, still suspecting it was a cover-up. 'But first I need to settle Colin in the other room, then we can talk in private. And if can get you a coffee while I'm gone ….'

'No way! This is not a social visit, I'll have you know. I'm here to extract your solemn promise that you'll never lay eyes on my husband again or have any sort of contact with him whatever. And if you break that promise, I'll be forced to hire a detective to keep an eye on the pair of you.'

Deeply shocked by the threat of a detective, and even more so by Colin having overheard such incriminating words, Veronica could only play for time, so, taking her husband's arm, she manoeuvred him back to his own lair, the process maddeningly slow and cumbersome, as she wrestled with his sticks and cursed his persistent tendency to lurch and lose his balance.

'I want *Pearl*,' he bleated. 'Where's Pearl?'

'She'll be back tomorrow, darling.'

'But where is she now? I want her now.'

Only a family-sized carton of his favourite caramel-crunch ice-cream managed to allay his protests, along with the DVD of a newly released movie he particularly wanted to see (which she'd been deliberately keeping for an emergency situation – although never in a million years expecting so dire a crisis.) Even then, however, she left him with the deepest apprehension. Without her there to keep any eye on him, he might fall and break another bone, or raid the drinks-cupboard, or access the most blatant of the porn channels and play them at full volume.

She returned to her opponent so on edge, her voice sounded jerky and uncertain as she tried to stand her ground. 'You're asking me to promise something, when I have absolutely no way of knowing whether what you're saying is true or not. Alex swore blind you two were divorced and I had no reason to doubt it.'

'In fact, you have *every* reason,' the woman snapped, refusing to sit down, her hostile position in the centre of the room – arms akimbo, face a mask of fury – increasing Veronica's sense of dread. 'Don't *all* cheating husbands claim to be divorced, or say their wives don't understand them? Well, I understand Alex all too well. Just for the record, I'm his third wife and, fool that I was, I failed to learn any lessons from his two previous marriages, when, from all accounts, he played the field in just the same reckless manner. But I was very young when I met him and assumed I could make a leopard change his spots. I also wanted children and, although he was so much older, I saw that as an advantage, because he'd be stable and mature and thus a very good father. God Almighty – how wrong I was! Our younger son was only two,' she added, with a bitter laugh, 'when Alex started straying and he's rarely let up since. We only stay together for the kids. Which is not exactly fun for any of us, but still seems better than a very messy public split and all the subsequent disruption for the boys.'

Veronica was fast losing any sense of what was reality and what untruth. From all she'd read about stalkers, they could be either pitiful neurotics, in the grip of an obsession, or ruthless psychopaths, determined to damage innocent lives. So should she hear this woman out, or simply send her packing, threatening her in turn, not with a detective but with an instant call to the police? But hadn't Alex himself already shopped her to the cops, sworn blind that they were on the case and Fiona would never, ever harass him again? So, was the vindictive shrew simply switching targets and pouring out invective on another hapless victim?

But, suppose she *was* a genuine wronged wife? She certainly sounded bitter and must be pretty distraught – if not close to cracking up - to spew out all this private, personal stuff to a virtual stranger. And what about that reference to the 'freebies', which had certainly hit home, since how could she, Veronica, deny the expensive treats and tickets she had accepted from her lover? Yet, if he was divorced, why shouldn't he share the perks of his profession by dint of generous largesse to his friends? For all she knew, *his* account could be the true one: that Fiona/ Louise/ whoever was a disgruntled colleague, out to get revenge. 'Look, I've no idea whatever whether you're telling me a pack of lies or ….'

'For God's sake, woman!' was the irascible retort. 'Do you want me to go home and fetch my marriage certificate?' With a snort of derision, she added in a contemptuous tone, 'But what I *can* show you, here and now, are some recent photos of our sons, so you can see them for yourself. And, since you're so obviously suspicious, all of them are date-stamped, which should clear up any doubt about their ages.'

As she swiped a succession of photos on her phone, Veronica was confronted, over and over, with two miniature versions of Alex, so similar to him in their features, colouring and general appearance, she could no longer doubt they *were* his and, yes, judging by the date-stamps, most definitely still *little* boys. Seeing their vulnerably innocent faces, her first thought was horror at the prospect of breaking up a family. Throughout her own childhood, she had lived in terror of her mother abandoning her, to live 'unencumbered', as she put it, with one of her many lovers. The dread had been so intense, only a monster would inflict it on this pair of hapless children.

Wrestling with her conscience, she was suddenly aware of a disturbance outside the door, as Colin struggled to come in, all but reeling in an effort to keep his balance, and in the grip of a racking fit of hiccoughs that rendered him speechless and clearly close to panic.

Rushing to his aid, she steered him to the sofa and supported his shaking body, as it erupted again and again with the pitilessly insistent noise. Hiccoughs were the stuff of farce, yet she herself was close to tears, not of laughter, but of chagrin and humiliation. How could she possibly continue this life-and-death exchange, in the presence of a husband rendered incoherent by those non-stop disabling spasms? His last bout, a month ago, had lasted the entire day, on and off and, if this attack was similar, she had no option but to stay with him, to ensure he came to no harm – hardly the appropriate setting for a conversation that involved her whole future happiness, now set against that of Alex's sons. Yet the very fact she was committed to a husband meant she had no right to be seeing Alex at all - least of all in these new circumstances - thus proving her accuser's point.

However, the woman herself had clearly reached the conclusion that any further discourse was impossible, because, turning on her heel, she marched to the door, her cruelly spiked high heels making angry little indentations right across the carpet. 'I was hoping we could thrash this out in private, just between the two of us, but since that's not on, I have no option but to contact my solicitor. You'll be hearing from him soon, OK?'

And with that – and no goodbye – she stalked down the hall

and slammed the front door behind her, the noise reverberating through Veronica's head, competing with the heartless gunfire of the unremitting hiccoughs.

Yes, her world was erupting, in discord, in bombardment, and all she could do was shut her eyes, sink down into the stained fabric of the sofa and, still holding Colin firmly, in an attempt to reassure him, feel his explosive spasms throbbing though her own body, along with the torment of these new, raw, unexpected, Alex-inflicted wounds.

CHAPTER 26

The illuminated clock-hands mocked her with their callous slowness. Not quite two a.m., yet it seemed she'd been lying sleepless for an entire despairing week. But, every time she shut her eyes, Alex's two sons appeared behind her eyelids, their fatherless faces accusing and rebuking her. She longed to phone him, not just in the probably hopeless hope that he could prove Louise/Fiona wrong, but simply to hear his voice and feel they were still connected, soul and body, that his desire for her, his love for her, were in no way dimmed. Yet she dared not get in touch, for fear that some detective might already be on the case, listening in to her every phone-call, monitoring each email. And, as for the ballet, a mere four days off now, how could she possibly drive to Sussex for a long weekend with Alex when his furious wife was on the warpath?

Yet the arrangements were still all in place. Pearl had willingly agreed to come and stay from this Thursday till the Sunday, glad of the extra money, and having long ago sorted out the complicated business of providing alternative care and company for her daughters – or four of them, at least. The fifth and youngest, had pleaded with her mother to let her stay at Clapham, too, thrilled by the prospect of living for four days in a big house with a garden and a tree to climb and the rare, unalloyed delight of having her own bedroom, rather than sharing with four siblings. Veronica had readily championed the idea - which made it all the more impossible for her to cancel now, when the child was so excited. Even if she cancelled but offered to pay Pearl anyway, not only would Pearl refuse (opposed on principal to taking any favours), but Kerissa would still be bitterly disappointed. Indeed, it would be patently unfair to all concerned to expect Pearl to change her plans at such short notice, so she, Veronica, would have to stick to her original proposal and get out of the house on some other pretext – go to a hotel, perhaps, or stay with poor, long-suffering Megan. However, the thought of relating the whole sorry saga to Megan was dismaying in the extreme, because, although her friend had always encouraged her affair, she had also strongly warned against the danger of living in a totally unrealistic romantic bubble, inspired by *La Bohème*.

The memory of that enchanted evening was almost too painful to endure, and she groped out her hand in the darkness and switched on the bedside light, to dispel the murky shadows in the room – shadows similar to those now darkening her whole life. Megan, she reflected, was just too down-to-earth to understand the pull of passion - a pull like the tides: powerful, irresistible and dictated by some force of nature.

On an impulse, she sprang out of bed and opened her top dressing-table drawer, where she'd stowed the transparent black-lace nightdress bought for the Sussex trip, along with a new matching bra-and-pants set, even more provocative than those she'd bought for her first rendezvous with Alex. As she held the nightie against her body, the thought that he would never see her in it, never peel if off with audaciously slow and sensuous hands – worse, that all such intimate encounters were now totally out of the question, was so unutterably bleak, she gave up on sleep altogether, banged the drawer shut, and dragged herself downstairs. If she was going to lie awake till morning, then better to keep busy and put in some work on her online fund-raising course.

It proved impossible to concentrate, however, because fund-raising brought yet more reminders of Alex, who was now so enmeshed in the warp and woof of her life, it seemed every train of thought led back to him. If some surgeon were to cut her open, he would find her lover's name printed through and through her every cell and fibre, as if she were a stick of rock with an everlasting 'Alex', decreed to last till the final lick.

She paced up and down the hall, regret and loss suddenly giving place to fury at the thought of his double-dealing, the way he'd disrupted his innocent family without a thought for their future or their peace of mind, woven a web of deceit, like a cunning spider intent on entrapping them - as well as her - in its relentlessly sticky coils. Yet, every bit as potent as her anger was a persistent desperation to see Fiona as the guilty party – not Louise, not a legal wedded wife, but some neurotic interloper who would stop at nothing to incriminate Alex, including photoshopping those pictures of her sons. She continued wrestling in her mind between the two positions, longing for certainty, for clarity, for a return to the blithe contentment of just two days ago.

Hearing a crash from Colin's room, she rushed to investigate, relieved to find he'd simply knocked the clock off his bedside table, rather than fallen out of bed himself - one of her constant fears. And the noise hadn't even woken him, as he continued peacefully sleeping, Peter clutched tightly against his chest. Suddenly, a new and different fury erupted in her mind, Lava-flows of indignation now directed against his deep affection for a dilapidated toy Dalmatian – a devotion never shown to *her* - along with bitter resentment of his sexual timidity and complete ignorance of how to use his mouth or fingers in the ingeniously erotic ways that Alex did, in addition to a long-buried rancour at him losing interest in sex so early in their marriage, with no reference to *her* desires.

Wresting Peter from his arms, she hurled the creature across the room, feeling a reckless satisfaction as he landed with a thud on his stupid, grubby face. Yet, immediately, she deplored her own base violence, feared she was becoming inhuman, venting her rage on a stuffed animal, because life had been cruel to *her*. Horrified, she went to retrieve him, and stood clasping him to her chest, tears streaming down her face.

Then, all at once, a horrific scene flashed in to her mind – a scene she had deliberately censored for thirty-eight years, determined to block it out of her consciousness, deny it ever happened. Yet, despite those decades of denial, every detail was still unequivocally sharp, as the appalling incident replayed in her mind: Colin lashing out at his son in a sudden fit of fury and frustration, on a blisteringly hot, temper-fraying August day – a day etched in black on the calendar, despite the flood of golden sunshine pouring from a febrile sky. All that week, the boy had been unusually distressed, plagued with a bad attack of eczema that had erupted on his face and chest in an itching, burning rash - a new cross to bear on top of his more serious disabilities. When his ceaseless wailing and writhing showed no sign of letting up, despite her own frantic efforts to soothe and distract the boy, Colin's patience had finally reached breaking-point.

She heard, again, the vicious slap reverberating through the room, as he aimed his hand against Tom's already red and swollen face; heard, again, Tom's howls of discomfort change to roars of pain. So forceful was the slap, the boy's face was deeply imprinted with the outline of Colin's hand, the abrasion slimy with snot and tears. She, too, had felt knocked off-balance on that scorching, shameful day, as if Colin had turned on *her* next and she was floundering helpless on the floor, torn between comforting her stepson, forbidding her husband any further access to him, and ringing the GP, to ensure no lasting damage had been done.

No – impossible. The very thought induced new fear because, if word should get around that Tom's father was capable of violence, Social Services would be on the case immediately, remove the child and put him into care. And she knew instinctively that, whatever else, she must save him from further disruption in his life, ensure he never suffered the terror of his second mother disappearing, in addition to his birth-mother. If he were shoved into care, no one would give him the individual attention he'd come to enjoy, and even expect: the nonsense-rhymes she recited each day, the nightly ritual of *This Little Piggy*, as she strove to wiggle his poor, stiff, distorted toes, before tucking him into bed. And, since he'd began to trust her, at last, after his initial hostile suspicion, the timing would be fatal and might threaten his entire future sense of security.

So, whatever the horror of Colin's violence – and she'd glimpsed his expression of incandescent rage as he hit out at a disabled six-year-old - she'd had no choice but to stand by her husband and hush up the whole crisis. That process had involved a host of lies and subterfuge, as she contrived to keep Tom away from all medical appointments and all sessions with physios and occupational therapists, until the livid purple bruise had completely faded, otherwise they'd be forced to take action in accordance with what they saw as their basic duty of safeguarding. Despite the strain, the plan had basically succeeded, thank God, and no one till this day ever suspected what had happened. Colin himself, though, must have felt a deep unease, since, from that day on, he had withdrawn from any part in bringing up his son and left the task to her - which, in a way, was easier.

Only now had the memory broken through her self-imposed embargo, and so distressing was its impact, she vowed to seal it over once more, bury it in the deepest vault of her mind, never again to be uncovered. Otherwise, continuing to care for Colin throughout his eighties - maybe even nineties - would be fraught with newly resurrected resentment, making it still harder than normal. If Pearl saw him as an 'angel' and a 'pussycat', then so be it. It was certainly far easier to wipe an angel's bottom than that of an aggressive brute.

Her mind still frantically churning, she crept back to Colin's room, found him breathing in the same deep, even manner, with the same tranquilly blank expression. Dementia could be a friend, in some ways, by erasing unwelcome memories, simply plucking them out of existence, and she almost longed to be equally disoriented, so that she could annihilate Fiona/Louise, along with her two young boys, and reinstall Alex as a long-divorced man, living a bachelor existence with two all-but-grown-up sons.

Working on autopilot, she smoothed the covers on Colin's bed, as she frequently did on her nightly checks on him, before tucking him in more securely. Normally, she'd ensure Peter was beside him, but she had left the dog on the dressing-table, from where he seemed to meet her gaze with an imploring, soulful eye. On impulse, she took him back to her own room and, realizing sleep was out of the question yet too exhausted to use the time in any useful fashion, she climbed wearily into bed again and just lay quietly with Peter in her arms.

'I'm sorry', she whispered to the poor, shabby, impotent creature. 'What I did was unforgivable.' And, as she cradled him against her body in a gesture of apology, Peter's flaccid, feeble paws seemed to undergo an extraordinary transformation, transmuting to Alex's skilfully sensuous, ever-inventive hands, as he clasped her close and safe against his body.

CHAPTER 27

'Now, I'd like us all to be gerbils,' Katy instructed, 'so imagine you have lovely twitchy noses and long, expressive whiskers.' She demonstrated with some exaggeratedly exuberant grimaces and a series of shrill *ee-ee-ee-ee-ee* sounds. 'Right, can everyone join in, please.'

The *ee-ee-ee-ee-ees* were soon drowned in giggles, as members of the choir endeavoured to out-twitch each other. The general air of hilarity was increased this evening by the fact it was both Keith and Catherine's birthdays and the proceedings had begun with two rousing renditions of *Happy Birthday*, one for each of them, followed by *S/He's a Jolly Good Fellow.*

However dutifully she tried to join in, Veronica's voice seemed to have disappeared completely, along with Alex himself, as if all her months of progress as a singer had been annihilated at a stroke and she was back to kindergarten status, capable of little more than a discordant, tuneless croak. Yet only fairly recently had she come to regard singing as a natural, God-given ability - a notion that now seemed arrogant, if not plain deluded. As for being a gerbil, the whole exercise struck her as so stupidly childish, she could barely believe that once – indeed, just last week - she had relished this very sense of becoming a carefree kid again and indulging in uninhibited play. Without Alex in her life, play, fun, indulgence, or even any grain of future happiness, was simply inconceivable. In fact, such was her misery, she'd resolved to miss this rehearsal, as she'd originally planned to do on account of the ballet. Megan, though, had overruled her – and in no uncertain terms. 'Yes, you can come and stay – no problem with that - I completely understand you don't want to disrupt the arrangement with Pearl. But I insist we go to choir together first – and no arguments, OK? However badly Alex has behaved, you mustn't let him destroy all the other good things in your life, and the choir is one of those, no question.'

Had been, she thought bitterly, but now there seemed nothing good left in the whole arid universe. What really rankled was, when she'd finally plucked up the courage to give Alex a ring, he'd tried to deceive her yet again, apparently ignorant of the fact that his wife had turned up on her doorstep and put her right about the facts. So, there he was, pathetically claiming that he'd had to cancel their Sussex trip because he'd gone down with a really nasty virus, when a quick check with his PA confirmed that, far from languishing in bed with a high fever, he had rescheduled an important meeting for this very day of the ballet - the tickets, no doubt, passed on to another of his women. Maddened by his deceit, she had rung him back a mere ten minutes later and confronted him with Louise's revelations. Even then, he had tried to excuse himself: admitting yes, he had lied, but only because he'd been driven to it by his wife's intransigence and by the fact that she, Veronica, had proved so irresistibly appealing. Such fulsome flattery, she realized only now, was one of the tools he'd employed right from their first meeting – just another way, presumably, to ensure he got his leg over, to use Louise's own crude term. And, as for his wife's intransigence, wouldn't any wife be intransigent in face of serial adultery?

Her thoughts were interrupted by the chorus of *ee-ee-ee-ee-ees* rising on all sides, still punctuated with giggles and accompanied by ever more extravagant twitches. She joined in reluctantly and only because Megan was standing right beside her and nudging her if she failed to participate. Yet, never before had Larks Ascending - normally, a haven of pleasure - seemed so puerile and pointless. And those few uncongenial members, whom she usually accepted as just a mild irritation, now set her nerves jangling like the screech of chalk on a blackboard. Although, when it came to screeches, Barry's near-hysterical ee-ee-ee-ee-ees outdid everyone and everything.

'The reason we do this,' Katy explained, 'is because *ee-ee-ee-ee* is a closed vowel and so puts the mouth and tongue in the correct position to find our head-voice in the easiest way. And that enables us to sing higher notes without the risk of damage to our vocal cords, and also increases vocal flexibility and helps loosen us all up before we start our singing proper. So, just two more minutes, Gerbils, but make sure you give it all you've got this time!'

Barry needed no such encouragement, but even Megan's *ee-ee-ee-ee-ees* were so ear-splitting and her twitches so exuberantly comic, Veronica was forced to make an effort herself, however much she might long to be on her own, away from this circus, so she could lick her wounds in private.

'Brilliant!' Katy declared. 'In fact, that was so well done, I want you all to give yourselves a hug.' She demonstrated by wrapping her arms around her chest and squeezing tight, repeating several times, 'I love *me*, I love *me*', with an expression of unbearably self-satisfied contentment.

Although everyone else followed suit, Veronica found it impossible to say she loved herself. She loved *Alex* – still did, despite his treachery. Yet because his fervent embraces would no longer be forthcoming, self-hugs, it appeared, were all she could expect now.

She glanced up at the artwork on the walls of the church hall, done by the kids at the church-run primary school, and which reflected the changing seasons. In spring, there'd been nesting birds perched on budding trees, in summer, beach-scenes, with wonky deckchairs and out-of-proportion sandcastles, in autumn, leaves so riotously red they beggared all belief, but now, in cruel December, only bleak, snow-stifled landscapes and gauntly naked trees. Despite the cosy fug in the hall, the cold of the collages had crept into her very bones, and she was shivering as Katy announced, 'OK, it's time we learned a new song, so I want you to choose between two alternatives: *You've Got a Friend* and *Burning Love*. I'll play each in turn on the backing-track, then we'll have a rough show of hands to assess which you prefer.'

As You've Got a Friend began resounding through the room, half the choir immediately joined in, seemingly word-perfect and note-perfect, some clapping enthusiastically, or even gyrating around in time to the tune. Only she, the dunce, had never heard of either song, nor even of the singer on the track - someone called James Taylor, who was apparently a household name, as well known as the Beatles. Clearly, she'd been plunged back to her first weeks at Larks Ascending, when, lacking all knowledge and any shred of confidence, she'd assumed she could - and would - never sing in tune and was so pitifully unmusical she had no right to be in a choir at all.

And *Burning Love* was worse, not just because everyone, again, seemed familiar with the song, but because she couldn't help interpreting its every word as addressed from her to Alex, as she assured him of her burning, flaming, sizzlingly intemperate love. But all that was in the past now - love, sex, confidence, self-respect - whereas the present barren winter held only bitter pain and disillusion. And, once the choir had voted for *Burning Love*, as against *You've Got a Friend,* she could hardly bear to learn the lyrics, stressing as they did the full flame of scorching passion, in contrast to her present ice-cold shred of an existence.

'Veronica, you really must stop over-reacting like this. OK, Alex has proved himself a shit, but, even so, that's not the end of the world. You have to learn to survive these things, to quote your favourite choir-song – yes, even if you're betrayed and sold down the river. It's happened to me loads of times, but the secret is not to let the buggers destroy you. You pick yourself up, dust yourself down and simply move on in your life.'

Veronica had never felt more out of sympathy with Megan – indeed, never heard her sound so sharp. How could she 'simply move on in her life', when life itself seemed no longer worth living?

'And I insist we have something to eat, OK?'

'I've told you, I'm not hungry.'

'But I am and you ought to be. It looks as if you're losing weight already, judging by your haggard face – and frankly, Alex isn't worth it. Why starve yourself to death just because that bastard has had his comeuppance? Anyway, I've already made us quite a decent salad, with avocado and walnuts and mushrooms and what-have-you and, if you like to come and join me in the kitchen. I'll rustle up an omelette to go with it.'

Reluctantly, Veronica dragged herself up from the sofa, although, once the omelettes were ready, the mere smell of cheese and butter was enough to turn her stomach. She sat toying with a lettuce leaf, while Megan tucked in heartily, alternating each mouthful with more unwanted advice.

'The problem is, if you don't mind me saying so, is that, right from the beginning, you ratcheted up this love of yours to an impossible degree. It was the Greatest Love of all Time, outshining Tristan and Isolde, Romeo and Juliet, and every other lover known to history. Except it *wasn't*. Alex was just a thoughtless bloke, long past even the excuse of a mid-life crisis, using you for his own selfish ends. You ought to feel fury with him – damn him to hell, rather than ache for his return. But I've noticed you find anger very difficult, so you direct it all inwards and it becomes self-destructive depression.'

Veronica shrugged in annoyance to hear Megan now sounding like some unpaid therapist, but she was clearly in full flow, and impossible to stop.

'I want you to think of the *good* things, instead on focusing on all you've lost. At least you had the courage to move out of your marital rut and embark on an affair at all, and that's real progress, considering how tied down you were by your caring role, with no spark of fun or sex to ever brighten your existence. In fact, you've always had great courage, if only you could see it. I mean, bringing up a disabled child must have taken huge amounts of guts, and, just when you'd nursed him through his final cancer, you were then landed with Colin, and had to cope with all *his* deficiencies.'

She tried to force down a small morsel of avocado, its rich creamy taste inducing another twinge of nausea. 'Oh, come off it, Megan, any half-decent wife or stepmother would do those things.'

'No, they bloody wouldn't! *I* wouldn't, for a start. And, from what you said, even Tom's own mother couldn't cope with him. And, as for Colin, he simply washed his hands of his son and left you to be both Mum and Dad. And you never credit yourself for the fact that, during all those years, you were solely responsible for every single aspect of Tom's life, which must have been a hell of a lot of responsibility. But things have changed, thank God, and you no longer have that sort of burden, so you simply must move on.'

Megan paused a moment to remove a piece of walnut-shell from her salad, but any respite was short-lived, since she returned instantly to the attack. 'There are other people now, to help you out, love, and I don't just mean Pearl, who's obviously a godsend. I'm talking about life in general, and I suppose the choir's a sort of metaphor for what I'm trying to say. You see, none of us sing solo, which means if we want to take an extra breath, or even a real break, that's OK, because the others will fill in for us. And even singing a wrong note is not a problem, because most people will sing the right one and cover up our mistake. And I've come to see that's true of many things – we're *not* entirely alone, and life shouldn't be a constant struggle, as it appears to have been for you. And, talking of mistakes, they're simply part of life, along with uncertainty and shitty men and all the endless stuff we can't control, like illness, or the weather, or the whole political scene, or even trains and buses running on time. We have to just accept all that, and also accept that none of it will kill us. In fact, in your case, it can make you stronger, as you develop your own needs and opinions and stop being such a sponge, soaking up everyone else's views and values.'

She winced at the description, but Megan was on her hobbyhorse, even ignoring her omelette, to make her points more vehemently. 'You have huge strengths already, as I keep on telling you, but, instead, you're always going on about your shortcomings. Take the Fund-Raising, as just one small example. You're doing a great job there and everyone applauds you for it, yet you keep saying you're not up to the role. As far as I can see, though, you've learned loads in a short space of time and given it everything you've got, and that role will carry on, even in Alex's absence, as will the choir itself, of course.'

Veronica abandoned the avocado and crunched a walnut instead, the bitter taste of its skin more in tune with her mood than Megan's saccharine platitudes. But her friend seemed determined to rally her, regardless, and now set off on a new tack. 'And don't forget Sebastian. You stood up to him, refused to let him mess you about any longer, and proved you didn't need him. Well, the same applies to Alex. You can learn from the whole debacle by ensuring that, next time, you choose a man who cares about you and puts your interests first.'

'You say "next time", Megan, as if men are lining up in droves for me to have affairs with them!'

'Yes, but you do have libido, and that's quite rare at our age. I doubt if *I* could be bothered to undo as much as my top button, if George Clooney himself was standing naked in my bedroom, literally gagging for it! And lots of older women don't feel the slightest tingle of desire, so you're blessed in that respect. And, believe you me, your libido won't simply vanish. If it's there, it's there, and I assure you there'll be other men.'

I don't want other men, Veronica didn't say – for me there's only Alex. But Megan had sowed a seed of new anxiety in her mind: perhaps there was something wrong with her to be sexually avid at the age of almost sixty. Maybe she'd inherited a gene from Den and would spend her older age leapfrogging from one loser's bed to another, becoming more pitiable and sluttish with each one. The prospect was so unlikely, even comic, she suddenly burst out laughing, the sound jolting her as much as Megan.

'That's better, love! I thought you'd never laugh again.'

She refrained from saying that her laughter was perilously close to tears, as she reflected on the fact that poor Den had died in her mid-fifties of a heart attack, and so hadn't even had the chance to enjoy a lecherous old age, still flashing her substantial boobs at randy pensioners. The memory brought a different type of grief, in that she'd been so busy with Tom at the time, she hadn't put enough thought or effort into her mother's funeral.

But nothing would stop Megan from pursuing her upbeat line. 'And just because it was Alex who introduced you to opera and ballet and the like, doesn't mean you can't enjoy them without him being there. London's bursting at the seams with theatres and galleries and exhibitions and, now you have Pearl, there's nothing to stop you exploring them all on your own, rather than insisting you have to have a man in tow to make anything worthwhile. OK, it might feel odd at first - I remember it did for me, after my first divorce - but you soon get used to being more self-sufficient. And to start you off, I've taken the liberty of booking three tickets for a ballet at Sadlers Wells, because I've come up with a plan: I want you and me and my niece to go together to see Matthew Bourne's *Cinderella*. Then, at least you can claim to have seen your first ballet and, as for Lavinia, she's a ballet fan already, so she's chuffed by the idea.'

Despite her annoyance with Megan's sermonizing, Veronica was deeply touched by her friend's sheer thoughtfulness. 'Oh, Megan, that's really sweet of you – and incredibly generous, too.'

'Not generous at all. It's something I'm dying to see myself. Have you heard of Matthew Bourne?'

Veronica shook her head, ashamed, as usual, of her ignorance.

'He's a true original, brings his own take to everything he does. In his *Swan Lake*, for instance, all the swans are male – really menacing creatures, not the pretty little frilly swans in tutus we're more used to. It caused a sensation when it was first performed, and his *Cinderella* is equally offbeat, with the traditional Prince in the fairy-tale becoming a dishy but traumatized RAF pilot. Prokoviev wrote the score in the Second World War, you see, so Bourne relocated the plot to the London Blitz, complete with demolished buildings, scouring searchlights and even a bombing-raid that apparently reduces the stage to rubble and flames!'

'Lord, that should be a sight!'

'Well, whatever else, it'll be different. And it's been seven years since the last production, so tickets were like gold-dust. I just hope you're free on January 6, which is the one and only date I could get three seats together in a row. I'm afraid it's a Saturday matinee and I know Saturdays are difficult because Pearl is off at weekends, but the Box-Office guy said if I didn't book them there and then, they might well have been snapped up by the time I rang back.'

'Oh, Megan, I'd adore to go! You *are* a sweetheart. And don't worry about Pearl. She's so easy-going, I'm sure she'll oblige, especially as she's having the whole of Christmas and New Year off.' Frankly, having Pearl at all was little short of miraculous, all the more so in her vacant, Alex-less future, when otherwise she'd be stuck with Colin, on her own, each and every day. But why stew in self-pity any longer, when Megan was being so decent – not just laying on this supper and providing a refuge for these desolate few days, but invariably supportive and willing to pick up the pieces when things went wrong? OK, her friend just couldn't comprehend how deeply Alex had wounded her, but she was still a friend – and a sterling friend at that, one who genuinely cared, even if they didn't always see eye to eye.

'I'm afraid it won't be as swish as Convent Garden – no Royal Boxes or chilled Moet in the Champagne Bar! But I reckon the three of us can still have a good time. And, anyway, I've been wanting you to meet Lavinia for ages.'

'It's a wonderful idea and something to look forward to.'

'Yes, you can leave the Old Year behind and start the New one on a happier note.'

Although Veronica doubted that anything would ever be happy again, she owed it to Megan to be a less miserable guest, to finish her supper - even show some sign of pleasure in it - savour her wine and try her hopeless best to damn Alex to hell, to use Megan's own words, rather than ache for his return.

And Megan must have picked up her change of mood, because, all at once, she broke into *I Will Survive*, singing the opening lines in her husky but still tuneful voice.

Veronica chipped in with the next lines, although more from duty than conviction, since any sense of strength and survival seemed as unlikely as a hailstorm in July.

Yet, as Megan cocked her own head into a position of jaunty confidence, Veronica followed suit, determined to *look* the part of an indomitable survivor, whatever her drained, depleted mind might actually be signalling.

CHAPTER 28

'Glenys and Robert, today you celebrate one of life's greatest moments and give recognition to the worth and beauty of love, as you join together in matrimony.'

Although the ceremony had barely started, Veronica was already struggling to maintain a calm exterior, overwhelmed as she was by the stark reality of a bride and groom, both battling terminal cancer, embarking on the journey of marriage, with no notion of how much – or little – time they might have together as man and wife. Yet both looked radiant. She herself had played her part in effecting Glenys's transformation, insisting on taking her shopping (as Megan had done for *her*, pre-*La Bohème*), and eventually helping her choose this ice-blue, full-length, figure-hugging sheath-dress, which did indeed look stunning. Her hair – or rather lack of it – had posed more of a problem, but they had finally settled for a matching lace turban, complete with a short but frothy veil that concealed the ugly rashes on Glenys's neck. And she personally had taken charge of her make-up, disguising her friend's pallor and dark circles with a variety of natural-looking concealers and foundations. Robert, for his part, was still unhealthily pale, but he, too, looked dapper in a smart grey suit and ice-blue tie, completing the picture of a perfectly matched bride and groom.

Yet the pair were eclipsed by the celebrant herself - not the usual faceless official Veronica had expected, but a tall, willowy woman, with a cascade of ash-blonde hair rippling down her back. Despite her colouring, she was actually Italian, a ravishingly pretty Neapolitan by the name of Gabriella. And even the venue bore little resemblance to some of the bleakly characterless registry offices Veronica had seen in her time. This room might be small, but it was supremely elegant, the shimmering gold ruched curtains seeming to glow in the soft light of the chandeliers, and a heady scent wafting from the elaborate flower-arrangement of roses and Madonna lilies.

'Robert Arthur,' Gabriella pronounced, in her lilting voice, 'do you take Glenys Helen to be your wife?'

'I do.'

As he spoke, Veronica looked up at the groom, whom she had met only briefly before, running into him occasionally on her frequent visits to Glenys. All four of the wedding principals had, in fact, twice arranged to meet before the wedding, for the specific purpose of getting to know each other, but the plan had gone awry both times, first, because of Robert's latest medical crisis (now fortunately resolved) and then because Glenys's chemotherapy had been suddenly rescheduled for the day of their second get-together. So, it was not until today – the day of the wedding itself - that they all four had the chance to exchange more than a few words.

'Do you promise, Robert, to love, honour, cherish and protect her, forsaking all other and holding only unto her?'

The phrase 'forsaking all other and holding only unto her' stirred such bitter memories of Alex's betrayal, Veronica had to make a ferocious effort to bar him from the room. This was a joyous, celebratory day, so any taint of grief or loss must be strictly prohibited from tarnishing so golden an occasion.

Gabriella now addressed the bride. 'Glenys Helen, do you take Robert Arthur to be your husband?'

'I do.'

Glenys's voice was unwaveringly strong, as she smiled up at her groom, then each in turn recited the vows they personally had written.

‘I, Robert Arthur, take you, Glenys Helen, to be my wife, my partner and my one true love. I promise to laugh with you in times of happiness, and to strengthen you in times of need. Through the best and the worst, I will trust you, honour you and be faithful to you. I commit myself to you for the rest of my life.’

Before Robert had even finished, Veronica was wrestling once more with inappropriate emotions. Having kicked Alex from her mind, she was now confronting Colin and her own wedding forty years ago. Far from being the happiest day of her life, she could remember only how Daisy’s tragic death had black-bordered the occasion, and how loudly the hammer-blows of Den’s disapproval of her daughter marring a man twenty-two years older, with a seriously disabled son, had resounded through the day. And, as for Colin laughing with her in times of happiness, she could barely recall any such times, let alone any laughter, only the many ‘times of need’, when, in fact, he had signally failed to strengthen her. But envy and resentment must be as strictly barred today as unhappiness and regret, whatever self-control it might demand.

Once Glenys had spoken her version of the vow and the couple had exchanged rings, Gabriella called on Skip and Veronica to give the readings chosen by the bridal couple. As both rose to their feet and stood side by side, Veronica felt distinctly overdressed compared with the casually tieless Skip, who wore a crumpled jacket the colour of dried-up mustard, teamed with designer stubble and hair in serious need of a cut. She, however, had felt duty-bound to make a splash for Glenys’s special day, and had followed Megan’s advice to buy new, flattering clothes for her own self-gratification and not simply for Alex’s sake. So, in a conscious effort to change her thinking, she had foresworn the sexy styles and provocatively vibrant colours that had seemed to please her lover, in favour of a subtly understated dress-and-jacket in the palest shade of duck-egg, that complemented but by no means competed with Glenys's stronger, more shimmery blue.

With his trademark cheery grin, Skip unfolded his sheet of paper for the reading. She still felt stupidly shy of him, despite his easy-going nature, and had been struck when they met by how little he resembled his sister, his sandy hair and greenish eyes a contrast to Glenys's darker colouring. She and Skip were, in fact, the only two guests, because, exhausted by their cancer-treatment, both bride and groom had more or less insisted on a small-scale, low-key wedding, as requiring far less energy to organize than a more elaborate affair. Besides, the minute they started inviting people, those not included might feel piqued or resentful, so, deliberately, they had kept the occasion a secret. Glenys also feared that if word should get around, some might criticise the very notion of their marriage as intemperately hasty or ridiculously romantic. Far from being either, to Veronica it seemed utterly right and, anyway, speed was of the essence when the future was so uncertain and when both needed to be well enough to go through with the ceremony, rather than risk a relapse on either of their parts by any sort of delay. In fact, she felt deeply privileged to be a witness at all and, although she wondered why, of all the people Glenys could have chosen, it happened to be her, she viewed the honour as compensation for her own unhappy wedding-day. It also confirmed her recent insight that love did not have to be romantic and exclusive, but could be a precious bond between friends as much as partners. Yet, once Robert began his reading, her shaming stabs of self-pity resurfaced with his words.

'Now, we will feel no rain, for each of us is shelter for the other. Now, we will feel no cold, for each of us is warmth for the other. Now, there will be no loneliness, for each of us is soulmate to the other ….'

So overpowering was her longing for such closeness, she could barely concentrate and had to call up Megan's constant reminders that dependency and lovesickness could be highly dangerous rather than empowering. Yet she had learned from Alex how central passionate love was in the context of art and literature and, despite her own heartbreak, still regarded it as inherently superior to cool, clear-eyed common-sense. At this particular moment, however, it was clear-eyed coolness she needed, as she started her own reading, the final part of Phillip Pullman's *The Amber Spyglass*. Every time she'd practised it at home, she had broken down in tears, because she was addressing it to Robert, on Glenys's behalf, yet tragically aware of Glenys's situation in committing herself to a marriage that might last only months. In a last-ditch hope of a cure, the hospital had enrolled her in the trial of an experimental and possibly dangerous new drug, and she was just one of twenty terminally ill and increasingly desperate guinea-pigs, determined to clutch at any straw.

She commanded her voice to stay steady as she recited the first line. 'I will love you forever, whatever happens. Till I die and after I die ….'

Even Skip looked moved, his usual roguish grin now replaced by a sombre expression.

'And, when I find my way out of the dead,' Veronica continued, 'I'll drift about forever, till I find you again. I'll be looking for you every moment, every single moment …' Catching sight of Robert's anguished face, she all but stumbled on the next few words. 'And when we do find each other again, we'll cling together so tight that nothing and no one will ever tear us apart ….'

When she finally returned to her seat, she gave silent thanks that she had got through to the end, with only one brief catch in her voice. But there was no time for reflection, because all four principals were now instructed to sign the Register, which they did seated at the elegant inlaid-walnut desk. Then the Registrar took over – a plumpish, grey-haired, cosy-looking woman, in contrast to the glamorously slender Gabriella. Once the paperwork was completed, the latter took centre-stage once more, to make a few concluding remarks and send off the bridal couple with an uplifting maxim.

'May all that you are always be in love, and may all that is love always be in you.'

'Amen!' Veronica longed to shout, knowing that, despite decades of Colin's indifference and despite the crushing fact that her one and only experience of consummate passion had ended in disaster, she somehow couldn't stop believing that love was still the ultimate goal in life.

Once they'd said their goodbyes to the celebrant and Registrar, the photographer took over, a cadaverous-looking man, whose lavish, soot-black Van Dyke beard seemed to compensate for his thinning, greying head-hair. He was clearly relieved to have Skip as an ally, since the latter's spontaneous laughter and appallingly bad jokes were already dissipating the tension of the ceremony and helping them all relax. And, once they were grouped outside on the steps of Chelsea Town Hall, Skip also proved a dab hand with the confetti, showering the bridal couple with several boxes of the stuff and producing a veritable Niagara of miniature horseshoes, hearts and flowers.

Despite the joyous occasion, they were all four shivering in the bracing cold of this mid-December day, all the more intense after the velvet fug of the overheated room upstairs. Skip's shivers were, of course, comically exaggerated, as he pretended his teeth were chattering and that he was suffering from terminal frostbite.

'I'm really chuffed you chose me as a witness,' he remarked to Glenys, with a final dramatic shudder. 'I mean, you could have had one of those super-smart Chelsea Pensioners in their flamboyant uniforms, rather than your shabby little brother!'

'Oh, you need to thank Robert for that,' Glenys joked. 'He didn't want anyone stealing his thunder today, and those cutesy old Pensioners just can't help taking centre-stage in their pillar-box-red and rows of medals!'

'Well, you could have had a couple of *dogs*,' Skip added. 'Apparently, one of the couples married here brought an Old-English sheepdog and a miniature dachshund as their witnesses, both wearing designer-sunglasses and cute little denim caps.'

Once they'd smiled their way through more of Skip's banter and at least two hundred different poses for the clearly obsessional photographer, it was time for Veronica to spring her surprise on the wedding party. Glenys and Robert were expecting little more than a brief drink in conclusion, but she had secretly arranged a proper wedding breakfast at the nearby Chelsea Garden pub, part of the Ivy group of restaurants. Only through Alex had she even heard of the apparently world-famous Ivy but, since she did want to choose a stylish and upmarket venue, she had allowed her much-mourned lover to influence that decision. Megan, though, had also played her part, in constantly urging her not to keep economizing, as if Den were still alive and still fearing destitution. 'It's high time, love, you broke with all that early conditioning. Your situation's entirely different now and, with that big house in Clapham, you're hardly likely to end up on Skid Row!'

And, yes, Veronica had reasoned, it did make perfect sense

to splash out on a decent reception for a couple facing struggle and uncertainty.

'So, where are we headed?' Skip asked, brushing a scurf of confetti from his thatch of hair. 'I quite fancy a Big Mac myself!'

'We're headed here!' Veronica announced, coming to a halt as they reached the entrance to the pub. 'There *is* a MacDonald's further down the King's Road, so if you're really gasping for a burger, we can go on there afterwards!'

'No way!' Skip was already halfway through the door. 'This looks seriously posh, and, so long as I'm not paying, that's fine with me!'

The manager greeted her effusively by name, well acquainted with her now, since she had been in several times to finalize the arrangements, book a table by the log-fire, and ensure the champagne would be suitably cold by the time their party arrived. She had learned a lot from Alex about doing things with panache, but, once again, she was forced to turf him out of her mind, and out of this genteel establishment, whose very elegance and refinement couldn't fail to stir unwelcome memories of the places he'd frequented with her.

Fortunately, she was too busy to give them head-room, in her role as hostess and her desire to put the others at their ease. She was aided by their waiter – exuberantly young and charmingly foreign Felipe – who showed them to their table, poured the champagne and passed around plates of canapés: miniature works of art in their intricacy and elaborate decoration.

'May I propose a toast' – Veronica raised her glass – 'to Robert and Glenys, to wish you both every possible happiness.' She left it at that, since any mention of a long life together or even of the future would hardly be appropriate.

They all clinked glasses, Skip draining his at a gulp, before starting on the canapés.

'Go easy, Skip,' Glenys warned him. 'I know you're always ravenous, but do leave some for Veronica!'

'Don't worry,' Veronica reassured her. 'These are only a few preliminary nibbles before our proper food.' When it came to the main course, however, she had in fact eschewed heavy, filling dishes, in favour of a series of mini-plates, aware that neither Glenys nor Robert had much appetite these days and that she herself would probably be too churned up to eat and certainly too preoccupied. She hadn't reckoned with Skip, though, who, having polished off the canapés, now turned his attention to the succession of plates the waiter had just carried in. She suppressed a smile as she thought of Colin's reaction to this pretentious food: goat's-cheese-stuffed courgette flowers, asparagus in aspic, crab-and-scallop puffs. He'd have much preferred bangers and mash, and, although he now had no objection to even the most esoteric of Pearl's Jamaican dishes, that was only because his beloved carer was feeding him and fondling him. It was a relief that Pearl would be with him all day today, leaving her free to concentrate on the wedding, rather than worry that he might have pooed his pants or had another fall.

'Oh, Veronica,' Glenys exclaimed, 'I've never seen such gorgeous food! But you shouldn't have gone to so much trouble and expense.'

'It's nothing,' she demurred, conscious of the kick it had given her to lay on a party at all. There had been no parties in her childhood and, once she married, only business entertaining, the latter often marred by the uncouth manners of Colin's associates, who flicked cigar-ash on the carpet, talked with their mouths full and always drank too much. But today, everything was gracious, including the ambience. The windows of this Chelsea pub looked out at a lush conservatory filled with exotic plants, there was interesting art on the walls, smartly dressed waiters were gliding from table to table, and the clientele, all worthy of Alex, exuded an air of prosperity and privilege. Even the crackling of the log-fire seemed to purr its pleasure, its comforting heat thawing the last frisson of cold from their limbs.

'I'm just sorry,' Glenys said, biting into a venison Scotch egg, topped with slivers of horseradish, 'that Robert and I can't do the food full justice.'

'Don't worry,' Skip assured them. 'In my job, I barely have time to eat, so I'm more than happy to make up for that today!'

'What work do you do?' asked Robert.

'I'm what they call a barista – which is posh-speak for us losers who work in coffee-shops. Some of my fellow workers brag about their artistry in sculpting perfect hearts in latte-foam, but what they forget is that we also do a hell of a lot of washing-up and sweeping floors!'

Veronica wondered why on earth he should work in such a lowly job at his age. Although Glenys's 'baby brother', he must be pushing fifty, whereas most baristas seemed to be much younger, or even students planning to move on to better jobs in the future. There was so much she didn't know about Skip, yet, if she were honest with herself, she had no great urge to find out. He simply wasn't her type, and the comparison with Alex was too painful even to contemplate. 'So how come you got your name?' she asked, moving to what she hoped was safer ground.

Glenys answered for him. 'Oh, that goes back to when he was just a tiddler. If he had to go anywhere, he never simply walked, always skipped along in this really jaunty manner, as if he were off to a funfair, even if in reality he was headed for the dentist, or to buy boring old school shoes! His real name is Albert, would you believe?'

Skip clapped his hand to his forehead in a gesture of Byronic gloom. 'Yes, that's my cross in life – one of many!'

It struck Veronica that perhaps there was genuine sadness behind the banter - often the case with inveterate jesters. However, the conversation had now moved on to Christmas, a mere ten days away. Glenys, of course, had Robert to help make the festive season a little less bleak and accompany her to her chemotherapy session scheduled for the day after Boxing Day. As for Skip, he was going climbing with a friend in Snowdonia, happy to forego Christmas dinner for the sake of challenge and adventure. *Her* only challenge would be keeping Colin reasonably content in the absence of his beloved carer. But she was determined to make it a decent Christmas for him and, if she couldn't prise Pearl from her family, at least she could lay on lots of presents and all his favourite foods.

While Skip expounded on the perils of Snowdon in the winter, Veronica was conscious that Glenys and Robert were beginning to flag. They had made it clear at the outset that, in their debilitated condition, they couldn't stay too long, so she needed to prime their waiter to bring in the wedding-cake, in order move on the proceedings. She had ordered not the traditional cake – far too big and rich for them – but a small heart-shaped confection, iced with Glenys and Robert's names, and topped with a miniature marzipan bride and groom, each holding a candle twice the size of the figure itself.

The waiter carried it in with a flourish, the flickering candles drawing delighted exclamations from the bridal couple. Once the pair had cut the first slice, Felipe remained at the table to divide up the rest and serve it on delicate bone-china plates.

'Veronica, you really are spoiling us!' Robert sat admiring his slice, the piece with his name on, iced in blue on white, and enclosed in a miniature icing-heart. 'Glenys and I were just expecting a quick coffee, not this lavish feast.'

Veronica shook her head vehemently. 'But this is a very special day – and special for me, too. I've never been a witness at a wedding before & I know I'll remember this for ever.' 'Ever' was a perilous word as far as Glenys was concerned, so she quickly changed tack and rummaged in her holdall for the couple's wedding-gifts. The choice of a gift had proved difficult. At their age, they both had enough possessions as it was, especially with their uncertain future. She had thought of tickets for a concert, since both were very musical but, whatever date she chose, they might be having treatment or feel too unwell to go out. Finally, she'd settled for a framed print of old Chelsea and a book of *The World's Greatest Love Poems*, the latter a work of art in itself, beautifully illustrated with reproductions of famous erotic masterpieces. She had wrapped both gifts in William Morris wedding-paper – another name she knew only through Alex. Who would continue her cultural education now he was no longer in her life?

'You don't need *him* to teach you,' Megan's disembodied voice countered, sharply. 'You have all the skills to learn stuff for yourself.'

Veronica begged to disagree. How could she have acquired all that subtle sexual experience without Alex's tongue and hands and amazingly agile body?

She dragged her concentration back to Glenys and Robert, who were both still thanking her effusively. Embarrassed, she waved their thanks away, knowing she owed more to them than vice versa, since arranging this reception had been the only thing pleasurable enough to distract her, at least temporarily, from the torment of losing Alex.

'I'm afraid my present can't compete.' Skip handed over a cardboard box, labelled 'Bride and Groom Survival Kit', and slit it open with the cake-knife. Robert and Glenys both dipped in, withdrawing a succession of tiny gifts, each bearing a tag: a miniature bottle of whisky ('to calm your nerves'), a sewing-kit ('sew in love'), a pair of earplugs ('did you know he snores?'), two pairs of socks ('in case you get cold feet'), a box of matches ('the perfect match') and other jokey items, all of which proved the perfect choice in that they made everybody laugh, and also provided the chance for Glenys and Robert to leave, claiming they needed the earplugs right away, as they planned to sneak off for a nap.

'That's the best excuse I've ever heard for a bit of hanky-panky,' Skip quipped. 'But no problem, Sis, I don't begrudge you your honeymoon!'

Once Veronica had seen them off, with their presents and the rest of the cake, expertly boxed by the waiter, she returned to their table, wondering how to make her own excuse to leave. She, too, was tired and, frankly, had no wish to stay any longer with Skip. He, however, had ordered coffee for them both – coffee she didn't want and which took a while to arrive. When it did, she sipped it dutifully, but then pushed back her chair and said firmly she must be on her way. She was in fact in no hurry to return to Colin, but an idea had just occurred to her: to sneak back to the Town Hall and indulge in a crazy but surely harmless fantasy. If no one barred her way, she'd go right upstairs to the wedding-rooms again and pretend she and Alex were standing there, hand in hand and indelibly in love, pronouncing their own solemn vows, swearing everlasting devotion to each other.

‘Oh, no, do stay,’ Skip pressed her. ‘It’s early as yet, so why don’t we go on to the ice-rink at the Natural History Museum? It’s only a stone’s-throw from here and it’s opened specially for the Christmas period. I haven’t seen it in person, but, judging by the photos, it looks pretty magical, with a huge great Christmas tree and loads of fairy-lights and skaters gliding around as if they’re in the snowy wilds of Russia rather than Central London!’

‘But I’ve never skated in my life,’ she objected. ‘I’m more likely to fall flat on my face!’

‘You won’t with me – that I guarantee. Though I says it myself, I’m quite a whiz on the ice and if you just trust yourself to me, I’ll make you feel you’ve been skating since you were born.’

She continued resisting the idea, despite seeming to hear Megan’s reproving voice again.

‘For God’s sake, *go*, Veronica! The last thing you need is to keep mooning around after Alex, when he’s dead and buried now. Leave him behind in the past and move on with your life, instead of indulging in hopeless fantasies. And, if you’ve never been skating, here’s your chance to give it a try.’

‘But I’m not keen on Skip,’ she countered, continuing the silent argument with Megan in her head.

‘If you mean you’re not passionately in love with him, and never likely to be, that’s neither here nor there. Just go because you’re free to and because you might actually enjoy it. I remember once being asked to dance the tango with a guy I barely knew. I told him I had two left feet and could no more dance than fly, but he himself was such an ace mover, he made it ridiculously easy and I performed so well, I’m surprised they weren’t imploring me to appear on *Strictly* that very week!’

‘So, are you up for it, Veronica?’ Skip asked, rising to his feet and taking her arm, as if the matter were already settled.

‘OK,’ she said, through gritted teeth and more from duty than from any wish to test her balance on an ice-rink. After all, Glenys might expect her to look after her ‘baby brother’, rather than dash off home and leave him high and dry. Besides, she need only stay half an hour. The minute he saw how little she resembled Torvill and Dean – or whoever their modern equivalents were - he’d be only too glad to bid her a hasty goodbye.

CHAPTER 29

'Happy Christmas, darling!'

As Veronica set down Colin's morning tea, she found him tightly cocooned in the sheet and two white blankets, looking for all the world like an Egyptian mummy. He always managed to tangle his bedclothes around him during the night, which meant that if he pooed or peed the bed - having torn off his incontinence-pad through perversity or confusion – all the bedding would be soiled and stinking and have to go straight in to the wash. But this morning – Christmas miracle – there wasn't the slightest stain on anything, or even a trace of odour, so she helped him along to the bathroom before her luck could change.

Once he was back in bed and settled with his tea, she passed him a couple of the mince pies she'd made last night, having decided to be more ambitious than simply buying shop ones, as she'd done last year. They looked a tad misshapen, but Colin wolfed them down with no complaint and, since today was Indulgence Day, she wasn't going to worry about them spoiling his appetite for breakfast. Indeed, if he wanted to gorge on sweet things all damned day, she didn't intend to nag.

Having cleared up the crumbs from the bed, she embarked on the long, demanding process of getting him showered and dressed. Once in the shower, he winced with pain and, on examining his leg, she found the ankle was again badly swollen and tender to the touch. Clearly, she'd have to make an appointment with his GP, as soon as Christmas was over - the thought triggering some measure of anxiety, since he'd slowed down considerably since his operation and she feared any further deterioration. However, once she'd given him some painkillers, strapped the offending ankle and led him along to the sitting-room, his face noticeably brightened once he saw the transformation she'd effected in the wee small hours. She had deliberately waited till he was fast asleep, so as not to spoil the surprise she'd planned for Christmas morning: a six-foot-tall Christmas tree, decorated with fairy-lights, coloured baubles and sparkly ornaments. The childish pleasure he showed in it made her trouble seem worthwhile – all the more so because he so rarely reacted with pleasure to anything these days, apart from porn and ice-cream.

In a bid to maintain his cheery mood, she ensconced him in his chair and brought him his pile of presents, most, inevitably, food-based: Turkish delight, brandy-snaps, chocolate truffles, marzipan fruits. She had also bought him a couple of DVDs, a bottle of aftershave (which he'd probably try to drink), a pair of Christmas socks adorned with reindeer, and a recording of Christmas carols. As she helped him remove the wrapping-paper - he ripping at it wildly - she remembered her mother saying that gift-wrap was an unnecessary luxury, when an ordinary paper bag would do every bit as well. Not that there had been much in the way of gifts in her childhood. Den was always hard-up and any spare cash she might have squirreled away would be used to buy her current lover a present, despite the fact that most of those lovers would have stormed off in a paddy before they'd barely worn the tie or used the wallet she'd chosen.

Aware her thoughts were straying, she recalled her promise to Megan to debar both Den and Alex from intruding on her Christmas Day. Both were in the past and she was about to embark on a New Year, in which, according to Megan, the 'now' must be savoured - the 'now' being each and every moment as it sprang into existence. And one of the things worth savouring at this very instant was the number of cards on the mantelpiece – more than she'd ever received in her life before. Most were from members of the choir, some of whom had also given her gifts. She was saving those for her own private present-opening, so as not to detract from Colin's, since this was *his* day and she'd need to work hard to compensate for his carer's absence. She handed over Pearl's present, in the hope it would make some small amends and, once he'd unwrapped the Christmas sweater from its layers of tissue paper, she explained that Pearl had knitted it for him specially. On the front was not the usual reindeer or snowman, but a white dog with black spots that bore a strong resemblance to Peter. Although it was difficult to know these days how much he understood, she was rewarded with a smile as she eased the sweater over his head, in place of the shabby grey one she'd just put on and steered him to the mirror to admire himself.

'Peter,' she confirmed, pointing to the knitted dog.

Then, since they were in Peter mode, she went to fetch the stuffed equivalent, along with Peter's doggy-stocking and, once she'd returned him to his chair, helped him extract the contents. He immediately tried to eat the bone-shaped biscuits and chocolate doggy-drops - although fortunately not the dog-chews - and she tied the final item, a black-and-white striped scarf, around the toy dog's neck. And there the two of them sat: Colin in his Peter sweater, and Peter himself looking distinctly fetching in his scarf. She vowed to maintain this upbeat start to the day, rather than crave more company, despite the fact it had struck her several times already how much better Christmas Day might be with a brood of excited children, perhaps, or a tribe of loving relatives. Many in the choir simply took their families for granted – a spouse to converse with, kids who visited, someone always there, in every sense – and had no notion of how marooned one could feel trapped in the lonely bubble of one's self. But why pine for what she'd never had, instead of focusing on the fact that this Christmas was infinitely better than last, when she'd had far fewer friends, much less confidence in her singing and, most important of all, no Pearl to help her out?

Reminded of the choir, she got up to play the recording of carols, starting with *White Christmas*, which they'd begun practising last month at rehearsals. Once the cheery sound filled the room, she was emboldened to join in – indeed, even to exult in her new ability to hold a tune without a single wrong note. It was imperative to keep distracted, rather than let thoughts of Alex gate-crash into her mind. One particularly distasteful image kept bypassing her self-censorship system: a naked Alex waking on Christmas morning entangled with his wife in bed and, even as she watched, continuing his lovemaking in so passionately exuberant a fashion, the word divorce seemed a total travesty.

'Any man who can lie so blatantly,' Megan's voice cut in, 'pass off his wife as a stalker and his two wee boys as teenagers is not even worth regretting. You should simply say "Good riddance!" and thank your lucky stars you no longer have such a shyster in your life.'

How could she *not* regret? Yet she had to admit she already had far too many regrets, stretching way back into her past, like a series of potholes along a rocky road. Nonetheless, Megan had insisted that she could choose, coolly and deliberately, to leave them all behind. And, to emphasize her point, she had quoted the phrase 'the highway of regret', from the song, *Make You Feel my Love*. 'If you're on a highway,' she'd said, 'that means you have the option of turning off on to a quieter, less perilous side-road.'

Tempted to ring her friend, if only to get reinforcement for her resolve to stay upbeat, she quashed the urge immediately. Christmas was a family-day and it would be bad form to intrude on it, even with a phone-call. Besides, Megan would be busy, since she'd offered to stay with her niece as a live-in babysitter for the whole of the Christmas week, so that Lavinia and her husband were free to go out for any jamboree where an infant might prove an encumbrance.

To fill the gap, she went to fetch the Christmas stocking Megan had made for her, which had prompted the idea for *Peter's* stocking. Colin instantly pounced on the contents, assuming it was for him, or maybe a second one for Peter, shaking everything out first, then picking up each item in turn, displaying a touching avidity, as if expecting a good-as-new ankle or a sharp and agile mind. Far from being agile, though, he managed to drop the old-style sixpence that had been stuffed into the toe, and spent several frustrating minutes trying to retrieve it. Then, having paused to peel and eat the tangerine, he wiped his messy fingers on his new sweater, and began unwrapping the variety of small, individually wrapped gifts Megan had chosen for *her*. He, however, seemed perfectly content to be given a new scarlet lipstick, a bottle of glittery nail-varnish, a pair of frilly lace pants, a lavender-scented bath-bomb and a sachet of cucumber face-mask.

She sat gazing at the treasure-trove - all extra bounty, on top of Megan's main gift of the ballet tickets for *Cinderella*, and the promise of lunch before the matinée performance on January 6. Pearl had promised to Colin-sit and would be back in harness by then – and, indeed, the whole endless Christmas shutdown would be well and truly over for another year – both such heartening prospects, she found herself joining in *Jingle Bells*, now playing on the track.

Through the fields we go
Laughing all the way.
Bells on bobtail ring
Making spirits bright ....

And, yes, she thought, with something akin to amazement, her spirits *were* bright, and even Colin, Pearl-less and in pain, was still gazing with satisfaction at his pair of frilly lace pants.

She carried in the macaroni-cheese - a decidedly offbeat Christmas dinner, but she knew Colin would refuse point-blank to eat turkey (let alone Brussels sprouts), and would want ice-cream on everything, including his roast parsnips. His sweet tooth was now so pronounced, even Pearl had started adding mashed banana and desiccated coconut to his favourite Jamaican dishes, and she herself had put condensed milk in the macaroni, in the hope he might get it down. The pudding, however, was definitely more festive: an old-fashioned trifle, comprising sherry-soaked sponge, strawberry jelly and custard in a lurid shade of yellow, lavishly sprinkled with hundreds and thousands. Much to her chagrin, though, he refused to touch it, *or* the macaroni, and, even when she tried to feed him, immediately spat out each mouthful, presumably missing the comfort of Pearl's over-sized, pillowy breasts.

'*Peter's* hungry,' she told him, 'Let's feed him, OK?'

Holding the spoon first against the dog's mouth, she quickly transferred it to her husband's, but, refusing to be fooled, he knocked it from her hand and reached for his sherry-glass. She had already allowed him two small aperitifs – probably a mistake, since they had destroyed the last of his appetite. Nor had it helped that he'd made serious inroads into the Turkish Delight and even attempted to eat the bath-bomb.

Removing the glass from his reach provoked a howl of protest, followed by a gigantic yawn.

'Time for your nap,' she announced, relieved that he did seem tired and allowed her to guide him back to his bedroom, peel off his

Christmas sweater and settle him under the covers. She needed a break, if he didn't. The morning had seemed interminable, with little on the television except simple, happy families doing simple, happy things. Soon bored with the Christmas carols, he had refused to watch either of his new DVDs and seemed restless in general, continually calling for Pearl. Perhaps an hour or two's sleep would restore his former good spirits and, fortunately he sank down against the pillows, with a sigh of exhaustion, Peter, scarf and all, clasped tightly in his arms.

She used the respite to open her presents, touched to receive her own hand-knitted sweater from Pearl, with a red-cassocked choirboy on the front, mouth open in full voice. What a skilful knitter the woman was, on top of all her other talents! Her gifts from fellow choristers included a book on Medieval Music, courtesy of Clive and Michael, a box of rose-geranium toiletries from Charlotte, and a pair of luxurious sheepskin slippers from Glenys and Robert. And it had given her great pleasure to reciprocate, setting off for the West End just before Pearl's Christmas break, with a much longer Christmas list than usual, and picking out unusual things for Pearl herself and all her five daughters, for Megan and her other friends in the choir, and those in the Fund-Raising group who'd been particularly supportive - each gift a gratifying reminder of how much her life had opened up of late.

The last present in the pile was from Catherine, but for Colin, not for her – a large box of Liquorice Allsorts, which happened to be his favourite sweets, although, having never met him, she couldn't possibly have known. Catherine was, in fact, unwell and having to spend Christmas Day in hospital under observation. And several others in the choir would be fighting pain and nausea and unable to leave their beds, or struggling to cope with the other unpleasant side-effects of radiation and chemotherapy. *She* was extremely lucky in comparison, yet, somehow, couldn't shift the feelings of isolation that seemed to swamp all else, the total silence of the house making her feel cut off from the rest of the feasting, revelling human race. And past Christmases had been little better, as she miserably recalled: Colin often escaping to the pub, alone but drinking hard, while she, unaided, sought to give Tom at least a reasonably festive day. Or sometimes Colin had feigned work as an excuse to miss what she'd optimistically hoped might be a family Christmas dinner, shutting himself upstairs in his room and not emerging till late on.

His recent dementia, however, had greatly increased her sense of solitude, since it rendered all normal communication totally impossible. He no longer had any grasp of her interests and concerns, no notion of her as an autonomous person, with a life beyond his own. Like a child, he was fixated on himself – his needs, his frustrations – she existing solely to meet those needs or assuage those frustrations. In her childhood, she had felt a different sort of loneliness, if Den was spending Christmas with a lover, or had invited some man home. His presence meant that she, the child, must creep into the background or simply fade away into silence and discretion, while the visitor was feted.

She mooched over to the window, to look out at the weather: a sullen drizzle falling from a lumpy-porridge sky. Nonetheless, she longed to be outside, striding briskly across the Common, breathing in deep lungfuls of fresh air. No way, though, could she leave Colin on his own, so, instead, she turned on the radio – always a faithful companion – and, tuning through a myriad of over-cheery stations, eventually settled for a nature programme.

'Murmurations of starlings,' a melodious male voice announced, 'flock together in thousands for safety and security, sleeping in reed-beds as part of a great tribe.'

She imagined herself a starling, no longer alone, but bolstered by a community, a fellowship of birds. Or, maybe - even better - one special mate to roost with, deriving warmth and comfort from the proximity of another body, the beating of another heart.

Despising her own self-pity, she resolved to put the time to good use by reading a few more chapters of the textbook she'd recently purchased for the Institute of Fundraising's Diploma Course, having finally decided to enrol for their next online course, commencing in March. She could barely believe her chutzpah in applying - a source of mingled pride and terror - and the cost of the course still seemed a shameful indulgence. Megan had pointed out, though, that the more she learned, the more valuable she would be to the choir and the more donations be able to secure, to guarantee its future. And, indeed, even the fifty pages she'd studied so far had greatly increased her knowledge of trusts, foundations and legacies, and of codes of practice in the field, and taught her really useful stuff about how to recruit, retain and manage volunteers. And work, as always, proved highly beneficial in distracting her from Den, Colin, Alex, Skip – and from the nation as a whole in its relentlessly celebratory mood.

All at once, her concentration was shattered by panting cries of orgasmic lust, rising full-volume from the sitting-room. She dashed downstairs to find Colin stark naked, unabashedly masturbating on the sofa, a look of bliss on his face as he watched a bevy of voluptuous young porn-stars rapturously pleasuring each other.

'*Colin*!' she shouted, aware he'd stained the sofa with faeces from his ever-productive bottom, and was now adding sperm to the curdled mix as he ejaculated over the new silk cushions, with a final cry of satisfaction.

He seemed neither embarrassed nor contrite as she led him to the bathroom for a clean-up, put on a fresh set of clothes, then toiled back to the sitting-room and tried to tackle the mess with fabric-cleaner and a succession of clean cloths. While she scrubbed at the stains, she allowed the porn to play on. If he preferred *Lesbian Lovelies* to the new *Pirates of the Caribbean*, there was little point acting as policewoman and risking more rebellion on his part. She would simply have to act as chaperone and at least ensure he kept his trousers on. Yet, inwardly, she couldn't help but fume, as she reflected on Colin's apparent avidity for sex. If he had so strong a libido, even at the age of nearly eighty-five, then why the hell had it never extended to *her*? The irony was she herself was yearning at this very moment to be back in Alex's bed - yes, despite his treachery – burning to feel him thrust inside her again, as she bucked and moaned above. Their affair, however brief and misguided, had given her the precious sense of feeling sexy and desirable, lent her a certain lustre, in that a high-status, cultured, deeply sensuous man craved her company, her body. Colin, in contrast, had ignored her needs throughout their marriage, preferring on-screen ersatz sex to his living, breathing, aching-to-be-awakened wife.

All at once, the porn cresecendoed, as if, cussedly, he'd turned up the volume, and the soundtrack – foreign, for some reason - reverberated through the room, the ululating, guttural voices reminding her of rutting pigs, snuffling and honking in their cesspit of a sty. Why, she thought indignantly, should *they* be allowed to couple on and on in drooling ecstasy, while she was shackled in a straitjacket of celibacy?

Suddenly, her mobile rang, shrilling through the orgiastic braying, like another wanton voice. She rushed to turn down the television, not that she was expecting any calls on Christmas Day, nor was in any mood for polite conversation or, even less, an exchange of festive greetings. Before picking up the phone, she put a finger to her lips to warn Colin to keep quiet – a probably pointless gesture, knowing his total unawareness of other people's wishes.

'Skip!' she exclaimed, surprised to hear his voice, since he had disappeared from the radar after their skating session – not a call, not a word, not even a Christmas card. Although his silence had been wounding, she had refused to let the snub prey on her mind, since they had been drawn together solely for Glenys's wedding and it was only natural that they would now go their separate ways. He was clearly not her type and he probably felt much the same about her.

'Sorry I haven't been in touch,' Skip continued in his cheery tone. 'You must have thought I'd vanished into a Black Hole. And it *was* a Black Hole, believe me, because I went down with this ghastly flu - and I'm not talking about "man-flu". I had such a high temperature, I couldn't lift a finger, let alone get out of bed, and just lay there aching and sweating. I only hope I didn't give it to you.'

'No,' she said, struggling to calm her inner turmoil, as she deliberately turned her back on the screen. 'I'm fine. Although really sorry to hear you've been in the wars.'

'Don't worry – I'm right as rain now. In fact, I'm ringing to ask if you fancy going skating again tomorrow.'

'Tomorrow?' she echoed, feeling distinctly non-plussed, having assumed she would never see him again.

'Yes, Boxing Day - the perfect day to go whizzing around the ice!'

For him, maybe, but *he* wasn't stuck at home with a cantankerous spouse. 'I'm afraid I'm not free until my carer comes back on January 4 and, in any case, that's my choir-day. And I already have an engagement for Saturday, the sixth, then my carer's off on the Sunday, so I couldn't even think of going anywhere until Monday the eighth.'

'No problem. Let's make it then. It means we'll have to go to a different ice-rink, because the one at the Natural History Museum is only a seasonal thing and closes on the seventh. Mind you, I'm glad we went when we did, because it looked so picturesque with all those fairy-lights glittering in the trees, and that gigantic Christmas tree shimmering with golden baubles. My local rink at Queensway is not so glitzy, but it's open every day of the year and I know it really well, so it's the obvious choice for Monday.'

'But I feel I'm simply not good enough to continue with this skating lark.'

'Nonsense! You're a natural. In fact, I could hardly believe that you'd never skated before. And I'll have you know it's not a "lark", it's a skill. And, since you clearly have an inbuilt talent, I'm dying to develop that and teach you a few new turns and twirls.'

She couldn't help but be heartened by his words. The skating had, indeed, proved unexpectedly successful and enjoyable, despite her trepidation at the start, which had resulted in a few mishaps and several outright falls. But falls, he'd said, were simply part of the process and actually had to be practised, so she could learn the proper technique for getting up again. He'd continued to encourage and instruct her - 'Don't look down!', 'Lean forward', 'Bend your knees a little', 'Yes, that's great. That's brilliant!' 'But put your arms out at the sides to keep your balance'.

Then, once he'd taught her how to stop, how to steer with her hips and shoulders, and how to use the edges of the blades, he'd taken both her hands in his and skated backwards, his own expertise and the solidity of his body providing essential support, as she dared to keep gliding forwards, guided by his hands. And, gradually, eventually, she had come to realize that if she followed his moves, relinquished control to his superior skill, she wouldn't trip or stumble, but slowly gain in confidence. And, much to her astonishment, and despite being such a novice, that had actually happened, as she began to get the knack of gliding - or at least of no longer falling flat on her face.

In truth, the experience had proved something of a revelation, in that Skip seemed to have become part of her body, taking it over, lending it a grace and speed she'd had no idea she possessed. In certain ways, it reminded her of sex, requiring the same trust, the same readiness to let go and abandon herself to the sensation of the moment, and rely on her partner to achieve undreamed of heights. Yet that very analogy, along with the unexpected physical contact, made her somewhat wary. She didn't fancy Skip and knew she never would, because, despite all Megan's admonitions, her heart still belonged to Alex. And, continually, unfairly, she couldn't help comparing the two: Skip, younger, less sophisticated, less alluring altogether, and with none of her ex-lover's sheen and status.

'Veronica, are you still there?'

'Er, yes,' she mumbled.

'Well, are we on for the eighth? I can't wait to see you again!'

Still she hesitated. Was it even fair to agree to another meeting, when she felt so little for him? Yet the prospect of male company other than her husband's was undoubtedly a draw - as was having another outing to look forward to, once the ballet was over. Besides, hadn't

Megan urged her to start the New Year by savouring all new experiences, and skating was certainly new, another thing she'd never done, even as a child. And if Skip was right and she did have a natural flair, then maybe she could build it into a new, late-life achievement, like the singing.

'Veronica, did you hear? I asked if we were on for the eighth.'

'Yes,' she said, surprising herself. As usual, she'd been focusing on the downside, but one more session on the ice didn't mean that she and Skip had to land up in bed together – in fact, committed her to nothing. Wiser to view it as just a passing pleasure, a few hours out of her life, to add a little lustre to the short-of-daylight, post-Christmas hibernation.

'Yes,' she repeated, a tiny tinge of excitement already gilding her cinders-grey Christmas. 'I'd really love that, Skip.'

CHAPTER 30

Veronica all but jumped out of her seat as a wailing air-raid siren cresecendoed through the theatre, followed by a Pathé News announcement, advising nervous citizens as to what to do in the event of a bombing raid. And, as Prokofiev's score resounded from the orchestra-pit, photos of crumbling buildings were flashing up on screen, along with footage of heroic firemen, pitting their hoses against the fiercely gluttonous flames. Yet those flames were often the victors, consuming vulnerable homes in their path like so much puny matchwood.

London, 1940, read the subtitle – the year her mother was born. Indeed, Den had always claimed to remember the carnage in vivid, photographic detail – a claim Veronica had never believed. How could a babe-in-arms have such graphic recall? Only at this moment, seated safely between Megan and Lavinia, in the front row of the stalls, did her mother's tales take on a poignancy and desperation she had been unable to imagine before.

And her thoughts remained with Den even when the scene changed to Cinderella's family home, the two ugly sisters and the evil stepmother joined in this offbeat production by three malevolent stepbrothers. Den had been an only child, as *she* was, yet also something of a Cinderella in that her parents had used her as a workhorse and a skivvy. until finally throwing her out, once she'd brought shame upon the household by falling pregnant as an unmarried teen. The rest was history – *her* history.

A rat-tat-tat on the stage front-door forced her concentration back to the proceedings, as the famous invitation to the ball was delivered, creating much excitement for all except excluded Cinderella. But, when the scene changed once more to the foggy streets of night-time London, they were again assaulted by sirens, searchlights and traumatizing explosions, as desperate characters in gas-masks dashed for cover, in disoriented confusion. Despite all Megan had told her in way of preparation, she'd somehow still been expecting a conventional ballet and basically a fairy-tale, not this stark account of destruction and devastation. Nonetheless, it was shot through with gleams of hope, especially in the persona of the Angel. And, yes, here he was again – this way-out equivalent of the traditional Fairy Godmother - garbed in a shimmery silver suit, lustrous silver shoes and a startling wig of silver-blonde hair - handing Cinderella her coveted invitation to the ball.

Neither Cinders nor Veronica could contain their excitement as a cohort of white-suited airmen began flying through the sky, like a squadron of heavenly pilots, the music itself seeming to take on a celestial, otherworldly quality, at least to her untutored ear.

She remained rapt until the interval, when Megan ushered her and Lavinia along to the bar, where their pre-ordered drinks were waiting at a table – not just prosecco, but raspberry-lemonade in an upbeat shade of pink that matched her mood.

'Auntie, this production's so original!' Lavinia clinked her glass against Megan's. 'I must have seen half-a-dozen *Cinderellas* in my time, but never anything as daring as this.'

'Well, it's my first-ever ballet,' Veronica told her, 'so I've nothing to compare it with, but I know I shan't forget it as long as I live!'

'And what a wonderful dancer Paris Fitzpatrick is,' Lavinia continued.

'The Angel,' Megan prompted, knowing Veronica was unlikely to know the soloists' names.

'I studied ballet for years as a child,' Lavinia explained, 'so I know from experience what hours and hours of practice and sheer hard graft it takes to move with that seemingly effortless ease.'

'I'm surprised by how many children are here today, considering how traumatic some of the scenes are.' Veronica glanced at the adjoining table, where three small girls in party-frocks and ballet-pumps were sitting with their parents, fizzing with excitement. She tried to imagine growing up in a world where ballet lessons and visits to the theatre were part of normal existence and where, from an early age, one imbibed through one's very pores music, drama, stage-plays, probably even opera. Yet, today, she was no longer concerned about her own cultural desert of a childhood. Much as she missed Alex, there had always been that shaming gulf between them: she the ignoramus, he the expert and the aesthete. In contrast, there was a sense of relaxation in being with Megan and Lavinia, since neither expected her to sparkle, shine, or contribute any profound remarks to the conversation. She could simply be herself and enjoy the buzz of exuberant chatter rippling through the bar, and the feeling of being part of an occasion.

As she watched, one of the little girls sprang up from her chair and executed a spontaneous mini-dance routine, applauded by both parents.

'Well done, Abigail!' the mother purred. The second daughter, refusing to be outdone, got up in her turn and started whirling around in a series of clumsy pirouettes.

'Be careful, Fleur,' the mother cautioned. 'Don't get in people's way.' She spoke, however, with the utmost of indulgence, while the father sat gazing at his three young prodigies with something close to adoration.

How amazing, Veronica thought, to be so idolized by a parent, and how pleasing to be called Fleur or Abigail, rather than plain, ugly Ron. She felt no tinge of envy, though – not now. OK, she had started her cultural education at the age of fifty-nine, rather than at three or four, but at least it *had* begun and her horizons were expanding by the day.

They continued to talk about ballet - or at least Megan and Lavinia did – and only when there was a lull in the conversation did Veronica change the subject to motherhood. How was Lavinia coping?

'Not well at all.' Lavinia gave an embarrassed laugh. 'In fact, without your help, Auntie Megan, I think I'd have simply collapsed. My own mother passed away last year,' she explained, turning back to Veronica, 'but Megan's been the most fantastic substitute.'

'Hardly!' Megan demurred. 'When it comes to babies, I'm a complete and utter novice. Having never had children of my own, I couldn't even put Flora's nappy on, at first. They're only disposables, so it should be easy enough, but I couldn't even tell which was the front and which the back, and Flora would keep wriggling, so the whole kibosh kept slipping off!'

Veronica thought back to the huge, bulky nappies Tom had worn as an adult. Despite years of practice, she'd always had to be careful not to stab him – or herself - with the safety-pins. She suddenly remembered the sound of the washing-machine, endlessly churning and tumbling those nappies, like an alternative lullaby in the otherwise silent house.

'Don't put yourself down, Auntie,' Lavinia, chided, adding, to Veronica, 'she's a natural mum, I assure you. Flora screams her head off with me, but Megan only has to pick her up and she starts gurgling and cooing, like a different child altogether. I have to say, though, it has been bloody tough. I had a bad case of post-natal depression and just sat and bawled my eyes out for whole hours at a time, so no wonder poor wee Flora did the same!'

Veronica's thoughts now switched to Den. If even Lavinia found new motherhood hard-going, with a loving, supportive husband, a spacious, comfortable house and a doting auntie on hand, then how much worse it must have been for a single parent, alone, abandoned and penniless. 'I guess we can all tip over into despair,' she said, 'when we're faced with a demanding new challenge. I know I did with Tom. Like you, I was pretty clueless about children and, as for a disabled child, with endless needs and problems ….'

'I don't know how you coped at all. If Flora had been born disabled, I think I'd have left her in the labour ward, run full-pelt as fast as my legs would carry me and not stopped running till I reached Lands' End!'

Yes, Veronica recalled, there'd been numerous occasions when coping with Tom had seemed a matter of basic life-and-death survival, with both of them at risk of going under. Gradually, however, she'd come to terms with his many disabilities and even grown used to the hostile stares, cruel remarks and finger-pointing from other (luckier) kids, although it had always been hard to accept that her own child would never be free of suffering. About to reassure Lavinia that the situation with Flora was fundamentally different and that things were bound to improve, given time, she was interrupted by the sound of a bell.

Ladies and gentlemen, please return to your seats. The second act of Cinderella will be starting in five minutes.

'Oh, this act should be quite something!' Megan told them. 'It's set in the Café de Paris the night it was bombed in 1941. First, we see it devastated – just a scene of wreckage, strewn with broken bodies - then time reverses and the ballroom springs back to life again, with the band triumphantly playing and all the couples waltzing and jitterbugging.'

If only, Veronica mused - despite knowing that thoughts of Alex were dangerously counter-productive - *she* could reverse time, undo the bombshell of Fiona's revelation, and make her ex-lover available again: free, divorced and with not one single lie to stain their future.

Once they'd waved Lavinia off at Waterloo, on her train to Godalming. Megan and Veronica returned to the Northern Line to continue on to Clapham. Megan had invited her in for drinks and nibbles, insisting the whole day should be her treat. And it *had* been a treat, leaving her both exhilarated and chastened, as she reflected on the ballet's themes of life and death, hope and despair, good and evil, free will and destiny – all disturbingly relevant to her own life and past and experience.

'I never knew,' she said, once they were settled with their drinks in Megan's stylish sitting-room, 'that a ballet could be so .... so *serious*. I'd mugged up all that stuff on nymphs and shepherds, because I thought I'd be seeing *Sylvia*, so I just wasn't prepared for bombed-out streets and hospital-wards full of the maimed and wounded.'

'It's not surprising, though, when you realize Prokofiev wrote the music while the war was raging on, with new horrors every day and half of Europe falling under Nazi occupation.'

'Yes, I kept thinking about Den, who was not only born then, but living in the thick of it. She and her mother were eventually evacuated to the wilds of Yorkshire, but they stayed barely a month up North. Apparently, my grandma couldn't stand the tedium of the countryside, after growing up in all the buzz of Hackney, and said she'd rather she and her baby were bombed to smithereens than die of boredom in a muddy wasteland, with only cows for company! And it was actually the ballet that made me see what a horrendous risk she was taking and how selfish it was to endanger her child like that. And the production also put Den's life in context – especially those perilous early years. I thought it was hard for *me*, but Den had no father, either. He was killed in the very early stages of the War and her mother went to pieces trying to cope on her own and scratch a living without a proper breadwinner.'

'That was no excuse, though, for the way she treated *you*. I mean, by the time you were born, the war had been over for ages, so she could hardly blame it for her own incompetence.'

'Oh, it wasn't that bad, Megan. In fact, watching Cinderella's wicked stepmother, made me realize that Den was a saint, in comparison. At least she never tried to suffocate me!'

'Yes, that scene was really chilling. I thought Cinders was a gonner when Sybil put that pillow over her head!'

'But, seriously, Megan,' Veronica said, sipping her chilled wine, 'I'm beginning to feel I need to make amends to Den. Her life was pretty crappy, right from the start.'

'So was yours, remember,' Megan put in, quietly.

'No, I was born in peacetime, and that makes an enormous difference - no rationing or bombing-raids or terrifying feeling that every day could be your last.'

'Still, from what you've told me, there wasn't much actual peace – not with all those lovers coming and going.'

Veronica sat, glass in hands, reflecting on her past. 'But don't you think that's really rather pathetic? I mean, Den's craving for a man was so intense and reckless – *any* man would do, it seemed – she must have appeared quite desperate to her boyfriends, and that obviously scared them off.'

'I wonder why you continually make excuses for her. You're allowed to be angry, you know! Den's bloody lucky you didn't wash your hands of her when she was older, rather than always being there for her.'

'But I *wasn't* always there for her. And, when she passed away, she was only fifty-six– that's younger than I am now – and I'd no idea she was near the end. And, because, at that time, I was up to my eyes with Tom and also trying to fit in a lot of business entertaining for Colin, I rather neglected her, much to my shame. And it still haunts me terribly that I wasn't actually present when she died. I'd visited her in hospital that day, but I had to rush back for Tom and the ward-sister told me she breathed her last just half-an-hour after I'd left.'

'Hardly *your* fault, love.'

'Maybe not, but, you know, I even made a hash of her funeral.'

'I wish you'd stop blaming yourself for everything! Here, have another drink and let's try to leave your mother in her coffin.'

'OK, but, talking of coffins, if I had my time again, I'd give her a much better send-off. I haven't even scattered her ashes yet. She said she wanted them thrown off Beachy Head into a wild tempestuous sea, and, instead they're still sitting in an urn in a dark, dank cupboard I deliberately avoid.'

'Well, it's not too late to scatter them now. And Beachy Head isn't far. Why don't you and I go down there together and enact a little ceremony for Den? We could read a few poems, even sing one or two of our choir-songs and give her a proper send-off.'

'Oh, *would* you, Megan? I'd love that!'

'Just suggest a few dates and I'll work on it. If she wants a tempestuous sea, I'll need to check the long-term forecast. But it mustn't be too windy, because a strong south-westerly will make the ashes blow all over the place, instead of directly down to the Channel. And I'll dig out some nice readings for Den and maybe record some solemn music for us to play on the clifftop, if the gulls don't drown it out!'

'Megan, you're an angel – as I've told you countless times. More than that, I'd say you're the equal of Matthew Bourne's Angel.'

'No way. I don't have a single silver garment in my wardrobe, and I certainly can't fly!'

'Yes, but you're the best Fairy Godmother anyone could ever have – and I mean that.'

'Don't embarrass me. In fact, I'm going to fetch the nibbles, to spare my blushes.'

'Well, only very few. I'm still full from that delicious lunch.'

Once on her own, Veronica glanced around with pleasure at the spotlessly tidy room, with no ineradicable stains on chairs or carpets. She was so used to Colin's clutter – empty whisky bottles, clothes flung on the floor, drawersful of ever-accumulating junk, dirty incontinence-pads left anywhere and everywhere – Megan's place seemed an oasis of serenity. And even the fretful wind outside, hounding clouds across the darkly troubled sky, appeared to know its place, rather than rattling at the windowpanes, as it would surely do at home.

When her friend returned with a platter of charcuterie and various cheesy dips, Veronica forced herself to ask - although with undisguised awkwardness - her advice on something else.

'If it's something to do with Alex, don't waste your breath! No second chances or special pleading for *that* shit!'

'No, it's to do with another man.'

'Ye gods, that's fast work! Did he pick you up at the ballet, when Lavinia and I went to the ladies' room?'

'No. The only person I spoke to then was those doting parents, who boasted about their three daughters the whole time you were gone. One's a little Einstein, the second's a Shakespeare-in-waiting and the third has an IQ of 155!'

Megan laughed. 'So, who's this new guy?'

'He's not actually new. He's the one who took me skating – you know, Glenys's brother.'

'Oh, the famous Skip, you mean?'

'I don't know about famous, but to cut a long story short, he's asked me to go skating again and yesterday he popped round to my house – although "popped round" isn't quite the phrase, since he lives miles away and must have made the journey specially. He certainly didn't warn me in advance, just turned up at my door with all this skating gear.'

'*His*, you mean, or for you?'

'For me. You see, the first time we went skating, we were both dolled up in posh wedding clothes, so we stopped off at his place first – except that's another misleading phrase, since we were in Chelsea at the time, whereas his place is in Westbourne Grove – quite a little trek. Anyway, he lent me some jogging-bottoms and this great big hairy sweater, although I felt a bit of a Charlie, to be honest, because the clothes were far too big and hardly flattering. But, this time, he went overboard and gave me the full works: a padded fleecy jacket and matching leggings, even gloves and knee-protection pads. I was really nonplussed at first, not just because he'd turned up out of the blue, but because I know he's short of cash, so why on earth should he spend so much on *me*? In fact, I tried to insist on paying him back, but he wouldn't hear of it and assured me he'd got them dirt-cheap in a clearance-sale.'

'Well, what's the problem? He sounds a rather decent sort.'

'If you really want to know, the problem is that, before he left, he kissed me – and I don't mean just a peck on the cheek, but a real full-on lover's kiss. I don't fancy him in the slightest, Megan, but the awful thing was that, instead of pulling away, which obviously I should have done, I found myself responding - well, almost passionately. I've no idea why, so I can only conclude that I've inherited Den's promiscuous gene and will start kissing all and sundry, now that Alex has broken through my barrier, so to speak.'

'Oh, Veronica, you're priceless!' So uproarious was her laugh, Megan all but choked on her drink. 'You've had one affair in all your fifty-nine years and you call yourself promiscuous. After my second divorce, I must have slept with half-a-dozen blokes in just eight months. If you enjoyed Skip's kiss, why worry? You don't have to be in love with him or see him as some divinely ordained soulmate. And, if he fancies you, so what? At least he's fit, compared with all those poor guys in the choir, who are taking so many female hormones, they don't have a scrap of libido left.'

'But I barely know him, Megan. And, anyway, he's not my type

- sort of jokey and laid-back.'

'What's wrong with that? The trouble with you, Veronica, is that you seem to be attracted to difficult men with overriding needs, and you personally don't tend to feel fulfilled unless you're catering to such needs. It's time you started believing that you're worthy of a decent, loving man and don't always have to "pay" for the slightest whiff of affection by taking on some burden in return. And this Skip may even cater to *your* needs, for a change. In fact, judging by all that gear he bought you, he appears to have done so already. And the very fact he's unmarried and childless means he won't expect you to look after any bolshie little brats, or to fit in with his lifestyle and play second fiddle to his wife. For God's sake, be warned by Alex and try to avoid all entanglements like that again.'

'Yes, but Skip's ten years younger than me, which is quite a big gap.'

'And quite a big advantage, judging by the number of blokes who seem to have trouble getting it up, long before they hit sixty. Anyway, just thank your lucky stars you haven't lost a breast and aren't disfigured by scars, like so many in the choir. Most of us couldn't even contemplate an affair, because we wouldn't dare undress.'

'And *I'm* not contemplating one either, or intending to undress. The most I'll take off will be my elbow-pads! I've simply agreed to the skating because I want to learn a new skill.'

'OK, I'll drink to that,' Megan said, refilling both their glasses and raising hers in a toast. 'Here's to your success as the next Tonya Harding, fully clothed and strictly vertical!'

CHAPTER 31

'No! I can't, I *can't*!'

'You *can*, Veronica. Just hold on tight and I'll guide you, OK? You need to simply trust me, then I more or less promise you'll be able to do a spin.'

Blindly, she obeyed, struggling to recall all he'd taught her in their long morning session at the rink – 'Think confidence, success ... Don't look down … Keep your weight on the ball of the foot … Push off with your body and use your arms to launch into the spin and then to control the rotation …' – and somehow, drawing on his own confidence, as well as using him as bulwark and bedrock, she managed the first manoeuvre in what Skip called a Simple Spin. As her knees began to tremble and her heart beat alarmingly fast, there seemed nothing remotely simple about it. Skip's left arm, however, was positioned firmly behind her back and his right hand held her own so tightly the two had become fused in one. So, she couldn't fall, could she? *Could* she?

Nonetheless, the spinning move seemed terrifying - unnatural even, to trust oneself to a mocking expanse of ice just waiting for her to crash down full-length and maybe drag Skip with her. Yet, miraculously, they both remained upright as he steered her into the spin and, all at once, her terror vanished and she was actually revelling in the sensation – all the more so because, a mere hour or two ago, she had deemed the movement totally impossible, and even Skip had admitted that it would be unusual to accomplish it when she'd had so little practice as yet. Indeed, the sense of achievement was so heady and so satisfying, she longed to go on spinning for ever, to spin away from her present constrained life with Colin, into a waltzing, whirling, humming-top of a future, in which all handicaps, restrictions and shackles melted magically away.

'That was brilliant!' Skip enthused, guiding her towards the rail, his arm still a reassuring extension of her backbone, his hand still clasped in hers. Such intimacy felt not a little worrying, but she was too elated to care. Besides, if he was her skating-coach, then, presumably, these were just necessary procedures, with no element of right or wrong.

'You must agree you did well?' he insisted, as they paused to rest a moment, allowing other skaters to hurtle past, showing off their skills in what Skip explained were split-jumps, twizzles, spread-eagles and back-scratch spins - all mystifying terms.

'Only thanks to *you*, though.'

'Not at all. I couldn't possibly teach you these manoeuvres in so short a space of time if you didn't have an inbuilt flair and also a fantastic sense of balance.'

'You're flattering me!'

'I *never* flatter, Veronica. I see it as a form of dishonesty. Well, how d'you feel? Do you want to try again?'

'To be honest. I'm so hungry, maybe we should refuel first. It seems ages since our hot chocolate this morning.'

'It *was* ages,' he confirmed, glancing at his watch. 'It's getting on for half-past three now.'

'In that case, let me buy you a late lunch. No, Skip, I insist. After all, if I were paying you for skating lessons, I'd owe you a fortune by now!'

He raised his brows in a comical expression. 'So, do you think I ought to change careers – swap coffee-making for skating tuition?'

'Absolutely. And, if you want a glowing reference for your website, you know where to come.'

He gently propelled her into action again, guiding her towards the exit, the pair of them still joined at the waist. 'If you're really sure about treating me to lunch,' he said, 'why don't we go to the restaurant here? I've never actually set foot in it, but they say the burgers are exceptionally good and, because it's on the premises, we can be sitting down devouring one in less than fifteen minutes, once we've taken off our skates and had a quick wash and brush-up.'

As they entered the restaurant, the noise from the jukebox was so rackety, so relentless, it seemed to threaten deafness to anyone daring to compete with it. Not that Skip seemed bothered, as he strode into the gloomy cavern, with its psychedelic black-and-white-painted walls and garish red ceiling-lights. She couldn't help but think of Alex as they seated themselves on spindly wooden chairs at a functional Formica-topped table, on which the only items were plastic tubs of ketchup, mustard and an unconvincingly acid-yellow mayonnaise. Where was the array of glasses and cutlery, the fulsome Maître D', spreading starched linen napkins over their laps, as he purred an obsequious welcome? The serviettes here took the form of a roll of basic kitchen paper, from which Skip tore a strip to mop a forgotten beer-spill from the table.

'What do you fancy?' he asked, passing her the menu – not an Alex-style menu in an embossed leather cover, but a single sheet of laminated paper, adorned with offbeat drawings. Apart from a few veggie side-dishes, there was little choice beyond burgers, chicken and fries, so she plumped for something called Monkey Fingers, described as 'chicken fillets in batter, slathered in our home-made buffalo sauce.' Alex had once amused her by giving her a list of words that usually spelled culinary disaster, 'slathered in' and 'smothered with' being two of the offenders, along with dewy-fresh' and 'morning-gathered' and, yes, 'home-made', which, he said, often signified that it had been highly processed in a factory, with no loving touch from Mum.

'Would you mind if I went for the "Bubble Trouble"?' Skip asked. 'Although it seems a bit of a cheek, when it's the most expensive item on the menu.'

'For heaven's sake, don't worry about that.' A quick glance at the menu proved that this 'most expensive item' was still considerably cheaper than most of the mere starters on the pricey establishments Alex frequented.

'It sounds wonderfully filling,' Skip explained, 'which is exactly what I need. I seem to feel permanently ravenous - so much so that Glenys used to say I had a tapeworm! It's partly my own fault, because I've never learned to cook and, anyway, I can't be bothered to eat once I get back from work.'

'Don't they feed you there, though?'

'Well, in theory they're meant to give us proper food-breaks, but if we're short of staff or there's a crisis in the kitchen, those go by the board.'

It struck her again how odd it was that, at the age of almost fifty, Skip should be living like a student, doing a basic, low-paid job, living in a house-share in a grotty part of London, with, apparently, no responsibilities or dependents, and being unable to cook.

'And what would you like to drink?' she asked, wishing she could pose more personal questions about his lifestyle and his past, get to know this man and his complexities, below his seemingly agreeable but strictly superficial surface.

'Oh, tap-water's fine for me.'

'No way,' she said suddenly wanting to spoil him, as Alex had done with her. 'Why don't we push the boat out and order a couple of cocktails? I never touch them normally, but I love the names of these: Silver Angels, Dead Hippies, Alleycats,' she spelled out from the menu.

'Well, if you're sure we've finished skating for the day. I wouldn't trust either of us on the ice if we're reeling from a lethal mix of vodka, gin and rum. Oh, listen!' he interrupted himself, 'this is one of my very favourite tracks – George Clinton singing *Atomic Dog*.'

A powerful, driving beat was now throbbing through the restaurant, outdone by screaming guitars and a backing vocal track that sounded, frankly, insane, with repeated 'bow-wow-wows' and 'yippie-yo-yippie-yeahs', and even doggy noises like panting and barking.

'Are you into Jazz Funk, by any chance?' Skip asked.

'Er, no.'

As he began to explain its roots in straight jazz, but with an added heavy back-beat, known as the groove, she doubted if she would ever be *au fait* with all the different styles and genres of music. Now that she was more alert to music generally, it seemed that everyone but her had grown up with a passion for some band or singer or classical ensemble and, even if they hadn't learned to play an instrument, had still been grounded in a basic musical knowledge and familiar with an extensive repertoire. But at least she was learning *now* and, indeed, Skip seemed as keen to share his musical expertise as he was his skating skills, and began expatiating on Clinton with a zeal and enthusiasm she only wished she could share.

'He's sometimes called the King of Jazz-Funk,' he said, gesticulating wildly with his knife, as if it were a conductor's baton, 'and his music draws on science fiction, psychedelic culture, surreal humour and outlandish fashion. He had a huge influence on rap and hip-hop, and was even inducted into the Rock & Roll Hall of Fame.'

Barely had she digested all this, when he switched to another of his passions: soul.

'Basically, Soul mixes Gospel, funk, jazz and Blues. But there are loads of different types …'

As he reeled off the list - Detroit Soul, Memphis Soul, Chicago Soul, Philadelphia Soul, Psychedelic Soul, Blue-Eyed Soul, British Soul, Northern Soul - every item on it increased her sense of ignorance.

Fortunately, he was interrupted by the waiter. 'A Dead Hippies and an Alleycat,' the swarthy guy announced, setting down their cocktails, although for all she knew about Soul, they could just as well be part of Skip's long list.

The drinks looked deceptively innocent, with their healthy cargo of pineapple chunks, cucumber-curls and slices of kiwi-fruit. Her very first sip, however, with its warming jolt and potently frisky kick, contradicted that impression.

'Let's drink to your skating success.' Clinking his glass to hers, he took an appreciative gulp, before launching into an exposition of what he called 'Soul's plethora of sub-genres', confusing her still further. 'I'm sure you already know how all the different elements intertwined in Soul – first slavery, then the Blues, then the Church and Gospel, then secular jazz, then rock'n'roll, then jazz rock, jazz fusion, funk, neo-soul ….'

'No, I don't know,' she admitted, 'and I'm amazed at all your own knowledge. I mean, how and where did you learn all this?'.

He shrugged. 'Just picked it up along the way. And I started very early, which always helps. I was barely out of my teens when I founded my own rock-band and, less than a year later, began building my own guitar. You see, I found this old wood discarded on a rubbish-dump and, since I was already learning woodworking skills at school, I put the two together and started hunting down old carpentry tools from junk-shops and car-boot-sales, and searching all the pawnshops for old, used guitars to cannibalize. To be perfectly frank, I must have been an obnoxious little nerd, spending every free minute mugging up technical stuff about frets and dowels and –'

Again, he was interrupted by the waiter, this time bringing their food, Skip's burger-bun overfilled and oozing cheese and relish, and accompanied by sides of plumply greasy chips and battered onion-rings. She could scarcely believe the passion with which he bit into the bun. Forget jazz-funk or Soul or making guitars – this was the basic passion of a starving man for sustenance. She was forced to suppress a smile as she thought of Alex nibbling on an asparagus spear, or toying with a miniscule portion of delicate crayfish mousse. Skip, in contrast, seemed to be hoovering up a week's rations in ten seconds flat. Yet she couldn't help but warm to his enthusiasm – no shallow food-snobbery, or critical comments on the lack of finesse in the culinary department, just an unabashed relish as he wolfed down every last morsel on his plate, including even the parsley garnish.

Only half-an-hour later, after eating both his own dessert (a coconut-and-marshmallow concoction, called, inexplicably, Filth Pie) and most of hers (Jägermeister Ripple ice-cream, which seemed more hard liquor than cream), did Skip seem replete and, once she'd settled the bill – remarkably low – they finally left the restaurant, exiting the back way, straight into the bowling-alley.

'Hey! Let's go bowling one day,' he suggested, pausing to watch a devoted Dad teaching his little-more-than-a-toddler daughter how to launch the ball. That 'one day' seemed to augur a long future association, which, again, made her feel uneasy, although, secretly, she would, in fact, like to try her hand at bowling. There were children in droves at the alley, most in small giggly groups without their parents, one such group sharing out a birthday cake as they took it in turns at the lanes. In her own childhood, she reflected, even birthday parties had been only for *other* children - children with friends, and fathers, and mothers who had cash to spare. But why dwell on the past when, right now, she was a happy adolescent, out with her kid brother and with coins jingling in her pockets to spend on any hobby she chose, be that skating, bowling, or learning the ukulele?

'But let's postpone that for another time. What I suggest right now is we go back to my place for a coffee.' Skip had already taken her arm and was steering her upstairs to street-level. 'It's only a shortish walk away and I can play you some of the music I've been telling you about.'

Instantly, she tensed. This *wasn't* her kid brother, but a man who had kissed her passionately and lingeringly just a few days ago. If she went back home with him, what else might he try on, especially encouraged by two cocktails? Indeed, she herself felt dangerously relaxed after her second Alleycat and feared she might do something she regretted, however strongly her rational mind was cautioning her against it.

'Is that OK with you, Veronica? I've just bought this new recording – well, it's really an old one, but it's been remastered – Jimmy

Smith playing *Back at the Chicken Shack*. He's the funkiest guy to hit the Hammond organ since they invented the thing and I reckon it'll bring out the inner tiger in you!'

Exactly what she feared and, if it was anything like Atomic Dog, she ought to be super-cautious. The Clinton song, as far as she'd made out, seemed to stress the bestial element in men: rutting dogs, constitutionally unable to stop chasing females (cats). And this song sounded worse: if Skip were right, inciting *her*, as well, to follow her animal instincts and go wild. About to tell him emphatically that she had to get back for her husband and had been absent quite long enough already, the words seemed to stick in her throat, as she contemplated the prospect of returning tamely home to silence, mess, spills, porn and Colin's complaints about his ankle. She was, in fact, concerned about the ankle, but there was nothing she could do until his hospital appointment (which the GP had arranged, thank God, in the blessedly short time of just ten days), except strap up the foot and apply an ice-pack, which valiant Pearl would already have done this afternoon. And, anyway, when she thought about it further, she realized that her fears about going home with Skip were almost certainly unfounded, since his four house-mates would all be returning home from work – and this particular week, they had offered a bed to a friend visiting from Australia, who was camping out in Skip's room on a futon – so, with no privacy or space to themselves, Skip would be forced to observe the proprieties, rather than turn into some crazy rutting dog.

'OK,' she said, 'but only a brief visit.' She would listen to the record, hope to God it was not a spur to any sort of pursuit, then have a strong coffee to sober up completely before taking over from Pearl. She had no intention, however, of giving Skip the notion that she was his for the taking – or ever would be.

CHAPTER 32

'I have some exciting news for you all,' Katy announced, having called for silence before beginning the rehearsal. 'We've been asked to sing at a prestigious event at London's City Hall, which is definitely a feather in our cap. *And*' – she paused dramatically – 'there's even better news. We'll be singing, for the first time ever, with a real live orchestra!'

'You're kidding,' Charlotte cut in. 'I can't believe that the Berlin Philharmonic or Royal Concertgebouw or whoever you've signed up would deign to perform with little old Larks Ascending!'

'Well, not those two, maybe, but the up-and-coming London City Orchestra are really keen to support us. They've performed all over the world, to rave reviews, and, although their conductor's only thirty, he's worked with lots of famous singers, and you should see his CV! Talk about a *wunderkind*!'

'It all sounds too good to be true,' Samantha commented. 'I tend to agree with Charlotte that he'll find us a bit underwhelming compared with the super-stars he's used to?'

'Not at all,' ever-loyal Katy responded. 'And, anyway, we'll be joining forces with Tenovus, whom I'm sure you all know run the best-known of the Cancer choirs. They're based in Wales, but have branches everywhere and both their London and their Sutton branches will be coming along that evening, to help to swell our numbers. Tenovus have been going strong for decades, starting with just ten brave souls - hence "ten-of-us" – and gradually branching out into more and more different fields, but with their focus increasingly on cancer. Just last year, I attended one of their presentations, explaining the research they've done on the link between singing and good health. And I have to say I was thoroughly impressed.'

'When is the gig?' Barry interrupted, adding in his usual flippant fashion. 'I can't miss Spurs, so most Saturdays are out for me.'

'Don't worry, it's a weekday and actually quite some way ahead – April 6, in fact, which is just after Easter and after the clocks go forward, and means we'll have an extra hour of daylight that evening. And, once we're into April, the weather should be warmer, so we can also celebrate the coming of spring. Please put the date in your diaries and, between now and then, we'll work hard on our repertoire, including a new song, *Sing For Life*, which was written especially for Tenovus and has now become their anthem. But they've kindly said we can adopt it ourselves, since our choir's whole ethos and purpose is so similar to theirs.'

'I actually heard them singing it in Cardiff,' Michael chipped in, 'when Clive and me were holidaying there last year. And I wasn't far off tears, however much of a wimp that makes me sound. You see, it was written by cancer-survivors, like so many of us here, and the words obviously come from the heart. And the choir itself was bloody good, so we'll have to pull our socks up!'

'We're every bit as good,' Katy reassured him. 'But, to put you all in the picture, the gig has been organized by a leading politician whose wife has cancer and is herself a member of Tenovus's London Choir. So, there'll be loads of VIPs in the audience and masses of media coverage, which, of course, will raise the profile of our own choir.'

'Where *is* City Hall?' Patricia enquired, tossing back her ponytail – one of the few females present who had long, strong, healthy hair. For some, having any hair at *all* was a cause for celebration.

'On the South Bank, between London Bridge and Tower Bridge.

It's a really striking building, which you could call iconic, if the word wasn't so overused. It's rarely open to the public and then only a small part of it, so it'll be a chance for those who don't know it to see inside. But forget any architectural bonus. What matters is our performance, so I'll need you to give it all you've got and sing with real joy and panache.'

Two words, Veronica mused, unknown to her until she joined the choir: joy non-existent, panache a dangerously exhibitionistic concept, not for the likes of her. How wonderful that things had changed!

'Do we wear our formal gear, or just our Larks Ascending T-shirts?' Samantha enquired.

'Oh, formal dress, definitely, but we can discuss all that at a later stage. Right now, before I finish the announcements, I want to remind you of another, slightly later event – the London Marathon on 22 April. One or two of you have already signed up as runners, but we also need some volunteers to help organize the post-race reception.'

As acting Chair of the Fund-Raising group, Veronica already had both dates in her diary, since she needed to consider how she could capitalize on their money-raising potential, perhaps making contacts with any glitterati at the gig who could be persuaded to donate, or arranging for choir-members to go round with collection-tins at and after the Marathon. There was a definite sense of satisfaction not only in her expanding horizons, but in the fact that she, personally, had done a huge amount to save the choir from disbandment through lack of funds. Of course, her success was due mainly to Alex's magnificent donations - one of the indisputably good things to have arisen from her otherwise disastrous affair.

'OK,' Katy said, 'let's get down to work, but before we start the rehearsal proper, I want you to introduce yourselves to one person you don't know or haven't yet spoken to. We're blessed in having quite a few new members, but we need to be sure they all feel welcome and at home. So, I'll give you just three minutes to make yourselves known to a newbie. Say your name and why you joined the choir and share one of your ambitions in life, be that winning the Lottery or being the next Mother Teresa.'

'The Lottery for me, please,' Barry said, with his vulgar, hooting laugh,

Veronica decided to move to the far end of the hall, to mingle with the sopranos, since, on the whole, she knew them less well than the tenors and basses she sat amongst. There was one soprano in particular she had never seen before, a shiny-bald woman on crutches, wearing a long compression-sleeve that encased her arm from hand to shoulder – one of the standard treatments for lymphedema.

'Hi, she said, with a smile. 'I'm Veronica and I joined the choir after my stepson died from cancer. And my ambition is to be less of a musical dunce.'

'Join the club! I can barely sing in tune. I'm Evelyn, by the way, and I'm here because my breast cancer has recently metastasized to the brain, so I feel I need to be with people who understand. And my ambition is to live long enough to see my first grandchild born. He or she is due in mid-July.'

A mere six months away, Veronica reflected, as she expressed her sympathy to Evelyn and, glancing at the children's artwork on the walls - all wintry snowscapes and skeletally bare trees – she willed this woman to live on until the drawings changed to billions of bright summer flowers blooming beneath a cloudless sky.

'Well, it's good to meet you, Veronica, and I have to say you do look glamourous.'

Veronica shrugged off the compliment, invariably embarrassed by such praise, which always seemed totally unwarranted, when, underneath, she was still shabby, ugly-duckling Ron, not elegant swan, Veronica. Most choir-members appeared blind to that fact, though, and often admired her sense of style or her knack of putting clothes together. Her present outfit, more daring and youthful than usual, had been a nonsensical purchase, since she'd bought it on impulse for no other reason than she felt it would appeal to Skip. But why attempt to please him, when she was still adamant that there could never be anything meaningful between them, and when Alex still consumed so much of her mind and heart?

Remembering her manners, she thanked Evelyn for the compliment, then suddenly, and again on impulse, enfolded the near-stranger, crutches and all, in a gentle, compassionate hug. Far from recoiling, as she'd feared, the woman responded with obvious warmth and pleasure. Hugs were important here – the only place she herself ever received them, or indeed, ever had. The bond of illness that united them all – their own or other people's illness – seemed to weaken the usual constraints and made everyone more willing to share, confide and, yes, physically reach out.

A sudden memory, from decades ago, flashed into her mind: Colin kneeling on the floor, teaching Peter to do a doggy-hug, the creature's front paws scrabbling to reach his shoulders, while his ecstatic pink tongue licked his master's hands and face. Such intimacies were forbidden to a mere wife. In fact, as far as she knew, her husband had never hugged another human being.

Once they had all returned to their normal seats, Katy urged them to their feet again. 'We're running slightly late, so, to get us started, I thought we'd combine a singing-exercise with a bit of limbering up. We're going to sing *My Bonnie Lies Over The Ocean* and, with every B, I want you to get up from your chairs, then sit down again with the next B. For those of you unwell or not too mobile, just raise your arms above your head for each B, and down again for the next one.'

The exercise prompted much hilarity, as people missed or mistimed their Bs, or even bumped into each other, but, amidst the giggles and apologies, Veronica was thinking how a choir-leader's skills weren't that different from a fund-raiser's. Both required an ability to galvanize people, sufficient tact to control time-wasters or calm dissension, without causing any offence, a need to praise and encourage, and also to bear in mind that some members of the group would be physically or mentally unable to participate to any large extent. The next fund-raising meeting had, in fact, been scheduled for the following Thursday and she would, as always, go on to visit Glenys afterwards, so that her friend didn't feel excluded from what should have been *her* role. Sadly, it looked increasingly unlikely that she would ever resume that role, since, far from improving on the experimental drug, she actually seemed worse - so much so that she'd recently been admitted to a hospice.

She experienced, right here and now, the same sick churning of her stomach as when she had first heard the news. And her horror had, of course, been augmented as she imagined Robert's distress that his wife of barely a month might not last until the spring. She had, indeed, arranged with Robert to visit the hospice this evening, after choir, and had come laden with grapes and clementines, a selection of books, and an extremely challenging jigsaw – although whether Glenys would be well enough to eat, read or concentrate on puzzles was worryingly uncertain.

She longed to share her worry with Megan, but she was away in

Cape Verde, on a last-minute bargain-break, in search of winter sun. She had gone with an old work-colleague, first suggesting that Veronica join them. For a moment, she'd been tempted, until common-sense and duty put paid to her wild fantasy of a fortnight in a luxury hotel, with nothing to do but stretch out on a sun-lounger, or paddle in a turquoise sea, fringed by tropical palms. Colin's still painful leg made it impossible to leave him even for two days, let alone two weeks.

She forced her mind back to the rehearsal, as they continued with *My Bonnie*, increasing confusion ensuing as people bobbed up from their chairs, often out of time with each other and the song, she herself one of the worst offenders. She couldn't stop her thoughts from circling back to Colin and their recent unsatisfactory visit to the hospital, where a rushed and offhand junior doctor had done little beyond prescribing stronger painkillers.

Skip was also on her mind: the whole complicated dilemma of whether she should be seeing him at all – something she certainly wouldn't mention to Glenys, since she felt distinctly awkward about being involved with her brother. She and Megan, however, could thrash out the issue in detail, once she'd brought her up to date with the latest developments, although one thing she would censor were her disturbingly sexual dreams, in which a man with Skip's body, weirdly combined with Alex's face and voice, was thrusting wildly into her, his abandoned cries echoing her own. She had not yet had the slightest glimpse of Skip's naked body, but, in all the dreams, it was muscular, hirsute, and as agile in the sack as on the ice.

'Right,' said Katy, 'I can't say that was brilliant, but at least we had a good laugh and a useful bit of exercise. And now I'd like us to start learning *Sing for Life*. If you didn't take a copy when you first came in, then here are some more to distribute.'

Veronica took two extra, one for Glenys, whom she liked to keep au fait with all the choir proceedings, and one for Megan, to await her return.

'First of all, I'll play the song right through, so you can get the gist of it. And, once we're more proficient – in a few weeks' time, I hope – I thought it would be really nice if we all sang it for Glenys and sent a recording to her at the hospice. I'm sure the words will mean a lot to her.'

And, as those words reverberated through the room, most people seemed struck by them, some listening with barely disguised emotion.

Sing for life, sing for love,
Sing for all the things that you are dreaming of.
Sing for hope, sing for strength ....

Life, love, hope, strength – who here didn't crave them, she wondered? And parts of the song seemed to have been written for those like Glenys and Evelyn, struggling with terminal illness.

Keep singing till the end, however hard life gets .....

All at once, and to her acute embarrassment, her mobile shrilled through the recording. With a brief word of apology, she slipped out to the kitchen to take the call, alarmed to hear Pearl's voice.

'Sweetheart, I know you said I mustn't ring you, except in an emergency, but this *is* an emergency. Your husband had another fall, you see, but it didn't seem too serious – no obvious injuries, as far as I could tell. And I hate to disturb you when you're busy, so I rang the paramedics, just so they could check him over and assure me he was OK. Fortunately, they were here in just ten minutes, but I'm afraid to say they think he's had a DVT.'

'Oh *no*!' The gasping cry had been unintended, since she had no idea, in fact, how dangerous a DVT might be - except that, at Colin's age, any new medical problem might pose a risk.

'The paramedics didn't want to hang around and wait for your return, so we're on our way to the hospital right now. But I suggest you leave immediately and join us in A & E.'

'OK,' she said, adopting, for Pearl's sake, a calm, measured tone of voice. As soon as she'd rung off, she scribbled a brief explanatory note to Katy and slipped it into her hand before creeping out of the hall.

And, emerging into the bitter January cold, she heard the reprise reverberating after her.

Sometimes, it's the smallest things
that help us survive.

So keep on singing, however hard life gets .....

CHAPTER 33

'Pixie! Pixie! where *are* you?'

As Colin's panicky voice jolted her from a deep but troubled sleep, Veronica sprang out of bed and pelted down the stairs, to find her husband blundering along the hall, lurching like a drunk. But who was Pixie, for heaven's sake? They had never known anyone called Pixie, not even a cat or dog. Could he be searching for Pearl, perhaps, but had forgotten his carer's name, apart from its initial P?

'It's all right, darling.' She rushed towards him, took his arm reassuringly. 'Pearl's at home with her family today, but she'll be coming again in a day or so.'

'Oh, Pixie, you're *here*!' he cried, his tone changing to one of deep relief, as he clung to her like an abandoned child.

'My name's Ron,' she reminded him, although he appeared not to hear and kept repeating, 'I couldn't find you, Pixie. I've been searching everywhere.'

'Well, you should be fast asleep.' She tried to lighten the atmosphere with a laugh that, even to her, sounded unconvincing. 'It's the middle of the night, so let's get you back to bed.'

'No, don't leave me,' he pleaded, terror-stricken once more. 'Don't leave me.'

As she led him back to his room and tried to settle him into bed, he kept clutching at her wildly, then attempted to rip off his pyjamas. She couldn't help but wonder if his week in hospital had made him revert to a dependent, child-like state, or even unhinged him in some way.

'Colin, lie down, and calm down!' Adopting the brusque, authoritative tone of the formidable charge-nurse on his ward seemed to make him more compliant, as he finally allowed her to pull the covers over him.

'I'll stay with you, OK? I can doze on this chair beside you, while you try to get back to sleep.'

Having pulled the chair alongside, she retrieved Peter from the floor and tucked the creature beside him under the blankets. 'Sleep well, Peter,' she murmured in a consolingly lullaby tone, relieved when he repeated it. At least he knew his dog's name, if not his wife's.

'Did you have a bad dream?' she asked. Perhaps Pixie had been a dream-figure, some evil fairy or wicked witch.

'Mm-hmm,' was his only reply, an interjection he'd started using in just the last few days, during his stay in hospital, and which he'd continued intermittently since she'd brought him home yesterday. Once a DVT had been confirmed, they had kept him in almost a week, because, when he'd gone on to develop breathlessness and chest-pains, they had feared a pulmonary embolism, which had necessitated further tests and close monitoring. He must have picked up 'Mm-hmm' from the Ghanaian nurse, Yaayaa, on his ward, who used it as her standard response to any question, comment, or idle piece of chitchat. Yet, however maddening it was in its non-specificity, many dementia sufferers lost their power of words altogether and resorted to total silence, so she was lucky in the fact that Colin had a fair amount of speech left. Nonetheless, she suspected that the medications were worsening his condition – not that he could stop them, since both the injections and the Warfarin were vital to prevent another thrombosis. He'd been instructed not to drink whilst on the drugs, but he'd become so severely agitated without his daily fix, she feared the stress would harm him more than a glass or three of the hard stuff. Yet his resultant incoherent state was taking its toll on her and she so dreaded the prospect of another drink-related fall, or even a full-blown stroke, she was beginning to feel she could no longer sleep in her own room, but must watch beside him each and every night.

Soon, she heard his breathing deepen, envying his ability to blank out any trauma. Indeed, in the taxi home this morning, he appeared to have totally forgotten the hours they'd spent in A & E, a mere seven days before. Once Pearl had returned to her family, *she* had stayed on in Emergency, tired, hungry and increasingly apprehensive as she pushed a fractious Colin in a wheelchair from one medic to another, unsure in some cases who they even *were*, if they were too fatigued or casual to introduce themselves. Then, as now, she had struggled through a convulsion of emotions, not least a deep concern about the future. Although, to her great relief, he had *not* had a pulmonary embolism, there was little doubt that his health had deteriorated, so was now the time to consider putting him into care? And should she sell the house to pay for it? Or, with Pearl's sterling help, could she continue to cope at home? Suppose Pearl left, though, lured away by a better job, or because one of her daughters developed some overriding health or personal problem.

She jumped up from her chair, now experiencing sharp twinges of guilt, as she reflected on her laxity in allowing Pearl to become so intimate with Colin: fondle him and feed him, as he nuzzled against her bosom. She had taken the line of least resistance simply in her own self-interest, because it ensured her husband's docility. And her guilt was increased by the large amount she was paying Pearl, to keep her in the job, when, in point of fact, *she* should be doing all the caring, not palming it off on someone else. Megan thought differently, of course. 'You've done enough caring for half-a-dozen lives! For God's sake, give yourself a break, love, and *spend* your money, rather than leaving it to some half-baked donkey sanctuary!'

Megan notwithstanding, more guilt flooded in as she pondered on Skip again. Although nothing had happened between them yet, there was no denying she *wanted* it to happen, however ambivalent her feelings about him in general. As a married woman, it was indisputably wrong to experience such jolts of pleasure when, during their skating sessions, he had clasped her hips, even touched her bottom and thighs, claiming he needed to demonstrate exactly where, as she skated, she should feel specific muscles working. Those muscles apart, though, she had felt far less innocent sensations in parts of her body completely unrelated to an ice-rink.

In an effort to distract herself, she returned in her mind to the glare and bleakness of the A & E department, a Limbo-like transit-station on the way to either discharge home, or a stay in hospital, or – worst case – to the mortuary, and a place where all normal sense of time had vanished. The other patients had mostly waited in silence, huddled into themselves, alone with their own troubled thoughts, no one attempting a smile if they happened to catch each other's eye, or striking up a friendly conversation. Her sense of isolation had gradually intensified, so that, after what seemed like aeons, she greeted a volunteer doling out custard-creams and plastic cups of juice like the last surviving human in a post-Apocalyptic universe, all but hugging him in her sheer relief at hearing a kindly voice.

Colin's whimpering jerked her back to the present. He was now awake and trying to tell her something more or less indecipherable. Perhaps he, too, was hungry and thirsty, but if she went to fetch him a midnight snack, he might flounder out of bed again, thrown by her apparent disappearance. Instead, she decided to sing to him – the new track they'd started learning last week, *Sing For Life* – purely on the grounds that, according to Katy, with a nod to Elton John, music had definite healing power. And at least Colin wouldn't and couldn't judge how weak her voice might be, or how sketchy her grasp of the tune.

In a second, life can change.
Don't let it slip away.
We've only got today .....

Megan, she reflected, might have written those words herself, being a great believer in *carpe diem*. Indeed, judging by the postcard that had just arrived from Cape Verde, she was seizing the day even on her holiday, no longer content simply to laze on the beach, but now trying her hand at wind-surfing and planning an expedition to Shark Bay.

Whatever Colin thought of the sentiments, the actual singing appeared to soothe him, despite several gaps and hesitations, where she could remember neither the lyrics nor the tune. And because she'd had no choice but to miss today's rehearsal, she was bound to fall still further behind. Nonetheless, she could still recall a number of lines that seemed to speak to her specifically.

Don't wait for life to choose.
It all begins and ends with you.
So, what will you do?

As the question hung in the air, her immediate, instinctive response was 'Go to bed with Skip', and she closed her eyes a moment to picture his body, which, weirdly, wasn't naked, but clad in his skating gear of tight-fitting black trousers, with a scarlet stripe down the side, and matching black-and-red blouson jacket that showed off the pert curve of his bum. And, in her fantasy, he was wearing his skates to bed: serious-looking, macho-black skates, with a daring splodge of scarlet on the toecaps. And the soundtrack playing was, of course, jazz-funk, which she'd been playing on YouTube as part of her 'Skip induction-course', goaded by its syncopated beat, by the wild, pulsing rhythm that made her want to dance until she dropped, by the explosive bursts of notes from instruments she couldn't name that sounded both aggressive and seductive. And now they were *both* dancing to that unsettling, inciting groove and his hands were straying everywhere as he twirled her, whirled her, twizzled her, then extended her outstretched leg between his own firm, muscular legs, clamping it tightly with his thighs, and finally bending her body back – mere putty in his hands – and pressing his right against it, groin to groin.

And, as they came together in a rocket-shower of black-and-scarlet thrills, she continued singing with new passion:

Sing for all the things that you are dreaming of ….

3 a.m. Colin was asleep again, but a fitful, restless sleep this time, so still she dared not leave him, or even dare to try to sleep herself. The last two hours had been so silent and slow-footed, she was again experiencing that desolate sensation of being alone in an uninhabited universe, and also struggling with self-reproach for having imagined *Skip* in bed, instead of Alex. It was the latter who, until very recently, had monopolized her heart and thoughts and longings, so, if she could switch her desire so easily to a completely different man, she must be

the sort of female her mother called a brazen hussy. It had, in fact, often struck her as ironic that, if anyone was a brazen hussy, then surely it was Den herself, but, alas, her mother was sadly lacking in self-knowledge. She just hoped she hadn't inherited such blindness, but, when it came to Den's promiscuity, she could certainly see the parallels and feared she might go on to become a bawdy, bed-hopping sexagenarian, however much Megan scoffed at the notion.

Such a prospect was so unwelcome, she decided to take the risk of darting back to her bedroom, just to grab her phone and divert herself by watching the News and checking Facebook. She also needed tangible proof that there was another world beyond this wee-small-hours wilderness, and that she was part of it. Resisting the temptation to ring her friends at such an unearthly hour, she did, however, dial the number she'd saved on her mobile after seeing it in the ladies' toilet of the A & E department. The notice on the wall had read: 'Does someone close to you make you feel afraid or isolated?', inviting callers to ring for help and support at any time of the day or night.

'Isolated' was exactly the word and, although 'afraid' hinted at domestic violence, she was afraid in different ways: afraid of being unable to cope if Colin deteriorated further, yet equally afraid of being all alone in the world. Maybe she could share such fears with the Helpline, at least make contact with another human being. However, all she got was a recorded message, despite their offer of support twenty-four/seven. Annoyed on behalf of those who might actually be suffering violence, she rang again and, much to her surprise, was rewarded this time with the voice of a real, live person. Yet, instantly, she terminated the call. What right had she to any claim on the service when she was merely feeling lonely – a condition shared by millions worldwide – and not in the slightest danger of assault, aggression or rape?

Switching off her phone, she got up from her chair to ease her aching back, then stood by the window, staring out at the dark, lowering sky and repeating over and over:

Keep singing till the end, however hard life gets .....

That must be her mantra, from now on.

CHAPTER 34

'Ye gods!' Megan gave a histrionic shiver, as she alighted from the warm fug of the taxi to the cruel knife-edge of the wind. 'It's perishing up here! Trust you, Veronica, to choose a day when inbuilt pain and suffering can be more or less guaranteed.'

'I *didn't* choose it,' she countered, hurt by Megan's barb. 'It was you who said today would be the best day, in terms of the strength and direction of the wind.'

'Yes, the best this week, but I never imagined we'd be making this trip in February. We should have postponed it until it's just less bloody cold.'

Aware of the sharpness in Megan's voice, Veronica felt her usual guilt, realizing, too late, that it had been selfish to insist on scattering her mother's ashes in the dead of winter. Yet the very bleakness of the season seemed more appropriate for Den than a time of caressing sunshine and benignly blue skies. And it would have seemed disrespectful to enact so important a ritual during the height of the tourist season, with Beachy Head full of hikers and day-trippers. It also struck her as right and fitting that the place should be so deserted. They hadn't glimpsed another human soul so far, and there was not one single boat on the wide expanse of sea stretching far, far below. Even birds seemed non-existent today. She had expected flocks of raucous gulls to be wheeling overhead or diving down towards the beach in a frantic hunt for food. Instead, the silence was absolute, as if the whole place was holding its breath or had been becalmed beneath some Sleeping Beauty spell.

'I'm sorry,' she said, giving Megan's arm an affectionate squeeze by way of an apology, although shamingly conscious of the fact that, since her friend was giving up a whole day to scatter the ashes of someone she had never met and appeared strongly to disapprove of, she owed her much, much more than just a casual 'sorry'. 'You're an absolute saint to do this trip with me and the last thing I want is you freezing to death!'

'Oh, I'm just being a grump – ignore me! It was that train that really got me down – I mean, stopping dead every ten or fifteen minutes, just as it had managed to put on a spurt, as if to say "Ya-boo! Did you really think we'd ever make up lost time?"'

No, the journey had not gone well. Apart from the serious delay, the heating in their carriage had been little more than tepid, and the cramped space full of rumbumptious, restless kids (whose mothers clearly believed in a child's Divine Right of self-expression, rather than in parental discipline) and, to cap it all, there had been no buffet car or trolley-service to supply so much as a packet of crisps, let alone a hot drink.

'Anyway,' Megan added, blowing on her rapidly numbing hands, to warm them, 'now we're here, we might as well enjoy the view. I've never actually seen it before in winter. We used to come up here as a family in the summer holidays, for hikes across the clifftop, or picnics and what-have-you. I was mad about wildflowers as a child, and my Dad was a bit of a botanist and could identify them all for me from his collection of nature books. I still remember some of the poetic names: Lady's Bedstraw, Queen Anne's Lace, Sheep's Sorrel.'

'Well, there's not a thing in bloom now,' Veronica said, experiencing a twinge of envy at such happy family outings: hikes, picnics, nature books and, best of all, a hands-on Dad. 'And look at that poor stunted tree. It's leaning so far sideways, it's totally lopsided. It must have been chivvied by the wind, winter after winter, so now it's twisted permanently out of shape.'

'Yet all the plants here have such determination. I remember as a child marvelling at flowers that were literally growing on the very edge of the cliff, as if clinging on for dear life.'

She herself had often felt that same sense of vulnerability, especially when her mother came back frighteningly late from some tempestuous tryst, and disturbed her with slammed doors, altercations, and insults shrieked full-volume at the latest hapless lover. But she did her best to suppress the thought, since it would surely be remiss to dwell on Den's deficiencies whilst disposing of her last remains.

'Right,' said Megan, gazing out at the seascape, 'this is the path we need to take. It leads directly to the point above the lighthouse that your mother specified.'

`As they set off along the grassy track, Veronica could hardly bear to look down, so precipitate the drop down the sheer face of the cliff, and she was nervily aware of the number of suicides this spot appeared to attract. No great feat to scatter a few ashes, but to hurl your *self*, body, blood and bone, five-hundred feet down to the treacherous rocks below, must take courage and desperation in equal parts. Despite the oppressive silence, she seemed to hear their anguished cries, followed by the sucking gurgle of the water, submerging their bloated bodies with a sublime indifference, as if they were of no more import than odd bits of flotsam and jetsam.

'I suggest we stay here on the level,' Megan said, 'while we do the readings, and not clamber down off the track until we're actually ready to scatter the ashes, otherwise we'll get vertigo or fall headlong into the sea!'

They had already discussed the readings on the train, both of them disappointed that they had failed to come up with more appropriate texts, and shocked by the sheer amount of execrably bad verse and sentimental trash on all the ash-scattering websites.

Your life was love and labour,
Your love for your family true.
You did the best for all of us.
We will always remember you,

Apart from the lame scansion, the sentiments were just plain wrong for Den, whose life was less love and labour than lust and lamentation. And, as for all those verses titled *Mother*, they were even more unsuitable, stressing as they did a lifetime of selfless devotion.

She listens to your stories and
she wipes away your tears.
She wraps her arms around you
and she understands your fears.

Her own mother's way with tears and fears had been to deride them as weakness rather than seek to assuage them – although today, of all days, it seemed disloyal to keep denigrating Den. Yet, she was wretchedly aware that the grief she felt – or rather dared not feel – was not only a deep sadness at Den's unhappy life, but also sadness for *herself,* in that her mother had fallen so far short of the stable, affectionate, caring 'Mum' she had craved in all her fantasies.

All at once, she stopped dead in her tracks, riveted by an initial letter 'D', constructed out of smooth white pebbles and shining in her path. Whilst surfing the websites, she had come across references to Signs and Portents From the Deceased - special stones or coins glinting in the grass, or a feather from some exotic bird floating down from on high – all deliberately placed there by the One Who Had Passed On, to indicate that they were still watching over their loved ones. Megan had dismissed the idea as arrant nonsense, adding that it seemed highly unlikely Den would be messing about with stones and feathers, rather than flaunting her booty in a bid to attract the denizens of Heaven.

Such flippancy had hurt and, now, faced with this mysterious 'D', Veronica couldn't be entirely sure that the notion was nonsensical. Why, out of all twenty-six letters of the alphabet, should it be a 'D'? *Could* it be a Sign, or was she simply clutching at straws, wanting a mother who, even after her death, would care so deeply she could somehow bring up pebbles from a beach five-hundred feet below and arrange them meaningfully and directly in her daughter's path? Unseen by Megan, who was striding on ahead, she gathered up the pebbles and slipped them into her holdall. At least they had weight and solidity, unlike the powdery ashes.

Megan had stopped to let her catch up and now pointed down the cliff-face to the red-and-white-striped lighthouse, diminished to toy-town size by its sheer dizzying distance below. 'Right, I suggest we do the readings from here. You start, Veronica.'

In truth, Veronica felt distinctly awkward reciting poetry for a mother who had frequently dismissed it as 'froth and gush'; nonetheless she withdrew the sheet of paper from her pocket and unfolded it against the jeering wind.

Remember me when I am gone away, she began haltingly, aware that the Christina Rossetti poem was not particularly apt for Den. But would any poem be apt, and at least this one was well-known, well-written and possessed pleasing weight and solemnity, which she did sincerely want for her mother's final send-off.

The wind rudely blew her words away, reminding her that she and Megan were just two paltry, pinprick figures amidst this daunting seascape, trying to immortalize a mother who'd been burned to her dregs twenty years ago. And, when Megan launched into her own reading, *Do Not go Gently Into That Dark Night* – again inappropriate, but another doughty classic - the constant reiteration of 'Rage' only served as a reminder of Den's own frightening rages. If only, she prayed to some non-existent Power Above, this pitifully inadequate ceremony could be transformative enough to undo a whole 'wrong' lifetime, make things eternally right. Yet, once Megan finished her reading, and she herself began edging her nervous way towards the cliff, now carrying the urnful of ashes, an element of farce crept in, as she realized she needed scissors to open the tough plastic bag inside. They *had* no scissors, yet to chuck the plastic bag itself directly into the sea seemed not only environmentally irresponsible, but a rebuff to Den who had cherished the romantic notion of being carried on the wind.

In a whisper, she explained the dilemma to Megan, who rummaged in her capacious handbag and eventually came up with a miniature manicure-set, which contained not scissors but a tiny pair of nail-clippers. Suppressing a blasphemous urge to giggle, Veronica began jabbing at the plastic with the ineffectual clippers, Megan joining in with sharp stabs from the nail-file, until, at last, they had punctured the bag and could now release the ashes.

Experiencing a sickening surge of vertigo, as she crept still closer to the cliff, Veronica decided to crawl on all fours for the final dizzying stretch. However, undignified the position, or messy for her clothes, it was preferable to merely dumping the ashes on the path. To fulfil her mother's wishes, they must go over the clifftop and rise on the breeze, if only briefly, before drifting down to the sea. The manoeuvre wasn't easy, and she had to stop herself from sliding forward on her stomach, as, bit by bit, she shook out the bag, astonished by the sheer quantity of ash. How could her tiny five-foot-nothing of a mother have produced so much residue? What she hadn't reckoned with was her sense of aching loss as the last of Den dispersed on the wind and all hope of a true bond between them – one that might outlast death – seemed to vanish in the churning ocean-currents far below.

Tears were streaming down her cheeks, as the final handful of ashes blew back in her direction, a grey, gritty powder sticking to her face, even clinging to her hands. Yet it seemed disrespectful to wipe her mother off on her coat, or try to find a tissue to clean up her face, so she remained grey-cheeked and grey-handed, like some weirdly substantial ghost.

'Be careful,' Megan warned, 'before you throw the flowers down. It's a heavy bouquet and you don't want to lose your footing.'

Veronica had deliberately bought hothouse roses, a dozen out-of-season beauties that Den would have called wickedly expensive. But all the more reason to indulge a mother who had never had the wherewithal to indulge *herself* on this, her Memorial Day – hence the taxi to the clifftop and the extravagant lunch to follow soon, at the newly revamped Beachy Head Restaurant. No long waits for buses, she'd decided, or cheap snacks in some low dive of a caff.

The roses felt weighty in her arms and she was forced to crouch close to the ground before she let them go, or she, too, might have followed in their arc. They plunged down to hit the narrow strip of chalky strand rising directly below the cliff, rather than reaching the actual water.

'Don't worry,' Megan soothed, sensing her disappointment. 'The tide will soon lift them off and bear them out to sea.'

Her tears continued to flow, however, and, as she returned to Megan and to the safety of the path, she was weeping as much from discomfort as from grief, her whole body bone-achingly cold, as if it had just been taken from the freezer like a great hunk of frozen meat. And, suddenly the gulls, silent until now, broke into screeching dissonance as if expressing her own turmoil of emotion. One bird swooped so low, she could see its dagger-beak and merciless red eye, and had the disquieting feeling that it might be another Sign, a portent of some threat to come.

'I feel so guilty, Megan,' she sobbed, 'that I wasn't a better daughter, especially when Den was older and had lost a lot of her former force and fire. I didn't visit as often as I should.'

'But you weren't free for endless visits when you were so tied up looking after Tom. And, in any case, it was quite a trek from Clapham.'

Veronica was barely listening, more intent on self-blame than on exculpation. 'When I think how much she suffered, Megan – things I've never told you, like her parents' acrimonious divorce when she was only ten or eleven, after years of quarrels and shouting-matches and even physical violence. And then her own mother died when Den was only fifteen and she was packed off to some odd relative, who used her as a skivvy. Was it any wonder she found life so difficult after all that early trauma?'

Megan leaned across to mop up her tears with a Kleenex, as if *she* had become the mother, in place of Den. 'It's a tragic story, I agree, but no way was it *your* fault. In fact, your mother was bloody lucky to have you! Once you'd left home. you could have simply washed your hands of her, or even murdered her, for God's sake, but you stayed dutiful until the end.'

'But I was always a disappointment. My very birth, for heaven's sake, destroyed her entire happiness and health.'

'So she said, but I'm inclined to think that, if she could disapprove of *you*, she'd disapprove of any daughter, even a plaster-saint. And, anyway, the whole thing is completely arbitrary. My mother thought the sun shone out of my arse, so she imbued me with great confidence, whereas your mother thought the opposite. And the problem is, our mothers' opinion of us has an almighty influence on how we go on to see ourselves, so, if they continually find fault with us, it becomes an incontrovertible truth that we're flawed and hopeless or whatever. But it's not the truth – far from it. *I* overrate my good qualities, and *you* underrate all yours, not because of the facts, but because of what we were told and how we learned to see ourselves. But that false opinion isn't set in stone.'

'It feels like it is, though, and, even now, I still hear Den's voice in my head, like a constant undermining refrain.'

'But you do actually have the choice to cut it off, refuse to listen, break with that whole era. Remember that bit in *Cinderella*, when Cinders has to leave her childhood home, as the only way to find a better life for herself? Well, it seems to me you need to do the same - metaphorically, of course – jettison the past and move on beyond your mother.'

'But, Megan,' she said, trying to dodge the wind, blowing her hair into insolent disarray, 'you don't know the whole story. I didn't even know it myself until just last night, when I finally dared to open an old shoe-box I've been keeping since Den died. It was labelled "Strictly Private", you see, so I presumed it would relate to her lovers – their letters, maybe, or photos - and I just didn't want to be reminded of all that angst, or of Den's constant disappointment in her men. But it was nothing to do with the men. It was all stuff connected to *me*: my hospital tag from the day I was born, and my childhood drawings and homework, and even my first baby-shoes, tiny, pink-suede ones, rather badly scuffed, as if she'd had to buy them second-hand, to economize, as usual.'

As she was speaking, Veronica withdrew the box from her holdall, opened the lid, and thrust each item into Megan's hand. 'I was absolutely astonished,' she continued in a rush, 'that she should have kept this stuff through all our dozens of house-moves, and I couldn't help feeling she must have felt *something* for me.'

Megan, too, seemed visibly moved as she examined the crayoned pictures, neat school-exercise-books, and grubby pair of miniature shoes. 'You're right,' she said. 'These must have been really treasured possessions if she continued to move them from pillar to post and held on to them until the day she died.'

'But that makes me feel all the worse. I mean, look at this – a record of my weight from birth to the age of five, for heaven's sake! The very fact she bothered to keep it updated for so long shows I must have been wrong about her and should have realized years before that I wasn't a total disaster in her life.'

'How could you have realized if she never said, and never praised you to your face? But, even if you *had* done something remiss - which I don't believe for a second - well, just accept, as I do, that everyone screws up and stop being so bloody hard on yourself. Even the famous Thomas Edison once electrocuted an elephant, would you believe!'

'Well, at least I've made you smile,' she added, handing Veronica back the shoe-box. ‘I suggest you keep this stuff, if only to remind you that what your mother felt for you was – I’d hazard a guess - profoundly more positive than what she said to your face. But, what you must get rid of is that festering load of regrets, rather than tote them around for the rest of your life. Remember after the Alex fiasco, we agreed to ditch our regrets, because they’re useless and self-punishing and drain us of all energy. So, I’m going to count to three, OK, and when I reach three, every regret from your birth to this moment must be dumped into the Channel. Right …..’

At the count of three, Megan mimed the gesture of emptying a huge sackful of boulders over the cliff-edge and Veronica followed suit, seeming to feel their oppressive weight suddenly tip into emancipating nothing. Then, physically unencumbered, they both broke into a run, away from the dangerously steep drop and the dangerously dark past, and towards the cheering light and warmth of the Beachy Head restaurant.

CHAPTER 35

'And what to start with, madam?'

'No starter for me, thanks,' Megan told the waiter. 'My main course sounds so filling, I doubt I'll have room for much else.'

'Megan, I insist'- Veronica passed her the menu again – 'It's a three-course lunch for both of us, strictly in Den's honour!'

'Well, all right, if you're twisting my arm, I'll have the duck-liver parfait.'

'And for you, madam?' the waiter asked, turning to Veronica.

'The scallops and chorizo, please. Since we're literally on top of the sea, the scallops should be wonderfully fresh.' She then consulted the wine-list, ordering the most expensive bottle, still wanting to make recompense for her mother's actual funeral, which, looking back from this vantage-point, now seemed too low-key.

'I can see we're pushing the boat out!' With a contented smile, Megan sank back in her chair.

'It's the least you deserve, coming all this way with me and letting me bore you stiff with all that guff about my mother.'

'If anyone's bored anyone, then it's me going on and on about my holiday for almost the entire train-journey – apart from when I wasn't griping about the delay!'

'But I love hearing about your holidays, if only so I can enjoy them vicariously.'

'I'm determined you'll enjoy them in reality, as soon as you're less tied down – all those places you simply have to see, like Venice and Istanbul and Marrakesh and even Timbuktu!'

'That's a tad ambitious! I'll happily settle for Paris, first-off.'

'Well, in actual fact, that should be easy enough, so long as Pearl is willing to hold the fort. Why don't we go together, just for a weekend?'

They were interrupted by the waiter bringing their wine, which he opened with a flourish befitting its vintage.

'To Den,' Veronica said, clinking her glass to Megan's, once the fellow had glided off again.

'To Den!' Megan echoed. 'May she rest in peace, and may *you*, her faithful daughter, enjoy peace in your own life hereafter. But, look, you haven't said yet what you think of my Paris idea.'

'I'm sorry, Megan, but it's out of the question at present. Colin's quite a bit worse and I couldn't possibly leave him at night. I've had to move into his room, you see, and doss down on a sleeping-bag, otherwise he gets panicky and thinks I've disappeared and keeps clambering out of bed to find me.'

She didn't mention the more intractable problem of his faecal incontinence and the distressing fact that, despite his tendency to diarrhoea (not helped by his excessive alcohol intake), he continually ripped off his absorbent pad, allowing puddles of poo to leak through his trousers or pyjama-bottoms and plop directly on to the carpet. It was hardly a suitable subject for the lunch-table and, as for her recent outburst, when, exhausted, frustrated and close to breaking-point at yet another poo-gush, she had yelled a stream of abuse at him, she was far too ashamed to admit that to a soul. Indeed, even recalling the words she had used shocked her to the core: a stream of expletives she didn't even know she knew. Megan had already seen her at her worst, way back in September, and would be aghast to know that the harridan she'd become that evening had resurrected just last week and, once again, she had lost control, screaming like a fishwife and literally shaking with rage at Colin's sheer perversity. Megan kept stressing that anger and resentment were only natural in her situation, yet the dementia literature told a different story, constantly reiterating that calmness and patience must be stoically maintained in the face of more or less any provocation. However, she couldn't help wondering, heretically, who had actually penned that literature? – probably not the spouses at the coalface, at serious risk of crack-up from the mounting daily strain.

Megan stretched her legs luxuriously in the warmth of the log-fire. 'It's really toasty in here. And I love the fact we can still see a wide expanse of the Downs, but without that vicious wind.'

Veronica followed her gaze through the large, scenic picture-windows that afforded a perfect view of the undulating grassland stretching far beyond into rolling, blue-hazed hills. In truth, though, she was still finding it hard to remove her mind from the problems with both Colin and Den. For some unfathomable reason, she was now dwelling on the disturbing fact that, on her honeymoon, she had actually missed her mother, felt deracinated and insecure without the one figure who had dominated her life to date, never before giving her any leeway to separate herself, be her own person, or cut the apron-strings. Colin had seemed so alien, so male, so silently self-sufficient, compared with the bosomy, ever-nagging, ever-present Den.

'There's still so much we need to catch up with,' Megan said, sipping her wine appreciatively. 'How's Glenys, for example?'

'Not good. I went to see her in the hospice last week and, to be honest, she looked awful. I feel desperately sorry for Robert. They've only been married two months, yet he's already in danger of losing her.'

'Oh, Lord! Is it really that bad?'

''Fraid so. At least I managed to distract her a bit, and she seemed to want to talk and hear everybody's news, but I could see what an effort it was for her and how much she'd deteriorated.' She herself had felt distinctly awkward, burning and bouncing as she was with illicit fantasies about Skip, whilst in the presence of his fast-fading sister. And, again she'd reflected how hard it was to open up completely, even with one's friends. Some things just had to be concealed, as she'd learned decades ago, when Colin had turned on Tom and hit him with the full force of his fist. She herself still had vivid flashbacks to that traumatic night: Tom's bruised and baffled face rapidly reddening and swelling from the blow, as the poor lad did his best to try to comprehend why his own father had attacked him. But never, ever, could she reveal such a thing, without destroying her husband's credibility as a caring parent and decent human being.

She was relieved when the waiter appeared and dispersed the troubling memories that threatened to wreck her pleasure in the meal. And, as he set down their starters, she tried to focus on them instead: the scallops sizzling in a rich, buttery sauce, and Megan's parfait served on a trendy slab of slate, with what looked like half a crusty loaf and enough salad for a tribe.

Megan raised her eyebrows at the spread. 'I intended to invite you back for supper this evening at my place, but, after this little lot, I'm not sure I could eat another thing!'

'Well. It's sweet of you, Megan, but I couldn't come anyway. I've left Colin quite long enough as it is, and I worry about Pearl.'

'I can't think why. She's earning a fair whack and she and Colin seem as thick as thieves, so what's the problem?'

'The problem' was the alarming fact that Colin had recently exposed himself to Pearl in an act of deliberate sexual provocation – another thing she couldn't possibly admit. Pearl had handled it brilliantly, with a mixture of firmness and humour, but, if it happened again, the woman might give in her notice, which would mean an end to any more time with Skip. She desperately wanted to discuss Skip with Megan, yet felt embarrassed about admitting the urgent attraction she felt to his lithe, athletic, agile body, perfectly displayed in the nimble way he skated, combining mercurial dash and élan with a skilful, imperturbable control.

'Is everything all right, ladies?' the waiter enquired, stopping at their table.

'Perfect,' Megan said, although Veronica fastened on his use of the word 'ladies', which reminded her of Den's constant injunction to her as a child to 'be a little lady'. Now, as an ageing adult, the advice struck her as a tad ironical in light of her mother's own anything-but-ladylike raucous promiscuity, and she also realized that, as far as Skip was concerned, she had no desire whatever to be a little lady; rather yearned to be a wild, licentious hussy.

The waiter had topped up their glasses and, emboldened by draining hers at a gulp, she suddenly found herself embarking on the subject she'd vowed to avoid, knowing it was now or never, because at least it was reasonably private here, compared with the crowded train home. Ignoring her scallops, she put down her fork and said, awkwardly, 'Can I use you as an agony-aunt again?'

'Sure. Go ahead! No – let me guess. You've met a new bloke at choir, who's a famous opera-singer and filthy-rich, with a string of racehorses, and lavish properties in Santa Monica, Biarritz and Dubai.'

'I wish! No, this is about Skip again, who doesn't seem to own so much as a brass farthing and is famous only for his lattes.' She felt profoundly disloyal even saying it. True, Skip was hardly a catch in conventional terms, but she couldn't deny the strong appeal he held for her personally, not just his physical attractions, but his very unassuming boyishness, his enthusiasm for a host of things from skating and jazz-funk to chess, bowling, water-sports and even boxer-dogs – although his landlord, he claimed, drew the line at even a goldfish.

'I haven't actually seen him for ages – you know, what with Colin being ill and ….' The sentence trailed away. How could she even consider sleeping with a guy she barely knew while her husband was still struggling to recover from a major blow to his health? Suppressing the thought, she added, 'But he has invited me out tomorrow, in fact, and tomorrow happens to be Valentine's Day, so I'm not sure if I should go.'

'Why ever not? Personally, I'd be thrilled to have a date for Valentine's, rather than sitting on my own, watching *Celebrity Big Brother*.'

'Yes, but that sort of date yokes any couple together as an item, since all the restaurants go overboard with hearts and flowers, and lashings of romance laid on like whipped cream.' Although not, she reflected, the places Skip was likely to frequent: basic burger bars, or atmospheric dives where unheard-of jazz musicians played in Stygian gloom, with not a heart or rose in sight. 'And I'm also a bit disturbed by what Glenys told me recently.' She had deliberately broached the subject of Skip, finding it hard to understand how two siblings could be so different – Glenys a graduate and civil servant, with an expensive flat and substantial pension, and Skip more like a student. Indeed, he and his younger house-mates had seemed endearingly like undergrads, with nothing to eat in the cupboards, unmade beds, piles of dirty crocks in the sink, but an everlasting supply of japes and banter, and a refreshing informality and high-spiritedness that had given her a taste of her own non-existent student days, now long overdue. And there was the same lack of privacy she assumed most student houses shared, so that Skip was unable to kiss her until they were on their way out. Then, all at once, he lured her into the broom-cupboard, shut the door behind them and clasped her in a scorching embrace. Far from objecting, she had found herself responding like the free-and-easy seventeen-year-old she had never been allowed to be.

'So, what did Glenys say?' Megan prompted, spreading a lavish portion of parfait on a chunk of warm, seeded bread.

'Well, she was a bit wary at first of saying anything, but she did eventually confide that he'd been engaged years ago to a beautiful, artistic girl who worked as a painter and engraver, but who killed herself just weeks before the wedding. Apparently, she took a hefty overdose and it was poor Skip who found her, stone-cold dead. And, according to Glenys, he's never quite got over it, and always blames himself for not having realized just what a dire state she was in. And her family blamed him, too, turned on him as a convenient scapegoat and have never spoken to him since. And Glenys also hinted at some drug problem. She clammed up at that point and refused to say any more, but I have to admit I can't help worrying.' All the more so, she omitted to add, because Skip had told her, with apparent approval, that his much-admired George Clinton had written most of his work while on acid.

Megan was shaking her head, in both warning and concern. 'I don't like the sound of any of it. You want to be really careful, love, before you get involved with anyone who could land you in the shit again, like Alex.'

Veronica said nothing, unable to admit that, even if Skip were a full-blown heroin addict, she still longed to go to bed with him. Something must be wrong with her, to feel such tigerish lust at her age. Besides, suppose *he* were an 'Atomic Dog', chasing any and every alley-cat on heat?

'As I'm forever telling you, Veronica, you're worthy of a decent relationship with a man who loves and respects you. And this is the perfect time to look for it, because you've just this minute broken with your mother's script, which means you don't have to settle for some highly neurotic bloke, or one who just wants his own selfish needs met.'

'You seem to imagine,' Veronica retorted, with a sigh, 'that, at the age of almost sixty, I have an infinite choice of devoted, loving, normal, stable men!'

'Well, maybe not infinite, but there's no reason why you shouldn't meet one halfway decent guy.'

'Skip *is* halfway decent – much more than that, in fact.'

'But you said yourself he's an unknown quantity. If I were in your shoes, I'd ask myself why his fiancée killed herself. Did he drive her to it, maybe?'

'That's totally unfair Megan.'

'Maybe. Maybe not. But I suggest you give yourself longer to get to know him. I mean, the whole Alex thing was very spur-of-the-moment and you don't want a repeat of that.'

She couldn't deny that it was Alex's uncanny resemblance to Leonard that had first attracted her, thrown her nonsensically off-balance, re-ignited her childhood passion for the first man she'd ever met who was kind, loyal, caring and responsible. The fact that Alex himself was none of those things meant her judgement had been seriously amiss, so how could she trust her feelings for Skip? Admittedly, Skip was nothing like Leonard, in age, appearance, interests, income, or profession, but that had absolutely no bearing on whether he was either suitable or safe.

'I suppose you could say,' Megan continued, reflectively, 'it's rather like learning a new song at choir. At first, it's all a bit uncertain and confusing, and then we gradually learn more, and finally decide whether we like the song and if it suits our particular voice and gives us real pleasure to sing it.'

Veronica failed to find the analogy convincing. Getting to know a song was entirely different from getting to know a person. Most songs were fairly transparent, whereas people could be secretive, even devious, present a façade completely at odds with their true self. Yet, in point of fact, that only justified Megan patently wise advice to be circumspect and cautious in her dealings with Skip, since he might be hushing up a whole covert, transgressive side, just as she herself did, and, for all she knew, might give vent to furious outbursts in private, or feel duty-bound to hide a weird relationship with his mother behind a show of cheery normality. But, even if both were true, she still found it hard to take heed of Megan's warning, because some deeper, almost basic instinct craved to get closer to him, to become his soulmate, someone who mattered deeply to her, as she to him. So many in the choir took their partners and children for granted. They were simply *there,* a rock-solid source of support, conversation and built-in company. Even Pearl had big, cuddly Renardo, not to mention their five daughters and, although Megan might live alone and declare she had no interest in meeting husband number-three, she actually had Lavinia and Flora to endow her present life with meaning and ensure her future was less lonely. She herself was extremely blessed in having Megan, of course, but a friend and confidante, however loyal and committed, wasn't the same as a sexual relationship. The latter, as she'd learned with Alex, could bond a couple in a unique and special way, only possible when *bodies* were involved, with all their wayward idiosyncrasies and sheer tumults.

'Here, try a piece of this,' her friend urged, passing her a chunk of bread, spread liberally with parfait. 'You haven't touched your scallops. Are they all right?'

'Yes, delicious.' Veronica quickly swallowed her first, along with Megan's offering, hoping no more warnings would be issued over Skip, since they only increased her confusion.

Megan, though, returned to the attack. 'Don't forget you have a lot to offer, love, so don't sell yourself cheap, OK? And another thing I've told you over and over is that having a strong libido is a definite pulling-point with most red-blooded men. Which means I'll have to settle for old age with a nice, companionable cat, since I've lost all interest in hooking up with anyone. In fact, my own libido is dwindling even further, so much so that when I read last week that the boffins have just decided there's no such thing as the G-Spot, I was mightily relieved, having been searching for mine in vain for all these years!'

Veronica laughed, deciding to change the subject as soon as she tactfully could. Without libido, how could Megan possibly understand her own fierce desire to go the whole way with Skip, however unwise it was – and, yes, even in a broom-cupboard, surrounded by mops and buckets? And, if he found her G-Spot in the process, she for one would rejoice.

*

'I just can't thank you enough,' Veronica said, as they alighted at Victoria and walked towards the barrier together, 'for coming with me today and making it so special.'

'It's me who should thank *you*. That lunch was out-of-this-world, although I'm beginning to regret that sharing-pudding-platter – I mean, six different puds, all wickedly rich and creamy!'

'Yes, Colin will be lucky to get a packet of crisps tonight! Which reminds me,' she said, contradicting herself, 'I'm almost out of cheese and bread, so I'd better pop into the M & S food-store here and stock up with a few supplies.'

'I'll wait for you outside, OK?'

'No, don't worry, I'll only hold you up. You see, I want to buy Pearl some flowers, as well, which means going up the escalator to the flower-shop on the upper level. The florists there do a fantastic job of wrapping the bouquets with bows and ribbons and stuff, but that does involve hanging around a bit. Yet, last time I treated her, Pearl was so over-the-moon with her great sheaf of gladioli, all decked out with silver ribbons and little iridescent butterflies, I'd like to do something similar today. After all, she has been holding the fort since early morning.'

'Well, I must admit I do feel pretty knackered, so, if you're really sure, I think I will push off.'

'Fine. I'll phone you tomorrow, OK?'

The two friends embraced and, as Veronica made for the escalator, someone touched her on the shoulder.

'Veronica! I *thought* it was you. Long time no see!'

She turned to see Sebastian, whom, indeed, she hadn't laid eyes on since feeling the full force of his fury five months ago, when she'd told him she was terminating her lessons. He still looked his usual dashing self, wearing knee-high black-suede boots, a trendy black jacket and an elaborately frilled white shirt. 'How *are* you?' she stammered, still feeling awkward at the thought of that last encounter.

'Never better. My professional life is going through the stratosphere! It's been non-stop bookings and engagements, and amazingly good reviews. I've been called a boy-genius, hailed as the next Fischer-Diskau - all that kind of thing. In fact, I'm just off this minute to Gatwick, to catch a flight to Basel, then on from there to Freiburg, to take part in a really prestigious music festival. I've landed the leading role in a ground-breaking new opera, and they're so impressed with my performance, they've already booked me for their next season.'

'Congratulations!' she said, grudgingly, riled, as always, by his boasting.

'And how are *you*?' he deigned to ask, although without waiting for her answer. 'I just hope you've parted company with that appalling choir you belonged to. As I tried to make clear long ago, any choir worthy of the name insists on holding auditions, to ensure a reasonable level of competence. And, as for admitting people who can't read music, well, it's totally counter-productive, since all they do is hold back the musically literate members and lower the general standard.'

'So you told me ad infinitum,' she retorted sharply, surprised by her own vehemence. 'But, as I've told *you*, ad infinitum, the whole point of our choir is not musical excellence, but the fact we're all bonded by our experience of cancer. It may seem heretical to you, but the singing, in and for itself, is almost secondary, because we're more interested in companionship and a sense of belonging and an improved ability to cope with our various stresses. During our rehearsals, we're encouraged to relax and release the tension that builds up every week for those struggling with their illness. And we all feel less isolated just by coming together and singing our hearts out, regardless of whether every note is perfect. I know you don't approve, but the whole ethos of Larks Ascending is that it's better to be "wrong but strong" than right but weak and timid.'

Sebastian's pursed lips expressed his distaste for such a notion. 'I certainly *don't* approve, Veronica, if only because it must require a huge amount of note-bashing to get your weaker singers anywhere near a basic minimum standard, and that holds back the rest, of course, and prevents the choir from shining.'

Commuters were streaming past them on the crowded station, travellers with bulky cases forced to skirt around them. Nonetheless, Veronica stood her ground, in all senses. 'We're not interested primarily in standards, or even in "shining", as you put it. Our particular choir's aim is to spread the word that singing is an inclusive activity, and an instinctive, inbuilt one, not an exclusive, elitist practice for a few especially talented stars.'

Sebastian gave a dismissive shrug, before glancing at this watch.' Sorry, but I'll have to run. I happen to be one of those stars you clearly love to disparage, so no way can I miss my flight. You see, *I* intend to shine at the all-important dress rehearsal tomorrow, even if your choir has no such laudable ambition.'

Although her natural inclination to take him to task for sheer arrogance, he was already speeding towards his train, so she herself soared up on the escalator, feeling a definite sense of triumph in having stood up to him with such assurance. Even a few months ago, she would have been incapable of taking so firm a line, or would have paid for such outspokenness with a sickening backwash of guilt. Now, there was no trace of guilt, only pride in herself, as she did what Megan had urged her to do during the journey back: keep acknowledging her many solid achievements. And, despite her embarrassment at Megan spelling out those achievements, there and then, in the crowded carriage, it had given her a kick to hear them listed, one by one: she had discovered her voice through the choir, developed new skills in her fund-raising work – leadership and organizational skills, as well as new digital expertise - and was now much better prepared to embark on the Diploma Course in less than a month's time. She had also made a start in breaking with her mother's negative script and, through her affair with Alex, even discovered she had a responsive, sensuous body. Admittedly, Megan always overpraised her, but her friend was undoubtedly right in warning her that she didn't want a repeat of Alex, so, instead of throwing caution to the winds and giving Skip the green light, she would wait a whole lot longer and first get to know him better.

CHAPTER 36

'No, Skip. I *can't.* I mustn't.'

Skip clasped Veronica tighter, as she tried to pull away. 'You said that about the skating and just one session proved you *can* and *must.*'

'Skating's totally different.'

'Not really,' he coaxed, pressing the length of his body against hers. 'They're both bodily experiences when it's essential to let go and surrender to the sensations, and where you have to trust your partner, trust your natural instinct.'

His achingly vulnerable smile seemed to reach his eyes and make them undermine her defences, especially in tandem with his caressingly persuasive voice. She should never have let him kiss her in the first place - a kiss so long and fierce it had knocked her completely off-guard, despite Megan's advice to be cautious, despite the fact she was married, even despite all the trauma resulting from her affair with Alex.

The thought of Alex brought her to her senses and she put a safer distance between her and Skip on the clapped-out, rickety divan. The contrast between the two situations struck her as almost comic: instead of Alex's king-size, super-sprung bed, they were stuck with this junk-shop affair, already creaking as they sat on it and which might well collapse if they engaged in any energetic encounter. And, instead of a luxurious flat, they were confined to the stark basement-bedsit Skip had borrowed for the evening from one of his barista friends. No panoramic vista through floor-to-ceiling glass, just one small window looking out at a brick wall; no exotic nibbles or expensive vintage champagne, only a bought-in pizza and instant coffee; no designer aftershave, just Skip's cheese-and-Nescafe breath as he leaned towards her again; no sense of space or privacy, but an uneasy awareness of the people in the flat above, their voices and footsteps resounding overhead. So what would *they* hear if she said yes, instead of no, and obeyed her body rather than her mind?

'I want you to meet Albert,' he said, still with that diffident, uncertain smile.

'*Who?*'

He unzipped his jeans, allowing his engorged and rampant penis to flounce free of its captivity – a shock and provocation. Yet, being only the third penis she had ever seen in her life (bar Tom's pitifully small shrimp) she couldn't help but gaze at it with a fascinated curiosity.

'Albert's my real name, as I think I told you the first day we met, but this is Little Albert.'

Flaunting there only inches from her face, it appeared anything but little, rather insistent and peremptory. They were going far too fast and her undeniable desire for him was doing battle with a sense of danger, almost of exploitation. 'No!' she said, more severely than she'd intended, deliberately getting up from the bed and moving towards the window, as if to look out at the non-existent view.

Instantly, both he and Little Albert seemed to shrink, abashed. 'OK,' he said, rezipping himself, with a crestfallen shrug. 'I obviously misread the signals. The last thing I want is to traumatize you for life by forcing myself on you!'

Despite his jokey tone, it was clear he was alluding to the recent media buzz about consent, abuse, and the fact that couples nowadays were meant to have grown-up, pre-sex conversations, to ensure whatever happened in bed was approved and endorsed by both parties.

She had never in her life had such a conversation and had no idea how to even start one. Indeed, wouldn't the very notion douse any romance or spontaneity? Yet now they seemed to have reached an impasse and she was at a loss as to how to proceed. If she made her excuses and left, it would be a slap in the face for Skip, when he'd gone to all the trouble of setting up this Valentine's date. In truth, however, she'd been expecting an innocuous meal out at MacDonald's, not a pre-arranged seduction. On the other hand, she was equally to blame for having led him on, responded to his kisses with undisguised enthusiasm.

Fortunately, he came to the rescue by suggesting they listened to some music instead. 'I want you to hear another George Clinton number,' he said, leaping off the bed to fetch his phone, 'one of my favourites, *Hit it and Quit it*, sung by Funkadelic.'

'Won't it disturb the people upstairs?' she asked, still aware of their noises through the ceiling: running taps, the clatter of dishes.

'I doubt it. Tony said they're very easy-going and, apparently, they're planning to go out for some big Valentine's bash, so I reckon they'll push off pretty soon, in any case.'

As the dynamic, febrile beat of the track erupted through the room, she only hoped he was right, since the noise was making the very walls shake and probably deafening not just the couple upstairs but all the inhabitants of any neighbouring flats.

'So, how did you like it?' he asked, once the track had skidded to an end, leaving a still vibrating silence.

'Like' was hardly the word. The music was blatant, in-your-face, and unsettlingly aggressive, like nothing she had ever heard before and, as for the lyrics, those she could make out managed to be both intriguing and appalling at once. The general effect, however, was exciting, arousing, and made her want to go bopping round the room like some teenager on Ecstasy.

As if tuning in to her thoughts, he moved purposefully towards her, and swept her into a frenzied, uninhibited dance. Dancing had rarely featured in her life, and never this anarchic freestyle, but she needed no persuasion to follow his lead, desperate for some release from the churn of contradictory feelings raging through her body and her mind. And, as she gradually relaxed, she found Skip, as with the skating, a compellingly expert partner, initiating movements so audacious and mercurial, she would never have dared them on her own, yet with no risk of a mis-step, because he was so totally in charge, his feet and body leading with such assurance, her own had no choice but to comply. As far as she could tell – and admittedly she was still pretty bad at identifying instruments - the rhythm seemed to be driven by the guitars: repetitive, insistent and, together with the powerful drumbeats, speaking to her body in some disturbingly primeval way, making it move faster and freer. And, undoubtedly, it provided a release, as she surrendered her control, fused her movements with his, as she'd done at the ice-rink, allowed his confident extroversion to banish her own constraint. And, as she slowly got the hang of the thing, she began to relish the sensations of swivelling hips, shimmying shoulders, pistoning arms, head flung wildly back and forth, as if she were loose on all her hinges and gloriously freed from her usual rigid posture.

At last, exhausted, they both slumped back on the bed, Skip kicking off his shoes and peeling back his sweater. The T-shirt underneath it had ridden up his chest, to reveal an expanse of dark, springy body-hair. Colin had never had much in the way of body-hair and Alex kept his waxed, so this secret pelt magnetized her eyes, not least because it was so different from Skip's head-hair, the latter being the colour of wet sand. And, although he'd now pulled down his T-shirt, his low-slung jeans afforded a glimpse of his navel, where the coarse, curly whorls of hair changed shape into a dark, straight line, as if deliberately and tantalizingly pointing to his penis. Her thoughts kept straying back to how urgent it had looked - inflamed and almost angry, the diadem of hair around it even darker than his chest-hair. How perverse of her to be craving it inside her now, when she'd said no with such conviction and actually pushed him away. Her body, though, in contrast, hot and loose and limbered up, seemed to be saying an emphatic yes. Hardly believing her own audacity, she laid a tentative hand across the zip of his jeans, felt him stir and swell beneath her touch. His eyes locked with hers a second, as if asking permission, asking if she'd changed her mind, and, silently she implored him, 'Yes, go ahead, I beg you. You're right – we *have* to do this.'

The sensation of him entering her was still something of a shock – no foreplay or fondling, just his irrepressible haste, as if they had reached the End of Days and had only seconds left if they ever wished to get together. They both still had their tops on and he, ridiculously, his socks, but that scarcely registered, because her attention was narrowed to that one, thrusting, tempestuous point where the two of them were fused. No more need to agonize about whether this was right or not; her body *knew* it was right, responding with a wildness she'd forgotten she'd possessed. She tightened herself around him, squeezing with her muscles, as Alex had once taught her, no longer even caring that she was using his techniques on Skip. What mattered was Skip's response: the quickened, frenetic tempo, the abandoned cries he was making – no, *she* was making, their two panting soundtracks merging into one.

Never before had she come so quickly and so completely, her eyes squeezing shut with the tension, her toes tensed and curling up, as if they, too, were startled by the sheer speed of the encounter, her hands clasping his waist so tightly, she feared she was leaving claw-marks.

And she, too, must be marked, where his designer-stubble had grazed so fiercely against her face, it felt as if had erupted in a rash. Yet she relished the fact that they had each left their imprint on the other, even wanted those marks to be permanent, to emblazon this moment for ever on their bodies.

Despite her elation, she also felt total exhaustion, as if she'd just run a marathon or competed in some gruelling contest, and could only collapse down on the bed, breathless, all but spent. Skip, though, seemed as energetic as ever, already on his feet, finding another favourite track on his phone, then rummaging in the cupboards and eventually coming up with a packet of biscuits and a giant bottle of Coke. Having poured them each a glass and ripped open the ginger-nuts, next he crouched above her and began kissing her ferociously, in one long greedy line, from her forehead to her feet. Almost too whacked to respond, she couldn't help noticing that his advances were less subtle than Alex's: no crafty tongue tracing the coils of her ear, circling her nipples, licking between her fingers. Skip was clearly more concerned with the sheer thrusting, coupling aspect of sex.

'Was Albert OK for you?' He spoke with a touching vulnerability, as if uncertain of his prowess and needing formal confirmation.

'Perfect.' She, too, had found the precipitate haste and sense of vehement onslaught unaccountably exciting, much to her surprise.

'Let's do it again as soon as I've recovered, which shouldn't take that long.'

He was clearly tireless, his energies unlimited - something of a turn-on in itself, suggesting as it did virility and youth.

'What do you call your cunt?' he persisted, sneaking his hand between her legs.

‘It’s never had a name,’ she said, his own four-letter word striking her as provocative and boorish both at once.

‘But that’s appalling! Let’s christen it right now. Any ideas?’

‘Victoria,’ she suggested, longing to close her eyes and take at least a short breather. The last twenty-four hours had been challenging, to put it mildly, with all the emotion over Den, her mounting worry over Glenys’s failing health, and her unwarranted but nonetheless acute anxiety about this very meeting with Skip.

‘No - too close to Veronica. How about Rose? Or Petal?’

‘’I’d prefer Susan,’ she said, suddenly recalling that Susan was Leonard’s favourite female name, as he’d told her, decades ago. And she’d always imagined Susans as being sweet, feminine and obliging on the outside, yet feisty and even contrary underneath.

‘OK, Susan she is. Susan, meet Albert!’

She was forced to suppress a smile, since he’d only just said he needed a while to recover, yet was already unzipping his jeans again, to effect the introductions. As the dark, straight line of his hair pointing down to his penis was once again revealed, she traced it with her finger, then, still more brazenly, let the finger dally where it ended up. And, within minutes, he was inside her again, less stiff, this time, less urgent altogether, but still so satisfying, her tiredness simply vanished as the sensations began rippling through the length and breadth of her body, even tingled through her scalp, for heaven’s sake. Skip didn’t manage to come again, but *she* did – she, the once sexless woman, who had never dreamt of straying from the matrimonial bed, now experiencing a Vesuvius of an orgasm, complete with aftershocks, and indecently soon after the Krakatoa of the first. Indeed, despite her declared exhaustion, she now felt she could continue half the night, if only to celebrate Susan

- a name that linked her to Leonard and also gave her a new identity. beyond Ron, beyond Veronica. Susan was a sexpot, an easy lay, a hussy – all things she had once considered as alien to her nature as theft would be or violence. Except sex *was* a type of violence – at least sex with Skip seemed to be. Even his kisses were voracious, leaving her mouth ravished, bruised, astonished.

'You're amazing!' he said, tweaking her still erect nipple so eagerly it hurt. 'What I especially love is the way you look so demure on the outside – well-turned-out and bandbox-fresh and as if butter wouldn't melt in your mouth - yet underneath you're a wildcat.'

So, the tame, toothless, domestic moggy had become a ravening tigress – a thought as surprising to her as it apparently was to Skip. He, for his part, had already launched into his schedule for their future skating sessions, the manoeuvres he wanted to teach her, and some soon-to-be-opened ice-rink he planned to show her next month. She couldn't help but contrast his inexhaustible loquaciousness and general restless vitality with Colin's uncommunicative nature and endless sitting and staring at the box. And, despite knowing full well that it would be woefully inappropriate to mention her husband whilst lying here with a lover, she somehow found herself blurting out Colin's maddening habit of using 'Mm-hmm' as a shorthand for ordinary speech.

'He says it so often now, I can't tell whether he's settling for the easiest option merely out of laziness, or because he's forgetting actual words. I should be much more tolerant, but those endless "Mm-hmms" goad me like … like mosquito-bites and, before I realize, I'm snapping at the poor man, for something he probably can't help.'

Why, in God's name, she thought, had she allowed Colin's dementia to intrude into her private time with Skip? Yet, deep down, she knew the answer: after their physical closeness, she wanted them to be emotionally close, as well. He knew so little about her home situation, knew so little about her, full-stop. And she was equally ignorant about *his* inner self, *his* current concerns, so, when he started opening up a little, she listened with careful attention.

'I do sympathize, Veronica, because I once went to a therapist – Hope, she was called, would you believe? Though maybe she changed her name when she realized half her patients were *losing* hope! You see, she never said a thing except "Mm-hmm, Mm-hmm", repeated every few moments. I discovered since then that most shrinks use it as a standard device to show they're listening, without actually having to interrupt. But, to be honest, it drove me bonkers and, finally, after the zillionth "Mm-hmm", I walked out of her consulting-room and never returned.'

'Did she help you at all *before* that?' she asked, hoping he'd reveal a little more about his past, perhaps divulge his fiancée's suicide, all those years ago.

Instead, he answered with a shrug and began scoffing biscuits, as if the recent family-sized pizzas were just the dimmest memory. 'It's a dismal subject,' he said, through a ginger-scented mouthful, 'so let's not talk about it. I'd rather hear more about you. For instance, why don't you simply leave your husband?'

An issue she couldn't begin to explain – the whole tangled web of duty, pity, loyalty, dependency and sheer terror at being on her own. Yet, in one sense, she *was* alone, already. Dementia had made her a widow, without an actual bereavement. She had lost the man she married – a man who could converse and run a business and knew who people were and what was going on in the world – and was currently living with his husk, his outer shell. Despite her continuing qualms about broaching the subject with Skip, she had a shot at telling him at least a little, mainly in order to bond them.

'I shan't leave him, Skip – not ever. He's far too old and too far gone now to cope on his own, and he wouldn't last two minutes in a care-home, with all their rules and regulations. But I have to confess it can feel very lonely, not being able to communicate or discuss anything at all, whether Brexit, or the choir, or just the day-to-day chit-chat most couples take for granted. He hardly seems to know who I am these days, and it certainly wouldn't cross his mind to ask if I'm OK. I'm on a choke-chain, twenty-four-seven, as far as his needs are concerned, yet he hasn't a clue about my life or what I'm doing.'

'Just as well!' Skip joked, now running a lustful hand across her flank, 'especially as I plan to feature in that life – and Albert, too, of course. First off, it's my birthday in six days – the big 5-0 – and I wondered if we could spend it together – maybe start with a skating session at Queensway, then come back here again? Tony often stays overnight with his girlfriend, so this place is free at least once or twice a week.'

A dozen different responses came and went in her mind. She was, frankly, disappointed that he had failed to explore any further the situation with Colin, and blamed herself for bringing it up in the first place, since it was definitely disloyal to have whinged about a condition her husband couldn't help. On the other hand, if she couldn't speak honestly and openly, any bond she and Skip developed was doomed to be shallow and superficial. Yet, whatever the rights and wrongs of the relationship, she simply didn't have *time* for it, what with Colin's declining health, her ever-increasing fund-raising duties, and her frequent visits to Glenys, which she refused to curtail, now that her friend was so ill. She did, in fact, have the option of stopping this liaison with Skip here and now, before regret set in, as Megan feared it might.

She continued to lie silent, unable to judge whether the whole entanglement was unwise, unwarranted, or even dangerous. Suppose he'd been to several *other* therapists, for a host of intractable problems? Or suppose, as Glenys had hinted, he was taking drugs, which would help explain why he had so little money and owned so few possessions? And why had he never married in the long stretch of time between his fiancée's death and now? Could he be concealing some fatal flaw?

Yet all such speculation had little bearing on her principal emotion: a whooping delight that he wanted to spend a landmark birthday with her and that, despite being ten years younger, still appeared to find her a turn-on and was already planning a repeat performance in less than a week.

'So, what do you think?' he asked, anxiously, crunching yet another biscuit, with as much relish as if it were a prized black Périgord truffle, rather than a stale ginger-nut.

And, all at once, inexplicably and wonderfully, her worries dwindled as fast as the biscuits. 'I'd love that,' she said, daring to add, 'And I'm pretty sure Susan would, as well.'

CHAPTER 37

Lacrimosa dies illa
Qua resurget ex favilla ....

As the opening music resounded through the small overheated chapel, it seemed to weep and lament, in accordance with its name. Veronica didn't know the work - the *Lacrimosa* from Mozart's Requiem – chosen by Robert as one especially loved by Glenys. Yet the yearning but uplifting sound seemed the very essence of grief, high female voices soaring above the tenors and basses in an anguished cry from the heart, making her close to tears herself. However, crying was out of the question when, in just the next few minutes, she'd be giving a eulogy for Glenys, and it would be equally impossible to perform as part of Larks Ascending with a puffy face and husky voice. She and a dozen other choir-members were already positioned at the front, wearing their formal choir-dress in honour of the occasion, Megan standing close beside her, providing silent support.

Support she desperately needed, as she watched Robert and the three other coffin-bearers, process up the aisle and set down the coffin on the catafalque, supervised by the funeral director, She wasn't sure which was more painful: Robert's strained and stoical expression as he helped to bear his late wife to her final resting-place, or the sight of the coffin itself, its highly-polished mahogany and blatantly bright flowers a callous contrast to the skeletally thin, totally bald Glenys she had last seen at the hospice.

Once the four bearers had taken their seats in the front row, one of Robert's old friends, Oliver, who was acting as lay celebrant – moved to the lectern to introduce the service and welcome the guests. His tall, imposing figure and neatly cut silver hair endowed him with a gravitas in keeping with the occasion, as did his well-tailored suit, the colour of a dark night-sky.

'We are particularly grateful,' he began, in his deep, velvety voice, 'to all of you here for coming out in such appalling weather. The Meteorological Office may call this the "Mini Beast from the East", but for those of you who've struggled with blocked roads, snowdrifts and cancelled trains, it's anything but "mini", and I know Glenys would appreciate your efforts. She herself loved snow and, during the full-scale "Beast from the East" in February, she'd look out of her hospice window and admire the landscape totally transformed under its duvet of snow. Well, today, we have that same transformation and, however inconvenient it may be for us travellers, I reckon Glenys would feel at home here in this surprisingly beautiful place.'

Veronica, too, had been struck by the almost rural atmosphere of Breakspear Crematorium, despite it being only a short taxi-ride from Ruislip tube station. She and Megan had deliberately arrived early, to allow for any possible delays, and had used the extra time to wander through the peaceful, snow-hushed grounds, bundled up in coats and scarves, and having to keep hitching up their long black skirts, to prevent them dragging in the snow. Trees, shrubs and lawns were all blanketed in white, with a delicate tracery on twigs and leaves, and the duck-pond, with its bulrushes and water-lilies, iced to a plate-glass finish.

'I know you're still upset about Glenys dying on your sixtieth,' Megan had said, as they explored the Garden of Remembrance, 'but I feel it's an apt reminder that it's *you* who needs to carry on her fund-raising work and wholesale commitment to the choir, so, in that sense, it's a positive, not a negative. And, to let you into a secret, I'd been planning a surprise party for that all-important birthday and had invited all your mates, but we'll simply have to postpone it till the spring.'

'Oh, *Megan*!' she'd exclaimed, too touched to say any more. No one had ever planned a party for her, surprise or otherwise

'And it should be spring right now, for heaven's sake!' Megan had concluded, vehemently, as if directing her ire at the Meteorological Office itself. 'I mean, here we are, almost three weeks into March, yet it's still like bloody Siberia!'

Oliver's voice returned her to the present. Her mind was all over the place today, jumping backwards and forwards in time and from one subject to another, as she wrestled with curdled cross-currents of grief, anxiety, and a most unfitting, Susan-related elation.

'But, although we mourn for Glenys,' he continued, 'we must also remember that she is now at peace, after a long and gruelling illness. We were all inspired by her courage, but she was nearing the end of what she could endure and none of us who love her would want to see her suffering extended.'

Veronica, who had witnessed first-hand the intense pain, fatigue and nausea, nodded in silent assent, yet, whatever her relief that Glenys was now spared, her death had left a gash in the pattern of her life: no more visits to the hospice, or anxious vigils by the bed, as her friend struggled to speak or even, at times, to breathe. And it had reactivated the grief of other deaths: Tom's, Den's, her unknown father's, even Mozart's whom, Megan had informed her, had actually died in the middle of composing the Lacrimosa.

'Secondary cancer,' Oliver went on, 'not only brings pain, it also means one cannot plan ahead, not even for next week, let alone next year. But Glenys accepted that uncertainty with the same grace that she accepted ......'

Veronica was suddenly distracted by Skip, who, worryingly late, had just sneaked into the back of the chapel and slumped down in the very last pew. In contrast to Robert and Oliver, he looked anything but svelte, his face blotchy from tears, his hair, as usual, in need of a cut. And he must have borrowed his black suit, since it was too short in both the arms and the legs, giving him a truncated, scarecrow air. Although his face was inscrutable, she knew all too well the extremes of grief his sister's death had caused. Apparently, the pair had been exceptionally close as children and Glenys, the elder by twelve years, had taken on an almost maternal role, so that Skip now felt bereft, as if all his usual bounciness and his multitude of interests had been extinguished at a stroke, along with his appetite. She was so used to his mouth being ever-open – enthusiastically eating, drinking, talking, singing - she could barely believe this new, silent, self-starving Skip.

Only when Oliver introduced the choir, was Veronica once again brought back to the proceedings, and had to make a determined effort to keep her mind on the service and not on this worrying change in her lover.

'Larks Ascending,' he declared, 'meant so much to Glenys, and Robert himself has recently joined the choir, which Glenys particularly wanted. All this time, he's been hiding his beautiful baritone voice, and I'm sorry to say you won't even hear it this morning, as, understandably, he's declined to sing today. But the rest of the choir will now sing one of Glenys's favourite numbers: *Let the River Run.*'

Veronica took a slow, deep breath, as a preparation for singing, and also to calm her mind and alleviate the nausea induced by the reek of oversweet lilies wafting from atop the coffin. However, just the presence of the other choir-members was soothing in itself: Clive, Michael, Barry, Charlotte, Evelyn and Samantha, all there, as well as

Megan, and a youthful-looking Patricia, wearing a circlet of red flowers on her waist-length ponytail, and Christopher his usual dapper self in black dress-trousers and red bow-tie. These people were now her family, and she needed to concentrate on them, and on the song, rather than allowing herself to be distracted by all the complications arising from her ties with Skip. Although he was still huddled in his pew, with his head in his hands, it was imperative to ignore his pathetic figure, or her thoughts would stray again to the unexpected ferocity of his grief – a grief that seemed unfathomable, as he'd made no attempt to put it in into words.

Hitching her own voice to Christopher's powerful tenor, she let it ring out loud and clear, partly in homage to Glenys, partly in support of Katy, who had been hoping for a larger turnout than the brutish weather permitted, since some choir-members, struggling with their illness, had been forced to stay in the warmth and safety of their homes. Nonetheless, the choir made up in enthusiasm for what it lacked in numbers and, once the final note had died away, Veronica was aware that the mood in the chapel had lightened and lifted, in response to their heartfelt singing.

Next, Oliver called on Robert to speak, and she marvelled at his courage in being able to function at all, when his wife had died after a mere three months of marriage, yet, it was that very aspect of their relationship that Robert was now expounding.

'I want to salute my late wife for her bravery in agreeing to our wedding. As Oliver has just explained, everything was uncertain for us both. Once we'd fixed the date for the ceremony, we didn't even know if we'd be alive by then, and whether it was worth us buying new outfits, which we might never wear again. And should we book a honeymoon, or would we only forfeit our deposit? But Glenys kept me going by refusing to harp on all the ifs and buts and saying yes to everything, including the honeymoon, which I'm happy to say did in fact materialize. Admittedly, we couldn't travel far, but our three days in a cosy little B & B in Cookham were as special for us as three weeks at the Florida Ritz would be for many couples.'

Veronica couldn't help but wonder if sex had featured in that honeymoon, with both of them so ill and both on libido-deadening drugs. And, however shameful it was that her mind had wandered yet again and she was now thinking about sex in the middle of a funeral, worse followed when her thoughts then turned - still more inappropriately – to the occasion of Skip's birthday, when Albert and Susan had renewed their acquaintance. She had deliberately concealed the fact that her own birthday was a mere fortnight after his, because, when naked and thrusting with Skip, the decades simply fell away and she became instantly, magically, ridiculously young. Indeed, that birthday-sex had been very different from their eruptive, quick-fire first encounter: playful, this time, and giggly, more kittenish than Atomic Dog.

And only then had it struck her that she was more relaxed with Skip than she had ever been with Alex, no longer needing to worry about being unmusical, as well as unsophisticated, unable to tell a cadence from a coda, or a Malbec from a Merlot, and never having had a proper job in her life. For Skip, it was enough that she could enjoy a Big Mac and a pint of lager, and could dance until she dropped to his latest jazz-funk craze, and it was certainly a new, unknown thrill that anyone should see her, as he emphatically did, as the clever, achieving, superior one. He had also endowed her with a nickname: Susiekins, one he'd chosen in honour of 'Susan'. Since early childhood, she had envied classmates with endearing nicknames like Precious, Peaches, Sweet Pea, Cupcake, Chickadee, all suggesting affection and devotion, yet Susiekins was better still, with its undeniable tenderness and secret erotic charge. Never, though, would she reveal it to Megan, whom, she feared, would regard it as sickeningly cutesy and twee.

Again, she realized how far she had strayed from the agenda of the funeral, her butterfly-mind still flitting from distracting flower to distracting flower, rather than experiencing the emotions befitting so solemn a service. Her only excuse was that she'd been sleeping extremely badly - not just on account of Glenys's death, but because of Colin's increasing restlessness at night – which had clearly wrecked her concentration. Yet, if she permitted Colin's problems to kidnap her attention now, on top of all the rest, she might as well give up and simply walk out of the chapel. So, making a renewed attempt to focus, she forced her mind back to Robert's speech.

'Glenys taught me gratitude and acceptance – gratitude for tiny, short-lived things, acceptance of impermanence and the fact we have no control over most of life's ups and downs, but can enjoy it nonetheless.'

Megan had said much the same, urging her to grab whatever joys were on offer, rather than keep worrying they might not last. 'OK, I admit the situation with Skip is anything but perfect, but try to live just for the day – your next skating session or the next new funky band he starts enthusing about.'

Sound advice, maybe, but, when it came to their basic outlook, she and Megan were miles apart. Megan believed that, if a relationship didn't work out, you just shrugged your shoulders and moved on, accepting the fact you couldn't control the future, or control any man, or any quirk of fate. *She*, for her part, still desperately wanted permanence and a tie that went bone-marrow-deep. and found the concept of a soulmate infinitely appealing: someone who knew you through and through, shared your views and philosophy and, as an extra vital bonus, was sexually compatible. But perhaps, as Megan avowed, such an ideal was, in fact, impossible.

‘Let’s face it, love, most people dissemble, hide their worse sentiments and present a more acceptable façade to the world, so can you really know anyone in depth?’

The thought was undoubtedly troubling and, indeed, she couldn’t deny that had never truly known Colin, not in forty years, and he had even less concept of *her* innermost feelings, or private hopes and dreams, let alone her lusts and longings.

For God’s *sake*, she rebuked herself, all but speaking aloud in her frustration at being once again fatally distracted. At any moment, Oliver would call on her to speak in praise of Glenys, yet she was still mulling over the various issues with Skip, Albert, Susan and Colin, and even pondering the issue of soulmates, rather than paying Robert the courtesy of listening to his words.

‘Take yourself in hand,’ she ordered, silently, ‘and clear your head of every buggering thing apart from the deceased – Glenys’s life, death, courage, legacy, achievements.’

Nor shall my sword sleep in my hand,
Till we have built Jerusalem
In England’s green and pleasant land.

Once the last note of the final hymn had trumpeted forth, with a great outpouring of sound from the concluding organ-crescendo, everyone began trouping outside. The cold was a sharp slap on the face after the cosy fug of the chapel, yet, despite the Arctic conditions, a hum of conversation soon arose, as people took stock of who was there and started making introductions. Veronica was touched to see some of those she'd met at Glenys's hospital, not just fellow-patients, but the oncologist and specialist-nurse, who had both taken the trouble to turn out for the service, however busy their lives. Having greeted them both, she then squeezed her way towards Avril, who had often had her chemo at the same time and place as Glenys, and was easy to spot, dressed not in funereal black but in breast-cancer pink, even down to her puce-pink wellington boots and up to her clashing-pink mop of a wig. Veronica had realized in the chemotherapy-suite that, never once, had Avril had a friend or relative to sit with her and seemed sadly alone in the world, so she herself had started offering to run errands for her or bring in things she needed.

Despite the comfort of talking to someone she knew, Veronica made a conscious effort to circulate and talk to other people, knowing Robert would welcome support in his role as host, especially as Skip, far from providing such support, hadn't even emerged yet. For all she knew, he might be skulking in the gents', nursing a grief he could neither share nor communicate, whereas Oliver, in contrast, was clearly a born organizer and began urging people towards the Woodman Pub, which was hosting the post-funeral reception. Since it was only a few minutes from the crematorium, those without transport could easily walk the short distance, whilst Oliver arranged lifts for the elderly, infirm and those already too chilled to remain out here any longer.

Veronica deliberately dallied, loath to leave without knowing where Skip was and – more important – *how* he was. To her great relief, he appeared at that very moment, and, having reassured himself that everyone had left, clasped her in a fervent embrace and whispered in a compelling tone, 'Don't go yet – I beg you. There's something we just have to do,'

‘What?’ she demanded, more harshly than she’d intended, fearing he might be harbouring some crazy notion of making love in one of the lonelier spots of the crematorium grounds - a profanity too far.

‘I know you’ll say it’s crackers,’ he said, in a hoarse, faltering voice she barely recognized, ‘and that we should do our duty by going straight to the pub, but this is infinitely more important and, anyway, nobody will miss us, with that great crowd milling around.’

‘I’m sorry, Skip, but I don’t know what you’re talking about.’

He grabbed her arm, as if trying to impart to her the urgency of his request. ‘We have to build Glenys a snowman. I promised her we’d do it together – me and her, I mean – before she …. passed away. I realize now I should never have made such a promise, but I was stupid enough to believe the prospect might keep her alive. You see, when we were kids, she was the best snowman-maker in the world and taught me all this stuff about using pieces of coal for the eyes, and a carrot for the nose, and two rows of red kidney-beans for the lips, and a hat for his head and a pipe for his mouth and a long, woolly muffler, to wind around his neck.’

She stared at him in bewilderment. Could he be serious? She was dolled up in her best clothes - totally unsuitable for such a messy task – and, in any case, how the hell could she find coal, or carrots, or red kidney-beans in a well-groomed crematorium? But, as if in answer to her question, he rummaged in a large canvas bag she had failed to notice before, despite its size and bulk, and withdrew all the items he’d listed and, in addition, a spade, a shovel, two old ragged duffle-coats and two pairs of thick waterproof gloves.

‘I thought of everything in advance, so you wouldn’t get frozen-stiff, or spoil your fancy choir-gear. Of course, this isn’t the same as

Glenys herself building the snowman, but it's definitely the next best thing and I've tried to square it with her through sort of .... telepathic messages that I hoped might somehow reach her, wherever she is now.'

Veronica felt still more thrown. This wasn't the rational, sceptical Skip she knew, unless he was simply clutching at straws to help him through his grief. But the sheer intensity of his demeanour convinced her at some deep level that she had to go along with his idea, however weird or wrong or mistimed it was. If she suggested postponing the task, he'd only quote the forecast, which had predicted decidedly less snowy weather as early as tomorrow. Or, if she insisted on doing her duty by setting straight off for the wake, if only to help Robert, Skip would simply build the snowman on his own and might stay out here for hours, getting chilled to the bone and maybe seriously overwrought, without her to keep a watchful eye on him. It was quite a struggle, though, to ditch her normal dutiful self - whose place was by Robert's side at the wake - and fall in with Skip's madcap plan, and she had to make an effort of will to put the cleaner of the two duffle-coats over her formal choir-clothes, seize the shovel and Skip's arm, and let him lead her to the spot he'd already chosen, farthest away from any public area, and where the snow was deepest.

They worked in silence and, although she had rarely made a snowman in her childhood (Den invariably condemning such frivolity), she simply followed Skip's lead, as she had learned to do so successfully in the skating and dancing sessions and, more recently, in bed.

To her great surprise, she found a certain comfort in the process, the sheer physicality of the task not only soothing her but sending a welcome warmth tingling through her cold-as-marble limbs, as she worked with speed and fervour in obedience to Skip's instructions. First, he showed her how to shape the snow into balls, then roll them along the ground, to pick up more loose snow, packing the snow tightly and firmly, before stacking the balls on top of each other, to form the body and the head. Then, while Skip stuck in the coal-eyes and carrot-nose, she created a wide snowman smile with the kidney-beans, inserted the pipe through the aperture and set the hat at a rakish angle on its lumpen, dirty-white head. Finally, Skip wound what looked like a college-scarf, in stripes of emerald, mustard and maroon, around the thick bull-neck.

Nonetheless, she became increasingly impatient as Skip stood back with a frown, making tiny adjustments to the hat, the scarf, the smile, as if he would never be satisfied, and it was all she could do not to raise her voice and chivvy him on to the pub.

'Great!' he said, at last, despite the fact his frown still lingered. 'Glenys will definitely approve.'

She noted his use of the present-tense. Perhaps wise of him to keep his sister alive, if only in a grammatical sense. And she could sympathize with that. When the curtains had closed around the coffin, to mark the end of the service, she had unashamedly wept at the prospect of Glenys becoming mere dust and ashes, no longer a voice, a presence, a living, breathing friend. She had been buried in the gold silk turban Veronica had bought her as a final gift, which, although more luxurious than all the previous ones, would, by this time tomorrow, be also consumed in the flames of the furnace.

'Well, I'm glad you're pleased,' she said, taking his frozen hand in her warmer one. 'But we really must push off now. We can come back here afterwards, if you want, and pay our respects to Mr Snowman.' Anything to stop him staying out here on his own in such an unstable state.

'No wait!' he commanded. 'There's something else – something equally important.'

She tried to keep the annoyance from her voice. She had a duty not just to him, but to Oliver, Robert, Katy, her fellow-choristers and all the guests, and should be playing her part in making introductions and passing round refreshments, rather than turning up unforgivably late, windswept and dishevelled. 'OK,' she said, tersely, 'but we must be really quick.'

As if in answer, he pressed the whole force of his body against hers, as if determined to merge them into one, holding her so tightly she could barely breathe. 'I love you, Veronica,' he declared, and, although his voice was muffled by the close contact, she couldn't fail to note its high-flown tone. 'No, don't interrupt. And don't think I'm only saying this because of all the emotion of the last two weeks. Absolutely not. I feel it deep inside me. Susan's easy to love, of course, but what you couldn't possibly know is that I've always found it well-nigh impossible to love another woman after' – he paused, as if searching for the word, only to come up with a brutal phrase – 'Carole topped herself.'

After so intimate an admission, she could hardly rush off to the wake, however anxious she might be about any further delay. This was the very first time he had ever mentioned his fiancée's suicide, let alone revealed her name.

'You see, I feared I was the sort of guy who somehow couldn't make a woman happy, or – worse - might actively upset them in some way I wasn't even aware of. So, I suppose I concluded it just wasn't safe for me to get deeply involved with any female, for fear it might end in tragedy again. Do you understand?'

No, she wasn't sure she did and, anyway, could barely answer coherently, struggling as she was with yet more contradictory emotions:

a secret, shaming delight that he should declare his love so ardently, guilt that, as a married woman, she had no entitlement to such a declaration, fear of the implications of such love, when she herself still felt so ambivalent, still knew so little about this man - except he was clearly more disturbed than she realized.

She stood, uncertain, silent, until, all at once, he kissed her. His lips and face were so cold, it was if the snowman himself had initiated the kiss, yet, as the white heat of its fervour began scorching through her body, kindling even Susan, her prudence and her willpower both seemed to slip away and, despite all her misgivings, she responded with such intensity, the kiss became an electric current jolting through their bodies at a dangerous voltage that simply scorched away all guilts and scruples.

'I love you,' he repeated, pulling away, at last, 'and I want Glenys to bear witness to the fact. You see, she was my *first* love – not our mother.' He broke off with a jarring laugh. 'Mum was, frankly, pretty unhinged and, as for our Dad, we very rarely saw him. So Glenys and I were thrown together and my big, supportive elder sister was the only female I ever dared to love until I met my fiancée. But, of course, her appalling death made me see that love was dangerous, maybe even doomed, so I deliberately stayed well clear of it until *you* appeared, Veronica. Which means for me you're a bloody miracle.'

And then he kissed her again, and Glenys seemed to disappear in the sheer turmoil of the kiss, and, to her shame and triumph, she was conscious - solely, swaggeringly - of being, for him, 'a bloody miracle.'

CHAPTER 38

A ripple of excitement tingled through her body like a skittish breeze through a wheat-field – and that was before she had sung a single note, or the rehearsal had even started! Just watching the members of the orchestra arriving with their instruments was a new, fascinating experience: a young, hawk-nosed man wheeling in the timpani, closely followed by an anorexic girl, all of whose sustenance seemed to have bypassed her stomach and gone into her double-bass. Trumpets, trombones, horns, flutes, were being unpacked from gleaming cases or heavy-duty bags, some instruments tricky to identify. Was that a violin or a viola, an oboe or a clarinet? But she refused to dwell on her ignorance when, today, she was an integral part of a musical community: The London City Orchestra and no less than five separate choirs. For the last half-hour, the choristers had been trouping in: fellow members of Larks Ascending, and many she didn't recognise - presumably from the four Tenovus Cancer choirs: Chelsea, Sutton, Cardiff and Bridgend. There was no real division, however, between the different groups: everybody bonding, swapping names and details of their journeys here, the Welsh contingent joking - or complaining - about their enforced early start in getting to London in time.

They were also united by their dress: every performer wearing formal black, with a contrasting splash of red – a tribute to Larks Ascending's basic colour-scheme, which had been adopted universally. Veronica stood marvelling at the array of red accoutrements: two men in red brocaded waistcoats, one sporting racy red braces, one in a black-and-red striped shirt, and several in red socks and ties. And the females were variously adorned with red ruffles, red artificial flowers, red earrings, chokers, scarves, bandanas, and their own Patricia was showing off her new, high-heeled scarlet stilettos. The five choir-leaders were garbed in the same black and red, although their role today was very much secondary to the orchestra's conductor, and they would be conducting their own individual forces only in one number from the programme.

'Are you Veronica?' a voice called from behind, and she turned to see a shortish, chubby woman, whose dyed plum-coloured hair shrieked pleasingly at her crimson top.

'Hi! My name's Olwen and I chair the Sutton fund-raising group, so I wanted to say hello to my opposite number in the Clapham choir!'

The woman was so friendly and engaging, they were soon deep in conversation and, when Olwen mentioned her partner, Bart, who'd taught himself to build guitars from scratch, Veronica listened intently, recalling *Skip's* experience of making guitars as a schoolboy.

'The latest one was an undoubted hit,' Olwen continued, in her husky voice. 'Bart made it out of an old Jack Daniels barrel, so it had this wonderful whisky smell that seemed to add to its appeal. And the great thing for us is that he's raising a small fortune selling them in aid of the Sutton choir.'

Could Skip do the same, Veronica wondered? He certainly hadn't lost those technical skills, since he'd told her about another guitar he had made in recent years. She imagined him working with her on the Clapham choir's fund-raising drive, maybe making a bit on the side, to improve his own cash-strapped lifestyle. Her mind took a leap as she pictured him giving private lessons not only on guitar-making, but on a whole eclectic repertoire of different styles of music, harnessing his infectious enthusiasm for everything from Albinoni to Zappa, by way of Cage, Coltrane, Crumb and Clinton – all names that, pre-Skip, meant so little to her they might have been outlandish foods, or past American presidents. And, if *she* were to do the admin - confirm dates, chase payments, set up suitable venues, and gradually persuade him into professionalizing his talents – it might truly be a shared venture, even cement their relationship, affording them both a new sphere of mutual interest.

Eager to discuss such ideas with Olwen and also learn more about the Sutton take on fund-raising, she arranged to meet the woman for lunch, chuffed to realize how her life was opening up: the new things she was learning, new people she was meeting - all unthinkable in her narrow, pre-choir existence.

Most of the players had now arrived, shed their coats and instrument-cases, and were tuning up in frankly screechy discord. Despite the strident sound, she continued to relish the novelty of being so close to an orchestra. That very proximity made them no longer members of an elitist Higher Tribe, separated from the general public by their sheer professionalism, but here specifically to support the choirs – which included *her*, of course.

Her excitement ratcheted up a notch as the conductor swept in: Pablo Urbina, young, dark, dynamic, and already a legend at the age of only thirty, who had not only founded this orchestra, but had conducted distinguished orchestras all over the world. He welcomed the five choirs in turn, shaking hands with a few in the front row, she one of those so favoured. And, as the world-renowned prodigy gripped her awestruck fingers, she hoped some traces of his handshake would linger for ever and imbue her with the tiniest fraction of his talent.

'Now if everybody's ready,' he said, once he'd concluded his greetings, 'Let's start with *Sing for Life*. I know it's our closing number today, but we've worked out our own orchestration for the song, which I'd like you to hear before you join in. I'm aware that some of you have never sung with an orchestra before, so we need a bit of practice before we face our audience.'

He mounted the podium, called for silence and encompassed them all in a piercing glance that seemed to say, wordlessly, 'Concentrate, excel, give it all you've got!'

And the orchestra obeyed. Their jubilant sound whooped and thundered through the hall with such éclat, she felt instantly revitalized. And the dramatic architecture itself had an equally uplifting effect. This Chamber at City Hall, although only on the second floor, lifted the eye to the full height of the spiral staircase that wound its stupendous way to the very top of the building, breath-taking in its grandeur. The impressive glass façade not only gave a sense of transparency and space, but afforded spectacular views of the Thames, no longer sludge-brown or grungy-grey, as it had been most of the winter, but today sparkling in the early-April sunshine with glints and gleams of gold. And the Tenovus anthem, *Sing for Life*, seemed similarly gilded, as each instrument added its distinctive tone and timbre to the tune. OK, she might be deaf to all those subtleties, but, at a deep, instinctive level, she felt the music reigniting all the things she had learned to value since she'd left behind her former drab regime: love, romance, new horizons, even success and sexual passion. And the sheer vigour of the players – bows wildly flashing or gently feathering, fingers plucking, strumming, gliding, lips pursed, mouths puckered, drumsticks beating a tattoo – shot her through with a fierce infusion of energy, as if she'd been launched like a rocket and was whooshing up, up, up, through an infinite immensity.

'Congratulations!' Pablo said, as the last note died away. 'I love your tremendous zest, but, once the choirs come in, we need to keep a balance between instruments and voices, otherwise we may overpower them. Right, singers, are you ready?'

A murmur of assent ran round the Chamber, then a moment's taut silence before Pablo raised his baton again and the five sets of sopranos embarked on the opening verse with an impact impossible for Larks Ascending on its own. And once the altos joined in, and then she herself, with the five-strong contingent of basses, the sheer volume of sound swept away any lingering doubts she'd had about this project: would the various choirs succeed in gelling, with no one choir swamping the rest, would Pablo find it hard to control such disparate forces? But, in fact, the clamorous outpouring was so accomplished and assured - and her own newly confident voice so powerfully supported - she felt part of a vast musical tribe, united in one super-choir and one unforgettable enterprise.

Sing for life, sing for love,
Sing for all the things that you are dreaming of,
Sing for hope, sing for strength ,,,,

She realized, with a jolt, she actually had all those things – not just life, but love, hope and strength: things once way beyond her reach. So, she did her utmost to pour them into the song with such pizazz and passion, it would carry across the whole of London, surging through the wide expanse of glass and galvanizing every city-dweller, every seagull on the wing, even every dull grey pigeon scrabbling for scraps in the gutter. And her present tiredness, her worry over Colin, her still raw grief at Glenys's death, all unaccountably vanished, as the entire building resounded with life, love, hope, strength - and every dream fulfilled.

'That was brilliant, everyone! Thanks for your hard work. And now it's time for our lunch-break, which you all thoroughly deserve.' Pablo stepped down from the podium, mopped the film of perspiration from his face, and added, with a smile, 'A few of our thirstier members have already sussed out the local pubs, although I'm just hoping they haven't yet imbibed! Anyway, the general consensus is in favour of the nearest pub, The Bridge Lounge. Turn right out of this building, walk across Potter's Field Park until you hit Tooley Street and the pub's right opposite, just two minutes' walk from here. It's quite a sizeable place, with a second bar upstairs, but, because we're such a big crowd, we may need to spread ourselves out a bit. Don't worry, though, there are several other pubs on Tower Bridge Road, which is also very close. So, I suggest we leave the heavy stuff here and take just our coats and bags, OK?'

'Before we go,' Megan whispered, 'would you mind if we had a quick coffee on our own? There's a café right here in the basement, so it should only take a jiffy.'

'Yes, of course, that's fine.' Veronica, aware of the disquiet in Megan's voice, was concerned about her friend, who had turned up late for the rehearsal, and seemed uncharacteristically tense.

'I just thought I'd better warn you,' Megan explained, once they'd ordered their espressos and found a couple of seats at one of the long tables, 'I may have to dash straight off after the performance. I've had bad news, I'm afraid. Baby Flora was taken ill last night and rushed into hospital.'

'Oh, Megan, how awful! Why on earth didn't you tell me before?'

'I haven't had a chance yet. Lavinia's at her wits' end, so I was on the phone to her for ages this morning – in a bit of a tizz altogether, to tell the truth. I offered to go straight down there and join her in the children's ward – you know, to give her some support. But Stewart's with her at present. He's taken the day off work, so she's OK for the moment. But if they need him back in the office tomorrow, I'll go down then, instead, so you see, I'd prefer to be home at a reasonable hour this evening.'

'That's OK – don't worry. I completely understand. But what's wrong with the poor child?'

'Well, that's the worrying part. No one seems to know, except she's running a high fever and can't keep any food or milk down. I can't help dreading something dire like meningitis, but, of course, I wouldn't dream of mentioning that to Lavinia and, anyway, I'm probably just overreacting. But, look, I mustn't hold us up any longer. Now I've put you in the picture, let's go and join the others in the pub. Tell me quickly first, though, what's the latest with Colin?'

'Oh, you don't want to be bothered with that whole dreary saga.'

''Course I do. We're friends, for heaven's sake!'

Veronica lowered her voice, although the three people who'd just joined them at their table were so noisily involved in their own conversation, there was little chance of them eavesdropping. 'Well, to cut a long story short, his wounds have infected again, despite the shedload of antibiotics he's been taking. In fact, I didn't want to leave him today, but I'd already booked Pearl to come in from ten in the morning to ten at night, and I never like to cancel when I know she needs the cash.'

'Lord! I'm sorry, Veronica. What a sod that disaster should strike both of us when we should be concentrating solely on the gig.'

'Well, hardly disaster in Colin's case. Once they find the right antibiotic, it's bound to do the trick, whereas things with Flora are much more worrying. I mean, she's still only a babe.'

'Nonetheless, we both made it, despite the problems. So, now we're here, let's have a damned good shot at forgetting all those problems and push off to the pub this instant!'

As they walked arm in arm through Potters Fields Park, Veronica was soothed by the sheer gentleness of the weather, a soft, balmy breeze frolicking with the fringes of her scarf, in contrast to the savage winds of just a week ago stinging her face and tugging tetchily at her hair. The sky was summer-blue and one or two of the birch trees were already coming into leaf, and, although she feared those intrepid leaves might be blighted by a punishing frost, the overall mood was still one of spring and hope and radiance. Bright sunlight was flickering on the slender, silvery trunks, and spangling the glass panes of City Hall itself – a daringly futuristic building, slightly crazy-looking in its bulbous shape and the way it appeared to lean backwards from the river, as it might fall over. Architecture, like so much else, had never held much meaning for her, but in this, her new-hatched life, she was becoming more aware of many arts hitherto unknown.

'By the way,' Megan asked, as they crossed the road towards the pub, 'is Skip definitely coming tonight?'

'Oh, Lord, yes! He says he wouldn't miss it for the world. Granted it's been a real pig for him trying to get this evening off, but he's finally arranged for a fellow-worker to cover for him. And, even if all falls through, he's so determined to be there and support me up to the hilt, he said he'll happily risk the sack for my sake. Don't you think that's lovely?'

Veronica guessed from Megan's non-committal grunt that her

friend classed Skip's behaviour as irresponsible, rather than 'lovely', and was probably thinking that he would never get another job at fifty, even a lowly job like barista. And, yes, there were still a host of problems as far as Skip was concerned, not least his neurotic traits and uncertain future, with no money, prospects or ambition. Yet that cautious, downbeat voice, warning of trouble and disappointment in the relationship, was invariably drowned out by Susan's ecstatic cries when reunited with Albert. And, since neither Susan nor Albert had any concept of guilt, adultery or betrayal - only of delight and rapture - it was all too tempting to go along with them, rather than dwell on the negatives.

'I don't think we ought to drink,' she said to Megan, attempting to shift her mind and body from Skip's gloriously rickety divan, 'not until after the performance, in case it puts us off our stroke.'

'Oh, don't be such a Puritan! I intend to have at least one stiff gin. And I insist you have one, too – *my* treat. Trust me, love, far from putting us off our stroke, it'll turn us into Callas, Domingo and Pavarotti, all rolled into one!'

'Encore! Encore!'

The cry seemed to skitter up and down the spiral staircase – up and down, up and down - and then be reinforced by every voice outside: tourists, trippers, passers-by, ships' hooters, speedboat engines, the flap of heavy wings from some insomniac night-bird who should have gone to roost an age ago. Even the lively evening breeze was repeating 'Encore! Encore!', as was the drone of a passing plane. Despite a performance two hours' long, the audience was demanding more – a truly rare experience for Veronica, as was the fact of having an audience at all. She stored the elation in her mental store-cupboard, as nourishment for her older age, along with the dramatic view, the dark night outside dispelled by the bright lights of the tower-blocks on the opposite bank, and the gleam and glitter of their reflection in the river.

Pablo had already prepared and rehearsed with them several different encores – songs well known to all five choirs, or that had been sent out in advance for them to practise in their separate groupings – and now lifted his baton to conduct them in *Higher and Higher*: an apt choice, in light of their elevated spirits. While she waited for the basses' entry, Veronica gazed out at the tiers of seats, hoping – and failing – to distinguish Skip in the ranks of anonymous faces. Anonymous they might be, but by no means indistinct, so the fact he wasn't there probably meant he'd turned up late and decided to skulk just outside the Chamber, rather than disturb people by barging in right at the last minute. But, soon, she forgot even Skip, as the song was greeted with tumultuous applause, and she felt her individual inadequacies melt miraculously away in the mighty sea-swell of voices.

And, after two more encores, when the combined forces of orchestra and singers began, at last, to leave the performing space, eager members of the audience immediately surged forward to offer their congratulations.

'You were amazing …'

'Brilliant …'

'Phenomenal …'

'Awesome….'

Veronica added each and every adjective to her now bulgingly well-stocked larder, along with Katy's effusions – their leader positively bursting with pride in their performance, having never, so she claimed, heard them sing better in all her years with the choir. Veronica knew she needed such stores of provender to strengthen and sustain her when, sleepless on account of Colin, or anxious over Skip, supplies seemed woefully meagre. Megan, too, had clearly been transported by the sheer lustre of the evening, whispering to Veronica that she'd changed her mind about rushing straight back home and would stay on for at least the first half-hour of the mayoral reception.

'Great!' Veronica whispered back. 'I hear it's a posh do, with no expense spared. And the setting's even grander than this, apparently.'

As they joined the queue for the lift, to take them all – choirs, orchestra, guests and VIPs – up to what was called London's Living Room, at the very top of the building, Megan muttered sotto voce, 'So much for Skip and his promise to be here! I've been checking all this time and there's not a sign of him.'

Veronica stayed silent. She, too, had been scanning every face and was now ridiculously disappointed by his failure to show up. Because broken promises had been so common in her childhood, any in her adult life bored deep and sharp like knife-wounds. She did her best, however, if only for Megan's sake, to assume a 'Who cares?' attitude. And, certainly, once they reached the top floor, it was much easier to blank Skip out, simply on account of the impressive setting. The views were spectacular – London, old and new, jostling for pre-eminence: the upstart Gherkin determined to outdo the hallowed Tower of London, HMS Belfast leading the eye to the Walkie-Talkie Building, itself demoting St Paul's, the latter's structure totally concealed, apart from the very top of the dome. And, inside, a laser lighting-display cast ever-changing colours across the walls and ceiling: a firework fiesta of emerald, puce, gold and turquoise, twirling and circling with psychedelic brilliance.

She had to make an effort not to be distracted by so much richness, inside and out, since their host and sponsor for this evening's reception, the Right Honourable Winston Delaney, had just stepped forward to give a formal vote of thanks, his voice cracking with emotion as he described his wife's battle with advanced lymphoma – the reason he now devoted himself to the cause of cancer-research. And, next, the Mayor spoke, saying how gratifying it was to see choirs and cancer - both constantly in the News these days, albeit for very different reasons - brought together in so inspiring a performance.

Veronica stood, drinking in the scene, wishing her mother could be there, to witness her 'useless' daughter rubbing shoulders with mayors and politicians, and - once the speeches were over - with a whole tribe of arty people: film-producers, set-designers, scriptwriters, impresarios, theatrical agents, and every type of musician from lutenists to accordion-players. She, who had once barely known a harp from a harpoon, was now surrounded by movers and shakers who seemed keen to make her acquaintance - undoubtedly a thrill.

And, as Olwen squeezed her way through the crowds to introduce her to more Suttonites, she was soon part of a large circle – all chatting, laughing, connected – the sort of thing she could only dream about in her lonely, friendless childhood and in all the years with Tom, when she was closeted at home with her silent, suffering stepson, for long, claustrophobic stretches at a time. Indeed, she was so preoccupied, there was scarcely a chance to sample the canapés - exquisite creations, like works of art themselves. But she did grab a glass of bubbly from the proffered tray, although unable to believe that, on one so-called ordinary Thursday, she could sparkle even one iota more than her present frothy, fluttery effervescence. And Megan, too, was plainly on a high and departed only with the greatest reluctance, and much later than she'd planned, the two friends embracing warmly, as Veronica escorted her to the door. And hardly had she said goodbye, when a tall, uniformed man suddenly showed up at her side.

'Are you Veronica Matthews?' he asked, to her immediate disquiet. Could something have happened to Colin, and Pearl had summoned her back or – worse – summoned an ambulance?

Too uptight to speak, she nodded confirmation of her name, wondering how the official had managed to locate her in such an anonymous throng.

'There's someone to see you, madam – says it's urgent.'

It *must* be Pearl, forced to come in person, because, although mobiles were permitted here – in contrast to the Chamber, where they had to be switched off - she had deliberately kept hers on silent, knowing that, since Colin would be tucked up safe in bed, Pearl would have no further need to contact her.

'Follow me, please,' the man instructed, accompanying her out to the lifts, then down to the ground floor. There was no sign of Pearl, however, in the large reception area – no sign of anyone much at all.

'The gentleman wouldn't come inside. He's waiting out there by the river.'

'He' couldn't be Colin, who was now far too doddery and disoriented to go anywhere on his own. Unless it was *Pearl's* husband, dispatched in her stead, so that Pearl herself was free to tend to a stricken Colin.

Apprehensively, she ventured outside, bracing herself for bad news, but, instead of Jordan's arresting dreadlocks and well-upholstered figure, she saw, just outside the entrance, a different man entirely: pale-complexioned, with sand-coloured haired, visibly out-of-breath, and half-concealed by a huge bouquet of roses.

'*Skip*!' she exclaimed, relief, delight and surprise all blooming in her mind as brightly as the flowers.

'These are for you,' he panted, thrusting them into her arms. 'I'm completely gutted that I didn't make it in time. My friend let me down at the very last minute and I all but broke my bloody neck trying to get here for the start. And, yes, my brute of a boss *has* given me the boot, for even planning an escape without someone there to stand in for me, but the miserable sod says I have to go back anyway to collect this evening's pay, otherwise he'll dock it. But never mind all that – what's important is you're still here. I can't explain it really, but it seems desperately important that I haven't missed you, after all. Apart from anything else, I wanted to give you these. I knew you'd sing fantastically well, so I bought you flowers worthy of a diva.'

As she gazed at the long-stemmed beauties, she realized they must have cost him not just this one evening's pay but not far off a whole week's wages. OK, Megan would disapprove of his being unemployed and maybe having to go on benefits, but what counted for *her* was so romantically extravagant a gesture and the fact he had gone to such trouble and expense for someone he actually regarded as a diva - a word as unlikely for her as would be astronaut or lion-tamer. Besides, how could Megan possibly judge the relationship, when she knew nothing about Skip's declaration of love and very little about Albert and Susan's growing intimacy? OK, things between her and Skip were admittedly less joyous than the accord they achieved in bed and, maybe, as Megan feared, they had no future together. But at last, she'd come to accept the fact that things would rarely be permanent or perfect, so no point in pining for Happy Ever After. Indeed, on this enchanted night, it seemed stupendously sufficient that she had his love, these prima-donna flowers and a crucial promise kept.

She put the bouquet down a moment, so she could return his fierce embrace – an embrace that seemed to comprise the softest, sweetest rose-petals and the sharpest, cruellest thorns.

'I love you,' he whispered, his voice muffled as he crushed her against his chest.

'And I love *you.*' Never before had she dared such words - reckless words that scorched her mouth – yet she didn't give a damn. Megan herself had urged her to live for the moment, and this present moment seemed superlatively worth living for. In any case, it was too late to retract her first-ever avowal of love, which must be recorded in the aether now, woven into the fabric of this ever-to-be-cherished night.

'I wish I could stay with you all week and make love to you behind that tree, or on the deck of one of those boats, or on the very top strut of Tower Bridge, or even in the Thames, underwater, fully clothed! But my pig of a boss said if I wasn't back within the hour, he'd not only dock this evening's pay, he wouldn't even write me a reference if I tried to get another job. So, I simply have to dash, OK?'

With scarcely time to concur, she watched him go tearing off towards the tube, scarf flying, dingy sneakers drumming on the path, and her own smugly stupid smile refusing to fade one jot. Indeed, her mood was so benign, she had no desire to go straight back to the reception, but wanted to linger here awhile, applause still sounding in her ears, and the coffee-and-burger tang of Skip's intemperate kiss still tingling on her tongue.

Strolling on towards the bridge, she watched the river rippling and shimmering beneath the faint but heroic stars, thinking of its odyssey from the merest trickle in the wilds to this mighty thoroughfare. She pictured it growing stronger, wider, deeper, as it withstood floods, storms, lashing rain, searing sun, plastic-waste-pollution, until finally it merged with the wild waves of the sea. And, this evening, she was part of it – part of a mighty current, an elemental force.

All at once, on impulse, she broke into the opening lines of *I Will Survive* – the first song she had ever learned, the first she had ever performed at a gig. And, not caring if people stared, or if she wasn't quite note-perfect, she let her voice ring out, praying that all those she loved would survive, baby Flora in particular, but also Robert, Megan, Lavinia, gloriously imperfect Skip, and even maddening Colin, somehow managing to shamble on in his boozy decrepitude. The song embraced all uncertainties, smarted with betrayals and abandonments, yet spoke of strength and renewal, and thus seemed totally right as her individual anthem, stressing as it did the sense of being 'somebody new'. She did, indeed, feel transformed - newly born, newly reckless, newly accepting of all the possibilities fate might fling her way, as well as all the disappointments. And, as the words affirmed. she did have all her life to live and all her love to give - enough life left to prove herself, and so much love she craved to pour it out not just on Skip and all her friends, but on every tramp and down-and-out, every meanest citizen, every ill or suffering child, every broken body, broken heart. Such brokenness could be endured, so long as she – and all of them – stood firm and stayed the course.

'I will survive,' she repeated, her voice reaching up so high, it seemed to touch the witnessing stars. Then, for the last line of the song, all those as yet unborn, untried, added their weak voices to create an audacious strength of sound.

'*We* will survive.'

CRITICAL ACCLAIM FOR WENDY PERRIAM

Nobody does deep feelings better. ***Sunday Times***

Perriam writes brilliantly about fear and grief, but she is also hilariously funny. ***The Times***

Wendy Perriam is a consistently sharp chronicler of modern Britain and also an extremely entertaining storyteller. ***Sunday Telegraph***

Wendy Perriam is one of the most interesting unsung novelists of her generation. Intelligent and accessible, she is fighting for the same bit of turf as Joanna Trollope, but she is probably the more accomplished and varied writer of the two. She writes beautifully about relationships and hilariously about sex. Her work can be recommended without reservation for its honesty, its acuteness and its wide-ranging humanity. ***Sunday Telegraph***

Perriam has the knack of being explicit about sex without being crude or embarrassing. She teases us to the end with twists and turns in the plot, but just as accomplished is the novel's moral debate. ***The Literary Review***

Perriam writes passionately and movingly about the sad and the bad, but is brilliant on the funny side, too. Bravo! ***Daily Mail***

Perriam must be a strong contender for Britain's most underrated novelist. ***Daily Telegraph***

Perriam is sometimes very funny, sometimes very sexual, sometimes very painful, and always difficult to pin down. ***Standard***

Perriam is both clever and funny, as well as being a skilled artist with something to say about life. This is an author who has learned how to face the world and tame the horrors of life: we should be grateful for her optimism – it is infectious. ***The Tablet***

Each book is a magnificently orchestrated orgy in which her potent blend of sex, religion and humour takes the reader on a spiritual odyssey from the solid rocks of safety to the wilder shores of fantasy. ***Time Out***

Perriam addresses serious issues, but she writes with such verve and such delight in the language that the touch is light even when the themes are weighty. ***New Books Magazine***

Perriam makes waves with her novels because each of them is an unusually honest projection of her personality and each of them is sustained by a fine command of her craft. ***Glasgow Herald***

Perriam is rare among contemporary writers in the breadth of her canvas and the boldness of her colours: a sort of literary blend of Benjamin Haydon and Stanley Spencer. ***Books and Bookmen***

Perriam is one of the funniest writers around. ***Daily Telegraph***

Wendy Perriam is a real find. For she has that magical combination of a brisk, lively style and a literate intelligence. Her characters are vibrantly realistic; her understanding of human hopes, selfishness and absurdity sympathetic, but sharp and funny; the dialogue twists absolutely right. Perriam is a very welcome discovery. ***Sunday Express***

Perriam is not afraid of big themes. Indeed, she seems as a writer to revel in them. She almost rushes to embrace and dissect contemporary vices, yet any tragedy is mitigated by a fine line in black humour. Perriam can be wickedly funny with her dialogue, in her off-the-cuff social observations and in sketching minor characters and their mannerisms. ***The Independent***

Perriam's shrewd, sharp prose style is complemented by a marvellous talent for satirical observation. ***The Scotsman***

Never predictable, never sentimental, she is a terrific champion of the powers of the imagination to transform individual lives. ***The Tablet***

It is impossible to categorize this prolific novelist, whose work is a bizarre mixture of intellectual gravitas and sex scenes more steamy than any you'd find in a bonkbuster. Perriam has a pacy Polaroid pen. ***Daily Mail.***

Wendy Perriam puts the soul back into sex. ***Irish Independent***

Perriam is a skilled and sympathetic observer of contemporary life, so there is a lot of truth about contemporary morals, manners and fantasies. ***Sunday Telegraph***

Wendy Perriam is bursting with ideas about sex, death, grief, celibacy, the problems of old age, of guilt, of mother-daughter relationships … The problems of women of all ages are described in a flexible lucid style, with humour and exuberance. ***Irish Times***

It is Wendy Perriam's gift to set out a chessboard of conventional characters with whom the reader can identify, and move them, perfectly plausibly, into the most extraordinary situations. You settle down for a nice, undemanding read, then you are hooked and finally you cannot put the book down. ***Daily Telegraph***

Her books will surely live on as great literature long after she and the rest of us have gone. ***Surrey Comet***

Wendy Perriam was born to write. She looks at the world with a different eye from the rest of us. Her work refreshes and exhilarates. She gets to the heart of the matter, and there, lurking beneath the seriously mundane, we discover the spiritual underpinnings of the universe. I am her greatest fan. ***Fay Weldon***

Printed in Poland
by Amazon Fulfillment
Poland Sp. z o.o., Wrocław

50400090R00217